This is a work of Fiction. All cal
although based in historical settin   n
the story, it is a coincidence, or m

All rights reserved. No part of this book may be reproduced, stored in a retrieval system or transmitted in any form by any means electronic, mechanical, photocopying, recording or otherwise, except brief extracts for the purpose of review, without the permission of the copyright owner

Acknowledgements

Thanks to Dawn Spears the brilliant artist who created the cover artwork and my editor Debz Hobbs-Wyatt without whom the books wouldn't be as good as they are.

My wife who is so supportive and believes in me. Last my dogs Blaez and Zeeva and cats Vaskr and Rosa who watch me act out the fight scenes and must wonder what the hell has gotten into their boss. And a special thank you to Troy who was the Grandfather of Blaez in real life. He was a magnificent beast just like his grandson!

Copyright © 2022 Christopher C Tubbs

THANK YOU FOR READING!

I hope you enjoy reading this book as much as I enjoyed writing it. Reviews are so helpful to authors. I really appreciate all reviews, both positive and negative. If you want to leave one, you can do so on Amazon, through my website, or on Twitter.

About the Author

Christopher C Tubbs is a dog-loving descendent of a long line of Dorset clay miners and has chased his family tree back to the 16th century in the Isle of Purbeck. He left school at sixteen to train as an Avionics Craftsman, has been a public speaker at conferences for most of his career and was one of the founders of a successful games company back in the 1990s. Now in his sixties, he finally writes the stories he had been dreaming about for years. Thanks to inspiration from great authors like Alexander Kent, Dewey Lambdin, Patrick O'Brian, Raymond E Feist, and Dudley Pope, he was finally able to put digit to keyboard. He lives in the Netherlands Antilles with his wife, two Dutch Shepherds, and two Norwegian Forest cats.

You can visit him on his website
www.thedorsetboy.com
The Dorset Boy, Facebook page.

Or tweet him @ChristopherCTu3

The Dorset Boy Series Timeline

1792 – 1795   Book 1: A Talent for Trouble
Marty joins the Navy as an Assistant Steward and ends up a midshipman.

1795 – 1798   Book 2: The Special Operations Flotilla
Marty is a founder member of the Special Operations Flotilla, learns to be a spy and passes as lieutenant.

1799 – 1802   Book 3: Agent Provocateur
Marty teams up with Linette to infiltrate Paris, marries Caroline, becomes a father and fights pirates in Madagascar.

1802 – 1804   Book 4: In Dangerous Company
Marty and Caroline are in India helping out Arthur Wellesley, combating French efforts to disrupt the East India Company and French sponsored pirates on Reunion. James Stockley born

1804 – 1805   Book 5: The Tempest
Piracy in the Caribbean, French interference, Spanish gold and the death of Nelson. Marty makes Captain.

1806 – 1807   Book 6: Vendetta
A favour carried out for a prince, a new ship, the S.O.F. move to Gibraltar, the battle of Maida, counter espionage in Malta and a Vendetta declared and closed.

1807 – 1809   Book 7: The Trojan Horse
Rescue of the Portuguese royal family, Battle of the Basque Roads with Thomas Cochrane, and back to the Indian Ocean and another conflict with the French Intelligence Service.

1809 – 1811   Book 8: La Licorne
Marty takes on the role of Viscount Wellington's Head of Intelligence. Battle of The Lines of Torres Vedras, siege of Cadiz, skulduggery, espionage and blowing stuff up to confound the French.

1812   Book 9: Raider
Marty is busy. From London to Paris to America and back to the Mediterranean for the battle of Salamanca. A mission to the Adriatic reveals a white slavery racket that results in a private mission to the Caribbean to rescue his children.

1813-1814   Book 10: Silverthorn
Promoted to Commodore and given a Viscountcy Marty is sent to the Caribbean to be Governor of Aruba which provides the cover story he needs to fight American privateers and undermine the Spanish in South America. On his return he escorts Napoleon into Exile on Alba.

1815-1816   Book 11: Exile
After 100 days in exile Napoleon returns to France and Marty tries to hunt him down. After the battle of Waterloo Marty again escorts him into Exile on St Helena. His help is requested by the Governor of Ceylon against the rebels in Kandy.

1817-1818   Book 12: Dynasty
To Paris to stop an assassination, then the Mediterranean to further British interests in the region. Finally, to Calcutta as Military Attaché to take part in the war with the Maratha Empire. Beth comes into her own as a spy, but James prefers the Navy life.

1818-1819   Book 13: Empire
The end of the third Anglo-Maratha war and the establishment of the Raj. Intrigue in India, war with the Pindaris, the foundation of Singapore. Shipwreck, sea war and storms.

Contents

Chapter 1: Paris

Chapter 2: Intervention and Assassination

Chapter 3: The Squadron Reformed

Chapter 4: New Allies

Chapter 5: Best of Friends

Chapter 6: The Nile

Chapter 7: Crossing

Chapter 8: Complications

Chapter 9: Revelations

Chapter 10: Consequences

Chapter 11: Try and Try Again

Chapter 12: Filiki Eteria

Chapter 13: Diplomacy?

Chapter 14: Passage

Chapter 15: Retribution

Chapter 16: Calcutta

Chapter 17: Society

Chapter 18: Bethscapades

Chapter 19: Gun Running

Chapter 20: Pursuit

Chapter 21: The Enemy

Chapter 22: To Catch a Spy

Epilogue

Historic Notes

Chapter 1: Paris

It was early September 1817 British Intelligence had information that factions in Paris would make an attempt on the Duke of Wellington's life within the next month and had sent their best man and his team to eliminate the threat. Marty thought, sourly, that the agents they had in Paris already were more than capable of protecting Arthur, and saw his mission as more about tracking down and eliminating the groups at source.

Marty and Caroline were taking the opportunity for a pleasure trip alongside his mission now that travel in France was allowed. She wanted to catch up on the latest Paris haute couture and perfumes while looking for more outlets for her precious stones.

The Shadows had come along of course but they were still a man down. The loss of Wilson and John, the last time they were in Paris was still raw. Adam, Marty's steward and valet, was a defacto member now and they had added Zeb who was John's half-brother, but they were still missing the muscle that Wilson had brought to the team.

This trip Caroline had insisted that they bring one of their own coaches.

"Those wrecks they call coaches for rent in France are uncomfortable and are always breaking. We will ship our own over," she had insisted.

Consequently, their larger, enclosed carriage was being unloaded from the Pride at Calais along with a team of four matched Suffolk

Punch horses. These big drought horses had the stamina to walk all day and wouldn't need changing on the way to Paris. Two of their own coachmen would drive the carriage taking turn and turn about every two hours when the horses were rested for thirty minutes.

The Shadows has mounts that were all former cavalry horses. Since the end of the war these had become readily available in France as the new government reduced the size of the army to peacetime levels.

The children had been left at home. Beth and the twins were in Cheshire with their pet leopards, Rhaja and Princess. Marty had given in and allowed them to be kept as the cats treated his ten-year-old twins like playmates. Beth, who was now fifteen, oversaw them and made sure that the twins kept them in their specially made enclosure when they weren't walking them out on their leads.

The estate workers had been terrified when they first saw the cats. They had never seen anything like them before but when they saw the twins walking them down the lanes, like they were dogs, they started bragging to other estate workers at the markets about the 'big cats of the Purbeck estate'. Ryan and Louise, who were acting as stand-in parents while Marty and Caroline were away, had instructions to ship the cats to the Tower menagerie if they showed any signs of getting out of control.

James, their son, was graduating from naval college this year and had asked if he could be a midshipman on a frigate. Marty had offered to ask Fairbrother of the Suffolk if he would take him on, but James had rebelled against that and had asked if he could be taken on the Leonidas under James Campbell.

"Have you made up your mind whether to let James join the squadron?" Caroline asked as they jolted over the atrocious roads in France.

"It is not unheard of for a son to be a midshipman on one of his father's ships, so his request isn't out of line, but, with his grades and being captain of the year, he could have his choice of any ship in the fleet."

"You think he could do better?"

Marty barked a short laugh, "That's a trap question if ever I heard it. James Campbell is a fine captain and trains his officers as well as any man in the navy. If he wasn't part of my squadron, I would jump at the chance for James to serve under him."

"Oh, so you are worried it would be seen as nepotistic."

"It could be seen as such."

"Not by James Campbell."

"No, he would be honoured."

"Then you are worried about what others think?"

Marty sighed, "I am worried about the effect on his career."

Caroline feigned looking out of the window and said casually, "He wants to follow in your footsteps."

"So does Beth."

"Touché, but she has Louise as a mentor."

"I suppose if he were in the squadron, he could learn some of the more unusual skills that we employ."

"And James could be his mentor."

Marty harrumphed and slid down into his heavy coat, so the collar covered his ears. He needed to think about all this.

Paris was damp and dreary, there was a heavy mizzle that chilled and even their stoic horses trudged along without a lot of enthusiasm. The town had a feeling of occupation and they saw many Prussian troops in their black uniforms. They crossed town to the Élysée Palace and took rooms in a hotel Marty used the last time he had been there.

The desk clerk was the same man and looked sharply at Marty when they approached,

"Parlez vous Englais?" Marty asked with a strong English accent.

"Non." The clerk looked confused.

"Jai suis Viscount Purbeck et je desirez un suite pour mon femme et mois." Marty smiled brightly as if he had given a grand speech. Caroline was quivering as she tried not to laugh at his deliberate mispronunciation.

"Un grande chambre, sil vous please," Marty said louder as if to emphasise what he wanted.

The clerk was now convinced he was faced with an idiot English aristo who knew enough French to strangle his beloved language. But he obviously had money as the coach outside was decorated with a coat of arms. He rang a bell, and a suited man came out of the office behind him. He muttered in his ear and the man stepped forward.

"My Lord Purbeck?" he said.

Marty nodded.

"My name is Serge and I am the manager of the hotel, my clerk, unfortunately, does not speak English so I will look after you myself."

"Excellent!" Marty crowed clapping his hands together, "I would like a suite for my wife and I."

"Do you have servants?"

"Only my carriage drivers."

"That's perfect, we have a communal room where they can stay. I have a suite on the top floor for you. It has recently been redecorated, overlooks the Palais and has a bathroom and one of the new flushing toilets."

"Sounds perfect," Marty said, "can you see to our baggage?"

"It will be brought up directly. The room has its own butler and maid who will unpack for you."

"Perfect! A bath, then dinner, what?"

"You sounded like some old general," Caroline laughed.

"Did I? I was going for Admiral Hood, but it will suffice."

"That poor clerk was convinced he knew you when we first walked in."

"I know. We stayed here the last time we were in Paris. Same room as well."

Caroline sobered and took him in her arms.

"It's alright, John and Wilson never stayed here." He buried his nose in her hair.

There was a knock on the door.

"Come in!" Caroline said.

It was the butler and maid who ushered in a line of bellboys with their luggage. Marty decided he would be better off elsewhere.

He met the Shadows at the hotel they had taken in the Rue Nicolas Flamel, which was a brisk thirty-minute walk away. Troy came with him and enjoyed the new smells and sounds. Several dogs checked him out from a distance but his size and the way he stayed close to Marty's hip, kept them at a distance.

"What I want is for you to circulate around the bars and cafés and see if you can get any hint of pro-Napoleon sentiment. The bars where ex-soldiers congregate will be the most likely places but follow your instincts and cover as much ground as possible. Do it in pairs. I do not want to have to mount a search party to find one of you lying in a sewer or down in the catacombs," Marty said.

"Do you want me to go as well?" Zeb asked.

"No, neither you nor Adam speak French, so you will be better served coming back to my hotel. They have never seen you before and you can act as liaison to the rest of the team."

"Thank *gould* for that," Zeb said, "I was wonderin' how I was supposed to know what them Frenchies was jabberin' about."

Adam schooled himself into a Spanish persona, basing the accent on the Jerez region he pretended to be a trader and Zeb his assistant. He dressed in a foppish suit with frills around the cuffs and neck. Lisping his s's and making a 'th' out of 'c', he led Zeb to the desk.

"I want a room for my man and me to stay in while we are in town," he said to the clerk in heavily-accented English.

The clerk raised his eyes to heaven in a 'why me' gesture and rang the bell.

The manager came out, took him in at a glance and said, "Sir, how can I help you?"

"Please, it is very simple, I need a room for my man and me."

"Certainly, Sir, one or two beds?" The inference was plain.

Adam swore and spewed out a stream of Spanish, cursing the dirty-minded Frenchmen. Marty, who was conveniently reading a paper in one of the lobby chairs, stood and asked in Spanish, "May I be of assistance?"

"Thank you, Señor, I want a room for me and my assistant, but this oaf thinks we are homosexuals!"

Marty smiled and turned to the manager. "Mr?" He looked at Adam with his eyebrows raised in question.

"Rodriguez."

"Mr Rodriguez, requires a room for his assistant and himself with two beds or two single rooms for the same price."

"Aah now I understand. I thought…"

"Yes, Mr Rodriguez understood what you thought."

The manager coughed and bowed to Adam. "My apologies Sir, we have only one room available, but I believe it will suit your needs. It has two beds, and you share the bathroom with the other rooms on that floor."

Marty translated and Adam pretended to be mollified.

"He will take it."

The clerk handed over the key and Adam signed the guest book with a typical Spanish flourish.

With a reason established for the two to talk in future, Marty left them to it and went back to his paper.

It was two days before the first report came in, Zeb had met Antton at a prearranged time and place, in this case a café, and reported the conversation to Marty via a note discretely passed as they crossed each other in the lobby.

"Interesting," Marty said as he read it in their room.

"What is?" Caroline said from where she was sketching the skyline.

"Hmm? Oh, this note, from Antton."

When it was clear he wasn't going to say anymore Caroline said, "Well? What truths does it reveal?"

"Oh, nothing much, only that they have identified two establishments where Boney's die-hard supporters seem to gather."

"I suppose that they will infiltrate them then."

"No, they can't. The people who attend are ultra-nationalists and Basques are not welcome. They were thrown out under threat of a beating when they tried."

"That counts out Chin and Sam as well then."

"Indeed." Marty looked thoughtful for a minute. Caroline waited expectantly.

"Let me guess," she said when she got tired of waiting, "you will have to infiltrate them with Roland."

"You read my mind!"

"Not hard," Caroline laughed.

"I will need a new identity."

"How about Monsieur Alfred Chabal."

"Good name! Now what does he do?"

It was Caroline's turn to look thoughtful.

"How about he is a former policeman from somewhere like Lyon. You can do the accent from there."

"Why is he in town?"

Caroline was getting into this now and she put aside her sketchpad.

"He was a big supporter of Napoleon and thought he was the answer to keeping France from falling back into the terror. The country is being overrun with the conquering armies and their former vasal states. On top of all that, the Bourbons are back and it all seems to have been for nought. Now he is looking to join with like-minded people to work towards a true republic."

"Brilliant! Let's get Zeb to create his papers."

A discrete meeting with Adam and Zeb got the forger working on the necessary then Marty set about working up a disguise. He got Caroline to curl his hair using tongs heated in the fire and stuck on a goatee beard and moustache from his disguise kit. He dressed in a suit that was of a style commonly adopted by civil servants.

"Your own brother wouldn't recognise you," Caroline said and sketched him so she could consistently reproduce the look. "How are you getting out of the hotel?"

"There is a back door that the staff use, it is never locked and unguarded."

"Hmph, so much for security." Caroline went to a trunk and opened it. She ran her fingers along a seam and pressed down when she felt a bump. A secret panel opened. Inside were her pistols complete with cleaning kit, powder horn and ball. She took them out, loaded and primed them. She hiked up her dress hem revealing her legs that were clad in thigh-high silk stockings held up by garters.

"Lovely!" Marty sighed looking at her admiringly.

Caroline blew him a kiss and slotted a pistol into each of the garters which had special loops fitted just for this purpose.

"I can get to them through slits in my dress but it's easier to get them in the loops this way."

"A brand-new way to carry muff pistols. I love it!"

She threw a pillow at him.

Marty met Roland in the street, and they made their way to the first address. It was a bar in the republic area of the city, it served traditional peasant food and rough wine. Marty and Roland walked in and were immediately confronted by a brute of a doorman.

"You have to be a member to come in here," he said.

"Since when do you have to be a member to enter a bar in Paris?" Marty asked in a thick Lyons accent.

"Since this became a bar for members."

"I was told this was the place to come to talk to like-minded people."

"That depends on what you want to talk about."

"I was hoping to talk about preserving the republic, throwing out the Bourbons and getting our emperor back."

"That's dangerous talk in Paris."

"It's dangerous talk anywhere," said a tall intelligent-looking man who approached after listening to the exchange. He nodded to the doorman who went back to his table just inside the door. "You are evidently not from Paris?"

"Came in from Lyon recently."

"You are a friend of the republic?"

"Napoleon brought stability and now we have the bloody king back. Was the revolution all for nothing?"

"That didn't answer my question."

Marty glowered at him and barked, "Yes. I am a friend of the republic."

The man held out his hand and Marty took it. He was unexpectedly pulled close and the man said quietly in his ear, "If you are lying they will find your body in the Seine."

Letting him go he said, "My name is Jean-Pierre Brissot."

"Alfred Chabal, out of Lyon. Are you related to Jacques-Pierre Brissot?"

"He was my father."

"He died a hero to some of us."

Jacques-Pierre Brissot, Marty knew had been an active member of the assembly and National Convention. Had led a faction called the Girondins who were in favour of a constitutional monarchy. He was executed after unsuccessfully declaring war on Austria and Prussia.

"He was wrong on one count," Jean-Pierre said, "the monarchy had to go."

"I agree that fat bastard is just a leach," Marty spat.

They were accepted into the 'club' after a careful examination of their papers and giving a complete history. Marty was sure that their stories would be checked out, but it would take several days if not weeks to get a man to Lyon, check out their story and report back. He would have Antton and Matai go to Lyon and look out for anyone asking questions in a bar that Roland had identified as a traditional hub of discontent.

They were given stamped metal pins with an odd design on them which they wore on the back of their left lapels. These gave them entry to the meetings of the Republican Brotherhood. The second address the boys had identified wasn't one of the locations the Brotherhood used and turned out to be a rival faction's meeting place.

"How come you don't merge all the factions?" Marty asked Jean-Pierre.

"That group are militants and anarchists, they want to bring back the terror. They don't want an emperor or any kind of government. They hate the British as well. In fact they hate all foreigners."

"I see," Marty said.

The Brotherhood held regular meetings in the backrooms of bars and even a disused warehouse. They debated and gave speeches but didn't talk about revolution or assassination. Marty concluded rather quickly they were relatively harmless. The other group was, however, a problem.

They couldn't get anybody in, the group was aggressively paranoid, and intruders were beaten up as a matter of course. Membership was apparently only at the recommendation of an existing member and he, or she, was held responsible for the new person for the entirety of their membership. The other thing was once you were in, you didn't leave, not alive anyway.

Marty had the boys keep a watch on the anarchists from a safe distance. Antton and Matai arrived back from Lyon and reported that they had intercepted and disposed of the man that was sent to check Marty's back story.

"We found him in the bar that Roland mentioned, he was asking all sorts of questions and not getting answers that he liked. He had an accident."

"Oh? What kind?" Marty said.

"Stepped in front of a dray wagon, the wheels nearly cut him in half."

"Witnesses?"

"None, no one saw Matai push him. The policeman who attended decided it was an accident and reported it as that."

Garai joined them. "Somethings going on with the anarchists, they dispersed last night, and the bar is deserted today."

"That probably means they think that whatever is going to happen is going to bring the authorities down on them. Are you following any individuals?"

"Yes, we are following two who seem to be prominent members."

"Antton, Matai, you are with me. Garai, get back to the boys, I want to know where their new meeting place is."

Marty, in his own persona, paid a visit to Arthur Wellesley,

"Hello, Martin, I wondered when you would come and say hello," Arthur said in his typically haughty manner which didn't fool Marty for a minute.

"I should have stopped by before but have been a tad busy," Marty grinned.

Arthur smiled, "I won't ask what you have been up to."

Marty became serious, "We think the anarchists will make a move very soon."

"Against me?"

"You or the king."

"Do you know how?"

"Something dramatic I expect. They will want to make a statement. The problem is we haven't been able to infiltrate them."

"So how do you know what they are planning?"

"They have abandoned their meeting place and dispersed. A good sign that whatever they are going to do will attract the wrath of the authorities."

"Are you going to disappoint them?"

"I want them all in one place so if I can stop whatever they are about to do and get them back into one place, then I will."

Chapter 2: Intervention and Assassination

Marty was supplied with the schedules for both Wellington and the king for the following month and he tried to put himself in the mindset of the anarchists as he looked for likely opportunities to make a splash.

"The king has nothing in his schedule that lends itself to any kind of attempt, but Arthur has three occasions where he will be very visible, and an assassination attempt would be possible."

"Do you know how they will do it?" Caroline asked.

"The anarchists like bombs, they make a statement, and they don't care if they kill a few innocents when they do it."

"How would they get one close to Arthur?"

"They would have to carry it." Marty thought that through, and his soul suddenly froze.

"They would sacrifice one of their own," he said in horror.

"What do you mean?"

"They would have one of theirs sacrifice him, or herself, for the cause and carry the bomb right up to him."

"What?" Caroline said, still not appreciating what Marty had said.

"They will get someone to carry the bomb right up to him and detonate it."

"But that is suicide!"

Marty scanned the event schedule and one stood out. "Arthur is attending an open-air opera on March the 15th."

The significance wasn't lost on Caroline. "The Ides of March!"

"Yes, the death of Caesar, killed because he was emperor."

"They see Arthur as an emperor?"

"He is the man who defeated their emperor, so that makes him the emperor by conquest."

"That is insane."

"No, that is the logic of the fanatic."

Marty looked out of the window, his brain formulating a counter strategy.

The next morning, he went to see Arthur.

"Good morning, Purbeck!" Arthur called from the back of Copenhagen his favourite charger.

He's in a good mood, Marty thought but responded in kind.

"Morning, Wellington, may I join you?" Marty was mounted on a palfrey which suited his riding style.

"Of course! Where is your dog?"

"Over there!" Marty whistled shrilly and Troy bounded over.

Arthur had a pair of foxhounds and Troy eyed them warily before wandering over and exchanging sniffs.

They trotted out, heading into the Champ du Mars.

"I believe there will be an assassination attempt on you at the open-air opera event at Le Hotel National des Invalides this evening."

"Really? And who will try to enact this devious deed?"

"The anarchists. They will send in one of their own to get close to you and detonate a bomb."

"But that would be suicide."

"Exactly."

"How will you stop it?"

"Maybe I will let them blow you up."

"Funny, and I can have you shot."

Marty laughed, he really enjoyed sparring with Arthur.

"Actually, I am serious."

"What?"

"Well not you but a double. I wouldn't want to endanger you and we need them to commit before we can stop them."

"Let me see if I understand. You want to put a double in my place at the opera so you can let the assassin get close, so you can stop them."

"That's about it."

Arthur thought that through.

"Everyone around me at that opera will be in danger as well."

Marty nodded.

"Then I cannot abdicate the role to a double."

"I was afraid you would say that."

Marty took a pipe from his coat and put it to his lips. He blew and Arthur slid from his saddle to be caught by two of the Shadows. They carried him to a coach that had been pacing them.

A figure, dressed identically, left the coach and mounted Copenhagen who fidgeted as he registered the strange seat on his back.

That evening the Duke of Wellington left his apartments at the appointed time. His wife had cried off going to the opera, so he was alone. The carriage ride through Paris was uneventful and he arrived precisely on time. The crowd variously cheered or booed as he made his way to his seat. As usual he didn't react to either. As there was a vacant seat, Lord Purbeck sat next to him. The two men chatted while servants served them drinks and brought snacks. The performance of Rossini's *Il barbiere di Siviglia* was in two acts and the audience waited in anticipation for its debut in France.

Marty enjoyed the opera and watched the audience which was predominantly made up of the wealthy. Vendors circulated, selling drinks and snacks from trays. Marty kept a wary eye on any that got close. They were ushered away when the first act started. The crowd applauded.

The act passed without incident and the interval saw the return of the vendors. Marty was pleased that his servants had moved to stand in a rough half circle waiting for him or Wellington to require attending on.

A vendor was working his way up and down the rows four from their seats. He was selling dainties, sweets and pastries. Marty noticed he was sweating despite it being a cool evening. The man moved up a row and was moving down it towards them. He was reaching under his coat when he suddenly cried out and collapsed.

Marty leapt to his feet and rushed to his assistance. "Move back, give him room!" he shouted. He checked the man's pulse in his neck then sat back on his heels.

"He is dead, I think he had a heart attack." He beckoned to two of his men to carry the unfortunate man away.

The second act started, and Marty resumed his seat. There was no need for something as trivial as a vendor dropping dead to interfere with it.

Arthur was furious.

"You drugged me! How dare you!"

Marty was unrepentant. "I couldn't risk your life on the chance we got to the assassin before he detonated the bomb, as it was it was too bloody close for comfort."

"You risked yours!" Arthur snapped with all the cold haughtiness he was renowned for.

"That, with all due respect, is my job."

Arthur hmph'd, "Who doubled for me?"

"Cyril Vaughn, the actor."

"He is in Paris?"

"His troop are performing at the La Comédie-Française.'

"You got him?"

"The bomber? Yes, Antton hit him with the same type of dart I used on you. He had a bomb strapped around his waist which would be detonated by a small pistol that was built into it."

"Where is he now?"

"In the basement of the palace, the boys are working on him."

Arthur winced, he knew Marty's interrogation techniques and could almost pity the man.

Garai and Matai had taken the prisoner to Marty's coach and from there to the Élysée Palace. There was an empty storeroom in the cellar, it had no dungeon, which they made into a holding cell. The room was bare, no cot or stool, just a bucket. There were no windows and they had lined the walls with cork so it was soundproof.

The prisoner woke when a bucket of water was poured over his head. He was dragged to his feet and forced to kneel in the puddle, blindfolded with his hands tied painfully behind him. He had no sense of time, just the pain in his knees and the pain building in his back and shoulders.

He knew he was a prisoner, he assumed it was the police, he had no idea how he had gotten there. A rough slap delivered randomly kept him awake. Sleep deprivation and stress took its toll, he imagined he heard things and random images started to pass before his eyes. His world compressed into pain and darkness. He could hear a door open and close periodically.

Suddenly there was a soft voice. "Who are you?"

"What?"

There was no reply.

"Hello?"

Still no reply.

Silence and darkness, he started to cry.

"Who are you?"

"Robert."

"Robert who?"

"Robert Dupuis. Can I stand up? My knees hurt."

Silence. There wasn't a sound for what seemed like a lifetime.

"Robert." The voice was very soft again and he strained to hear it.

"Yes?"

"Who made the bomb?"

"I can't tell you."

The silence returned, he had nothing to eat or drink, he started to hallucinate. Bats, he imagined bats were flying around his head. He shit himself.

"Who made the bomb, Robert?" He was dragged to his feet and forced onto a chair; the blindfold was removed. A bright light shone into his eyes.

"Who made the bomb, Robert?"

"They will kill me!"

"You are dead, they cannot kill you."

He believed the voice; he must be dead he was about to fire the bomb when everything went black. *Was this hell?*

"Am I in hell?"

"Yes, this is hell. Who made the bomb?"

"Henri, Henri Bartolomie. Will he join me?"

"Yes, Robert."

He could feel heat.

"Where is he?"

"He is an apothecary on St Germain Street."

"Who else was involved in planning the assassination?"

He must have been successful!

He gave them names; he was so tired he couldn't think.

The blindfold was replaced, and he was lifted to his feet, his legs could hardly take his weight. His trousers were ripped from him, and cold water hit his body, sluicing away the filth. He was half carried half dragged back into his cell and thrown onto a cot.

"We have a list of names. I will eliminate them all," Marty said to Arthur.

"Can't the police just arrest them?"

"That just makes martyrs of them. This way they just disappear."

Arthur looked like he had sucked a lemon.

"You know your business. Can't say I like it though."

Marty and two of the Shadows raided the apothecary's shop that night and found bomb-making equipment. Henri Bartolomie was asleep in his apartment above the shop next to his wife. When she woke the next morning, he was gone. It was a busy night, men all over the city disappeared or were found dead by their own hands. Only a few knew they were anarchists and they decided to stay very, very quiet.

"Your job here is done?" Arthur asked as Marty sipped tea.

"Almost."

"I'm surprised the newspapers haven't picked up on the number of deaths and disappearances in one night."

"Oh, they have." Marty tossed Arthur a copy of *Le Moniteur*.

"Good grief, an inter-faction war?"

"Yes, the Brotherhood of the Republic has made a claim that they have retaliated against the anarchists because they took out one of their members."

"Who?"

"Alfred Chabal."

"Wasn't that the name you used?"

Marty just smiled.

"I hope you enjoy your visit," Serge the hotel manager asked as Marty settled the account.

"Yes, it was quite entertaining, thank you, and the room was splendid."

"Your wife was happy with the shopping I see."

"Quite, I have had to purchase two extra trunks. She has made up for lost time."

Serge had counted the coins as Marty had passed them over and swept them into the cash drawer. Marty tossed him an extra half louis. "That's for the butler and maid."

"I will make sure they get it."

Marty was sure they would only get half but that was the way the world turned.

The boys formed up around the coach as it left the hotel, and they made their way out of town. They had said their goodbyes the evening before when they treated Arthur to a sumptuous dinner in the best restaurant in Paris. He had forgiven Marty for drugging him but had warned him never to do it again. Marty had promised, with his fingers firmly crossed behind his back.

As they passed the Élysée Palace, a group of protesters waved placards and chanted slogans. Marty recognised several as members of the Brotherhood of the Republic. Democracy was alive and well in Paris.

Chapter 3: The Squadron Reformed

"There is something perverse about the navy," Marty thought as his coach pulled into Plymouth. His squadron had been sent there to assemble and it was as far away from London unless they had designated Falmouth. It had taken him over a week to coach down and he was feeling grumpy.

The only mitigating factor as far as he was concerned was that his son, James, was joining the Leonidas as a midshipman. His choice as a reward for being top of his class at the naval college for three years in a row.

James Campbell had taken him on his complement on the condition that he got no favours because he was the commodore's son. Something Marty welcomed. He was constitutionally against nepotism and had opposed James joining the squadron fearing that would be how it was seen. Caroline had argued that, as his son wanted to follow in his footsteps, it was the best course. Even now he had doubts but with both his eldest wanting to follow him into the intelligence service he was at least able to ensure one had the grounding they needed.

His oldest, Beth, who was maturing far faster than he was prepared for, was being mentored by Louise Thompson: the former spy known as Linette. She had his talent for languages and was studying politics, anatomy and all the skills needed to be undercover. She had demonstrated her acting skills by disguising herself as a maid and waiting on him at their Cheshire home without him realising for half a day. Beth had been delighted and didn't hesitate to rub it in.

The coach clattered across Stonehouse Creek Bridge and pulled up at Devonport's gates. The dockyard was enclosed by a fortified wall on the landward side. A marine corporal stepped up smartly, looked into the coach and saluted.

"Your papers, please, Sah," he barked.

Marty passed him his commission which he studied before passing it back. Marty doubted he had read it until the marine said, "The Unicorn is moored in dock three with your squadron commodore. Have a good voyage," he said and snapped a salute. After handing the papers back he directed the driver where to go. Marty liked dockyards, the smell of tar and wood overlaying the usual stink of humanity was like coming home in a way. After entering through the gate, they turned left before the Ordinance Board building and entered Mount Wise Parade Ground.

There were a lot of marines in Devonport, it being one of their home bases, and they marched up and down the parade ground to tunes played by a marine band. Marty smiled; Devonport felt much more 'Navy' than Chatham because of the marines. Chatham felt more like a repair yard in comparison.

They passed the two-hundred-and-sixty-yard-long ropewalk before entering the South Dock. The coach pulled to a stop directly beside the Unicorn, he took his time gathering himself to allow Wolfgang to organise the mandatory reception committee. What he didn't expect was Midshipman Stirling opening the door and saluting him out. An honour guard of marines was lined up on the quay either side of the gangway with Captain O'Driscol in full uniform stood in front with his sword at the present.

"Good afternoon, Captain," Marty said and touched his hat to return the salute. He couldn't fail to notice that he had a magnificent black eye. Suspicion blossomed as he turned to inspect the guard. O'Driscol dropped into step half a pace behind him to his left.

Marty started at the right-hand end of the line and as he progressed, he noticed that every man had evidence of battle written clear on their faces: black eyes, bent noses, split cheeks along with broken and bruised knuckles gripping their rifles. However, they all stared fixedly ahead and held their heads proudly.

"Very good, Captain, a very smart turnout," he said, straight faced, and made his way up the gangplank.

He could see Wolfgang and the rest of the officers stood in a line with another contingent of marines that came to attention with a crash of rifle butts and a cloud of pipeclay. It was obvious they were all having a hard time supressing grins. The bosun's whistles trilled their Spithead nightingale call and Marty saluted the quarterdeck. "Permission to come aboard, Captain," he said.

"Permission granted, Sir," Wolfgang said and shook his hand. As they were being so formal Marty went along the line and greeted each officer by name and shook his hand. When that was done, he and Wolfgang walked to the quarterdeck leaving Lieutenant McGivern to retrieve his baggage.

Sam was waiting for him, and Marty greeted him as an old friend. Once they were out of earshot of the others he turned. "Now, Wolfgang. What the hell is going on?"

"Sir?" Wolfgang said, oozing innocence.

"Don't 'Sir' me. Why all the pomp?"

"Ah well, there was a bit of a disagreement between members of the squadron and some of the regular navy types in a pub in town."

Marty looked at him steadily until he continued.

"The regular navy types taunted them that our squadron was a second-class unit made up of the dross of the service, fit only to ferry cargo. They also said that we couldn't fight our way out of whore's embrace."

"I take it our boy's objected?"

"Yes, Sir."

"Officer's as well?"

"Separate incident, outside the Wardroom."

"The damage?"

"The pub was wrecked, a large number of regular navy were hospitalised and the shore patrol were called in. I made reparation with the landlord."

"The Wardroom?"

"No damage there, the disagreement occurred out the back in the courtyard."

Marty stared him down then asked, "Any casualties on our side?"

"No, Sir, only bumps and bruises."

"The port admiral?"

"Was persuaded to let us take care of punishment by Mister Fletcher."

Marty raised an eyebrow, the purser had something over almost every shore-based officer in the navy and he wondered what had been traded to get that result.

"Is the squadron ready to sail?"

"We are in all respects ready for sea."

"We will leave on the tide in the morning. I wish to have all captains join me for dinner this evening. I assume that Roland is already here?"

"Aye, Sir, the Shadows arrived yesterday."

"Have Mr Fletcher attend me in my cabin."

Fletcher, dressed in his usual smoker's jacket and hat, visited Marty as requested.

"Commodore," he said respectfully.

"I wanted to thank you," Marty said and poured glasses of Armagnac for them both.

"For what?" Fletcher replied.

"Intervening with the port admiral."

"Oh that. It was nothing."

"Tush, you must have used up a significant bit of leverage to do it."

"Ah, I see. Well, I didn't exactly use it up, more like I mentioned I knew something that he would rather have kept quiet. I still know it so it's still available."

Marty grinned and said, "Don't let the crew know or they will take the town apart next time we are here."

Fletcher raised his glass and Marty said, "Please join us for dinner tonight."

The dinner was another triumph of culinary perfection by Roland who had spent the day since he arrived stocking up Marty's private stores. He had anticipated him wanting to entertain his captains and had prepared some special dishes.

"Gentlemen, I expect you would all like to thank Roland for this fine feast." The men applauded and gave three cheers.

"You will also want to thank Mr Fletcher, his intervention with the port admiral saved the whole squadron from facing court martial." he gave them his best gimlet stare. "He will not have to do that again." He sat back and continued. "I expect you all wish to know what our mission is going to be. It comes in two parts. The first is to assist the Ottomans in defeating the Wahhabi in Egypt. As usual, trade is the reason behind our government's generosity." Marty waited until the laughter died down. "But that is all a cover. There isn't actually much we can do to help apart from show our faces. The second part was communicated to me by Admiral Turner the night before I left London and isn't in the written orders. The Ottoman Empire is beginning to collapse, their problems in Egypt are symptomatic of a general rise in discontent with their rule. There has been a rebellion in the Balkans and Greece is building towards rebellion." He took a mouthful of wine, an extremely good Barolo. "We are to use our presence in the region as an excuse to visit Cyprus, measure the sentiment of the people there and, if we think it appropriate, aid them. Cyprus being a very strategically-placed island in the Eastern Mediterranean. We will also endeavour to make contact with the Greeks with the aim of covertly aiding them on to the road to independence."

"Is it the aim of the government to make Cyprus part of the British Empire?" James Campbell asked.

"If it keeps it away from an independent Greece, yes that would be a possibility."

"Do we know who is aiding the Wahhabi?" Captain Trenchard of the Endellion said.

"That's a good question, Philip, we have been told by the Ottomans other radical Muslim groups out of Persia are suspected of supplying weapons and even fighters."

"We won't be able to do much to counteract the arms from there," Arnold Grey, the master of the Unicorn, said, "not without sailing all the way around Africa."

"You are right, if there was a river we could utilise, we could at least get some gunboats down into the Red Sea," Marty said. He went to the map locker and pulled out a map he had bought in Paris. "This was created by Napoleon's surveyors and accurately depicts the Nile and the waterways in Egypt. Apparently, he had them looking for a dried-up canal built by some Pharaoh or another."

"Do you intend to dig it out?" James laughed.

"That's a thought, I could send you and your crew down there with shovels." When the men stopped laughing Marty focussed back on the chart.

"Arnold, the Nile is navigable by small craft all the way up to the cataracts, isn't it?"

"Aye, Sir. By anything up to and including a large dhow."

Marty looked at the map, picked up a magnifying glass and examined a certain section. He grinned and rolled up the map. "Well, gentlemen, thank you for your company. We won't be sailing for a few days. The men can have shore leave by watch. Any more fighting will result in no more leave for anyone and the culprits losing their rum and tobacco rations for a month. Trevor, please come and see me for breakfast tomorrow at seven o'clock?"

The men left and Marty could hear them speculating what the old man was up to. He smiled and went back to examining the map. He had an idea but had no idea whether it would be doable or not.

The next morning Trevor Archer of the Eagle was announced on the dot of seven.

"Come in, Trevor. Would you like some coffee?"

"Yes, please, Sir, especially if it's some of your own beans."

Bacon, sausage, blood pudding and eggs were laid out on salvers along with toast and a slab of fresh butter. The two men helped themselves while Adam poured coffee.

While they ate, Marty said very little, just chatting about the weather and the ships. He polished off his last piece of bacon and used a heel of toast to mop up the fat and egg yolk left on his plate. Adam cleared the table and as soon as they had space, he laid out the chart.

"I have a mission for you, and I want you to take the marine engineers with you." Marty had always ensured that a contingent of the marines were engineers. They were affiliated with the Toolshed, his inventive geniuses.

"I want you to take the Eagle up the Nile from Izbat Burj Rashid to here at Al-Bilaydah and drop off the engineers with an escort of thirty marines."

"The river passes very close to Cairo."

"Yes, that's why I have chosen the Eagle for this task. You can pass for American. You may well be scrutinised, but you should be able to sail up without interference."

"What will the marines be doing?"

"Surveying a route over which we can portage a pair of gunboats into the Red Sea."

Trevor sat back looking astonished then got hold of himself and said, "Am I to wait for them?"

"Yes. It's about sixty-five miles from the Nile to the sea at its narrowest so it will take them at least a month to find and map a route."

Trevor thought as he examined the map, "Can I ask, Sir?"

"Yes, ask anything you want."

"How are we to portage the boats? They are heavy beasts especially when armed."

"I have in mind using boats that are big enough to carry a pair of carronades, manned by twenty to thirty men and transporting them on wheels."

"Still sixty-five miles across the desert is a long way."

"Indeed, and it may not be possible in time, but we won't know until you go and have a look. When can you leave?"

"We are ready for sea, so as soon as the marines are on board."

"Good I have your written orders here." Marty passed him a sealed packet. "You will need an interpreter for the trip and I have signalled Admiral Turner for him to send us one. The marines should be ready in three to four days."

Turner didn't disappoint and a man from the Foreign Office arrived.

"Umbridge Falconer," he said and handed over a letter of introduction. Marty read it while Umbridge sat nervously on the edge of his chair.

"You speak Arabic and have spent time in Egypt?" Marty said.

"Yes, that is correct."

"You know the Nile?"

"I know of the Nile of course and have sailed it as far as Aswan."

"Perfect."

"Can I ask, Sir, what it is you need me to do?"

Marty smiled, "They didn't tell you, but still you volunteered?"

"Volunteer is not a term I would use. I was instructed to make my way here and be prepared to be at sea for a protracted period."

Marty understood, Turner and the Foreign Office had just found someone with the right attributes and sent him on his way.

"If I told you that you will be sailing up the Nile and helping survey a route from there to the Red Sea, would you be willing to go?"

His face lit up. "Oh yes, Sir, I have dreamed of returning to Egypt."

"Even if the natives are hostile?"

"Not all Egyptians are Wahhabi, Sir, many are friendly to outsiders and just want to live their lives in peace."

"He'll do," Marty thought.

The Eagle left and Marty gave Fletcher the task of finding the kind of boats he had in mind. Fletcher came up with a pair of oversized launches normally used by first rates. They came from a shipwright in the town who had built them for the navy only to be told they were no longer needed. He negotiated hard and got them for an exceptionally good price.

The thirty-five-foot-long boats had a wide beam and could carry up to nine tons of cargo. They were normally propelled by ten, two-man oars, but a mast could be stepped, and a Bermuda rig raised. They were the bastard offspring of the old longboats and modern ship's barges, and Marty thought they would be as agile as the galleys he had fought against in the Mediterranean when under oars.

They were stowed on the decks of the Unicorn and Leonidas. Meanwhile the Toolshed acquired two heavy-duty four-wheeled carts, normally used for carrying stone, which they cannibalised to fashion skeleton frames to transport the boats overland. The wide wheels were especially suitable for travelling over soft ground. They were stowed in pieces in the hold.

"You really think they can get those boats sixty-five-miles across the desert?" Wolfgang said as he and Marty circumnavigated the upturned hull on the Unicorn's deck.

"To be honest I have no idea," Marty admitted, "but we have to try. It really depends on what the engineer's report says. We will need to get horses or oxen in Egypt if they say it's possible."

Wolfgang changed the subject, "When do you want us to leave?"

"We are ready, so on the next tide."

Wolfgang excused himself and went to prepare his ship. Marty returned to his cabin and looked out of the transom window. Could he really get boats into the Red Sea from the Nile? He had his doubts, sand was a terrible surface to transport any kind of wheeled vehicle over and the heat.

Chapter 4: New Allies

The voyage to the Mediterranean was regulation. Without the French or Spanish to fight there wasn't any risk of attack and they could cruise. Marty didn't even particularly hurry as he wanted to give the Eagle as much time as he could. They stopped at Gibraltar as a matter of course and while he was there wanted to pay a visit to an old friend, Billy Hooper. He asked around for his location and heard he could be found in the more disreputable part of town. He dressed in civilian clothes and set off to find him.

"Hello, Billy, I hear you are at a loose end now Francis has gone home," Marty said as he approached the whorehouse that Billy was keeping door at.

"Hello, Sir! I never thought to see you again," Billy said with a beaming smile, "I still have that pistol you gave me."

He pumped Marty's hand, then spun to grab a drunk who was trying to sneak in behind him. A kick on the backside sent him on his way.

Marty waited for him to turn back to him and said, "I promised you that once Francis no longer needed you for protection, I would see about you joining the Shadows."

"Aye, you did, but I never thought you meant it."

"Well, I did, and now I've come to ask if you want to join?"

"Serious?"

"Yes serious."

"When?"

"Now unless you have something pressing to take care of."

"Naw, the old bird who runs this pigsty owes me two days money. She can go 'ang."

Marty grinned and turned to walk away. He stopped after three or four steps and looking back said, "You coming or not?"

Billy laughed and fell into step.

They collected Billy's meagre possessions and walked together through the town. Marty stopped at a clothes shop and bought him new clothes. Two hard-wearing suits, five pairs of undergarments, socks and other items. They then stopped at an armourer where he kitted him out with a proper fighting knife, a punch knife, a pair of stilettos and a pair of pistols. They eventually made their way to the steps where the Unicorn's boat waited. It was manned by the Shadows who called out in welcome, making Billy grin like the cat that got the cream.

They got him onboard and settled in, then Marty met him with the rest of the Shadows on the main deck.

"Billy, welcome to the team, your training starts now. Chin will instruct you in unarmed combat and sword play. Matai and I in knife fighting and Antton will work on your fitness. Zeb will show you how to pick locks and the finer arts of house breaking. They will all instruct you in the delicate arts of surveillance and counter-surveillance and being generally sneaky."

Billy looked surprised, then adopted a rueful grin.

"I suppose I should have expected that."

What followed was possibly the hardest day's work he had ever done. Marty had Antton run a full workout which included bench pressing bar shot, tossing cannon balls to each other, climbing rigging with and without the use of their legs. Every muscle was used and Marty was struggling.

"Come on, Boss!" Antton encouraged and set off up the ratlines for the fourth time. Marty dug deep and set off in pursuit, by his own admission he had 'let himself go'; spending too much time sailing a desk or riding a horse.

In his cabin he groaned as Adam rubbed his back with liniment.

"I really think you should have eased yourself back into the exercises, milord," Adam said and dug his thumbs into the ligaments either side of Marty's lower spine.

"Maybe, but I will get back to fitness quicker this way."

After a few especially hard digs Adam said, "I heard from a shopkeeper on Gibraltar that pasta was very good for energy."

"Probably an old wife's tale."

"The Italian's swear by it; I will ask Roland what he thinks."

"He is French and despises any cuisine that isn't."

"He is more open than you think."

Marty looked over his shoulder. "If he is, then get him to serve me an Italian meal tonight. If he doesn't, you are cleaning the heads for a week."

"Harsh, but I will take it."

His massage finished and smelling bad enough that Troy would have left the cabin if he had been aboard, Marty settled down to thinking about his mission and what he needed to do. It was true the Ottoman Empire was beginning to come apart at the seams, but it was not at the point of collapse yet and probably wouldn't be for many more years. The Greeks were showing definite signs of rebellion and there was a growing independence movement. Cyprus was a contested territory, being two thirds Christian and a third Muslim.

The Greek orthodox church controlled the Christian population, and the imams controlled the Muslims. This made Cyprus a split theocracy answering to Ottoman rulers. The problem was the Ottomans were corrupt, fragmented, factionalised and misruled almost every part of their empire. That led to resentment and fomented rebellion.

Cyprus was positioned in the perfect strategic position to dominate the Middle East. If the British could get a base on the island there was no part of it that wasn't in easy reach. In fact, between Gibraltar, Malta and Cyprus, they would be able to dominate practically all of the Mediterranean. His eye travelled over the map and settled on Crete. It was the missing link but was historically and firmly Greek. On the other hand, it might be worth a look.

To satisfy the fiction that they were giving support to the Ottomans, Marty needed at least two ships to patrol the coast from Alexandria to Lebanon. The Ottomans seemed to think that the Persians were helping the Wahhabi and if they were, they would probably be shipping contraband overland on the old camel route to Jerusalem, from there to the coast and then by sea to Alexandria.

The Ottomans had put large numbers of troops into the region, but it was like trying to seal up a sieve. There was always another route, and, anyway, most of their officers could be paid to look the other way. *"That was the trouble with having a corrupt leadership,"*

Marty thought, *"everybody ended up on the take."*

The Leonidas, Silverthorn and Nymphe would suffice for the patrol. That would leave the Unicorn, and Endellion free to investigate other possibilities. But, first, he needed to hear from the Eagle.

They sailed into Valletta and Marty went ashore to pay his respects to Sir Thomas Maitland, the governor. He walked from the Unicorn to St Georges Square with Billy and Zeb as bodyguards. Marty didn't feel he needed them, but it kept the Shadows happy if he let them protect him. It had been several years since he had cleaned up Malta and there would only be a few who knew him from those days. He doubted Sir Thomas would even know of him as he took the post in 1813.

It was certainly a more prestigious residence than the old one. It had once served as the Grand Master's palace and was known both as the Governor's palace and the Magisters Palace. As they entered St George's Square, they saw a long cream stone building with two arched entrances. Small square and rectangular windows lined the ground floor while the upper floor had tall windows with wrought iron balconies. The roofline was lined by a stone balustrade hinting at a flat roof.

"Which door do we go in?" Zeb said.

"The one with the guards," Marty said, leading them across the square. He was in full uniform and fairly glittered in the late morning sun. The guards snapped smartly to attention when he approached.

"Commodore Stockley to see the governor."

The guard looked him up and down, noting his honours, and the Waterloo medal.

"Please report to the clerk inside, Sah," he said in a parade ground voice that could be heard across the square.

Marty thanked him and stepped through the door into a cool foyer.

"How did he look you up and down without moving his ''ead?" Zeb asked.

"Practice, and that stock," Billy grinned, referring to the leather stock that soldiers wore on official duty.

A clerk was sat behind a desk and only looked up when Marty stood directly in front of him. Marty knew the type, little men who wallowed in the smidgen of power the post gave them. Well two could play at that game.

"Viscount Martin Stockley of Purbeck, Commodore of the Eastern Squadron (he made that bit up). I wish to see the governor," he said with authority.

The clerk ran his eyes over his uniform taking in the honours then looked into the eyes, he leapt to his feet.

"My lord, I will tell Sir Thomas you are here."

He scurried off, his feet slapping on the marble floor. As soon as he was out of sight, they heard him break into a run. He returned, his footsteps pattering rapidly until he reached the door when they slowed to a walk.

"The governor will see you immediately, please follow me," he said, trying hard not to pant. Zeb and Billy followed along as no one told them they couldn't, and Billy said loud enough for Marty to hear. "He needs more exercise."

The corridor was lined with suits of armour and Billy couldn't resist knocking on one with his knuckle to make sure it was empty. Marty kept a straight face and ignored him, but the clerk shot him a look as the hollow clank echoed down the corridor. Marty admired the walls which were sumptuously painted with scenes from the various sieges that the island had survived. It was impressive.

They finally stepped into an office where a uniformed captain stood waiting for him.

"Commodore, welcome. Captain Selwyn Johnston 1st Huntingdonshires adjutant to the governor at your service. The governor is waiting for you. Would your men like to wait here? I will order them some refreshments." He didn't bat an eyelid that they weren't in uniform.

"Wait here," Marty told them.

Zeb and Billy wandered over to a pair of armchairs and sat down. They were, however, watchful. Which wasn't missed by the captain.

Marty was led into another office, this one much larger and infinitely more ornate. Every wall and even the ceiling had been painted with murals, the colours exceptionally bright. The furniture was old and finely carved, a pair of antique suits of armour stood in the corner holding pikes.

"My Lord Purbeck how are you. I had a communique that your squadron was being tasked with supporting the Ottomans and expected you to stop by," Sir Thomas said, with a soft Scottish burr.

"Sir Thomas. It would be remiss of me if I didn't." Marty shook his hand.

They chatted about the end of the war and future challenges for the empire then Marty said, "What can you tell me about what you see going on with the Ottomans?"

"From what we hear from traders, things are warming up in Greece but could take years to come to a head. They are at the local uprisings stage. There isn't a clear unifying leader but there is an organisation called the Filiki Eteria, which roughly translates to Friendly Society, and is based in Odessa. The Russian Tzar has visions of a holy roman war and Greece features large in that."

"Interesting, and what about Cyprus and Crete?"

Sir Thomas paused and looked frankly at Marty. "I get the feeling you are up to more than supporting the Ottomans, do you want to tell me what you are really here for?"

Marty looked at him steadily and decided.

"I have your word it goes no further than this room?" he asked.

"Absolutely, old chap. I am well aware of your history on the island and your preferred solution to intelligence leaks."

Marty gave him his wolf grin, then got serious.

"The support for the Ottomans is a screen, it gives us the excuse to be here and legitimises some of our actions. For example, I have a ship surveying the Nile and a route by which we could get ships into the Red Sea from here."

"Good grief, that's ambitious."

"Quicker than sailing all the way around Africa. However, that's a side show. The real target is an independent Cyprus. Independent from the Ottomans and the Greeks that is."

"Under our control? Poof! That would be a coup," he said

looking at a large map of the region pinned to his wall.

"Yes, and one of immense strategic benefit. We would have control of both ends of the Mediterranean."

Sir Thomas steepled his fingers under his nose in thought then looked up and said, "Now I see why you were asking about Crete, that would give us the entire Mediterranean. But I think you will find Crete is Greek to the core and violently inclined to stay that way."

Marty looked at him quizzically.

"By that I mean they are only part of the Ottoman Empire because mainland Greece is. The Ottomans who dare to show themselves on the island have a habit of disappearing."

"I see. Well, a visit might not go amiss."

"Be careful, if they think you are a threat …" Sir Thomas left the rest unsaid. "On a more welcoming note, would you join me for dinner this evening?"

"I would be delighted."

"Of course! Shall we say seven o'clock?"

Sir Thomas had made it clear this was an intimate dinner with only a few people, so Marty took the unusual step of dressing in civilian clothes. The suit was made by a tailor on Savile Row in London and cut to the latest fashion. He wore no honours except his knights cross. He was, of course, armed and had Sam and Adam escort him.

They arrived at the palace and were admitted immediately on passing his visiting card. He was shown through the building to the private residence where the rooms were no less sumptuous than the more public area. The boys were shown to the kitchens.

Sir Thomas had invited a limited number of friends.

"Lord Martin, may I introduce Annabelle Scarratt, her sister Theresa and husband Sir Graham Hunter, Mr James Arbuthnot and his wife Lady Agatha and finally Miss Veronica Southerland."

It was obvious that Sir Thomas and Annabelle were together which meant that Veronica was along to even up the numbers.

The introductions given; a delicate fino sherry was served.

"This comes from Jerez in Andalusia and is made with the palomino grape," Sir Thomas announced giving Marty the hint that he considered himself somewhat of a connoisseur.

Marty sipped it, appreciating the delicate flavour. James Arbuthnot asked, "You are Commodore of the squadron that came in this morning? I must say they are fine-looking ships."

"Yes, I am, and thank you. I will tell the captains you said that," Marty replied.

Arbuthnot obviously fancied that he knew something of the navy. "Strange that you don't have second rate as your flagship."

"We are a highly mobile unit and often get used for diplomatic work. Frigates are better suited and less threatening," Marty said.

"A sailor!" Veronica chirped, she had a rich alto voice, "You must have many stories you can tell."

Marty smiled and she moved in closer, looking at him intently. Marty was about to reply when Lady Agatha pointedly said, "How is Lady Caroline? I haven't seen her for years now. Has she fought any more duels?"

Veronica looked askance when Marty replied with a laugh, "She is exceptionally well, thank you. Her swordsmanship is even better as she practises with my daughter, Bethany, and me regularly. Her reputation is enough to keep challengers at bay."

"My word! How old is Bethany now?"

"Fifteen acting thirty, you know how teenage girls are."

"How many children do you have?" Veronica asked, a slight note of disappointment in her voice.

Marty was about to reply when they were called to dinner.

"Did you serve under Nelson?" Sir Graham, who was an army major, said.

"I both served under him and knew him; he was a fine man. He attended my wedding." Then to turn the conversation away from his family he launched into a story of Nelson and the pursuit of the French before the Battle of the Nile.

The end of the evening came after an excellent meal, some very good wines and the ladies entertaining them with songs. Veronica had a very good singing voice. It was midnight before he got back to his cabin.

Midshipman Stockley stood on the deck of the Leonidas. He had the watch; he was the most senior officer aboard as everyone else had gone ashore. He only had an anchor watch to oversee and paced the quarterdeck to keep awake. A ribbon of cloud ran across the moon diffusing the light. It was approaching midnight; the moon was almost full, when he saw his father's barge leave the dock and head back to the Unicorn.

He was about to turn away for another circuit of the deck when a small rowboat left the dock and, once clear, spun around a couple of times then headed towards the Leonidas. James watched it, noted the inexpert way it was being rowed and expecting it to change direction, but it kept coming.

That's funny, all our boats are here, he thought.

"Boat approaching!" the port side lookout called.

"Hail it," James said.

"Boat Ahoy!"

There was no answer.

James reached behind his back and pulled a pistol from where it was clipped to his belt. He held it by his side as he waited.

The boat got closer.

"Whoever is rowing that ain't got a clue," Tug Wilson, the lookout, said.

It pulled up at the side, rather it ran into the side and a face looked up, "Mr Stockley?"

"Lor' it's a woman and she be asking for you," Tug said.

"Get down there and secure that boat," James ordered putting his pistol back on his belt.

Tug scampered down and leapt into the boat which was floating a few feet from the side. It rocked as he landed, eliciting a frightened squeal from the occupant. He threw up a rope and another hand pulled them in.

"We're going to need a chair, she's got dresses."

"What do you expect me to be wearing?" she said.

A bosun's chair was rigged and the lady brought up the side.

"Midshipman Stockley at your service, Miss, what can I do to help you?"

"Midshipman? I was expecting to find the commodore."

"My father, Miss, now what is your name and why have you rowed out to the Leonidas?"

"Leonidas? This isn't the Unicorn?"

"No, Miss, that's her over there." James pointed to the bigger ship.

She started to cry. James was now well out of his experience and comfort zone.

"Um, now, Miss, don't take on so. Why don't you come with me and I'll get someone to get us a nice cup of tea while you tell me what's wrong," he said lamely.

James took her to the captain's coach and kicked his steward out of bed to make tea. They sat at the dining table.

"You look like your father." She sniffed.

"They do say that. Can we start from the beginning? What is your name and how do you know my father?"

"Veronica Southerland, I work for British Intelligence, and I need to talk to him before you leave for Libya."

"Are you telling me you are a spy?"

"No! I am an agent." The last was said with a proud toss of the head.

The door opened and the steward served tea. James waited until he left.

"Why did you cry when you found out this wasn't the Unicorn?" he said, thinking now she had collected herself she was rather pretty.

"Frustration, I keep making stupid mistakes. Please don't tell your father. He already thinks I'm an empty-headed ninny."

"Your secret is safe with me. He will be abed by now. I can take you across in the morning if you would care to stay here, I can get a cot made up for you here in the coach."

She agreed and the put-upon steward was called on again. James left her and was just finishing his watch when James Campbell came aboard. He intercepted him and explained.

"Let me get this straight," Campbell said, "we have a British Intelligence agent aboard who has gone to the wrong ship. She is currently asleep in the coach which is part of my cabin on your authority?"

"Aye, aye, Sir that is correct," James said, standing rigidly to attention.

"And you intend to take her over to you father in the morning."

"That is correct, Sir, with your permission of course."

"Well, you had better get her over there at dawn as we will sail with the tide."

James understood. The tide would be at its peak at eight o'clock in the morning and the ebb would start a half after.

At six-thirty he knocked on the coach door. There was no answer, so he knocked again and pushed the door open. Veronica was asleep on the cot, her honey blond hair spread out like a halo.

"Miss Southerland. Wake up, we have to go to the Unicorn."

"What? Oh my!" She was startled and looked about in panic.

"It's alright, it's me James."

She calmed as she recognised him and her surroundings.

"Is it time?"

"Yes, we need to go now."

He got her down into a boat which was manned by grinning sailors.

"Sit here at the back," he said.

She went to move from the centre to the stern and lost her balance, falling towards James who stepped forward and caught her. She was in his arms when Captain Campbell looked over the side.

"Mr Stockley, if you can restrain your ardour, I believe the commodore is waiting," he said. James didn't see him smile as he turned away.

He got Veronica seated and ordered the men to bear away. He was blushing furiously and glared at the grinning oarsmen.

"Boat ahoy!" called the Unicorn's lookout.

"Midshipman Stockley and visitor!" James called back.

"Come ahead!"

"We need a chair," James shouted, "lady aboard!"

They came alongside and a chair was lowered so fast that James suspected someone had seen them coming. Veronica was loaded and hoisted aboard. James climbed the battens and was met by the Unicorn's first lieutenant.

"Good morning, Mr Stockley. What have you brought us this morning?"

"A visitor for the commodore, Sir."

"Indeed." McGivern watched as Veronica was lowered to the deck.

"Mr Donaldson, please give the commodore my compliments and tell him we have a lady…"He looked at James.

"Miss Southerland of British Intelligence."

"Miss Southerland of British Intelligence to see him."

The mid ran down the stairs to the commodore's cabin while James helped Veronica from the chair.

"I look a mess!" she said.

"You look fine, and don't worry, Father is no ogre."

"I know, I met him at dinner last night but couldn't speak to him then."

Midshipman Donaldson returned and saluted the first, "The commodore will see her now."

Marty was curious. He had met Miss Southerland of course and she had come across as an empty-headed ninny. Now he was being told she was an agent for British Intelligence. The marine announced them: "Midshipman Stockley and Miss Southerland. Sah!"

"Enter," Marty deliberately drawled.

His son, smart in his new uniform, entered with Veronica who looked dishevelled but lovely.

"James, Miss Southerland, please take a seat. Now, tell me what is so urgent that you rowed out from the dock after midnight last night."

"You knew?"

"I was aware you were following me, and I saw you take the boat. I was somewhat surprised that you headed for the Leonidas rather than the Unicorn."

Veronica looked on the verge of crying again so James intervened. "Just tell my father what you need to."

Marty noted the protective stance of his young stallion to the older woman.

"I work for British Intelligence, and I am working undercover on the island which is why I could not say anything at the dinner last night."

Marty acknowledged that and rang a bell. Adam came in and he ordered coffee for them all.

"You must have something of importance to tell me."

"I do. I was told that if I found anything I was to tell you when you visited the island."

Marty raised his eyebrows in surprise at that as he had only decided to call in when they were on route. Somebody was second guessing him, and he had a good idea who.

"I have been circulating amongst the merchant fraternity in Malta. One group, the Russians, has been doing a lot of trade with Egypt. I allowed one to befriend me and encouraged him to share his business secrets with me. I found out he is not actually a Russian, but a Greek Cypriot called Andreas Vlachos who trades under the name of Vigor Sidorov."

Marty sat forward; this was getting interesting. "Go on."

"He represents an organisation based in Odessa."

"The Filiki Eteria?" Marty said.

"Yes! How did you know that?"

"A lucky guess, go on."

"Well, they are supplying weapons to the Wahhabi."

Marty sat back. "Damn that has just made things very complicated."

He looked at his son,

"Go back to your ship and give my compliments to James Campbell. Tell him that I wish him to take the Leonidas and the Nymphe down to Lebanon and assume a patrol from there to Cairo. I would like him to offload the launch and leave it here. If they make contact with the Eagle, direct them here."

James looked like he would object but a look quelled the impulse and he saluted as he stood.

"Aye, aye, Sir!" He turned to Veronica, "It was a pleasure meeting you, Miss."

She blushed as she stood and curtsied, "Thank you for your help."

James turned away and Marty could see the tops of his ears were bright red. When they were alone, she said, "Why are you sending your ships to Libya? The gun smugglers are here."

"Aah now that is something to be discussed over breakfast, I am hungry as I am sure you are," Marty said and rang the bell again. Adam came in and Marty said, "Adam is breakfast ready?"

"Yes, Milord."

"Oh, I forgot, you were a viscount, your son is a lord too."

Veronica gasped.

"In the service he is just plain Midshipman Stockley."

Her brow furrowed as she thought about that then she said, "Should I call you Lord or Commodore?"

"Martin will suffice. Let's go through and eat."

Adam had set out breakfast. Wolfgang and McGivern were waiting for them. Marty made the introductions adding, "You can say anything in front of my officers, they are all members of Naval

Intelligence."

Marty loaded a plate of bacon, poached eggs and toast and Adam filled his cup with coffee.

"Is this your first mission?" he asked.

"Yes, I went through training and because I speak Greek and Latin as well as a little Arabic, they sent me here."

"To infiltrate the merchants and find out if any were helping the Wahhabi?"

"That and to find out if there were any groups actively working against British interests."

"A hard and dangerous mission for a novice. What is your cover?"

"I am an actress. I am here as a singer in the opera."

"Your singing voice was very good last night. I did wonder," Marty said.

Wolfgang asked between mouthfuls of bacon and kidneys, "What have you found out?"

"That the Greeks are helping the Wahhabi through a Greek Cypriot trader posing as a Russian out of Odessa."

"That complicates things," he said to Marty.

"That's the second time I have heard that," Veronica said, "what are you doing that I do not know about?"

"Our mission isn't to help the Ottomans. That is just our cover."

"Well, what are you here to do?" she said and then her eyes went wide, and her mouth formed an O as her brain caught up.

"Have you guessed?"

"If the fact that the Greeks are helping the Wahhabi is

complicating things then it is something to do with them."

"Almost, we are interested in moving the Cypriots away from both the Ottomans and the Greeks towards us at the same time as encouraging the Greeks to gain independence," Marty said. "How close are you to the merchant?"

"Andreas? I keep him infatuated but I'm not sleeping with him if that's what you mean." She looked offended by the idea.

"You may have to at some time," Wolfgang said.

She blushed and concentrated on eating an egg. Wolfgang looked at Marty and raised an eyebrow. Marty shook his head.

"As far as the Ottomans are concerned, we are ignorant of who the supplier of the weapons is. They have told us they suspect that it's the Persians. We will let them continue to think that."

"Oh, that is why you sent those ships to Libya!" Veronica exclaimed.

"Yes, they will maintain the fiction that we are actually trying to help while the rest of us fulfil the real mission."

They ate in silence until McGivern said, "I must relieve young Brazier. If you will excuse me." He bowed to Veronica.

"Your son seemed very young," Veronica said then blushed as she realised, she may have just accused Marty of nepotism. "Oh, I didn't mean—"

Marty grinned "He was captain all three years he was at Dartmouth. That could have gotten him a lieutenancy as his first posting, but he asked to be in my squadron under James Campbell."

She looked relieved; she was beginning to like Marty. His reputation at the academy had been larger than life and his exploits used as examples of what an agent could do if they applied themselves. The man himself was handsome, witty, urbane, and he had more than a hint of a West country accent. His work with the legendary Linette was the inspiration for her to progress through training and pass with high marks. Her attention was drawn back to him as he sat back and gazed at the ceiling. "I think I need to meet Andreas. The question is how?"

"Breaking and entering?" Wolfgang said.

"No, I don't think that will work," Marty said, "I want to be on his good side."

Wolfgang grinned, somewhat evilly she thought. "What about the old rescue gambit."

"Genius!" Marty said.

"What on earth are you two talking about?" Veronica said.

"All will become clear," Marty laughed. "When is the next time you will be stepping out with him?"

"Tonight, he is coming to the opera to watch me."

"Where will you meet him and at what time?"

"What are you going to do?"

"If I told you, it would spoil the surprise." Marty had a look on his face that she found annoyingly attractive, almost naughty boyish.

Veronica huffed and added annoying to her list of characteristics for Marty.

"He will collect me from my lodgings and walk me to the theatre." She gave him both the addresses.

"Good that sorts that out. Now to get you back on shore without being seen."

Chapter 5: Best of Friends

She was given a voluminous cloak to wear, which covered her completely, and taken up on deck. Stood in a group near the mainmast were some of the most frightening men she had ever seen. These had to be the infamous Shadows.

"Boys, this is Veronica. She is our contact on the island and needs to get ashore without being seen," Marty said.

"Leave it to us, boss," Billy said. Marty took his leave. Kissing her hand as he bowed goodbye.

A boat was brought up to the side away from the shore and the 'boys' manned it. Billy was left on deck with her and just watched while the others took up their positions. She looked around for the chair when he swept her up and threw her over his shoulder.

"Hold on tight," he said as he climbed over the side and started down the battens.

Veronica let out a high-pitched squeak, kicked her legs a couple of times then froze as she saw the boat and water below her. They reached the bottom and he gently put her down. Her legs gave way and she sat on a thwart with a thump. The boys were all grinning.

"Why is it that every time I get in a damn boat everyone ends up grinning at me?" she said in a genuine huff.

They set out at a casual pace and went straight out to sea. "Where are we going?"

"St Julian's Bay," Billy said.

"What? That's an hour's walk back to my place over a bloody great hill," she snapped.

"Fit girl like you will manage." Billy steered them out of the harbour and along the coast. It took them fifty minutes to row to the bay and they chose a landing well away from other people. She was surprised when Billy and the one called Antton joined her on shore.

"Keep the hood up. Antton will get us some transport," Billy said.

She kicked him in the ankle.

"Ow! What was that for?"

"Making me think I would have to walk."

He grinned and he suddenly looked boyish. In fact, as they had rowed, and the banter had flown around the boat she realised none of them were as scary as she first thought.

A clatter of hooves and wheels and Antton arrived in a cabriolet with the roof up.

"Nice, where did you get it?" Billy asked after they were all aboard.

"Hired it off a bloke in a big house two streets over. He was just putting it away when I turned up."

Veronica caught something in his accent. "Where are you from Antton?"

"I'm a Basque from the Montpellier region."

"Have you been with the commodore long?"

"I met Marty when he was a midshipman, I have followed him ever since."

"Is that the same for you, Billy?"

"Nope, I'm the new boy. I've known Marty since I was a kid and he always promised me a place when one came available. I joined this trip. I worked for Francis Ridgley before."

That was a name she knew well. "I know Francis, he was an instructor at the academy."

"Is that what he did when he went back to England? I didn't know."

"He taught counter espionage, but he always said the master was Martin."

They stopped talking as they entered the busier streets of Valletta. Veronica sunk back into the shadow of the hood. The cabriolet came to a halt and both men got out with a whispered "Wait" from Billy.

"All clear, dump the cloak and come out."

"You are two streets away from your house," Antton said as he climbed back into the cart.

"Take care," Billy said, and they were gone.

The street was empty when Veronica set off to her lodgings, but she had a feeling she was being watched. The feeling was comforting so she thought it was a friend. She smiled to herself as she opened the door into her building and caught a glimpse of a big man in a brown coat wearing a baker's boy cap leaning against the corner of the street.

She rested, she had only had three hours' sleep and that wasn't good for her voice. She had to sing in the chorus that evening so bed was the order of the day.

She woke in plenty of time to get ready, sponged herself down, arranged her hair ready for a wig and applied theatrical makeup. She had her costume for the night and she was expected to arrive in character. They were playing Don Giovani, which she enjoyed as she liked Mozart. It was lively. She dressed and donned the wig that completed her ensemble. A knock at her door precisely on time announced that Vigor/Andreas had arrived to escort her to the Teatru Manoel.

"My love, you look enchanting!" he said as she opened the door.

"Vigor, you are too kind!" she simpered.

They walked down the stairs and out of the front door together. She glanced around but couldn't see anybody, the street was quiet.

After fifteen minutes they were walking along the waterfront by Sa Maison Gardens when a pair of roughs came out of the shrubs that bordered the street. Vigor stepped in front of her and held up his cane like a sword to protect her.

The roughs ginned; one swung an iron bar while the other pulled a knife.

"'and over yer purse," the one with a bar growled.

"Come and get it," Vigor said.

Veronica was looking at the pair curiously, there was something about them…

She was suddenly grabbed from behind and a rough hand was clamped over her mouth. She reacted immediately and bit a finger – hard. There was a curse, and the hand was pulled away allowing her to scream.

She struggled but her captor was too strong.

"Give us yer purse and we let her go!"

Vigor had no choice; he reached into his pocket and took out his purse.

There was a shot.

"Let her go or the next one goes through your head," a voice said calmly from the shadows.

Her captor stiffened and slowly let her go, then all three bolted down the street.

She almost swooned and Vigor was there in a second to support her as their saviour stepped into view under the streetlamp.

"Are you hurt?" Marty asked.

"I think we are unharmed, just shocked," Vigor said.

"It was lucky I was on my way to the opera. Heard a scream and thought there may be trouble."

He still held a double-barrelled pistol. One of which had a whisp of smoke coming from it. It disappeared inside his coat.

"Commodore Martin Stockley at your service." He peered at Veronica. "Miss Southerland, is that you?"

"You know Veronica?" Vigor said.

"We met last night at the governor's mansion."

"Commodore, Martin, thank you for your help," Veronica gasped.

"I am on my way to see your opera. Can I escort the two of you there?"

"That would be most welcome," Vigor said.

"Lucky I was early," Marty said as they strolled along.

Veronica regained her equilibrium.

"Do you always carry guns to the opera?" Vigor asked, a hint of suspicion in his voice.

"I am always armed when ashore. Damned dangerous places ports."

"I have become comfortable living here. This is the first time I have experienced any trouble and do not carry arms. I think I might have to reconsider."

"A barker for your coat pocket is enough, most roughs don't want to argue with a pistol."

"Barker? What is a barker?"

"Short, barrelled man stopper."

"Aah, yes I could get one of those, do you recommend any particular maker?"

"You are not familiar with guns?"

"I know how to shoot of course but when it comes to selecting one for my own use, my knowledge is sadly lacking."

"Look, I will be in port for a while yet. Why don't I come with you to an armourer and help you select a brace."

Veronica listened as Martin spun his web, he kept his distance and wasn't pushy. He was sympathetic and helpful. Vigor agreed to meet Marty the next day and they would go shopping.

"Well, here we are, you should be fine now," Marty said as they got to the opera house.

"Thank you, Martin," Veronica said and dashed inside to get ready for her performance. Her makeup was smudged and lipstick all askew.

"Can a stand you a glass?" Vigor said.

"Sorry, old boy, but I am meeting Sir Thomas, but I will see you tomorrow so maybe we could have lunch?"

Vigor agreed and Marty went to find Sir Thomas. Step one had been made.

The opera was nicely performed, Aloysia Weber played Donna Anna and Francesco Albertarelli Don Giovanni, both of whom played at the premiere in Vienna. Veronica sang in the chorus as one of the young ladies.

Marty was humming the libretto as he climbed up the battens on his return to the Unicorn. He met the Shadows in his cabin.

"Nice work, lads, just the right balance of intimidation and cowardice," he said as they shared a glass.

"It worked then?" Billy asked.

"It did. How is your finger Matai?"

"Shelby put a stitch in where she bit it to the bone."

"You'll heal then. She sent an apology. You caught her by surprise, and she just reacted."

The boys had obviously been teasing him about it as he sipped his rum with a sour look.

"I will meet with Vigor or Andreas, whatever you want to call him, tomorrow to find him a new gun. I want a tail on him from then onwards, usual stuff, where does he go, who does he meet. Make notes and report back daily. Clear?"

"Aye, skipper."

"Good, look out for biters."

The Shadows laughed, drained their glasses to heeltaps and left.

The two met at the appointed time outside of the Gun Shop on Triq L'Imhazen near the waterfront. The owner was a Maltese gentleman of advancing years but with a mind as sharp as a rat trap.

"Gentlemen, how can I help you."

"My associate here would like to have a look at some pocket pistols for self-defence," Marty said.

"I have a selection if you would step this way." He led them to a glass-topped cabinet on the far side of the shop. Under the glass were a dozen different short-barrelled pistols. Marty scanned them and spotted a couple of makers he recognised.

"Can we have a look at the Sharpes and the Reynolds please." He turned to Vigor. "Both are sixty calibres by the look of them, that is enough to stop anybody."

Both guns were new and Marty expertly checked the actions and barrels.

"Which one fits your hand better?" he said and handed them to Vigor, who hefted first one then the other.

"I like this one better, but I would like to fire them before I decide."

"Can I suggest you try this one as well?" the proprietor said and handed a third to Marty. "It's by Bingham of London."

Marty looked it over, fifty-four bore, two-and-a-half-inch brass barrel, flip down trigger.

"We can try it."

The owner had a range set up in the courtyard and loaded the guns himself. Vigor tried the Reynolds first, it had quite a kick and he hit the target in the upper right corner.

"Don't worry about that. If you use it, your target will only be feet away."

The Sharpes came next. He did better and seemed to like the feel of it. Last he tried the Bingham.

"I like the Sharpes. It feels nice in the hand and doesn't have such a vicious kick as the Reynolds."

"You have a flask, tools and ball mould?" Marty asked the proprietor, who confirmed he did.

"You must let me buy you lunch," Vigor said.

"That's really not necessary," Marty said.

"I insist, you have been of great help to me."

Vigor took him to a lovely little restaurant with seating outside on the pavement as well as inside. They took a table. Marty noticed it was one where they could talk without being overheard.

"You are a commodore in the British navy, yet you only have two ships here in the harbour," Vigor said casually.

"Two others are patrolling West of Alexandria and a third is sailing up the Nile," Marty said.

"The British do not have interests at that end of the Mediterranean, do they?"

You're fishing, Marty thought.

"Not directly but the Ottomans are worried about the Persians running guns to the Wahhabi and, as a sign of solidarity to our trading partner, the government has sent me to stop them," he said with a deliberately bitter twist of his lips.

"You sound as if you disapprove."

"I'm no friend to the Ottomans. I am in trade myself and they compete with India in a lot of cases."

"A lord in trade, whatever next?" Vigor laughed. "Sorry for the generalisation but the British aristocracy are famous for despising those in trade."

"I have a rather unusual background, as do you."

Vigor sat back and looked at Marty, his face suddenly, carefully neutral. When it was clear he wasn't going to comment, Marty leant forward his elbows on the table.

"You are no Russian, I've met enough to know one when I see one. If I had to guess I would say you are Greek, or maybe a Cypriot."

"You are very observant."

"It's part of my charm."

Soup was served which stopped the byplay momentarily.

Vigor looked to be struggling with something and Marty let him make up his mind without interference from him.

"Do you believe that the Persians are supplying the weapons?" Vigor asked.

"No, but that doesn't matter, the Ottomans do so that is where I will send my ships. I will be honest with you and tell you that my government doesn't really care. The Ottoman Empire is crumbling and there is no profit in backing a dying horse, but they are the incumbent, so we make a play of supporting them."

"Where do you see it crumbling now?"

"The Balkans, Egypt, Greece. It's collapsing under the weight of its own corruption."

"Greece is a Christian country."

"And you are a Christian." Marty used his spoon to point to the cross that Vigor wore around his neck.

Vigor sighed, "Yes I am a Christian, I am a member of the Greek Orthodox church, and my real name is Andreas."

Marty smiled, finished his soup, and mopped his mouth with a napkin. "Excellent we have that cleared up! Now how can we help each other?"

Over the main course, Andrea told Marty about the Filiki Eteria and how they were supporting the growing rebellion in Greece and sending weapons to their brother rebels in Egypt.

"The Wahhabi aren't brothers with anybody, especially Christians," Marty said. "How did you persuade them to accept guns from you?"

"Aah that's where the belief the Persians are involved comes from."

Marty laughed in surprise. "You, tell them that the guns are from the Persians? Oh, that is famous! You know they will declare a Fatwa on you if they find out the truth?"

"Yes, we are aware of that."

A gifted amateur, Marty thought in delight. This was going to be more fun than he had thought.

"Our goals seem to be roughly the same. If I may, I would like to propose an alliance," Marty said.

"Can you do that without your government's approval?"

"I can if I think it will help with my mission. My orders are necessarily broad. We won't be able to tell anyone else about it of course."

"I understand, I will consult with my – colleagues and let you know."

"Interesting, he needs to get approval, maybe not as high up as he would like me to believe," Marty thought.

Andreas left after a coffee and Marty spotted Matai tailing him. Garai wouldn't be far away either. Things were moving along nicely.

That was until he got back to the ship and found a message waiting for him.

Chapter 6: The Nile

Trevor Archer raised an American Flag and entered the Nile delta. As he didn't have a clue where the navigable channel was, he waited until a large felucca sailed in and followed it. What wind there was came from astern and was light, so it was stifling hot as the apparent wind over the deck was almost nothing.

"Let's get some more shade up, get a couple of spare staysails and rig them as shades," he told Gerald Sykes, his midshipman.

Lieutenant Alexander Beaumont, commander of the marine contingent, joined him. He, like all the crew, was dressed in civilian clothes and had donned a rather strange broad-brimmed top hat.

"Where on earth did you get that?" Trevor said.

"All the rage in Paris, don't ya know," Alex said. "Keeps the sun off."

"Wish I had a hat with a brim, but all I've got is my bicorn."

"What about one of the sailor's boaters?"

"That's an idea, I wonder if the purser has any spares in the slops." He looked at the helmsman and barked, "Stay directly behind him in his wake! You will have us aground otherwise." The man adjusted their course to follow the curve as the felucca had.

"I will ask him." Alex wandered off down the deck to where their purser was leaning on the rail watching the shore drift by.

"It could almost be a pleasure cruise," the purser said as Alex joined him.

"Let's hope it stays that way, Mr Waggonfield," Alex said.

"What can I do for you, Lieutenant?"

"Not for me but the captain, he is in need of a hat to protect that handsome dome of his. Do you have any of the straw hats that the crew wear in the slops?"

"I can do better than that. I have a hat from our trip to Venezuela he can use, I picked up several at the time. I will go and fetch one for him."

He returned with a conical straw hat with a very broad brim that turned upwards at the edge. It had a coloured band around the head piece and a darker weave of straw around the edge of the brim.

"Captain, the good lieutenant tells me you are in need of some relief from the sun, will this suffice?"

"That will do handsomely, it looks like the hats we saw in Venezuela."

"Indeed, that is where it came from."

Trevor put it on and tightened the chin strap. It was a fair fit.

Umbridge Falconer, the Foreign Office man, came up from below. He looked around with owlish eyes and made his way to the side. He took a deep breath in through his nose and smiled, "The smell of Egypt, oh how I've missed that."

"Smells like camel shit and sweat if you ask me," a crewman who was coiling a rope nearby snorted.

Umbridge sniffed and made his way to the fo'c'sle where he watched the felucca. Midshipman Sykes came up to him. "Captain's compliments, Mr Falconer, but would you be so kind as to join him on the quarterdeck."

He followed the young mid and was surprised to see the captain in a broad-brimmed hat.

"There you are, Mr Falconer. Do you like me hat?"

"It's very, aah, nice, Captain."

"I think I will grow a moustache like the caballeros in South America. What do you think?" Trevor grinned then laughed.

"You are having a jest with me," Falconer said without a flicker of a smile.

Trevor sighed; he had tried. The man was fusty beyond belief and hardly ever smiled.

"We are coming up on a town. Do you know what it is?"

"That will be Rasheed, the river is quite serpentine above there. The locals often resort to sweeps."

"Bosun! Prepare the sweeps," Trevor called.

The bosun shouted orders and the long sweeps, four to a side, were unshipped from the rack on the centreline. They would be manned by two men each if they were needed.

The turn came up and turned them ninety degrees to port, the wind was now directly on their beam. Sails were adjusted and progress maintained.

"This ship sails better with the wind on the side than the local craft," Falconer observed.

"Different sail shapes and rigging. We can sail much closer to the wind than they can," Trevor said absently. He wasn't paying much attention to Falconer but focussing on the ship ahead.

"Hold us a little more to his port side, helmsman," he ordered. Then, "I want two men with leads in the chains. This water is so thick with sediment you can't tell what's in front of us." He was also very aware that the felucca drew less water than the Eagle did.

"How far to Cairo?"

"From here, about one hundred and fifty miles," Falconer said.

"At this rate we will get there in two and a half days. I'm not risking sailing at night."

As it happened neither did the felucca, as soon as the sun started to go down, they pulled into the bank and moored up. Trevor wasn't about to do that, he dropped anchor just off mid-stream and set a double watch. This was where the extra marines came in handy as he paired a marine with each sailor.

"Do not shoot unless you are sure that whoever you see is belligerent. We do not want to spark an incident," Alex told his men. "If possible, call the officer of the watch before taking action."

The night passed quietly apart from scratching heard through the hull. The marine and sailor that investigated got the shock of their lives when they discovered it was a curious crocodile trying to climb the side. The sailor took a boathook and smacked it hard on the end of its snout. It swam off indignantly. The next morning no one believed them until they pointed out the deep grooves it had left in the hull.

They set off as soon as the felucca made sail. Following it for another half a day until it docked at the village of Shubrakhit.

"This is where Napoleon had a battle with Murad Bey," Falconer announced, as animated as he had been the whole trip.

"Did he win?" Trevor said.

"Yes, I believe he did," Falconer said with a smile.

The men in the chains continuously called the depth and were replaced every thirty minutes. The lookout in the bows was replaced every hour. As predicted, they reached Cairo two and a half days later, only having to resort to sweeps once. They called in as any ship would. Falconer and the purser shopped for fresh food.

"Someone is coming down the dock. Looks like an official," a lookout said.

"Damn, Falconer is out with Waggonfield shopping," Trevor cursed the timing.

The official walked past the ship and looked at the stern, glanced up at the flag then walked back to the gangplank.

"Min ho kaedk?" he called up.

"I'm sorry we don't speak Arabic. Our translator is onshore," Trevor shouted, as if the louder he said it the more likely the man was to understand. The official turned his head to look at him and they saw that he had a silver rope with a strand of gold in a spiral around it holding his headdress in place.

"I said, who is your captain?"

"Oh, that will be me. Captain Archer at your service."

"Please, come down onto the dock."

Trevor thought it strange he didn't want to come aboard but walked down the gangway to the dock.

"I am the port official. Abdul Mohammed ben Khasi. You are American?"

"Yes, out of Boston."

"Why are you here?"

"To stock up on fresh supplies."

"That is why you are here in Cairo, why have you come to

Egypt?"

"Oh, I see, I want to travel the Nile, map it and see some of the antiquities along it."

"You will need a permit to travel further."

"Where do I get one of those?"

"From me."

Trevor understood. The man was looking for a bribe.

"What will that cost?"

The man grinned showing white teeth. "Two thousand piastre for the permit and five hundred for my time."

Trevor calculated that as twenty-five pounds or one hundred American silver dollars.

"Will silver dollars be acceptable?"

"Yes, then there is the mooring fee which is another five hundred piastre."

The man is a bloody thief, he thought but smiled and said, "I will get the money."

Trevor had a strongbox in his cabin which Marty had given him for bribes and supplies. It had British golden guineas, French Louis D'Or, American dollars, and Spanish reals. He counted one hundred and twenty silver dollars into a pouch and returned to the dock.

"One hundred and twenty silver dollars." He held out the bulging pouch.

Abdul took the pouch and handed over an official-looking scroll.

"You know we are at war with the Ottoman Empire?"

"I heard something about it."

"Where does America stand on this?"

"America supports all attempts to throw off the yoke of colonialism," Trevor said as sincerely as he could.

"Excellent, but please be aware that there are many who are intolerant of infidels in this country."

"Thank you for the warning."

Abdul looked along the dock and said, "Your purser and his friend who speaks Arabic are on their way back. I will bid you farewell, Captain." He genuflected with his hand over his heart and turned away. By the time Falconer and Waggonfield reached the gangplank with a train of porters carrying fruit, vegetables and several goats, he was gone.

"Was that the port official?" Falconer said.

"Yes, he gave me this."

"The permit to travel," Falconer said. "We stopped off at his office and bought one. It cost four pounds including the docking fee."

"You did what? Why that crook charged me one hundred and twenty dollars."

"He spoke English?"

"Yes."

Falconer laughed, the first time Trevor had ever heard him, he sounded a bit like a donkey.

"Welcome to Arabia."

They got the supplies aboard and shoved off. As they worked their way out and raised sail, Trevor saw Abdul stood on the dock. He waved and got a toothy grin in return as the man bowed.

"Fucking crook, may the dollars burn a hole in your—"

"Skipper?" the helmsman said.

"Nothing, get us into mid-stream."

It wasn't long before the river split into several channels and Falconer was called to guide them.

"That is the Ile d'Al-Warraq, stay to the left-hand channel. At the end of it there is Maadi Island, we need to go between them. Then stay to the centre of the river as there is a sandbar on the right."

They left the city behind and were soon travelling through agricultural land that bordered the river. Arab El-Saf came up the next day.

"Alex, this is where you and your boys get off. If you head East you come to the Red Sea."

"You will carry on up the river?"

"Yes, the commodore wants us to map it, we will return here in three weeks at the latest."

They shook hands, then Alex went ashore followed by Falconer.

The first task was to find a place where they could bring the boats ashore. They needed to find a beach or a place where the water was shallow enough and the bottom firm enough that they could float the boats onto the wheeled frames then haul them out. The river curved so they were on the inside bank and a survey, where two men waded in with sticks, showed it had a firm bottom that was the right profile for their needs. Riflemen watched for crocodiles constantly while the men were in the water.

The bank was mainly earth and clay and would be carved into a ramp and as soon as he was sure that it was suitable. The engineers began surveying the surrounding land. By that evening they had found a path East through to the edge of the farmland. Falconer negotiated with the farmers for access across the two and a half miles of land before the desert started.

"They aren't happy having us trample across their land, but I told them that we would pay double the value of any crops that were spoiled."

"We will need to make a road, when the boats arrive."

"I know and I laid the ground for that as well."

The next morning, they started to survey and map the desert. The terrain was rocky but firm, crisscrossed with wadis and rose gently to a ridge of hills in the distance.

"We need to find a pass and plot a route accordingly," Sergeant Gregory Hungerford, their chief engineer, said the next morning.

Alex took up a telescope and scanned the ridge.

"There looks to be a break over there just to the South. Why don't I take a small group and recce it while you finish the survey here?"

"That would speed things up, Sir. Do we want to split our force?"

"It seems safe enough this side of the hills, mainly farmers around here. We will risk it. If we march fast, we can be there and back by midday"

Alex selected four men, two scouts and two sharpshooters, to accompany him leaving Sergeant Bright in charge of the escort and set off to yomp the eleven miles. Yomping meant travelling at speed across rough terrain and was a term that had crept into the marine's vocabulary from an unknown source. They marched fast carrying just one day's rations, water, and ammunition and reached the hills in a couple of hours.

"The pass is slightly South of here, Bodmin and Tubb, scout ahead." The two scouts, both West country lads who joined the marines to avoid prison for poaching, set off at a trot. Alex and the others followed at a fast pace.

The temperature was rising rapidly as the sun got higher in the sky and soon the land shimmered with heat haze. Sweat evaporated immediately and their water was consumed rapidly.

Marine Tubb returned, and reported, "There is a dry wadi through the hills ahead which looks like it's fairly regularly used. We went about halfway through it."

"Any sign of the locals?"

"Not that we saw."

Tubb led them to the pass and Alex immediately saw its potential. It was a dry riverbed and snaked through the hills. A rock base, with a fine covering of sand and mostly wide enough for the carts. They would have to blast some rock away in places but generally it was good.

"I've seen enough, let's get back to the others."

The trip back was slower, the midday heat was brutal. They found the others by mid-afternoon.

"Damn this place is fierce," Alex said as he drank water. "We had better carry extra water as we didn't see any between here and the pass.

"The pass is suitable, Sir?" Sergeant Hungerford said.

"Yes, we will have to widen it in places but by my reckoning, we should be able to get the boats through."

The look on the sergeant's face said *we will see*.

They mapped a usable route from the river to the pass, surveying as they went. They wanted a gentle gradient and in the main the land rose steadily but at one point there was a step across the wadi which the trail skirted on a narrow ledge.

"It's four and a half feet high. Hardly anything in the big scheme of things but a mountain to the boats," the sergeant said.

"How do we get over it?" Alex said.

"Well, we could blast it into a ramp. However, drilling that rock will take a long time; it's a type of granite. The alternatives are to use A-frames to lift the boats, or build a ramp from stone and sand. Given the lack of usable timber I think building a ramp will be the easiest option."

"How would we do that?"

"Pile rock up with big rocks on the bottom and fill in with ever smaller rocks as we get to the surface then a covering of sand. That should make a stable ramp."

"We will need more men than we have now?"

"Yes, double the number to do it quickly."

"Sir, there is one of them caravans coming through the pass," marine Bodmin reported.

"Get the men hidden, we don't need to let them know what we are doing."

The men scattered up into the rocks either side of the pass before the first camel came into view. It was led by an Arab who walked beside it. Directly behind came a line of camels, each one tethered to the one in front of it. Strangely the last animal in the train was a mule which carried the cameleers' possessions. The camels were laden with large square packs slung either side of their humps. More men, armed with long-barrelled muskets, walked beside the train at intervals. All alert and looking around them. These guards were the focus of Alex's attention. He noted the guns but also the long knives and swords each carried.

One stopped, crouched and looked at the sand in front of the step. He called to one of his colleagues who came and squatted beside him. He traced a footprint, then looked around at the sides of the pass. Alex held his breath. After what seemed like an age they stood and followed the camels.

"There were over seventy camels in that train," Bill Murray said to his mate.

"Aye, and thirty armed guards," Finn McCormack replied as he cut a lump of dried meat from a strip to chew on.

"I wonder what riches they were carrying. Do you think it were silks and rare spices?"

"More likely dried fish."

Alex smiled as he listened to the byplay. If the men were bantering their morale was good.

They reached the top of the pass and could look down to the route ahead. They'd gone up over a thousand feet and should be able to see for thirty-nine miles on a clear day. Unfortunately, it wasn't. Haze and dust obscured the view after twelve miles or so.

"Well at least we can see where we will be going for the rest of today," Alex said. But they didn't get much further. The horizon to the Southeast developed a dark line which got darker and higher.

"That's a sandstorm and it's coming this way. We need to get everyone under cover," Falconer said.

"Get the tents up?" Alex said.

"No, get behind rocks and get a tarp or a groundsheet over your heads. The wind will rip tents to shreds."

Orders were given and the men obeyed. None had been in a sandstorm before and had no idea what to expect. Some were joking as they dug in but then the wind arrived. The laughing stopped and survival started.

It started as a gusty breeze and soon developed into a gale which grew to a tempest. The sun was obliterated, and it went dark. The sand was travelling so fast that if you raised a hand above the shelter the skin would be flayed from it. The tarps whipped and cracked, and the men struggled to hold onto them. Sand got in everywhere.

It lasted an eternity and was over suddenly. Once it was quiet men emerged from under piles of sand that had dropped on top of them. The world had changed. The sun had gone down, and the stars covered the sky, the milky way smoked across the heavens, clearly visible. The temperature was dropping. It was time to make camp.

The next morning, the pass was covered in a deep layer of sand and the route forward was only defined by a dip.

"That is not going to make life any easier," Alex said his hands on his hips.

"The wind will clear it," Falconer said from behind him.

"It had better, we will never drag a boat through that otherwise."

"It's a constant cycle, the one thing you can be sure of in the desert is the wind. It comes from the Northwest unless there is an event like last night so all this dust will be blown back to where it came from."

Dust it most certainly wasn't. It was fine sand that got in everywhere. It was in their food, guns had to be thoroughly cleaned and their clothes shaken out. It didn't help much as the wind picked up and the dust went right back.

The down slope was passable in the main but narrowed in several places. The surveyors measured the slope, the width of the path and the direction. From Alex's point of view, if it went downhill and generally East it was fine, and he began to chafe at the delays.

Things suddenly got more exciting.

"Horseman, Sir!" a marine shouted and pointed.

A lone horseman was silhouetted against the sky atop a hill to the South. He had a musket held upright, the butt resting on his thigh.

"Falconer, who is that?" Alex said.

"A Bedouin. There are nomadic tribes across the whole of North Africa. If we don't bother them, they will leave us alone."

Sergeant Bright wasn't as confident in the Bedouin's good will as Falconer and made sure his marines were on alert. He had the scouts well out in front and flankers two hundred yards out to the sides. Alex noticed him taking precautions and approved,

"Well done, Sergeant, let's not take any chances."

The Bedouin watched them for an hour or so. Alex was amazed he could keep his horse still for that long and was somewhat relieved when he left. His relief was short-lived when suddenly the horizon was lined with horsemen.

"Call in the flankers, and scouts, Sergeant," Alex said.

Marines Bodmin and Tubb came in and went straight to Alex. "Sir, we found a well up ahead, it's got fresh water."

Falconer appeared and said, "Did you touch it?"

"We took a drink and filled our bottles. Why?"

"The wells belong to the Bedouin, and they don't take kindly to trespassers."

"And you didn't think to tell us this before?"

"I didn't know there was a well on this route."

Alex snarled something incoherent then made a visible effort to control his temper.

"What will they do?"

The answer came immediately as with a shout the horsemen started down the slope and within a minute they were surrounded.

Alex called orders and the marines took a knee with their rifles to their shoulders, no one was to fire unless fired on first.

A single horseman came forward, he was robed in black and had a golden cord around his headdress. His horse's harness was decorated with beaded tassels and his musket was chased in silver.

Alex grabbed Falconer by the arm and stepped forward.

"Tell him I greet him in the name of the American president."

Falconer gave him a look but translated for him.

"He says you are trespassing on their land and have stolen water from their well."

"We apologise for any offence we may have inadvertently caused and are prepared to pay for a licence to travel and the water."

"Why should I not just take what I want?" the Bedouin said haughtily.

"That would force us to defend ourselves causing death and suffering on both sides."

The Bedouin grinned, revealing white teeth with a pronounced gap.

"I want a hundred piastre per man and another five hundred for the water."

"He expects you to bargain with him," Falconer muttered.

"I will give you fifty piastre per man and two hundred for all the water we want."

"You are robbing my children, eighty piastre a man and four hundred for the water."

"Sixty per man and two hundred and fifty for the water."

"Seventy per man and three hundred for the water."

Alex stepped forward and spat on his hand, "Agreed." He held it out.

The Bedouin looked confused until Falconer explained it was the American's way of sealing a bargain, then spat on his hand and slapped it against Alex's.

"Tell him we will be bringing boats across from the Nile and we will happily pay him his tax for them."

Falconer launched into a long explanation and the Bedouin roared with laughter and shouted something to his men who laughed and slapped their thighs.

"He wants to know how you will bring boats over the pass."

Alex explained and told them that they would have to widen the pass in places to get the carts through.

"How will you pull the carts?"

"Preferably with oxen, camels or horses," Alex said, getting tired of explaining himself to the over-inquisitive Bedouin.

"That is no work for horses or camels, you need oxen."

Something in the way he said it made Alex pay attention.

"Can you supply oxen?"

"At a price."

Chapter 7: Crossing

"Is it bad news?" Wolfgang asked Marty as he saw his face when he opened the letter which had been brought by the Eagle.

"Mixed, they have found and mapped a crossing."

"I hear a 'but'."

"But it will need blasting to clear it and the local tribe of Bedouin are demanding a tax to let us across their land."

"I didn't think Bedouin owned land."

"I think they consider they own whatever they are stood on."

"Alexander says we should send the boats to the landing. He is staying there to prepare the route and keep the Bedouin onside. He also says to avoid stopping at Cairo."

"At least we have a depth map of the river. How are we going to do this?"

"We will sail the Unicorn to the delta along with the Eagle which will take the second launch. When we get there, we will unload the launch from the Unicorn and the Eagle can tow it up the river. We can transfer the carriages to the Eagle now, she has room in her hold."

"I'll get started."

Wolfgang left and Marty considered the letter. He changed his mind. "Have Mr Archer and Mr Trenchard report to me."

Archer and Trenchard arrived promptly. "Phillip, I am thinking about sending the Endellion back with you which is why I have asked Trevor to be here. Tell us about the river."

Phillip gave a detailed report of the river and his findings. He had brought his log and a chart that his master had made. He also had some watercolours he had made himself.

"So, the river to the landing is easily navigable."

"Yes, the first cataract is a long way upstream. There is a shelving bottom on the East bank and the bank can be dug away to form a ramp. We can float the launches onto the carriages and pull them out. Alexander has negotiated for oxen with Bedouin."

"What? Since when have Bedouin kept oxen?" Trevor exclaimed.

"You know something of the Bedouin?"

"I read Carsten Niebuhr's account of his expedition of 1762. He was quite explicit about the Bedouin herding camels and goats which can survive in the desert. You only find oxen in the farmed area either side of the Nile."

"So, we can assume the nomads will either steal the oxen or buy them at a much lower price from the farmers. Either way it doesn't matter, we need the oxen and to keep the Bedouin onside."

"I don't know if we should send a second ship," Phillip said, "The authorities in Cairo are used to seeing the Eagle."

"You think you will have enough men?"

"We can take a few more marines in case the Bedouin turn nasty if you want."

Marty thought about it. They would leave sixty men behind to man the gunboats, the Eagle would be crowded enough having to carry them. It would be more comfortable all around to have the Endellion go along. They could tow a launch each which meant the Unicorn could stay in Valletta which suited his plans better.

"I think it's better we send both of you, the Eagle will be overcrowded with the boat's crews as it is. The Endellion can carry extra supplies as well as marines."

The launches from the Unicorn and Leonidas had been named the Shrike and Skua respectively and had their carronades mounted. Powder, shot, and stores were stowed aboard to ballast the big boats. The Eagle and Endellion would tow them and store the carriages on deck. The launch's thirty-man crews would travel on the ships apart from a helmsman and his mate who would man the tiller during the tow. Marty made sure there was at least three months of supplies aboard each. Lieutenant Richard Brazier would have overall command and have the Shrike, and Midshipman Donaldson would command the Skua.

Everything prepared, they set off for the Nile. The Unicorn sailing as escort, until they entered the river. Then the clipper and the schooner were on their own.

Richard Brazier was worried, this was his first command, and he was desperate not to let his mentor down. The Shrike was bobbing along behind the Eagle and a cable behind was the Endellion and the Skua. They reached Cairo and kept going. They timed their passing for just after dawn so passed largely unnoticed.

The one thing he had was absolute faith in Marty's judgement and if he thought that it was necessary to get a couple of boats sixty-five miles across the desert to the Red Sea, he would do his best to get there and fulfill his mission.

They reached the landing point, and they were greeted by cheering marines on the East bank. It was late in the day, and they pulled the launches up and loaded the carriage parts into them to get them ashore. They worked until it got too dark to do any more and resumed at first light. The engineers on shore assembled the carriages and had two teams of oxen ready to haul them. They wheeled one down the ramp they had created in the bank and out into the river. It floated. Riflemen kept a watch for crocodiles while nervous men ballasted the carriage with rocks to get it on the bottom.

It was a struggle to get the big boat into position above the carriage and pull the two in together, so the launch seated correctly. The current, although sluggish, tried to push the stern of the launch around and they resorted to attaching a cable from the Eagle's capstan to the sternpost to control it.

With a good helping of ingenuity and even more of brute force they married the launch and its carriage. The oxen strained and the whole assembly crept up the ramp. It slowed to a stop. It was just too heavy so they connected the second team and ran ropes for men to pull as well. In the end two teams of eight oxen and one hundred men got the launch onto dry land. Then they had to do it all over again for the Skua.

Once on firm land, eight oxen were ample to pull the carts, the axles were well greased with slush from the galley, and they carried extra in buckets for the journey.

Alex did not trust the Bedouin and decided to beef up their ability to defend themselves. Extra marines were added to the escort, and they all carried extra ammunition. The men were ordered to use corks to stop the ends of their barrels to prevent dust from getting in. Some ingenious men tied condoms over the ends of the barrels and explained that they could shoot without faffing around with the corks. After that the standing order was changed and condoms issued.

The climb up into the hills was slow but steady, the oxen only needing the help of the men on the steeper stretches. The marine engineers had blasted the trail to make it wide enough, which the caravaners welcomed. The step had also been made into a long gentle ramp and was negotiated without trouble.

It was all going well, until they had a visit one night by sneak thieves. Rations were stolen and a man was injured. The next night they caught several men in the act of trying to steal a cask of powder. The marine's justice was swift and terminal.

They were approaching the peak when the pass was blocked by a dozen horsemen.

"Men, watch the flanks!" Alex shouted.

Falconer stepped forward and said, "What do you want? We have a license to travel here."

"You do not have a license to kill my people!" the chief shouted.

"They were stealing from us."

"Then you should have handed them over to me for punishment."

"We are sorry, we did not mean to challenge your authority."

"You have insulted my people!"

"We meant no insult."

The chief swung his rifle down and fired, the bullet hit Falconer square in the chest.

All hell broke loose.

Alex took the situation in at a glance, they were surrounded. The Bedouin were in the rocks above them and shooting down on them. A marine cried out as he was hit, another cursed as a bullet narrowly missed him.

He aimed and fired, taking the chief out of his saddle. Then ducked behind one of the boats.

An ox fell, shot in the head. The others panicked.

"Cut the traces!" he shouted. A marine slashed at them with his bayonet. Freed, the oxen rumbled off down the path bellowing their fear.

They were pinned down and taking casualties. Then he saw Lieutenant Brazier and three men climb into the boat and uncover the forward carronade. Bullets smacked into the hull around them but miraculously none hit. They loaded and trained it around on the hill to the left.

BOOM, CHUFF, the carronade fired, and the hill was raked with canister. The smoke drifted down the pass and someone manned the second carronade. Now they were alternating and providing suppressing fire, the marines could move into the rocks and work their way up the slopes. Soon they were getting cover from the second boat's guns as well.

The Bedouin retreated; they weren't interested in a hand-to-hand fight with well-trained soldiers.

"We have five men wounded and two dead. No oxen for the front boat and we need to know what we will face if we can get it over the brow of the hill," he said.

Sergeant Bright looked up at the sun which had crossed its zenith. "I will send the scouts out; do you want to stay here for the rest of the day?"

Alex nodded, "We need to get the wounded and dead back to the ships. If we have to fight off Bedouin for the next fifty miles, we will need more men. We will stay here until the scouts return and we get reinforcements."

More bad news.

"The end of the pass is blocked; they have hauled boulders across and have men positioned behind them. Behind that on the plain is a camp," Marine Bodmin said.

"The whole bloody tribe is there and there are more joining. I think they will have a couple of hundred fighters by now," Marine Tubb said.

Alex had no choice but to defend his position, so he sent men up into the rocks either side of the pass. They would spend an uncomfortable and tense night there, but it couldn't be helped.

The next morning another marine was dead. His throat cut in the night without a sound. Alex went forward with the scouts to a point where he could see down to the end of the pass.

"Bloody hell, there's hundreds of them," he said.

The plain was a mass of tents, herds of goats and camels wandered, and riders moved back and forth leaving trails of dust.

"We'll not fight our way through that lot without losing more than a few men," Marine Tubb said.

"Tubsy's right."

"Let's get back. I've seen enough."

They made their way back to the boats and got there in time to meet the reinforcements led by Lieutenant Brazier.

"So that's the situation. I don't believe we can get through to the Red Sea under the current circumstances," Alex said.

"Not even by bringing up more guns?" Richard said.

"We can blast our way through, but then we have to get back and the boys who man the boats will not be able to land anywhere the Bedouin are. It will cost too many lives on both sides and could develop into a war that sucks in the Egyptian military."

The consensus was that they should fall back and take the boats back to Valetta.

So, this is what the sour taste of defeat tastes like, Alex thought as they started a tactical retreat. The first order of business was to get the boats down to the river floodplain. The oxen were unhitched, and men positioned above each of the wheels to man the lever brakes that were applied to the rims. More men manned traces on the uphill end of the boat to help regulate the descent. It took half the time to get them down as it took to get them up. The rear guard kept two hundred yards behind, then stayed at the bottom to prevent the Bedouin from following. They divided the remaining ox team between the boats and with some additional manpower got them to the river.

A marine messenger arrived with news. "The Bedouin have stopped at the bottom of the pass. It looks like the floodplain is out of their territory. They are taking pot-shots at the rear guard as they retreat."

"Any more casualties?" Alex said.

"No, we got away clean."

"We can dismantle the carriage, it would be a shame to leave them," Sergeant Hungerford said.

"Make it so sergeant but get a move on. The Bedouin might change their minds."

The launches were re-floated, and the carriages stored onboard. Then they embarked the men and headed downstream. Trevor Archer stood next to Alexander Beaumont on the quarterdeck of the Eagle.

"You know what? I think those bastards never had any intention to let us pass," Alexander said.

"What makes you think that?"

"They got all those extra men into position far too quickly. It was as if they were trying to provoke a confrontation."

"Do you think they will go to the authorities in Cairo?"

"They might I suppose. I did put a hole in their chief after all."

Trevor looked up at the pendant then took up his speaking trumpet. They were running with just forecourses set. "Let's have the main jib set," he called.

They picked up speed as they approached the city. The Endellion keeping pace a cable behind.

"Horseman galloping towards the city, Sir!" the mainmast lookout called down.

"Probably warning them we are coming."

"Shall we go to quarters, Sir?" said Midshipman Sykes.

"Yes, load both sides but do not run out. Keep the men down so they can't be seen. I don't want to provoke an attack."

A look back saw that the Endellion was preparing as well. Trevor wished he could get a message to Philip Trenchard, but he just had to hope he observed his actions and followed suit.

They could see the great pyramids ahead on the port side which meant that in the next couple of miles Cairo would be on their starboard side.

He decided to risk passing down the Western channel around the islands. The Giza side of the river was much less developed, and they were less likely to be fired on from there.

The Ile d'Al-Warraq slid by and suddenly Cairo was upon them.

"They are trying to barricade the river with boats, Sir," the lookout shouted.

"Run out the forward carronades and train them as far forward as they will go."

The barricade wasn't complete. The Arabs were rushing to get the last two boats into place, but the current wasn't helping them. On the other hand, the current was helping the Eagle make more speed.

Shots were fired from the far bank, but even the long-barrelled muskets weren't very accurate against a moving target.

"Permission to return fire," Alex said.

"Keep their heads down, try not to kill any," Trevor said.

Alex's right eyebrow rose but he turned on his heel and bellowed orders which were repeated by Sergeant Bright. The marines fired a volley over the heads of the men shooting from the bank. The looks on their faces saying they thought that was a waste of ammunition.

A bullet tugged at Trevor's coat. "Mr Beaumont, your efforts are not having the desired effect."

"Wipe that grin off your face, Marine Price!" Bright shouted. "Make them jump!"

The next volley kicked up dirt around the feet of the Arabs and sent them scurrying for cover. Alex turned to the quarterdeck and saluted. Trevor grinned at him and touched his forelock in return.

The barricade was approaching fast. The Eagle was carrying every stitch of sail she could sailing close to the wind and the trimmers had their work cut out keeping them taut and pulling.

The Egyptian boatmen had managed to get a rope between the last two boats but by the time the Eagle arrived, hadn't managed to tie it off.

"They should have run a rope across from one bank to the other," Trevor commented to the helmsman as he directed him towards the gap.

"Get ready to cut any ropes we get tangled in!" Trevor shouted and men took up tomahawks and axes.

They hit between the middle two boats, their prow rose over a rope that was low down and out of sight. For a second Trevor thought momentum would rip their masts out. Then there was a crack like a musket shot and the rope broke.

"Bugger! They did run a rope across the river," Trevor said as the Eagle surged forward. The barricade split and the current carried the boats apart. A short burst of chopping cleared stray ropes away, but they were too slow to cut one rope, onto which a boatman was holding. He was jerked over the side and dragged beside the Eagle; the rope wrapped around his leg.

""'ere we got a fish on a line," Seth Smith shouted from the side.

Trevor walked over and had a look. "Cut him loose, he's not big enough to keep."

The line cut, the boatman untangled his legs and trod water, shaking his fist and cursing them in Arabic.

The run down the Nile was nervous. The marines firing warning shots at anyone who looked like they were paying too much attention on shore. They didn't relax until they hit the open sea.

Valetta was a welcome sight; they dipped their colours, which were now British, to the castle as they entered the harbour and as soon as they were spotted by the Unicorn a signal went up with their numbers.

"Captain report aboard."

Chapter 8: Complications

Marty continued to cultivate the friendship with Andreas who carefully kept him away from his 'colleagues'. The Shadows, however, had him under constant surveillance and Marty had a very good idea who they were.

Christos Christofouru: Merchant, purportedly shipping leather goods and timber, actually running guns from Odessa.

Georges Hondros: Trader in olive oil going by the name of Victor Koblenko. Money man.

The boys had searched their homes as well as their business premises and even managed to infiltrate one of Christofouru's ships where they found a cache of weapons hidden under a cargo of timber. Andreas had a ship that to the untrained eye was identical and one night the ships mysteriously changed names.

"So that's how they are doing it. Andreas told me only his ships were able to get into Alexandrea at the moment and that's because he has convinced them that they are working for the Persians," Marty said when Matai reported, "Yes, they did the swap last night and Andrea's ship is due to sail today."

Marty recognised it as a similar trick to one the smugglers used in England. It worked, so he wouldn't knock it. He was more interested in getting to know the organisation behind it.

"The real question is who can we get to introduce us to the organisation in Odessa?"

"Andreas?"

"He is dragging his feet. I don't think he is the main man."

"Has Veronica been able to shed any light on it?"

"Not as such. Only that Andreas seems to have to report to someone."

"He visits Georges Hondros regularly."

"And Georges pretends to be a Russian. I wonder if he is the man we need to convince?"

The Eagle and Endellion returned to the harbour with the boats, much to Marty's disappointment. He invited the captains to report. They arrived almost at the same time.

"Gentlemen, I can see that the crossing was unsuccessful. What was the cause?" Marty said as soon as they were seated in his cabin.

"The Bedouin turned on us after the marines executed a couple of thieves," Trevor said.

"They executed a couple of thieves? What did they steal?"

"Powder and food," Phillip said.

"Who ordered the execution?"

"Lieutenant Beaumont. He wanted to set an example and deter any others who thought we were a soft touch."

Marty could understand his thinking but questioned the necessity. He kept his thoughts to himself.

"They will have closed off that route to the Red Sea, the Bedouin don't forget or forgive. What was the butcher's bill?"

"We lost Falconer, he was the first to be killed, five men dead and half a dozen men wounded. Young Brazier conducted himself with exceptional bravery and initiative. He manned a carronade while bullets were raining down around him and suppressed the Bedouin who had gotten above us."

"Damn that's an expensive failure. Well, we will have to look for another way."

He dismissed them after taking their reports and as they were leaving Trevor turned,

"Carsten Niebuhr talked about lakes and an ancient canal running North from the tip of the Red Sea from a place called el Souis. Maybe that would be an option."

Marty nodded and thanked him. It would be worth thinking about, but now he had letters to write. He always wrote a personal letter to each lost man's family and to the bank, where the squadron fund was held, to release the men's dues.

Veronica visited. This time she got a boat to bring her over.

"I have a message from Andreas. His superior in the Filiki Eteria has been informed about you and he wants to meet you."

"They took their time. Is that because Andreas was reluctant to tell them?"

"I think he wants them to think this was his initiative."

"That's alright, I am more than happy to let them. The important thing is to get into the organisation. When does he want to meet?"

"Tomorrow in the afternoon at the Upper Barrakka Gardens after the salute has been fired."

"A public place. Is he worried I will kill him or something?"

"Phht, that wouldn't stop you if you wanted him dead. At the academy they taught us how you kill with a stiletto. He would be dead before he knew it. No, I think he just doesn't want you to see where he is based."

Marty ignored the compliment.

"We know that anyway. The boys have been inside and searched it already."

Veronica looked surprised.

"You still have a lot to learn," Marty grinned, "they don't teach you everything at the academy."

"Did you find anything?" she asked, slightly put out.

"He is the moneyman; he has a large cache in his home hidden in a strongbox set into the floor under his bed. There were documents in Russian which we have copied but have yet to translate. There were others in Greek.

"I know of a man who speaks and reads Russian, Greek and Arabic who isn't connected to Andreas or his friends. He is a scholar and opera lover."

"Introduce me. I want to judge whether he can be trusted."

Veronica realised that Marty would want to do this even if one of his trusted men made the introduction, so swallowed the feeling of indignation that rose.

"Come to the opera tonight. He will be there."

Marty had seen the opera that was being performed that evening so spent most of his time observing people and how they interacted. He noted which butterflies swarmed around the governor and which around the mayor who was the de facto leader of the Maltese. He recognised there was a polarisation with only a very few who crossed between. None of the Filiki were present. He spotted a rather furtive group that orbited around a hard-faced, older man who they would approach, pay homage to, then slip away.

Marty was curious. If he had to guess, he would assume the man was a local criminal leader. The people paying homage were all furtive and he had an entourage of what could only be described as heavies.

Marty also noted that there was someone else watching the crowd as well. A moustachioed man in a plain dark suit sat several rows behind the furtive group who was paying more attention than his casual demeanour would suggest. Marty tagged him as a policeman and decided to introduce himself. Leaving his seat, he made his way to the row behind the man and sat directly behind him.

"Interesting crowd, what can you tell me about them?" Marty said.

"Commodore, I wondered when I would meet you," the man said without turning around.

"You have the advantage of me."

"Captain Mateus Falzon, Maltese police."

"Who is the target?"

"That is Henry Tanti, head of the local cartel."

"He knows you are watching him."

"I know, he expects me to. He would feel neglected if I didn't and I get to see the opera."

"How do you know me?"

"I was here when you were purging the island of French agents. I was clearing up bodies behind you for a week or more."

Marty smiled at that and moved back to his own seat.

After the performance he took a drink in the bar where Veronica joined him with an elderly man.

"Martin, this is Professor Allington. The man I told you about. Professor this is Commodore Stockley."

The old man sat and propped his hands on his cane in front of him.

"Veronica tells me you have need of some documents translating."

"I do, but I will need assurance that whatever you see will remain confidential."

"Veronica mentioned that. I give you my word as I do for all my clients. My fee takes that into account."

Marty nodded, acknowledging the professionalism.

"Where can I find you?"

"I have a small house on Triq San Gwann. There is a name plate by the door. You haven't asked what I will charge."

"I will pay your fee, whatever it is."

The professor studied his face.

"You were here before."

"Yes. Back a while now." Marty looked him in the eyes, challenging him to continue.

The old man pursed his lips, put his head on one side and decided to let that drop.

"Two guineas a sheet, single sided. Three for double sided."

"Agreed."

Marty stood as the professor rose. They shook hands. Then the old man grinned. "You don't look like the monster that they described."

"Who described?"

"The city merchants and traders you questioned when you were here before. I wrote quite an interesting account based on their stories. I think it was exaggerated."

Marty laughed and said, "I wouldn't bank on that."

"I will send you a copy, you can tell me if it is."

"Now why would you want to be talking to the professor?" Captain Falzon said to himself as he watched from a table in the corner of the room. A waiter approached and placed a glass of red wine on the table in front of him.

"Compliments of the commodore," he said.

Falzon looked across at Marty who was sitting with the actress. He caught his eye and raised the glass in salute. The commodore smiled and nodded.

"I will be keeping an eye on you," he thought as he sipped the wine. He smiled and held it up to the light. It was an excellent chianti from Tuscany. The wine was a deep burgundy colour and when he swirled the glass it held on to the sides showing it had body. He sipped some, swirled it on his pallet and tasted rich berry and a hint of old leather. The commodore certainly knew his wines.

He reviewed what he knew about Viscount Stockley. Apart from the obvious he was something to do with British counterintelligence. His antics on the island the last time he was here testified to that.

He thought on it.

If he was, then it was a safe bet that the squadron he commanded was as well or at the least on special duty. He was lost in that thought when a voice made him jump.

"Do you like the wine?"

He came back to the present with a start and saw that the commodore was sat opposite him.

"It's wonderful. Do you always move that quietly?"

"It becomes a habit. I am told you are the senior officer in the Maltese police."

"I am, but it's not much of a police force. We only have twenty-three officers across Malta and Gozo."

"Can you call on the army if you need them?"

"Only in an emergency like a riot."

"Interesting, so how do you deal with the cartel?"

"As long as they don't get out of hand, we leave them alone. I don't need a war with them; they outnumber me five to one."

"An unhappy peace then."

"You could call it that, but there have been rumblings that could upset it."

"Which is why you are here."

"Yes," he looked up suddenly, "and there is the man I have been expecting."

Marty looked up and saw a rotund man in a strange cross between European and Ottoman dress. He was wearing a red flowerpot-shaped hat with a black tassel.

"That is Abdula. He is an Ottoman of high rank and is head of the Ottoman community on the island. They have been here since the 1500's but I suspect they have close ties to the ruling party in Constantinople. Since the troubles in Egypt, they have been more active and are rubbing up against the cartel and trespassing on their territory."

Marty frowned. "Why would they want to start trouble? I don't see it's in their interest," he paused as a thought came to him, "unless they are trying to destabilise the island."

"Why would they want to do that?"

"To get control of this end of the Mediterranean and especially the trade routes to Alexandria. They can't overtly attack Malta because, on paper at least, they are allied to the British, but they can undermine it and cause unrest. That would force us to step in which they could hope would cause resentment amongst the locals."

"You think they would try and get us to invite them in to run the island? That would never happen."

"That may well be true but that has never stopped a hairbrained scheme in the past. Their empire is crumbling around them. The Balkans are in revolt, the Greeks are working themselves up to it, and Arabia is in danger of slipping away from them. They are fractured internally so this may not even be sanctioned by Mahmud the second."

"You think it could be sponsored by one of the factions?"

"I don't know, I am only guessing, but I think it's in both our interest to find out."

"As Commodore Stockley?"

"As a representative of His Majesty's Government."

"By that you mean the intelligence service."

Marty didn't reply, just sipped his wine and studied the new threat.

"You know they say, 'you should never judge a book by its cover'? Well, our friend Abdula is a prime example of that. See our friend Tanti? He is trying very hard to not reveal his true feelings but is having to steel himself to go over and greet Abdula. Who, quite deliberately, has sat in a position where he knows Tanti can see him and knows he will have to approach him in front of everybody."

"Why doesn't Tanti just ignore him?"

"Tanti isn't ready to confront him yet. He is still garnering support. I suspect that was what all that meeting, and greeting was about," Marty said with a frown.

"It was more than usual and included some people that I wouldn't expect to be so public about their affiliation. Are you sure you aren't a policeman?"

"I'm sure, but I do have experience with this kind of thing."

"As much as I hate to admit it, I am way out of my depth if they start an inter-faction war, I don't have enough resources."

"Lucky for you I do," Marty said.

"Am I going to be picking up bodies again?"

"Oh, come now, we didn't leave that much mess behind when we cleaned up the French network," Marty said with a smile.

"No, you were very neat about it, people died under what looked like natural or accidental circumstances, but someone still had to pick up the bodies."

"Fair comment. Oh, that's rich!" Marty laughed.

Tanti had stopped short of Abdula and, leaning on his cane, barely nodded to him. He waited, forcing Abdula to stand to get close enough to exchange pleasantries.

"Abdula looks like he sucked a lemon."

"I think Tanti is getting close to being ready, we need to move fast," Marty said with a frown. "Can you meet me on my ship tomorrow at eight in the morning?"

Falzon looked around the Unicorn as he stood on the deck and was impressed with the sheer firepower on show. The men looked tough, disciplined and fit. The officer that met him was young but had the look of someone who had seen combat.

"Captain Falzon?"

He nodded.

"Lieutenant Brazier. The commodore is expecting you. Follow me."

He was taken aft to a stair and down one deck. Then aft again to a door that was guarded by a marine.

"Captain Falzon for the commodore," Brazier said.

The marine knocked on the door, cracked it open and said quietly, "Captain Falzon, Sah."

"Enter," the familiar voice of Stockley replied.

Brazier bowed him forward as the door was pushed all the way open. To his surprise Stockley wasn't alone, nor was he in uniform.

"Captain! Welcome," Marty said. "Come in and take a seat."

The only chair available was between a big man with a toothy grin and a smaller but fit-looking dark-haired man with a Spanish cast to his features.

"Let me introduce you to my team. Next to you are Billy and Antton. Over there are Garai and Matai. The Chinese gentleman is Chin and that is Zeb."

A man who he took to be a steward entered with a tray of coffee.

"And that is Adam."

The coffee was served, and Adam lent against a wall.

"Nice to meet you, gentlemen," Falzon said.

Billy grinned at him. "I ain't never been called a gentleman before."

Marty smiled. "These men have all the skills needed to find out exactly what our friend Abdula and his friends are up to."

"You can gain evidence I can use in court?"

"If that's what you want, but I would prefer to stop the problem at source," Marty said.

"More bodies?"

"Not necessarily that is always a last resort, but—"

"You won't rule it out."

Marty just smiled and said, "Tell us what you know about Abdula and his activities."

"They are bringing in opium resin and are running at least two opium dens in the Marsa area where they are concentrated. That doesn't conflict with the cartel as they aren't into that, but they are running their own smuggling and prostitution rackets which does. He is also making himself the biggest fence on the island, and I have a suspicion that he is forging currency as well as there has been an upsurge in dud coins being handed in."

"Do you have one?" Zeb asked.

Falzon dug into his waistcoat pocket, pulled out a coin and flipped it to him. Zeb plucked it out of the air and examined it.

"Silver crown, dated 1809, looks almost mint. Weight about right but probably a little heavy as its impossible to get it spot on. This one has been hand struck and at a guess the metal is an alloy of nickel and tin with a bit of copper. It definitely ain't silver."

"Thank you, Zeb. Where would they make them?" Marty said.

"Somewhere the sound of hammers wouldn't be unusual."

"They have several gold and silversmiths in the area and a couple of places where they make copper pots."

"Zeb and Billy, go for a stroll around the area and see what you can find," Marty said and the two immediately got up and left.

"Chin and Matai, look into the opium dens and Garai and Antton the prostitution racket. Keep it low key, I just want to know where everything is and how many men they have."

Marty turned to Falzon who said, "Very efficient, you've done this before."

"We aren't finished yet. You, me, and Adam are going to pay a visit to Tanti."

"I thought you said Adam was coming with us?" Falzon said, looking around for the missing man.

"He is." Marty glanced up at the roof of a church.

"On the roof?"

"He has an uninterrupted view down into the courtyard of Tanti's house from there. He checked it out last night."

"And Tanti is known to prefer to meet people in the courtyard because he feels secure there."

"Exactly."

"It would be a long shot."

"Only two hundred yards."

"Only?"

Marty stopped at the door of Tanti's house and turned to him. "Adam can take the eye out of a fly at that range."

He knocked on the door with the silver head of his cane. It opened immediately.

"Come in. Sinjur Tanti is expecting you," the large, evil-looking thug who opened the door said. The two stepped forward and were immediately confronted by men with pistols. Marty held out his arms and when Falzon hesitated tapped him on the shoulder.

"They want to search us," he said.

Falzon grunted something unintelligible and held out his arms so he could be patted down. Weapons were removed. A pistol and a club from Falzon and a pair of barkers, his fighting knife and, what looked like, a knife handle without a blade from Marty.

"What is this?" the thug that patted Marty down said.

"A knife," Marty said.

"Where is the blade?" the thug said, turning it in his hands.

"Inside."

The man, who was obviously not gifted with a tremendous amount of intelligence, shook it then banged it against his hand.

Marty winced and said, "May I? Before you do yourself an injury."

Marty palmed it and pressed a concealed button with his thumb. The blade shot out forward and locked into place. It was double edged and razor sharp.

Three pistols were cocked and swung towards him simultaneously.

Marty held up his hands then passed the knife to the thug, holding it by the tip of the blade.

"Don't cut yourself it's very sharp."

When he took it, Falzon let out his breath with a whoosh.

"Please don't do that again," he said out of the corner of his mouth.

Marty ignored him. "Can we see Mister Tanti now?"

As predicted, they were shown into the courtyard. It was shaded and had a fountain which kept it cool. Marty remembered meeting Simón Bolívar in Columbia in very similar circumstances.

"Captain, you I know. You, I know of, Commodore. Your last visit cost me a couple of friends who were foolish enough to get involved with that French bitch."

"Nothing personal I assure you," Marty said.

Tanti nodded. "What do you want?"

"Blunt and to the point. I want nothing from you except some information."

Tanti crossed his arms. "What have you to trade for this information?"

"Advice on how to stay alive."

Falzon looked at him in surprise and was about to blurt

something out when Marty trod on his foot to keep him quiet.

"I am quite safe here," Tanti said.

"Are you? If I can demonstrate that you aren't, and from where, will you answer my questions?"

"Cover him," Tanti said to his men. Pistols appeared and were cocked.

"Oh, it's not me," Marty said, "although I am flattered you think I would be a threat."

He extended his hands in front of him and suddenly there was a playing card held between his fingers. It was the ace of spades. Tanti didn't look impressed at the simple sleight of hand.

"Would you be so kind as to hold this out at arm's length, here?" Marty said, flipping the card around so he held it between finger and thumb by a corner.

Tanti looked at him for a long moment then gestured to one of his men who took the card.

Marty moved around him and got him to hold the card where he had indicated to Tanti, which was at head height, three feet from where he was sat. He gestured to a man standing behind it. "Please move two steps to the right."

The man looked to Tanti who shrugged then nodded.

When all was set, Marty moved back to where he had been stood originally and nodded.

There was a distant shot and a hole appeared in the precise centre of the card.

Marty assumed the flood of Maltese from the man holding the card and Tanti was a string of expletives. He waited for them to calm down, being careful not to move as pistols were pointing pointlessly in all directions as they scanned for the shooter.

"You take risks, Commodore," Tanti said when things calmed down.

"Not really, my man doesn't miss, and if any of your men did try and shoot me, he would stop them."

"Where is he?"

"Will you answer my questions?"

"Damn you, yes!"

"He is two hundred yards away on the church roof over there."

Marty waved. Adam stood and waved back.

"He has an unobstructed view over more than two thirds of your courtyard, and with a modern rifle…" Marty left the rest unsaid.

"I need to take more interest in new weapons," Tanti said ruefully. He settled back into his seat. "What do you want to know?"

Marty asked him about what he knew of Abdula's operations and organisation.

"They started two years ago with one opium den. It was very low key and was mainly used by their own people and sailors. That was followed by a second and people in what they considered their territory were asked to donate to the security of the area."

"Classic protection racket?"

"More like a local tax as everyone had to pay it."

"Interesting, what happened next?"

"We found out they had set up brothels and were undercutting ours. They were bringing in girls from outside. Then the counterfeit coins started turning up."

"Where?"

"All over, they turn up all across the islands."

"Anything else?"

"They recently shut us out of their area. Several of my people were forcibly removed from their establishments and chased into our territory."

"Are their soldiers locals?"

"Interesting you should call them that. No, they aren't, they are professionals from the way they conduct themselves."

Marty had heard enough. "Mr Tanti, I think there is more to the Ottomans going into business against the cartel than just a desire to make some money. If I am right, then it's us that needs to take care of it. Would you be prepared to help?"

"You will remove Abdula and his organisation?"

"We will, how should I say it, neutralise him."

"That is good enough for me, we will help when you ask."

"I will keep you informed. My men will use the identification," Marty leant forward and whispered in his ear, "La Chaton."

Back on the Unicorn the Shadows gathered in Marty's cabin, Falzon was there with one of his men.

"This is Sergeant Patrick Doyle."

Doyle had the look of an ex-military man. Rugged featured with an impressive handlebar moustache. He sat upright, his broad shoulders dominating the space around him. Billy eyed him up wondering if he could take him. Doyle noticed, looked him in the eye and grinned showing he was missing one of his front teeth.

"Gentlemen, you have all been observing the activities in the Ottoman area of control. What have you seen?"

Zeb kicked it off,

"There is one goldsmith who has more people turning up to work than you would expect for the size of his shop. We couldn't get in during the day but it would be worth a visit at night. It looks like Abdula is fencing stuff himself. We saw several shady-looking characters enter his place with bags and leave without them."

Matai went next,

"Opium dens are what you would expect. Decrepit buildings tucked away out of sight. You can follow your nose to find them as the smell is unmistakable. Our guess is that they are smuggling it in with the other goods that they aren't declaring."

"What are they smuggling?" Falzon said.

"As far as we can tell from a short surveillance, wine, olive oil, gold, high value stuff."

"Thank you and good work," Marty said. "Antton, Garai?"

"We have more interesting information. They are smuggling in girls for their prostitution racket. The girls come from all over and you can take your pick of black, brown, white or yellow skin. The girls are mostly opium addicts, whether by choice or forced we couldn't say. But we did see that they are constantly under guard and when not working are locked up. They also have boys, mostly younger ones, and young girls. It's all very unsavoury."

Marty noted it all down and asked questions, filling in the gaps. He pulled out a map of the area out and laid it on the table.

"Please mark where you observed all those activities."

The boys took it in turn to mark on the map the places they had found. When they were done Marty examined the map.

"This is Abdula's house here?" Marty said pointing to the mark which was noticeably apart from the other marks.

"Yes, we followed him there." Zeb said.

"The rest of the operations are clustered around Triq Ix Xwieni. Near enough to the docks to get trade from the sailors. What's this over here?"

"Warehouses, they seem to be using a couple regularly and they are constantly guarded."

Marty considered his options.

"I would like to know who is behind this and which faction in Constantinople they are connected to. I would also like to know more about their prostitution business. Where the girls come from, whether they being held against their will, and where."

He looked at Falzon,

"Opium is not illegal, is it?"

"No but importing it without paying duty is."

"Falls under the heading of smuggling then."

"So, we have forgery, smuggling and slavery?" Falzon said.

"Yes, but first I want to find out whether this is just a local move, or a state backed attempt to destabilise the island."

"You want to visit his home?" Antton said.

"Going to need the whole team then, he has guards inside and out." Billy said.

"We will come along as well." Falzon said.

"Didn't know you had breaking and entering in your resume."

Marty said.

"I don't."

"Then you can't be part of that team, you would put us all in danger. We need to be in and out in the shortest possible time. You and your sergeant can play a role however."

Chapter 9: Revelations

Marty and Adam knocked on the door of Professor Allington's house. He sent a message that he had translated the documents that Marty had given him, and some interesting information was contained in them. Although Marty felt the Ottoman problem was a higher priority, he had time to find out what the old man found so intriguing.

"Come in, come in!" Allington said when he answered the door.

"Your message said you had found something interesting," Marty said as they entered the dim hallway.

"Indeed! Indeed! Most interesting and revealing."

They entered a cluttered living room that had a couple of shabby chairs and a low table. In the corner a large samovar steamed. Books were stacked around the floor and bookshelves covered one entire wall. Marty thought that the open flame heating the samovar amongst so much fuel, was a fire hazard.

"Would you like mint tea?" Allington said.

"Yes please," Marty said.

"I'll make it," Adam said.

"What have you found?"

Two of the letters you gave me, come from someone or something called Filliki, say nothing much. They are just general instructions, requests for accounts and reports on progress. The third is an instruction for someone called Georges to find out what the Ottomans are up to in Malta. It seems that their masters in Odessa have information that someone called Köse Musha Pasha is sponsoring destabilisation of the island in an attempt to discredit Mahmud II in the eyes of the British."

"Why would they want to do that? They are in enough trouble as it is without making more enemies."

"Our writer seems to think that the perpetrators are part of the ruling body but outside the royal family. It could be that they are trying to make Mahmud look foolish to garner support for a coup."

"What do you base that on?"

"I have been observing the Ottomans for the last thirty years and have watched them slowly tear themselves apart. There are factions within factions within the governing body. They are held together by the royal family, but it would only take one sign of weakness for there to be a coup."

"Have there been any attempts so far?"

"Several, but all were stopped at the early stage or before they got started, usually with bloody consequences."

Marty steepled his fingers under his bottom lip as he thought it through.

"If I were the Filiki I would want the Ottomans to fall out with the British, so what is Andreas doing getting friendly with me?"

"That could be a double game."

Marty looked at the professor, realising the old man probably knew more than he was letting on.

"If you have been observing the Ottomans for thirty years, how long have you been observing the Greeks?"

Allington laughed. "For close to fifty. My studies centred around Ancient Greek History."

"What do you think is going on?"

"My educated guess is that the Greeks represented by the Filiki Eteria would love the Ottomans and the British to fall out so that they could gain them as allies."

"Not very subtle," Adam said.

"They don't have to be. They can sit, watch and step in when the whole thing explodes," the professor said.

"Was there any hint in the letter that they know who I am?" Marty said.

"And just who are you?" the professor teased.

Marty laughed and said, "You were here in '06."

"Yes, I was. A young man and his team of men cleaned the French out of the island. They were led by a woman. Rumour had it that she died as well."

"She did. A lot easier than she deserved."

"Then Commodore Stockley I know exactly who you are."

Adam was reaching inside his jacket. Adlington noticed the move and held up his hands..

"Have no fear, I am on your side. My lips are sealed."

Marty looked at Adam and shook his head almost imperceptibly.

"Just what do you think you know?"

"You are a naval officer with some kind of remit for counterintelligence at a guess."

"I do undertake the odd mission for the government."

"Hiding in plain sight as a navy officer here to help the Ottomans."

"I am here to further British interests in the Mediterranean, whatever it takes."

"Beautifully obscure."

"Indeed, now how would Mahmud II react to the news that his people on the island are trying to destabilise the British hold on it?"

"He would probably react violently and root out the conspirators."

"I think it would be better if that information was complete with evidence of who is behind it," Marty said.

"That would please him no end, he is trying to reform the empire and these internecine rivalries are getting in the way. But why would you want to stop it?"

"Because Britain isn't ready to take advantage of the Ottomans falling apart just yet, we are almost bankrupt from the war with the French and need a trade arrangement with them to help rebuild our finances."

"I see, so what's the next step?"

"We get the evidence that we need to take to Constantinople."

Two nights later Marty and Zeb stole across the rooftops to the house of Abdula. The rest of the boys were pacing them across other rooves and in the streets below for protection.

An Iman called the faithful to prayers, his voice echoing across the rooftops. It was mid-

March, and the new moon was hidden behind a layer of cloud. They squatted on the roof of the house and waited.

Captain Falzon and Sergeant Doyle were in the street watching the house to see if Abdula went to the mosque. When he didn't, they went to his door and noisily banged on it. A servant answered it and Marty could hear them demanding entry to see Abdula.

There was a hatch that gave access to the roof and Marty slipped a slim jim between the hatch and the frame to shift the bolt. A little bit of gentle persuasion and the hatch opened. Marty peered down then stepped onto the ladder that he spotted leading down. Once inside he unshuttered a small lantern and shone it on the ladder so Zeb could follow him.

They worked their way through the upper floor checking each room at a time. Marty pulled back a heavy curtain covering a door and saw a large bedroom that was richly decorated and lit by candles. In the centre of the bed lay a woman. She was European and beautiful but her beauty was marred by bruises and the eyes that stared at him were haunted. Marty put his finger to his lips and stepped into the room. He saw a chain that was fixed to a ringbolt on the wall and ended in a manacle around her ankle.

"Do you speak English? Parlez vous Française?"

"I am English,"

"What are you doing here?"

"I'm his slave," she said and looked down ashamed.

"I'm here to find evidence to stop him, the men downstairs are the local police."

She looked at him blankly.

"Where does he keep his letters?"

She looked at a chest under the window.

Zeb went to it and picked the lock. He took out a sheaf of papers and looked at them.

"They'm all in that Arab writing."

"Can you memorise them?" Marty said. Zeb like his half-brother had an eidetic memory.

"Half a dozen."

Marty turned to the woman,

"Do you read Arabic?"

"That is how he found me. I was studying in Constantinople when he took me."

Marty had an idea.

"Can you select one letter that proves who his sponsor is?"

"Can you get me out of here?"

She wanted a trade, which was understandable.

"It would tip our hand too early if we took you now, but I will come back and release you as soon as I can."

"Will you kill him?"

"I will give him to Mahmud along with his co-conspirators."

"Then he will die slowly." She looked through the letters.

"This one is from Köse Musha Pasha and gives him precise instructions, it is six months old so he won't miss it. He was supposed to have burnt it but kept it for insurance."

Marty took the letter and slipped it into a pocket.

"Once we have verified the content we will be back."

Zeb replaced the rest of the papers in the chest and relocked the lid, then the two of them slipped away."

Professor Adlington unfolded the paper and, taking up a magnifying glass, studied it.

"This came from Abdula's house?"

"From his bedroom."

"This is from Köse Musha Pasha and gives instructions of what he is to do and what the pasha wants to see as a result of it."

He barked a laugh. "The final instruction is to destroy this letter."

"He kept it for insurance."

"It will be his death."

The next night Marty and all the Shadows crossed the rooftops. The hatch had been left unlocked and they quickly infiltrated the house. Simultaneously Captain Falzon, supported by a contingent of marines led by Captain O'Driscol, raided the two brothels and the goldsmith.

Marty, Adam and Zeb went to the bedroom while the rest swept through the house to take Abdula.

"You came back," she said, "I didn't think you would."

Marty worked at the lock of the shackle on her ankle,

"I always keep my word to a lady. What is your name?"

"Annabel. Annabel Crofton."

"Well, Annabel, I can call you that? You are free."

The lock gave and the shackle fell away leaving an ugly red sore behind. She looked at it as if she couldn't quite believe it. Shouting in Arabic came from below and then the sound of something smacking into flesh. Steps up the stairs preceded Matai who stuck his head through the curtain covering the door,

"All secure, he's in the bag."

"Get him to the ship and send a couple of the lads up to carry that chest away as well."

He held out his hand, "Would you come with me?"

"Where to?"

"Safety and freedom."

She took his hand and stood, her near naked body and its bruises plain to see. Zeb brought a blanket and wrapped her in it.

"What will you do now?" she said.

"Take Abdula and the evidence to Constantinople and present them to the sultan."

"I can give evidence," she said after a pause.

"Are you sure you want to?"

She nodded and with a determined look said, "And I want to watch his execution."

Chapter 10: Consequences

The Unicorn and her escort, the Silverthorn, sailed West towards Crete. Onboard were Miss Annabel Crofton escorted by Miss Veronica Sutherland. Veronica had first loaned Annabel a dress then taken her for a shopping spree funded by money Marty had found in Abdula's chest.

The raids on the brothels had freed around twenty enslaved females aged from fourteen to their mid-twenties. They were all nationalities, representing all tastes. There were a half dozen young boys as well. All under sixteen by their estimation. The raids had been resisted and the marines had gleefully slaughtered the guards, taking no prisoners.

The raid on the goldsmiths had revealed a veritable factory for manufacturing forged coins. Some dozen men and women were employed in striking coins using dies made by a pair of craftsmen. They found hundreds of pounds in forged coins ready to be distributed and it was estimated that they had already distributed several hundred pounds worth already.

Marty had suggested that an amnesty on handing in the coins might be a good idea and the governor was busy with putting one into action. It was hoped that most of the coins in circulation would be collected this way.

Abdula himself had been spirited away and, along with two men identified as his lieutenants, was held in the brig. They were all in chains.

Marty was on deck with Wolfgang. "Signal the Silverthorn to go ahead," Marty said after Malta had fallen below the horizon.

Wolfgang gave the order, and flags flew up the mast. Silverthorn acknowledged and set all sail with Adlington standing at the rail and waving as they pulled away. He and Captain Falzon had volunteered to go ahead and tell the sultan what had been going on to prepare the ground for Marty's arrival.

They reached Crete and turned North into the Aegean. Wolfgang got an itch between his shoulder blades.

"I want extra lookouts Mr McGivern and change them every hour. When we go to quarters at dawn, I want a full clearance fore to aft," he ordered

"Aye, aye Sir," McGivern said and bellowed orders.

"Expecting trouble, Wolfgang?" Marty said. He had heard him give the order through his open skylight and come up out of curiosity.

"A feeling." Wolfgang scanned the horizon.

Marty didn't say anything, he could feel a sense of anticipation running around the ship but had no presentment of danger. They saw nothing that day but at dawn the next, "Sail Ho, a point of the starboard bow," the mainmast lookout cried.

The ladies, kicked out of their cabin at an ungodly hour, had come up and stood looking around bleary eyed.

"What is it?" Veronica asked.

"We don't know yet," Marty said, "the lookout has spotted their topsails on the horizon. If they are headed towards us, we will know within the hour."

The minutes dragged and then, "Deck there, sail is a three master, and she has turned towards us."

"Are the men ready for action, Mr McGivern?"

"Aye, Sir, ready and willing."

He was right, the men had quietly gotten their guns ready, and weapons had been brought up from below and stacked along the centreline. The big carronades on the fore deck had been uncovered and the slides checked. The Azimuthal pivot and elevation thread given an extra dollop of grease. The smaller thirty-six-pound carronades on the aft deck were also swung back and forth on their pivots and greased by their crews.

"Any idea what she is yet?" Wolfgang called up.

"Looks like a warship, can't see the flag as it's hidden behind the sails."

Marty looked down the deck.

"Matai!" the Shadow looked around and Marty gestured to the mainmast. The Basque ran up the ratlines and was soon in the tops.

"Ottoman seventy-four," he shouted down five minutes later.

"Have they sent an escort?" Marty said.

"Why would they? We are a warship and there are no threats in this area," Wolfgang said. His bad feeling had gotten worse.

Marty had more to consider.

"We cannot assume he is hostile, but I don't want us caught napping either. We will not fire unless fired upon but that doesn't mean we can't be prepared for the worst."

Wolfgang knew exactly what he meant. "Mount preventer stays and chains, have boarding nets ready," he said. "Have the gunners sit by their guns out of sight and have the marines get up into the tops."

An hour later they could see the approaching ship from the deck.

"She has reefed mainsails," Wolfgang said.

"Out of the way of their guns?" Veronica said. She had stayed on the quarterdeck to watch what was going on.

"Could be, or they are in no hurry."

"On a fine sailing day like this? Not likely," Marty said.

"Mr McGovern, have the men ready to take in the mains," Wolfgang said.

Marty grabbed a glass and slung it over his shoulder.

"Commodore," Wolfgang started to protest.

"Fight the ship Wolfgang," Marty said and ran up the ratlines.

He settled on the topsail spar and brought the telescope around. A quick twist pulled the tube out to his focus mark, and he brought it to his eye. He scanned the horizon, then settled his view on the approaching ship.

She had her mainsails furled and a lot of men in the rigging as if she was about to manoeuvre. Her gun ports were down but that meant nothing. She was a two decker of a type the British had retired as obsolete. Marty wondered if she was one the ones that they had sold off. He focussed on her lines, bluff bow, sails British cut. Yes, she was most likely a former navy ship.

She was a mile away now and approaching fast. She showed no signal flags and looked to be going to pass about six hundred yards off their starboard side. He could see the captain stood on the quarterdeck.

Marty waited.

She came closer and then when she was just a cable away, her gun ports shot up and the guns started to run out.

"EVERYBODY GET DOWN!" he shouted.

It was just seconds later that the ships passed, and the seventy-four's guns fired.

They had aimed to cripple the Unicorn but had underestimated how fast she was sailing. Many of their guns missed but enough were on target to damage their rigging and knock a couple of holes in their side.

Marty hung on for life as bar and chain howled around him. He yelped as something hit his leg. He was almost afraid to look, fearing that he had been hit by a bar shot and lost it, but when he looked down, he could see that something had passed through his calf. He could also see Matai and Antton haring up the mast to his aid.

As they helped him down to the deck, men were already repairing the damaged rigging and Wolfgang had the ship ready to fight.

"Take him down to the orlop and into the care of Mr Shelby!" he ordered. Marty started to object but Billy picked him up and carried him below giving him no option.

Wolfgang was angry. The seventy-four, which he saw was called Jebel-Andaz, had damaged his ship. It was only the preventor stays and chains that had saved them from being crippled. They were not at war with the Ottomans, who had not even fired a gun in challenge. "Wear ship to port, load guns with double shot, carronades take down their rigging."

McGivern shouted the orders, and the men went into their well-rehearsed routines. The Unicorn spun on her heel, wearing faster than most ships could manage on their best day. The Jebel-Andaz was not so well manned and turned to reverse course much more sluggishly.

Wolfgang watched and assessed, then ordered, "Run out the starboard guns. We will cross their bow and rake her, then wear to port and take her with the port battery."

Below in the infirmary Marty heard the rumble as the guns were run out and felt the ship turn. Shelby had him strapped face down on the operating table while he worked on his calf.

"Looks like you took a ball through the calf. A musket if I'm not mistaken," he said as he probed the hole for debris.

Marty said nothing, he was busy biting down on the leather strap he had between his teeth. He had refused laudanum on the basis he wanted to stay aware of what was going on. He was regretting that decision at that moment.

Satisfied that the wound was clear of any large pieces of debris, Shelby took a large metal syringe and pushed the spout into the hole. Pushing down on the plunger he flushed the wound with half a pint of raw alcohol. Marty's back arched like a bow as the raw spirit hit raw flesh he strained against the restraints in pure agony.

"All done," Shelby said cheerfully and dusted the wound thoroughly with sulphur powder before packing it with boiled wadding.

Marty spat out the strap and started to curse him. Veronica, who had been sent to the orlop with Annabel, was wide eyed as she heard words that had never sullied her ears before. Marty could curse fluently in English, French and Spanish.

Up on the main deck the crew were preparing for their first broadside. The guns were loaded and run out; gun captains had the lanyards tensioned. They looked down the barrels lining up the V-notch at the back with the blade at the front waiting for the enemy ship to come into their field of view. They heard the order "Tack to port!" and tensed.

The guns started to fire from fore to aft and then the enemy ship came into view in Cyril Coombes' gun port, bow on, chunks of timber flying off as the guns to his left fired. He waited until his sights were just to the right of their foremast then pulled the lanyard. The flintlock sparked then the gun bucked and ran back, fire and smoke spewing from the barrel, blown away almost immediately by the apparent wind. The eighteen-pound ball found its mark, slamming into the foremast about a third of the way up.

"Wear ship! Reduce sail, let her come up on us!"

Wolfgang saw the fore mast of the Jebel-Andaz shudder as it was hit squarely.

"An extra rum ration to that gun crew, Mr McGivern. Ready the starboard battery."

He looked across to where Midshipman Sterling was attending to his carronades.

"Make them count, Mr Sterling," he said and got a grin in return.

He waited until the bigger ship was just half a cable behind him, "Wear to Port!"

The ship swung across her bows at almost point-blank range and the big sixty-eight-pound carronades on the foredeck coughed their loads of death across the scant fifty-yard gap. The smashers wreaked destruction along the length of the gun deck entering through the bow and hammering their way down the length of the ship. Followed by eighteen-pound ball, after eighteen-pound ball, guns were flung around and men smashed to pulp. Blood ran out of the gun ports.

Quinten Sterling knew his target was the upper deck and rigging and set his guns to do the maximum amount of damage to both men and ropes.

"Steady men," he said as the ship's bow approached. He was planning to fire just as his guns passed their starboard rail and take out the stays holding the mast on that side. He had loaded with cannister, bar and chain, a deadly mix. The musketeers on the other ship had gotten organised and balls slapped into the rail in front of him, one whined off the barrel of a carronade. He stood firm. His moment came, he was behind his foremost carronade and gave the order to fire before moving to the next in line. Each was fired at almost the exact same point and the repeated swathes of destruction did their job.

"Foremast is going!" McGivern shouted.

Wolfgang grinned, "The main isn't so steady either."

The Unicorn put on sail and accelerated away from their stricken foe. She might be wounded but she still had guns that could fire and needed to be treated with respect. Wolfgang's goal was to circle around and take her up the arse.

As they passed her beam, a thousand yards off, a half dozen guns fired and most of the balls splashed down in the sea abaft of them and short. One thudded into the side after skipping once.

"They aren't schooled on shooting a crossing target," Marty said.

"Commodore. Are you well?" Wolfgang said.

"Good enough."

Marty was using a pair of crutches to balance on one leg. Antton and Matai hovered protectively nearby.

"You will cross his stern?" Marty said.

"He will try to turn and stop me but that will put a lot of strain on his mainmast."

"He should strike."

"Have you ever known a Muslim to surrender?"

"They must be commanded by someone who is affiliated to the same faction as Abdula. In which case, they will be dead men if we take them back to Constantinople."

"Sir, there is smoke coming from the Ottoman!" a crewman shouted.

Sure enough, a rapidly-thickening column of smoke was rising from amidships.

"Is that something we started or are they burning their own ship?" Wolfgang said.

"Heave to behind her but keep your distance," Marty said.

The foresails were backed, and the Unicorn stopped in line with her stern a thousand yards off. The men lined the side and watched as flames shot up the mast.

"Her magazine—" Wolfgang didn't get to finish his sentence as the Jebel-Andaz chose that moment to explode. Throwing them to the deck.

When they had picked themselves up, Wolfgang ordered the boats away to search for survivors. The sea was strewn with flotsam and bodies. The boat crews had a grisly job searching through them. The seventy-four had carried over five hundred men.

"Got a live one 'ere!"

Midshipman Donaldson ordered the man brought aboard. He was badly burnt.

"Another over there on that hatch cover."

This one was more intact. He was dazed and in shock but had gotten away with a superficial head wound. In all they found twenty-three survivors. Most had jumped overboard when the flames had erupted and been in the water when the magazine exploded.

"What have we got?" Marty asked the surgeon once they were underway again.

"Twenty-two seamen and one officer," Shelby said. "Of them two are so badly burnt they will be dead before the morning."

"The officer?"

"He's fine apart from an excess of seawater. Doesn't speak a word of English though. None of them do."

Marty wished the professor was on board then he remembered that Annabel spoke Arabic or whatever the Ottoman's spoke."

"Ladies, may I enter," he called through the door to their cabin.

The door opened and Veronica invited him in. Annabel was sitting on the transom bench looking out of the window and Marty was struck with how beautiful she was now she was free and dressed in clothes of her choosing.

"Are you well, Commodore?" she said as she took his arm and led him to a chair.

"I am and I wish to apologise for my bad language in the infirmary."

"Oh, please don't worry about that," Veronica said.

"You speak French and Spanish very creatively." Annabel smiled.

Marty blushed.

"I have a favour to ask you, but you can say no if you wish."

"Ask I will do what I can."

"We have captured an officer from the ship that attacked us, but he doesn't speak English."

"You want me to translate for you?"

"Could you?"

"I can but it needs to be clear to him that it is you asking the questions, He would never answer a woman, especially a white one."

Marty had the man brought up on deck. He strutted arrogantly even with his hands shackled.

"Stand behind him," Marty instructed Annabel from the folding canvas chair where he sat with his leg supported on a stool.

"Wolfgang, if you can do the honours."

Both he and Wolfgang were in full uniform to impress, and Wolfgang towered above the Ottoman officer.

"What is your name and rank?" Annabel translated in an even tone neither adding to nor taking away from what was said.

"Lieutenant Omar,"

"Why did your ship attack us?"

He didn't answer and stayed silent when Wolfgang repeated the question.

"Bring him here and put him on his knees," Marty said.

Omar was dragged forward by Antton and Matai who as ever were in close attendance and Antton kicked him behind the knees to put him down onto the deck.

Marty looked at him for a long moment, his head cocked to the side. He could see the defiance in his eyes.

"I could give you to the sultan and let him have the fun of torturing you. I am sure he has people that are very good at it. But then again you attacked one of my ships so I think I will save that pleasure for myself."

Omar was surprised. He had been told that the infidel were soft and their Christian god forbade the use of torture. He was also surprised when a pair of trestles were set up and a wide plank was set on them.

"Up you go," Billy said as he and Garai hoisted Omar up and deposited him roughly on the board. Antton and Matai were standing by with ropes and quickly lashed him down so he couldn't move.

Marty lit a cheroot and appeared relaxed as if he was watching a play at the theatre.

"When you are ready, lads."

Matai had a piece of flour sack and laid it across Omar's face, holding it tight so he couldn't move his head.

"Ladies, if you wish to retire you can," Marty said.

Neither did, in fact Veronica was watching with professional interest and Annabel looked totally unmoved.

"Proceed."

Antton picked up a bucket of water and poured a steady stream over Omar's mouth and nose. He struggled but couldn't avoid it stopping his breathing.

"Enough," Marty said and gestured to Wolfgang.

"Why did you attack my ship?"

"Go to hell!"

Marty nodded to Antton who had collected a fresh bucket. This time Omar got two whole bucketsful.

"Why did you attack my ship?"

Omar was coughing and spluttering, gasping for breath, half drowned.

"Why did you attack my ship?" Annabel lent in close and spoke softly and added, "They won't stop until you tell them. They won't let you die."

Still, he wouldn't answer.

Veronica had moved around to stand by Marty, "They didn't teach us this."

"It's a method Chin taught us."

Antton poured again and again from buckets Billy handed him.

This time Omar took much longer to clear his lungs and get his breath.

"Why did you attack my ship?"

Omar broke and told them everything he knew.

The ship was part of a section of the Ottoman fleet that was loyal to Köse Musha Pasha. The captain was a family member and the crew carefully selected from those loyal to him. The Silverthorn had docked at Constantinople. The professor and Captain Falzon had successfully requested an audience with the sultan. The pasha's spies in the palace reported that a witness to his involvement was on his way from Malta on a British ship. He had dispatched the Jebel-Andaz to eliminate them and the witness. Marty asked how they knew that the witness was on his ship. The answer was chilling. They didn't and would have sunk and burnt every British ship they found heading to Constantinople.

Marty would have given him the mercy of a quick death, but he needed him alive to testify alongside Abdula. Even if it meant he was dooming him to a horrible end.

The Unicorn moored next to the Silverthorn in the Harbour of Sophia in the shadow of the great hippodrome. A reception committee waited for them on the shore.

"Captain, Professor. Nice to see you," Marty said.

"Commodore, may I present Selim the cousin of Mahmud II Sultan of the Ottoman Empire," the professor said

The richly-dressed and turbaned man bowed slightly and smiled showing a gold tooth. Behind him was at least a company of troops.

"We owe you our thanks, Lord Purbeck." He spoke in perfect English albeit with a distinct Ottoman accent.

"The least I could do to preserve the peace between our

Empires," Marty replied with a bow that matched his.

"Oh tush, don't be modest. Come, we need to present you to my cousin. You can hand the prisoners over to the major here."

An officer with a lot of gold braid stepped forward and gestured to, who Marty assumed, was a subaltern. He stepped forward and barked orders. A dozen soldiers marched forward and surrounded the four manacled men.

Selim invited Marty to join him in an ornate coach as an escort formed up ahead and behind them. Captain Falzon and the professor were next in line with the ladies in an open landau. The Shadows positioned themselves around the coaches much to the consternation of the major.

The prisoners were driven ahead of them, and they progressed at a walk on a road that ran alongside the hippodrome.

"A legacy of the Romans, they used to race chariots around it," Selim told Marty. "It is mostly used as a market now although it is a convenient place for grand spectacles."

"Such as public executions?"

"Occasionally."

"I have a written confession from the lieutenant. As they attacked my ship directly, I felt obliged to question him."

"Understandable, he looks in remarkably good condition for someone who has confessed."

"I can be very persuasive without drawing blood."

"You must tell me how you do it. Is that a Chinaman escorting those women?"

"That is Chin, one of my personal guards."

"I have never seen one before, exotic eyes. Why are the ladies here?"

"One is a colleague; the other is a witness."

"Confessions and witnesses. You come well prepared."

Marty just nodded. They had reached the end of the hippodrome and he got his first look at the Hagia Sophia. The Hagia was unmistakable with its huge blue dome and minarets. It was enormous and showed off the wealth of the empire for all to see.

"It was not built by us, you know. We converted it from a cathedral to a mosque."

"Did you now, when was that?"

"Three hundred years ago in the reign of Mehmed II, when we Ottomans conquered the city."

"When was it built then?"

"I don't know but it was renowned for centuries as a wonder before we arrived."

"Where are we going?"

"To the sultan's residence, the Topkapi Palace, it is situated on the peninsula to the North of the Hagia."

"We should have sailed around to a port on the other side."

"That is not permitted, the harbours on the North of the peninsula are restricted to our ships only."

The Topkapi Palace was another enormous complex. White walls, arches, domes covered in blue grey tiles. The palace sprawled before them, windows glinting in the sun, gold leaf sparkling. It was surrounded by a white stone wall and ceremonial guards in elaborate uniforms manned the gates.

The carriage pulled up and Selim said, "We walk from here," as a guard opened the door and placed steps for them. He noted that Marty was leaning heavily on his cane.

"Are you wounded?"

"A ball through the calf during our encounter with the Jebel-Andaz."

Selim barked an order and an officer moved out at a trot to return with an open sedan chair carried by a couple of burly slaves. He insisted that Marty sit and be carried.

"Impressive." Marty noticed the Shadows were looking hot after their walk.

"The Imperial Gate, entrance to the first courtyard."

"First? How many are there?"

"Just three. We will be going to the third. No one is allowed beyond that."

"Why is that?"

"That is where the harem is. It would be death to trespass there."

Marty looked around as they walked along a path lined with guards and dignitaries. Selim walked beside his chair and kept up a running commentary. A large building caught his eye as it was heavily guarded. Selim noticed and said, "The Imperial Mint, and over there the Hagia Irene." They were approaching a large gate bracketed by towers with spires on top. Marty noticed the towers were octagonal rather than round. "The gate of Salutation."

The prisoners were staggering now. Their shackles were heavy, and the guards were relentlessly driving them along, hitting them with rattan canes. Marty thought it politic not to say anything. A domed building was described as the Imperial Audience chamber. They passed it by and moved through the courtyard to another gate.

"The Gate of Felicity," Selim said as they moved into an impressive columned porch, the ceiling of which had a large gold boss from which a golden lantern hung. The amount of gold ornamentation effectively announced that that they were entering the sultan's personal domain. A rotund man approached and gave orders in a high voice. The prisoners were dragged to the side and forced to kneel.

"That is the sultan's chief eunuch. He is in charge of protocol."

"Eunuch as in?" Marty made a snip, snip, gesture.

"Yes. Eunuchs are the only men allowed in the harem and he is a particularly gifted organiser and administrator."

Marty saw that Veronica and Annabel were being taken to one side and given scarves to cover their hair. His attention returned when the eunuch approached and spoke to Selim. "We are to wait; the sultan is occupied at the moment." The slaves lowered the chair to the ground. Marty got out and stood, if he was going to be presented to the sultan, he would do it on his own two feet.

Marty knew a powerplay when he was presented with one, the sultan was making him wait to make it clear who was in charge. He had no idea for how long but was determined not to be seen to care.

He looked for the Shadows. They had been kept in the Second Courtyard.

"Do not worry your men will be being served refreshments and allowed to sit in the shade." Selim said.

The eunuch disappeared only to reappear fifteen minutes later and bark orders in his falsetto.

"Come, we can enter; you must remove your shoes and wear the slippers."

Marty did as he was bid and slipped his feet into the silk slippers that were offered to him. They were a surprisingly good fit and exquisitely made. As he stepped into the audience chamber, he realised why. The floor was tiled in delicate ceramics as were the walls, gold leaf was used in abundance and the lamps and ornaments were all solid gold.

He approached a large couch upon which reclined the sultan. He bowed as he would to his own king and stayed there until the sultan gestured, he could stand.

"Sultan Mahmud the Second bids you welcome and asks that you sit."

Marty looked around for a chair but realised he was expected to take a cushion which would seat him well below the sultan. He lowered himself down and crossed his legs. Selim took a cushion between him and the sultan and translated.

Marty was invited to tell his story and he did so as concisely as he could. The sultan listened and then asked what evidence he had of this perfidious act. Marty introduced the professor and captain who presented the letters they found in Abdula's house and the confession of the lieutenant. The sultan had the eunuch read them to him.

Then he asked to see Annabel. She was escorted in by a pair of men (Marty guessed they were also eunuchs). She kept her eyes down, not looking at the sultan. The chief eunuch asked her a question and she answered him directly. Selim looked surprised but said nothing. The questions came quickly but she never panicked and answered smoothly. She was halfway through an answer when a man was pushed through the door by a pair of guards.

"Aah, Köse Musha Pasha has answered the summons," Selim whispered seeming amused. He had been keeping up a whispered translation for Marty.

The pasha knelt and touched his forehead to the floor. The sultan ignored him and gestured for Annabel to continue. She completed her answer and stood with head bowed. The sultan said something, the first time he had spoken to her directly. She raised her head and looked him in the eyes. The chief eunuch looked scandalised which caused Selim to chuckle.

The sultan smiled and spoke. "She is truly a beauty; I could find a place for her in my harem," Selim translated. Annabel couldn't suppress a look of fright.

"I am sure she would be honoured, your majesty," Marty said, "but she has been promised to one of my officers as a wife." The lie was delivered as smoothly as the silk in the gown the sultan wore, and he was rewarded with a look of pure gratitude.

The sultan smiled again and spoke to the chief eunuch at length. It was obvious he valued the man's opinion. The discussion ended. The chief eunuch spoke. The guards grabbed the pasha and dragged him to his knees.

"You are sentenced to death along with the men from Malta, your name will be forever known as traitor, your lands are forfeit, your family will be eliminated to ensure your seed is not passed on."

He gestured and the guards dragged the pasha out.

"You and your people are invited to witness the execution," Selim said.

"How will it be done?" Marty said.

"The men from Malta will be beheaded, the pasha strangled."

"His family?"

"Will be dead already. They are here in the palace and the sultan's guards will have killed them all."

They were treated to a grand banquet that evening, even the Shadows, professor and captain were, there albeit seated as far away from the sultan as they could be. Marty was sat next to Selim who was obviously in the sultan's inner circle. The ladies were not in attendance as this was an all-male affair, except for the dancing girls.

The next morning at dawn they met in the first court. The executions were near a fountain which Marty was told was called the Fountain of Execution. The crowd were chatting cheerfully.

"Does this happen often?" Marty said when Selim appeared.

"More often than it should. Execution is a common punishment."

Four men with axes came forward and stood in a row beside wooden blocks, a fifth, the biggest of the lot, stood to one side.

"The executioners," Selim said unnecessarily.

"Soldiers?" Marty asked surprised that they weren't in uniform.

"Gardeners."

Marty's eyebrows rose in surprise.

A fanfare of trumpets, discordant to European ears, echoed across the court and the sultan was carried in on a litter carried by six massive slaves.

Marty was joined by the professor and Captain Falzon, behind them came Veronica and Annabel.

"That was all the trial they got?" Falzon said.

"Justice is swift in the Ottoman Empire, especially if you go against the sultan," Selim said.

The sultan's litter was placed gently on a dais and the people knelt, foreheads touching the ground. Marty nudged Falzon and made a leg. A glance confirmed that Veronica and Annabel, who had their heads covered in silk scarves and their faces veiled, had curtsied deeply. The tableau froze for a long moment then the sultan gestured, and everyone stood. It was a demonstration of absolute power.

Chief Eunuch stepped forward and read from a scroll, Selim translated. "Köse Musha Pasha, has been found guilty of the highest treason against his Imperial Majesty, the sultan. He is listing his sins, I won't bore you with the details. Aah, here we go with the sentence. He is sentenced to death by strangling as befitting his rank."

"Not a swift clean death then," the professor said, looking slightly green.

"That depends on the instructions the executioner has received."

The arrival of the four co-conspirators ended the chat. They were lined up behind the blocks. Their heads had been shaved except a top knot which Marty found strange. The eunuch made a short pronouncement, and the men were forced to kneel with their heads on the block. All of them had their heads turned to the side facing the sultan.

Drums pounded.

The executioners stepped into position and raised their axes. The sun glinted off the razor-sharp edges.

The rhythm of the drums increased in speed.

The executioner closest to the sultan swung his axe.

THUD, its edge bit into the block and the lieutenant's head dropped into a shallow bowl that was positioned to catch it. A fountain of blood exited his corpse.

"Messy." Marty said.

The executioner grabbed the top knot and raised the head high so everyone could see it. He retrieved his axe with his other hand and stepped away from the cooling corpse.

The next in line was Abdula, and Marty could see his body was shaking and he had fouled himself.

The axe rose and fell.

The macabre show was repeated until all four were dead.

The executioners dropped the heads back into the respective bowls and went to the fountain to wash the blood off their hands and arms.

Köse Musha Pasha's turn had come. Marty had expected they would use a contraption to strangle him, but the big executioner stood behind him and put his hands around his throat.

The eunuch made another speech and as he spoke the executioner started to squeeze. His bare torso shone with oil and the muscles bunched as he increased the pressure. Köse Musha Pasha's face started to turn blue, and his tongue poked out. The executioner's shoulders tensed as his feet started to kick and then he went still.

Marty was surprised it was so quick but then he saw that the head was at an odd angle.

"He broke his neck."

"Yes, the sultan decided on a quick death."

Marty wondered at the power needed to break a neck with hands alone.

The court was silent for a second then a cheer went up. The sultan's litter was picked up and he was taken back to the third court to the cheers of his happy subjects.

Chapter 11: Try and Try Again

The Silverthorn and Unicorn slipped back into Valetta harbour. The Unicorn showing the scars of combat. They had no sooner anchored than boats were sent ashore for supplies to complete the repairs to Wolfgang's satisfaction. None of the damage was below the waterline so they didn't need a drydock.

Marty and Falzon went to see the governor.

"I must say I am relieved you settled this before it got out of hand," Sir Thomas said when they gave him their report, "but I would have expected to be kept informed as the investigation proceeded."

"We thought you would rather not be involved with deals with the cartel," Marty said. "Not really the thing the government wants the governor to be involved in."

"That's as maybe but I will write to your commander and voice my concerns."

His nose is well and truly put out! Marty thought.

"That is your prerogative, Sir Thomas, but Malta is safe from internal strife for now and no blame can fall on you for the deaths."

"Deaths? There was no mention of deaths in the report!"

"Best left undocumented, if you know what I mean."

"Damn it man. How many?"

Marty looked at Falzon, "Was it eight?"

"Nine, I think. The Iman," Falzon said with a straight face.

"Oh yes. I forgot about him; fell off his minaret."

Sir Thomas looked aghast.

"We only included the casualties of the raids on the brothels and goldsmiths as they were legitimate; the others were more in the nature of a clean-up." Marty smiled and poured himself a cup of tea. His casual treatment of the subject chilled Sir Thomas's soul.

"That was priceless," Falzon laughed as they took a carriage back to the centre of town where they would have dinner with Annabel and Veronica. Annabel had taken a shine to Falzon. Much to Wolfgang's annoyance she had not reciprocated to his advances. Veronica had told Marty that Annabel didn't want a long-distance relationship which is all a navy captain could offer. Marty had to agree. It took a special kind of woman to live with the separation that navy life demanded.

Marty looked out into the harbour and suddenly sat upright.

"Something wrong?" Falzon said.

"There's a second rate coming into the harbour."

"Second rate?"

"A ninety-eight-gun ship of the line and she is flying an admiral's pennant."

"Do you need to report back?"

"Haven't seen it, and certainly haven't seen any signals," Marty said using a variation of the Nelson excuse.

The dinner was a celebration of the end of the 'Ottoman problem,' as Marty called it. Veronica had gotten them a table at the best restaurant in town which was run by an Italian from Tropea. The food was delicious.

When he got back to the ship a note from the admiral was

waiting for him.

"It's Rear Admiral Winter. Seems I am to attend him for dinner tomorrow at seven," Marty said to Adam.

"Do you know him?"

"No, never heard of him. Do you have the latest copy of the list?"

A copy of the list of commissioned officers that was only two months old was found and Marty searched the admirals section.

"Here he is, made admiral in 1815. Was the captain of the Boyne before that." Marty looked at the ship from his window. It was lit up like a Christmas tree.

At precisely seven the next day Marty stepped aboard the Boyne to the pipes of a well-drilled side party. The ship was seven years old but as shiny as a new pin. Gold leaf gleamed on scrollwork, brass was polished to an inch of its life and the paintwork was perfect.

A pretty ship, Marty thought disparagingly.

"Commodore Stockley, welcome. I'm Captain Stevenson, the admiral is expecting you."

He was announced. The admiral was sat at his desk and rose when Marty stepped forward.

"Stockley, nice to meet you," he said with a distinct Devonian accent.

"Admiral, the feeling is mutual. Though I am not familiar with your career."

"Nothing spectacular, mainly blockade duty at Brest."

That explained it, if the man had spent his career in second rates on blockade duty, his name wouldn't appear in *The Gazette* except when he was promoted.

The door opened and a steward entered. His face was familiar, and Marty knew exactly why.

"Your career is well known to me, and I must confess to being somewhat jealous of frigate captains like you and Cochrane dashing around getting all the excitement. But I did my duty and must say I came to enjoy the routine."

"My service has not always been as exciting as it may seem," Marty said. "There were long periods of running around delivering messages and suchlike, interspersed with a few minutes or hours of blood and death."

"But you saw combat and from the looks of the repairs being made to your ship and your cane, you still are. If the war had continued, I may have seen some," Winter said with regret.

Marty looked at him for a long moment, judging the man, then said, "Is that why you sent a message to Napoleon's supporters that he was being carried in my squadron?" Marty said.

It was as if he had hit him with a hammer. He stepped backwards, his hand came up to his heart, all colour drained from his face.

"How…?"

"How did I know it was you? I questioned the officers of the French ships that tried to free him and have an almost perfect likeness of your steward."

"You cannot prove that."

"I have written confessions; a portrait and, I'm guessing,

your man has been with you since you were a captain. The only reason I haven't tracked you down before this is because I have been under admiralty orders and too busy."

"By what authority do you accuse me?" he shouted, anger giving him strength.

"I act for the good of the service" Marty said softly.

Winter lost some of his bombast.

"What will you do?"

"Me? Nothing. I know who you are, that's enough. Napoleon is in exile on St Helena and will probably die there. Your treachery only gave my ships some well-needed practice."

Winter's eyes hardened.

"There was nothing listed in The Gazette."

Marty gave his wolf smile.

"Three rebel corvettes were taken after a short and bloody night action while my squadron was on a covert mission. It didn't make it to *The Gazette* because the powers that be didn't want it to. They were sold off in Gibraltar."

"I do not believe a word of it, there would be something made public."

"Not everything I do is in the public domain."

The admiral in Winter came to the fore and he stood straighter.

"Who do you answer to?"

"Admiral Turner and the first sea lord."

"But that means—"

"Yes, it does."

"Oh, my lord." Winter sat; his head in his hands.

"Cheer up, Admiral. The worst that will happen to you is you will be quietly beached on half pay."

"No publicity?"

"No trial, no publicity. Why would the government want to make an example of you? The war is over and the whole operation never happened as far as the public are concerned. Napoleon was just taken to St Helena. The fact that he still has supporters will never be acknowledged publicly."

"Does Turner know what happened?"

"Of course, it was all in my report which was circulated to the first sea lord and the Prime Minister."

"Can I persuade you not to tell them it was me?"

"No, I lost a few men in that action, and you have to answer for that."

Marty let him stew for a minute then stood. "I think dinner is out of the question now."

Winter just nodded.

Marty left and returned to the main deck. He waved to the Unicorn and waited at the side for his boat.

"Commodore. I thought you were here for dinner." Stevenson said noticing he was there.

"Something came up," Marty said, Stevenson looked uncomfortable.

"The Admiral is a good man."

"Why do you feel the need to tell me that?"

Stevenson sighed, "I heard what was said, I was in the coach.

I don't know what he has done but I know he would have thought it for the best."

Marty snorted his denial of that, then said,

"Keep him from doing something stupid, there is no need for any grand gesture."

A movement caught Marty's eye. The steward was advancing across the deck with a pistol in his hand. Murder in his eyes.

Marty stepped to the side to be clear of Stevenson.

The steward raised the gun and pointed it at him.

Marty's hand went behind his back inside his coat then shot forward. His fighting knife's hilt appeared in the man's chest just to the left of his breastbone.

He stopped; the gun started to sag as the strength left him. With the last of his remaining will he pulled the trigger. The ball dug a hole in the deck a foot in front of where Marty stood.

"What the hell?" Winter exclaimed.

Marty stepped up to the body and kicked the gun away.

"A pointless grand gesture," he said. "Go and look after the admiral, take his guns away."

"What am I to do with him?"

Marty rolled the body over and pulled out his knife, cleaned it on the steward's trousers and said, "Bury him. Write a report telling exactly what happened, no embellishments and no mention of anything you heard. Send it to the admiralty in the next mail. You can show it to Admiral Winter, but this is ordered in the name of the first sea lord."

Marty showed him his letter of authority.

As he was rowed back to the Unicorn, he wondered why he hadn't killed Winter. He certainly deserved it. The more he thought about it he realised he understood him. The need to prove himself in action, the disappointment that the war ended before he could do so.

"He must have thought the war had passed him by," he said to himself.

"Sir?" Sam said from behind him.

"Nothing, Sam, just thinking out loud."

Back in his cabin Marty wrote, then encoded a letter to Admiral Taylor. When it was done, he sealed it, wrapped it in oiled paper and called for Trevor Archer.

"You are to sail to London. Deliver this to Admiral Taylor and wait for his reply. Collect up the mail from the rest of the squadron and any other ships before you leave on this evening's tide," he said.

"Aye, Sir." Trevor knew better than to ask any questions. When Marty was in this mood.

"Get there as fast as you can."

Marty turned his thoughts back to his mission; it was time to deal with the Greeks. He needed to meet with Georges Hondras. The last attempt to meet had been interrupted by the Ottomans, so he set about repairing the connection. He sent a message to him apologising that he couldn't make the previous meeting and asking if they could meet at the same place the next day at two o'clock.

He got a message back an hour or so later agreeing to the meeting.

Marty walked along the path at the top of the Upper Barrakka Gardens. He was dressed in a light grey suit and wore a straw boater. His cane tapped in time with his pace. He didn't need it now as his calf was almost completely healed except for a pair of very pink puckered scars, but the cane was a disguised gun. One shot, but enough to buy him the time for the Shadows to close in if he needed them.

Georges was sitting on a bench that overlooked the harbour. Marty spotted at least three men loitering nearby. Probably there to ensure that Georges wasn't assassinated or that they weren't disturbed. Either way they were of little consequence. Adam was positioned on a roof some two hundred and fifty yards away, Matai was gardening not far to his left, Antton and Garai were pruning some bushes.

Marty strolled up and sat next to him.

"A wonderful view, one could never tire of it," he said.

"Indeed, and high enough to catch the breeze."

They sat quietly for a long moment.

"You have convinced Andreas that you are a potential ally," Georges said.

"I could be, but only as a silent partner."

Georges laughed, "I saw what you did to Abdula."

"A matter of maintaining public order."

"You didn't want a war between him and Tanti?"

"Why would I? It would destabilise the island."

"What became of Abdula?"

"He lost his head in Constantinople as did his sponsor."

"Your alliance with the sultan is assured then."

"Let's just say that trade will continue."

Georges laughed again, he was a jolly chap.

"You British. Trade is everything."

"It keeps the empire ticking along," Marty said.

"Why do you want to help us?"

"I have my reasons which I will explain to the Filiki Eteria in Odessa."

George got serious, "I cannot introduce you to anyone if I do not have something to tell them."

"Tell them I am willing to make a trade for our covert support. I can supply weapons and money."

"What do you want in return?"

"That I will tell them when I see them."

Marty stood and looked across at the ships. The Boyne had her yards crossed and looked pretty in the sunlight.

"Let me know when you have gotten their agreement and you can come with me on one of my ships to Odessa."

"Why not one of ours?"

"Too slow."

He turned and walked away.

Martin didn't expect an answer anytime soon so looked again at how to get gunboats into the Red Sea. The idea that there was a route directly from the Mediterranean intrigued him and he bought every map he could find. He went through each one and grouped the ones that agreed.

"Now I should have an accurate enough picture to gauge the possibility," he said to himself.

The maps all agreed that there was a lake to the North of the Red Sea. It was called the Bitter Lake or Lake Shieb and there was a river running down to the area called Suez or el Souis. There appeared to be a caravan trail or track marked on most of the charts from a town on the Mediterranean coast called Catieh. He measured off the distance and estimated it was between sixty and sixty-five miles.

He went to his door, "Please ask the watch to summon Captain Howarth," he said to the marine.

It only took Howarth thirty minutes to arrive.

"Commodore, how may I be of service?" he said expecting to be given messenger duty.

"You and I are going on a short expedition."

Howarth perked up, any expedition Marty had in mind would be more interesting than sitting around in port or running messages.

"Look at these charts. They all show a trail or a track running from the coast here to this lake."

"It's pretty direct."

"The reality may be somewhat different so we will go and have a look. I want a marine scout; the escort will be the Shadows. You and I will survey the route, so I want you to bring along your master."

"You don't want the marine engineers?"

"No, they took a battering on the last expedition and the temptation to shoot any Bedouin we come across may be too much."

"Will we be in uniform?"

Marty gave that some thought before answering, "No I think civilian dress will be more comfortable and practical."

"When will we leave?"

"Tomorrow morning. I want to be back when the Eagle returns from Britain."

He called Mr Fletcher to prepare rations for four weeks for twelve people. He would acquire horses on landing.

"No horses for sale anywhere?" Marty said to Annabel and Terrance Howarth who had been sent to buy some.

"None, there are camels, but we would need some locals to lead them," Annabel said.

Marty had realised he would need an interpreter at the last minute and Annabel had jumped at the chance to get away from the island. It turned out she wasn't as attracted to Falzon as he had thought. She was dressed in trousers that tucked into calf-length boots, a tan-coloured cotton blouse with a scarf that wound around her neck that could be used to cover her face. Her head was covered in a straw hat that was held on by another scarf that was pinned to it. Marty thought she looked damned attractive.

"Camels it will have to be," Marty said, "they can't be much different to ride than horses."

They engaged a local camel drover and caravanner who had enough camels to carry them and their supplies. He was no more than five feet tall, dressed in, what looked to the Europeans, like a nightshirt with a waistcoat and wore a desert headdress. He had two boys as helpers who Marty kept a careful eye on as he thought they would have sticky fingers.

Then came the moment of mounting. How nobody was seriously hurt Marty would never know.

"Jesus fucking Christ! I'm splitting me difference," Zeb cried as he threw a leg over his beast which had been persuaded to kneel. The next moment the back legs went up, throwing him forward, then the front legs extended, throwing his body back. He was so off balance that he exited by the back door and landed flat on his back on the sand.

The others fared almost as badly, even forewarned by Zeb's experience. The only person who didn't have at least one fall was Annabel. Marty took a tumble over his steed's head and narrowly missed a stream of green bile the beast spat at him. Garai pulled a pistol and threatened to shoot his, after he hit the dirt for the third time.

"Hook one leg around the saddle horn," Annabel told them when there was a collective groan about the width of the animals."

"What like ridin' side saddle?" Zeb said.

"Exactly, it stops you falling off when they get going. Their gait is nothing like a horse."

She was right. The camels walked with a rolling gait, not unlike a sailor on dry land, by moving both legs on a side together. Once they got moving the men found the more, they relaxed the more comfortable it was.

They covered twenty miles a day. The camels weren't carrying huge loads and there were wells on the route. The first village they passed through was Hahrash which was just ten miles down the trail and a good place to stop for lunch. The men had rubbed sores and Matai distributed liniment. Annabel helped them rub it in even when the sore spot was in a private place.

Her tender ministrations were greatly appreciated, and Marty wondered if she would make a good nurse. She had made it clear she was done with academia, it brought back memories she would rather keep locked away. He decided that when they got back, he would introduce her to Shelby.

The caravan route was relatively flat and wide for the first day and Marty stopped every two miles to pace off the width and test the firmness underfoot. Yates Bonneville, the Eagle's master, kept notes of headings and landmarks supported by sketches from which an accurate chart could be created.

The days were hot, and they got through a prodigious amount of water. Marty realised why the Arabs preferred camels. They could go weeks without water and food and carry two hundred odd pounds. When they did drink, they sucked up vast amounts which they apparently turned into fat and stored in their single hump.

The second day they passed along Hazer Wadi. It too was wide and in general the going was firm. They reached Asebee that evening just before dark where there was a well and made camp.

"So far, the trail looks ideal for bringing the boats over. The incline up to the wadi was gentle enough and about the same on this side. There are a few stretches of soft sand but nothing that mats couldn't cope with," Terrance said.

The mats were the idea of one of the marine engineers, they were tough rush mats that were about fifteen feet long and a foot wide.

They could be rolled up to be carried and stopped the wagon's wheels from sinking into soft sand.

"It's a case of so far so good. Much easier than the route we tried last time," Marty said.

"Could the boats be pulled by camels?" Terrance said.

"I don't know, let's get Annabel to ask the drover."

Annabel was eating at the second fire so Marty went and sat beside her.

"He says that they can but none of his camels are trained for pulling."

"Ask him if he knows where we could get some."

Annabel held a long conversation with the drover with much gesticulating and hand waving. He grinned as he answered, showing uneven yellow teeth. His two helpers thought the whole conversation hilarious and spent the time laughing and nudging each other.

"He says he knows men who have them but to get more than a couple will take time and a lot of money. He wants to know what you will transport that cannot be carried by a camel."

"He doesn't need to know yet."

"If you want his help you will have to tell him."

"I will tell him if we decide to do it."

Marty stood and, after thanking her for her help, walked away.

"Well really! That is one infuriating man," Annabel said.

"I heard that!" Marty's voice said out of the dark.

The third leg followed a river and got them to the head of the lake. Rather than find a boat to sail along it, Marty had them follow the shoreline around it to the river that emptied into the Red Sea. They needed to stop for the night and Marty asked how far it was to the shore. He was told, "Another day and a half."

"Thirty miles more," he told Terrance.

"From what I've seen the shallow draught boats should be able to run on the river."

"We will see when we follow it, but did you notice it looked unnaturally straight for a river?"

The next morning proved him right. They followed the bank which ran generally Southeast and had a consistent gradient. Annabel rode near to Marty and overheard him talking to Bonneville.

"You are thinking of bringing boats along this route to the Red Sea aren't you?" she said.

"My! You are persistent," Marty grinned. "Yes, we are. Gunboats, so we can patrol along the Red Sea to prevent arms being smuggled into Egypt."

She frowned, "Why? The arms aren't coming in from there."

Marty pulled up his camel.

"How do you know that?"

"Because Abdula knew they were being supplied by the Greeks."

"He knew?"

"Yes, he thought it was funny that the Greeks would support the Wahhabi. He thought the weapons were second rate and would be more dangerous to the user than to whoever they were shooting at."

"Did he report that back to Constantinople?"

"I don't think so, he thought they were doing more damage than actually helping."

Marty rode off muttering, Annabel caught some of it and blushed.

"You know this looks like it is a river that has been straightened into a canal," Bonneville said over lunch.

Marty remembered something and went to his camel, rummaged in his saddlebag, and pulled out his maps. He searched through them until he found the one he wanted. It wasn't one of the ones that agreed with others, but it had annotations in faded ink. He unfolded it and laid it between him and Bonneville.

"See here? There is an annotation which isn't on the other maps," Marty said. I couldn't really read it but didn't try that hard because it didn't appear on any of the others."

The two of them had spent minutes trying to read what it said when Annabel noticed and came over to see what they were doing. After watching them for a minute or so she went to her own bags before returning and kneeling beside Marty.

"This might help," she said and offered him a magnifying glass.

"Thank you," Marty said and took it.

He peered at the inscription and shook his head, "I still can't make it all out. Only a word that could be canal."

"Let me see," Annabel said. He handed her the map and glass.

She held the map up to the sun, so the light shone through the paper.

"Ptolomacus Canalis," she said then looked at the maker's mark.

"This was made by a Frenchman."

"Yes, one of Napoleon's surveyors before the Battle of the Nile."

"He must have been a scholar as well. Ptolemy was a king of ancient Egypt around the time of Alexander the Great. In fact, if I remember correctly, he was a Macedonian like Alexander was."

Chapter 12: Filiki Eteria

Back in Valetta Marty pondered what to do next. The route had proven to be viable. But, even if Abdula hadn't mentioned the fact that the Greeks were supplying arms to the Wahhabi to his superiors, it was a waste of time. The information was bound to be found as the sultan's intelligence service sifted through the pasha's records.

He was pacing the deck and noticed Annabel and Shelby sat beside each other, heads bowed over a book. He had introduced them when they had returned and suggested she might make a good nurse. She had been reluctant at first but after Shelby had taken her down to his infirmary and talked about his beliefs and methods, she became interested. Now you couldn't get them apart with a jackstaff.

Marty smiled, sometimes things worked out just fine. He went back to pacing as he thought his problems through. He was just reaching a conclusion when a shout went up. "Boat ahoy!"

There was a muffled reply and the lookout shouted, "Civilian, wants to come aboard."

Curious Marty went to see who it was.

"Let him up," he said when he saw it was Georges. "Bring him to my cabin."

Adam had the apothecary's pressure cooker working by the time Georges arrived.

"Georges, welcome," Marty said and held out his hand.

"I am not sure how to address you," Georges said.

"Just call me Martin." Marty smiled trying to make him feel welcome.

Georges looked around the cabin noting the rack with his swords and rifle. Then saw the portrait of Caroline which he openly admired. Adam entered with a silver tray and served them both coffee. Georges added four large lumps of sugar to his and stirred it. Marty looked at Adam and raised his eyebrows. Adam just shrugged.

"Is there anything else, my lord?" Adam said.

"No, that will be all. Thank you."

He sipped his coffee.

"You have been to Odessa?"

"Yes, I got back an hour ago."

Marty waited and sipped.

Georges finished his coffee and put the cup back on its saucer.

"The Filiki will see you."

"That is good news. When?"

"As soon as you can get to Odessa."

"Are there conditions?"

Georges smiled, rather wolfishly in Marty's opinion.

"You come alone, without your… what do you call them? Shadows."

"Can I bring my steward?"

"Yes, for the voyage but he stays on the ship when we get to Odessa."

"That sounds like I won't be using one of mine."

"No, we will go on the ship that brought me."

He pointed out of the transom windows. Marty turned and saw a ship about the size of a navy cutter but fully sloop rigged with raked masts.

"She looks fast."

"She is, it's the type the Russian navy use for carrying messages."

"Adam!" Marty called. Adam stepped through the door to the steward's room.

"We will be going on a trip, pack my small sea chest please."

"Will you require your honours?"

Marty thought about it. "No, let's keep it low key."

They left on the next tide and Georges had not exaggerated. The little ship was fast. Marty estimated they were making at least fourteen knots in a stiff breeze and were sailing close to the wind. The captain was a gnarled Russian who smoked the smelliest cheroots Marty had ever come across. The smoke smelt of tar and something else. "Old socks," Adam volunteered when Marty mentioned it.

"Probably; it is not something I would try anyway."

He looked around to see if anyone was within earshot, they were stood together by the starboard rail.

"When they take me ashore don't try and follow. If I don't come back, I want you to get word to home."

"What makes you think that they will let me go?"

"They probably won't, which is why you will make for the Endellion at the first opportunity."

"Endellion? I thought she was off carrying messages to the ships patrolling the Libyan coast."

"She should be already in Odessa, flagged as an American with a different name."

Adam laughed. "I understand now why you didn't pack anything that couldn't be replaced, and I why half dozen crewmen were dressed as the boys."

Marty changed the subject as the ship's first mate was approaching. He pointed to Marty, then to the stern. The ship had a through deck without a raised quarterdeck and was steered with a tiller manned by two men. The captain was there along with Georges.

"I guess my presence is required," Marty said and made his way aft over the deck clutter. He had seen tidier ships.

"Martin, the captain wishes that you join him for dinner," Georges said.

"It will be an honour," he said, although he wondered what kind of fair he would get. He had a cot in the captain's small cabin which he would sleep in for the next three nights. Adam would sleep on a bedroll on deck as the weather was clement.

At their current rate of progress, favourable winds, and no slowing at night they should be in Odessa in four days. But that could double if things turned against them.

Dinner was early by navy standards, around six o'clock. There was just Marty, Georges and the captain. The food was different, a soup called borscht that was hearty and contained chicken, potato, carrot, celery, onions and beetroots in a chicken stock. It also had little dumplings with carraway seeds in them.

While they were eating, the captain, whose name was Sergei, asked about his sailing experience. Marty told him some of the stories of when he was a lieutenant and captain. During the main course which was chicken breast stuffed with garlic and herb butter served with potato dumplings Marty told him about Lisbon and meeting Admiral Senyavin. Sergei got excited and Marty learnt that he had been part of the Admiral's squadron at the Battle of the Dardanelles.

He brought out a bottle of clear spirit and three small glasses. He filled the glasses to the brim and pronounced a toast to the admiral. Marty could do nothing but knock it back to heeltaps with the other two men. Georges made a toast to the Tsar and Marty to Nelson. The night became loud and very drunken with singing, dancing (a crewman was summoned who played a balalaika) and more storytelling.

Marty regained consciousness. At least his body did. His head was disconnected from his body and was being pounded on the inside by dwarves with large hammers. He tried to open his eyes and the light caused the dwarves to up the tempo and hit harder. He groaned.

"Are we awake?" a familiar voice said.

"Ngya," someone said. He wasn't sure, but it might have been him.

"There is a storm coming, you need to get up."

"Strrrm?"

"Yes, a storm."

He forced an eye open; the pain was intense.

"Adam?"

"Yes, my lord tis I,"

"Oh my god! I feel awful."

"Something to do with all the noise you three were making after dinner last night I expect."

Marty sat up and immediately regretted it as his head thumped and spun, his stomach flip flopped. He held on to its contents with a supreme act of will.

"Help me up."

Adam practically lifted him to his feet, the ship lurched as it hit a wave and the two ended up in a heap.

"Let's try that again," Adam said after he had regained his feet. He got Marty up with a bit of a heave. "Fresh air is the cure." He led him out of the cabin and up the steps to the deck.

The captain was showing no such signs of sickness. He stood foursquare on the deck shouting orders. The wind had picked up and the crew were taking in sail.

"Dobroya utro, Martin," Sergei shouted.

Marty hung on to stay and concentrated on staying on his feet. When Sergei saw his condition, he bellowed with laughter and shouted an order to a crewman. Ten minutes later the same man returned with a glass on a tray. In it was coffee, but not anything like he had ever had before. It was thick, very strong, and sweet. He sipped it and it hit his stomach like a hammer. Then the caffeine hit.

"Bloody hell! That stuff is kill or cure!" Marty gasped. He finished the glass, and another appeared. By the third he was ready for breakfast.

The storm came in from the North and they had to battle contrary winds for a day before things settled down again. Even then the wind now came from a far less favourable direction, and they were only making ten knots.

They reached the Bosphorus after three days. The captain ran up signal flags which were answered from a pair of fortresses positioned opposite each other to dominate the passage around halfway through. Marty knew they were being watched as he caught the flashes of light reflected from unshielded telescope lenses from the battlements. He used his own glass to examine the fortresses.

"They have forty-eight pounders on both," he told Adam. "It would be hard to force passage even with a liner."

"What's in the Black Sea that we would want to get to?" Adam said.

"Russia controls most of it and they want access to the Mediterranean through the Bosphorus for trade and their warships. While the Ottomans control it, they can shut it down. Those two forts aren't the only defences, and they can effectively close it whenever they choose. It's been the cause of multiple conflicts especially when the Ottomans start charging a toll as Russia exports most of its grain out of Odessa."

"They don't already?"

"Not per ship but the Russians have to pay a fee every year."

"Why are we sailing so close to the shore?"

"That's because the current flows out of the Black Sea and is so strong that it makes progress impossible. There are a couple of points where the current really increases due to a sudden drop in the seabed. The one we are passing right now is called the Devil's

Current, see how the surface is different over there?"

"How do you know all this?"

"I asked the captain," Marty said with a smirk.

Once into the Black Sea, they headed a half point East of North. It was as calm as any sea he had ever seen; the wind was steady, and their speed increased.

Georges came and stood with them, "We will be there in less than a day now."

"Excellent," Marty said.

"It's unnaturally calm," Adam said, "do they get storms here?"

"In the winter the storms can be very severe. Only the very brave or foolhardy sail then."

Odessa was protected to its South by a large fort which had a seawall extending out into the sea before curving to the North. There was a pier just to the North and another curved protective seawall to the North of that. The city was built at the Southern end of Odessa Bay, and from the deck, as they came in, Marty could see it was laid out in a grid pattern.

They docked on the pier and Georges took Marty ashore as soon as they tied on. He walked them briskly along the road to the city and Marty had the opportunity to examine the ships anchored or moored along the coast. There was a smaller fort near the Northern seawall and from there only warships could be seen. Marty concluded correctly that the port was divided in two with the commercial shipping kept separate from the military.

They entered the city; the houses were generally three storeys and ornate. Balconied windows overlooked the streets which were unpaved. Horses pulled wagons and carts loaded with goods for the port, but most people seemed to use shanks's pony to get around. They entered the cathedral square, the building itself had been built in 1794 according to Georges and was continually being added to with the latest extension completed in 1808. The house they were headed for was on the Western end of the square.

Georges used an ornate door knocker and moments later a man opened the door. He spoke to Georges in Russian then swung the door wide for them to enter. Inside was a plain hallway which they were led down past doors on either side. Only one was ajar and Marty glimpsed several men sitting in comfortable chairs.

They came to a staircase at the end of the corridor. They climbed up a floor and it ended in a large double door. Georges opened them without knocking and led Marty through into a large meeting or dining room with a massive oval table that could easily seat twenty people. The table was surrounded by high-backed Venetian-style chairs around half of which were occupied.

"Gentlemen may I present Commodore Lord Stockley of the British navy," Georges said in Greek, then to Marty in English. "This is the government of Greece in exile. Mr Iraklidis – the Prime Minister, Mr Drivas – The Chancellor, Mr Nomikos – The Minister for Law." He introduced all nine men, but Marty was only interested in the first three.

Iraklidis spoke, "Mr Hondras has told us that your government would be interested in supporting our cause for independence in return for something as yet unspecified. How is it you can speak for your government?"

Marty looked around the table at each of the men in turn and then back to Iraklidis, "Mr Prime Minister, I should introduce myself properly. I am Viscount Stockley of Purbeck, Commodore in His Majesty's Royal Navy and member of British Intelligence. I am here on the authority of The British Prime Minister. I am authorised to offer covert support for Greek independence which, if exposed, will be denied most strenuously. In return for that support, we ask for you to consider placing Cyprus under British protection. This will solve problems for both of us. With its large Turkish population Cyprus will be very hard to govern as a direct Greek territory, while the British can be seen to be even handed and neutral. For us it gives us a base from which to operate in the Eastern Mediterranean."

"What would you offer in terms of support?"

He didn't say no! Marty privately exulted.

"Weapons, money, intelligence."

"Training for our guerrillas?"

"That could be arranged."

"We already supply weapons to the Egyptians,"

"With all due respect, I have seen those weapons and they are more of a danger to the user than the target."

"What weapons would you send us?"

"Guns unmarked but made and proofed in England, that won't explode in your men's faces. Muskets and pistols, Swords, powder and shot.

"Money?"

"One hundred thousand pounds a year to finance the revolution."

"Intelligence?"

"Word of what is going on in the rest of the Ottoman Empire so you can judge the best time to revolt."

There ensued a lively discussion. Very lively with raised voices, wagged fingers, and the odd shaken fist.

"I seem to have caused some conflict," Marty said to Georges who stood quietly watching the proceedings.

"Don't worry this is normal. Greece is the home of democracy, and each will have their say."

After fifteen minutes Georges said, "We should go and get some tea. This could take a while."

They left the room and went downstairs to the door that was ajar when they entered. It was similar inside to a gentlemen's club and when he asked, Georges told him, "It is in a way; this building is owned by the Greek community here in Odessa and it is used as a gathering place and refuge."

He took Marty to a pair of chairs with an occasional table between them. A servant or waiter arrived, and Georges ordered. The tea was laced with mint and very sweet and came with pastries soaked in syrup.

"Will they take long?" Marty said.

"Anywhere from a couple of hours to a week."

"Oh," Marty said.

"As I said it's—.."

"Greek democracy at work." Marty finished for him and raised his tea glass.

It was late afternoon when word came that they had decided. Marty and Georges went back up to the boardroom and found a much more peaceful scene.

"Lord Stockley, we have verified who you are with the British Consul," Iraklidis said.

"I wasn't aware there was one in Odessa."

"There isn't, he is usually in St Petersburg but he is here for a visit to discuss trading rights."

"Who is he?"

"Sir James Fairley."

Marty knew of him, a junior diplomat in The Foreign Office.

"He doesn't know I work for British Intelligence."

"No, but he did confirm your identity and that you are a commodore."

"If you are indeed representing Robert Jenkinson then we accept your offer."

Marty produced his letter of authority and passed it to Georges who read it out. Once he finished Marty held out his hand and took it back.

"When will the first delivery arrive?"

"In the first ship that comes under the agreement that Sir James makes. There will be weapons and half of the gold hidden under the cargo."

"Why to here?"

"We couldn't possibly risk having weapons found on a British ship in Greek waters."

"I see. You seem to have thought of everything."

"I will provide training on the island of Cos."

"You will?"

"Not personally but I have men that can."

"How are we to get the men to Cos?"

"That, Mr Prime Minister, is your problem."

Marty stood and pulled on his coat and hat.

"Please pass messages to me through the governor in Malta. Sir Thomas will be able to get them to me or my admiral."

The trip back to Malta was just as difficult as the journey out, except the run through the Bosphorus which, going with the current, was exciting. They arrived back in Valetta a week later to find the Endellion in harbour.

"When did you get back?" Marty asked Philip after he had reported to his cabin.

"Two days ago, Sir."

"You made good time. Well done!"

"Thank you, Sir."

"You have the reply from London?"

"Here Sir and orders for Admiral Winter." Philip passed two packets over. "You are to hand him the orders yourself."

"Whose idea was that?"

"Admiral Turner's."

Marty snorted a laugh. His boss had a sense of irony. He opened his letter and read it. His head went to the side as he did, and his lips pursed in thought.

He looked up, "That's all Philip, please ask Wolfgang to attend me on your way to your ship."

"Sir!" Phillip said, did a smart about face and started to leave.

"Philip," Marty said before he got through the door. "Join me for dinner this evening at seven."

"Aye, aye, Sir."

Wolfgang arrived moments later.

"Philip said you had received orders."

"Yes, to return to England as soon as I had accomplished my mission. They have something else for us to do."

"When?" Wolfgang said.

"As soon as the squadron can be made ready. We need to recall the Leonidas and Nymphe. Send the Eagle to fetch them."

"Did they say what we will do next?"

"No. I will need my barge. Can you get it around?"

"Of course." Wolfgang knew when he had been dismissed.

Marty climbed that battens up the side of the Boyne and was met at the port by Captain Stevenson and a full side party.

"Commodore, an unexpected pleasure."

"Not so unexpected that you weren't prepared."

"I confess we have been keeping a watch on the Unicorn since you got back."

"Is the Admiral below?"

"He is, Sir. Come with me."

As soon as they were away from prying ears and eyes, Marty said, "How has he been?"

"Moody, depressed. As you would expect. Do you have orders for him?"

"Yes."

Marty was admitted to the admiral's quarters and found him gazing out of the stern window.

"Admiral," Marty said.

"Commodore. Have you come to announce my fate?"

"I have orders for you from the admiralty. I was instructed to deliver them myself."

"To witness my final downfall no doubt." He held out his hand and Marty passed him the packet.

Winter read the papers inside and when he had finished his hands dropped to his lap and he heaved a huge sigh. Marty waited, he would let him have all the time he needed.

"They have ordered me back to England. The Boyne is to stay here, and I am to travel back with you." Marty must have looked surprised.

"You didn't know?"

"Nothing in my orders at all."

"Then you also won't know that I am being made Admiral of the Yellow."

Ouch, thought Marty that was brutal. It inferred he hadn't served in the capacity of an admiral in service as normally only officers who made admiral when they retired joined the non-existent squadron. However, despite that he kept his silence. Winter passed him the orders and gestured for him to read. Marty scanned them noting the relevant parts.

"If you will get your steward to pack, you can move over to the Unicorn. When the Leonidas returns, you can transfer to her. I will sleep ashore so you can use my cabin." That met the requirements of the orders. The last paragraph of which was directed at him.

"I have a new man, but then you knew that didn't you."

"He showed you great loyalty. He just chose the wrong commodore to try and eliminate."

Winter didn't reply, he just stared into space, so Marty called the steward and told him to pack the admiral's things. While they were being packed, he went to talk to Stevenson.

"You are instructed to return to Gibraltar, here are your orders."

"The admiral?"

"He will accompany me to England."

"Will he face trial?"

"No, he is being retired."

"Whitewash then."

"Not really, he has been judged guilty and sentenced. It has just been done quietly."

The admiral appeared on deck, a pair of crewmen carrying his chest. He walked straight to the entry port and looked down into Marty's barge. Marty thought he was about to do something stupid and was braced to stop him when he turned and walked over to Stevenson and held out his hand. "Thank you, for all you have done Peter, look me up if you ever get to Petersfield."

They shook then Marty did him the honour of being last into the barge.

"Martin, can I talk to you privately?" Shelby asked. He had arrived unannounced at the hotel where Marty was staying while they waited for the Leonidas and Nymphe to join them. The fact he used Marty's

Christian name warned him something was up.

"Of course, what's on your mind?"

"Annabel."

Marty sat, and indicated he should join him.

"You have been spending quite a bit of time with her. How are her medical skills?"

"That's what I wanted to talk to you about. You see, she won't make a good nurse."

Marty was surprised he had been convinced she would take to nursing like a duck to water. Shelby took a breath and continued. "She is a highly intelligent woman and I believe she would do better to train as a doctor or physician."

Marty let his breath out in a "Pooof!" then said, "Has there ever been a woman trained in England?"

"No, never, they wouldn't stand for it."

"So how can she be trained?"

"I can teach her everything she needs to know."

"But she won't have a formal qualification."

"She can work beside me."

Marty waited; he had an inkling of what was coming next.

"If you would allow her to travel with us as my wife."

"Are you sure about that?"

"She has no concerns about being onboard ship."

"No, I meant are you sure you want to marry her?"

"She has the most beautiful mind; we match each other perfectly intellectually and I must admit I have become quite smitten with her. She is the first woman I have met who makes me happy since my wife left me."

"She reciprocates your feelings?"

"Yes."

"I have to ask. Is the marriage to your wife annulled?"

"Yes, I sued her for divorce. She agreed so she could marry her lover."

"Where is she now? Annabel that is."

"On the Unicorn. Why?"

"I would like to talk to her. I feel somewhat responsible for her."

Shelby looked like he was about to protest, but saw the caring look on Marty's face.

"Please do, should I ask her to visit here?"

"This afternoon, if possible, I don't want to hold this up any longer than necessary."

Annabel arrived on the dot of two that afternoon. Elegantly but simply dressed, bonneted, and escorted by Billy. Marty tossed him a crown. "I will escort Miss Crofton back to the Unicorn, get yourself a beer."

"I suppose you want to know if my feelings for Shelby are genuine," she said as she sat.

"Oh, I have no doubt about that."

She looked confused, "Then why?"

"Why did I want to see you?"

"Yes."

"When I freed you, I assumed some responsibility for you. I am, if you like, your surrogate father. As such, we should discuss what you want for your wedding and your dowry. Let's start with the service."

"Shelby said Captain Ackermann could marry us."

"He can, when the ship is at sea, but as we are in port it is more traditional to be married on shore."

"Oh, but I don't have a dress or anyone to give me away."

"I will give you away, and I am sure Veronica would be delighted to take you dress shopping."

"But I have no money."

"Didn't I just tell you I am your surrogate father? Here."

Marty handed her a purse. There was a long moment while she seemed unable to take it in.

"And as a wedding gift I will buy you a surgeon's chest with all the instruments. That is if you are serious about becoming a doctor."

"Oh, I am, it is a vocation I never expected or looked for but since meeting Nicholas I have discovered something in me I didn't know was there."

"Nicholas? Oh, Shelby! I had forgotten that was his given name. If he teaches you everything he knows, you will be a very fine doctor."

Veronica arrived. Marty had sent her a message that morning asking her to stop by and why. She was grinning fit to split her face. The two women embraced, and Marty could see there was a firm friendship there.

"Lord Martin tells me a wedding is in the offing and we need to go shopping!" Veronica practically purred.

"He is too generous." Annabel said.

"Go! Go and buy your wedding outfit. I will arrange for the ceremony to be held on shore."

That was a problem, both Annabel and Shelby were Anglicans and all the churches in Malta were catholic. After making enquiries he discovered that Anglicans traditionally married in the Governor's Palace which had a chapel. Curious, as he hadn't noticed it when he was there last time, he asked for an appointment with Sir Thomas.

"A wedding? Of course, we can. Come let me show you the chapel," Sir Thomas said when Marty explained. "It used to be the kitchen that served the Grand Master, but it was converted in 1800 or there about. There are two other chapels, but they are catholic."

Marty wondered what it would look like. It turned out to be larger than he expected with no trace of its former use visible.

"The Grand Master liked to entertain, and this was a substantial kitchen. With no Anglican churches on the island, the former governor had it converted to a chapel and consecrated."

It looked like many Anglican chapels in England. Whitewashed walls, a simple altar with a white and gold cloth, turned wooden candlesticks with silver collars and a wooden cross with the crucified son of God pinned in place. Pews made of ship's timbers. There was a plaque with the names of the governors who had worshipped there. A vicar came out of a side door when he heard them talking.

"Lord Martin, may I introduce our vicar, Clifford Wantage."

"Lord Martin, nice to see you here at last. I have heard much about you."

"Much ado about nothing, I am sure," Marty quoted the bard.

"Ha! A well-read man." Wantage laughed.

"Two of Lord Martin's crew need to get spliced to each other," Sir Thomas said, causing Wantage's eyebrows to raise.

"They want to get married, rather than need to," Marty corrected not catching the deliberate inference.

"Sir Thomas said two members of your crew?" Wantage said worriedly. Marty twigged and grinned.

"I fear he is teasing you. My surgeon, Mr Nicholas Shelby, wishes to marry his assistant, Annabel, and as we are in port it is traditional for them to get married in church."

"More than happy to officiate old chap," Wantage enthused relieved, "who is the bride?"

"Miss Annabel Crofton." Marty didn't offer any more information, he knew the prejudices the clergy could hold.

"Who will be acting for her?"

"I will."

A date was set for the bans and service. A small pouch of coins donated to the chapel fund. Marty was pleased with himself as he walked back into town. The girls would get back much later than he. He had time to visit a local apothecary who pointed him to a trader that could supply him with a fully-stocked, new, surgeon's chest.

By the time they arrived, Marty had reserved a room for Annabel, which turned out to be just as well as they had apparently bought most of the dresses and shoes in Malta. Marty told them about the chapel.

"Who have you got to decorate the chapel?" Veronica asked.

"Um. Do we need to?" Marty said.

Veronica rolled her eyes, hands on hips, "Men! I will take care of it. When is the service?"

"The vicar wants to do it on Saturday."

"Saturday? That's only three days!" She practically ran out of the door.

Saturday came and, with still no sign of the Leonidas and Nymphe, all the Unicorn's officers attended. It was quite a crowd that escorted the groom to the palace. Shelby had chosen Fletcher to be his best man, which was no surprise as they both lived on the orlop deck and had become firm friends. The palace staff were on hand to show them where to go and soon the chapel was full.

Marty was at the hotel with Annabel and Veronica who was maid of honour. He was not allowed in her room while Veronica and the hotelier's wife prepared her, so he waited in the lounge with coffee and brandy. The allotted time approached and with no fanfare she appeared. Marty was dazzled, Annabel was in a figure-hugging red dress with a flower garland around her head. Her face was subtly made up with just a touch of rouge to emphasise her cheekbones. She carried a posey of white forget-me-nots.

Marty stood and bowed, "You look spectacular my dear. Are you ready?"

"I am."

"Then your carriage awaits!"

She took Marty's arm and he led her out of the hotel. Outside was a beautiful landau carriage, decorated with white silk bows, highly polished, with a driver in a morning suit and top hat holding the reins of a matching pair of white horses. Marty handed her aboard, then Veronica before stepping up himself. A clatter of hooves and the Shadows formed up as an escort. Smartly dressed and polished to shining perfection they looked as smart as any guardsmen.

The trip to the palace was longer than necessary as Marty had the driver take a circuitous route, so they arrived precisely on time.

He led her through the palace to the chapel which was festooned in flowers and ribbons. He supressed a sneeze and led her to the alter. Shelby turned as he heard their footsteps and Marty saw the look of awe and admiration on his face as he beheld his bride.

Chapter 13: Diplomacy?

The squadron returned home to Chatham. A platoon of marines was put on standby to provide training to the Greeks under the command of Lieutenant Beaumont and the ships put in to have their bottoms cleaned and repairs made. The men were given shore leave.

Marty went to London to find out what he would be doing next. He had written to Caroline and would meet her at their Grosvenor house. He left the ship and hired a carriage. Adam rode with Roland inside with him. Zeb drove, with Sam riding alongside him and Billy sitting in the rumble seat at the back. The rest either rode horses or on the cart that carried their sea chests.

Marty had been warned by the port admiral that since the end of the war, the number of holdups on the road to London had increased. Unemployment was high with the influx of demobbed soldiers and sailors. He thought that a visible display of firepower would deter even the foolhardiest, so everyone openly carried pistols and rifles.

They took the toll road to Dartford and were making good progress when there was a shot. Things happened very fast from then on.

Marty exited the coach with pistols in hand followed by Adam and Roland. A volley of shots rang out from the Shadows and screams echoed from the bushes along the side of the road. Marty saw a man run and dropped him with a shot in the back. A bullet hissed past his head, and he focussed on the smoke that rose from behind a bush. He fired the remaining barrel on his right gun and the first of his left into the bush. The Shadows charged their horses into the margin on the side of the road, forcing those that were still able, to move out from cover or get trampled. Garai had one by the collar and kicked his horse forward dragging him onto the road. The rest were herded forward then into a bunch with the horses surrounding them.

"Skipper!" Zeb shouted and Marty looked up at the top of the coach. Zeb had his hand pressed over a hole in Billy's chest. Billy was slumped back in the seat, his face pale.

Marty clambered up on the roof but was pushed aside by Matai who examined him quickly.

"We need to get him to Shelby as fast as we can," Matai said.

Marty looked down, "Adam, take Matai's horse and get back to the ship as fast as possible. If you find Shelby on the road, bring him here. We will bring Billy back – slower." He turned to Matai as the thunder of galloping hooves told him Adam was on his way.

"What can we do?"

"Get him inside, gently."

Marty was tempted to shoot the prisoners out of hand but instead told the mounted Shadows, "Herd this rabble to the nearest town and place them in the charge of a magistrate. Take the wagon with you. If they give you any trouble, kill them."

As soon as the wagon had cleared the road, they turned the carriage around and started back to Chatham.

Adam rode his horse hard; they were ten miles from Chatham and if he was lucky, he would catch Shelby and Annabel not far down the road. He saw a dogcart coming the other way, but it wasn't them.

The driver shook his fist as he whipped his horse past them mud flying from its hooves.

Two miles from Chatham he spotted a landau with the roof up and slowed to a canter as he approached, then dropped to a trot as he recognised the driver.

"Mr Shelby! We have an emergency."

Shelby took in the state of his horse that was sweated up, head drooping in exhaustion.

"What had happened?"

"Billy has been shot, badly wounded in the chest. The skipper is bringing him back this way in the coach."

"How far are they away? Is Matai with him?"

"About ten miles when I left, the road's not bad so they should be making good time. Yes, Matai is with him."

"Then he is in good hands. We will return to the Unicorn and prepare the infirmary. Wait here, that horse is going no further unless you want to kill it."

Adam sat on the verge and waited. His horse chewed a mouthful of grass and looked at him accusingly.

"I'm sorry, alright!" he said.

The horse didn't look impressed, so Adam led him to a trough beside the road and let him drink. Not too much, as that could hurt him as well.

He heard an approaching carriage. It was theirs, and he mounted so he could ride alongside. His horse had gotten its wind back and could carry a trot.

"Mr Shelby is waiting in the Unicorn. He says Matai is all the help Billy needs until we get there," Adam said.

Marty had to agree, Matai had applied all the knowledge he had accumulated over the years working beside Shelby. Billy was resting easy on a pile of blankets and coats to cushion the ride. He was still grey with the pain, but he was as comfortable as they could make him.

They got to the dock. The Unicorn had been brought from its anchorage and moored directly to it. A double width gangway had been set up and a team of men stood by with a litter. Billy was gently extracted from the coach and carried aboard.

"Everybody out except Matai, Annabel and my boys," Shelby said as soon as they had him on the operating table.

Marty was about to object but a look silenced him. He went up on deck and waited.

Two hours later Annabel came up on deck. Her apron was bloodstained, and she looked tired. She saw Marty and smiled as she walked over to him.

"He is asleep," she said. "The bullet is out, and Shelby has repaired his lung as well as he can. He was lucky his ribs almost stopped the bullet by the time it got past them, so the damage was superficial although his lung was punctured."

"The boy is built like an ox," Marty said. "What is the prognosis?"

"Nicholas says that he will need weeks to heal, the ball broke two rips and to repair the lung he had to spread them further. He put in over one hundred and fifty stitches."

"Can he be moved?"

"Not for at least three weeks," Shelby said as he emerged from below.

"We will stay and nurse him," Annabel said.

"Thank you," Marty said with all sincerity. "When he can be moved, we will get him to the London house. I will see him before I leave."

Billy slept for two more days, aided by the judicious application of soporifics. Marty had messaged Caroline that he would be a few more days and sent a similar message to Admiral Turner by telegraph. The Shadows re-joined after dragging the hapless ambushers to Gravesend magistrate. They had tied their hands to the back of their saddles and delivered them in whatever condition they ended up in. A sheriff had arrived and taken statements.

"They will all hang," was his verdict.

Billy woke and Marty was first in to see him.

"Stay still," he said as Billy tried to sit up.

"We will move you to London when Shelby says you are fit enough."

Billy just nodded, he was very ill and sleepy.

"Shelby and Annabel are staying to nurse you and Matai will stay here to help them. You are in the best possible hands."

Billy smiled and closed his eyes.

They arrived at the house and Marty was enthusiastically greeted by Troy and the now ten-year-old twins. Beth, at sixteen, was more reserved and greeted him with a hug and a kiss on the cheek. Caroline was radiant with joy that he was home safely and promised a proper welcome home later that night.

There was a note from Admiral Turner asking him to report as soon as he got home.

"He can wait until tomorrow," Marty said after he read it.

"Good job in Malta, we will take that from here," Turner said.

"Why did you recall me?"

"The Prime Minister will explain when we see him in," he looked at a new clock above his fireplace, "forty minutes. We will see him directly he finishes today's cabinet meeting."

"No hints?"

"I don't know what they have in mind, they are keeping this very quiet. He and Stewart will be coming here."

"Very strange," Marty said. One thing the prime minister didn't do was run around after his intelligence services.

The two men arrived and once everyone was settled around the table, Robert Jenkins started the proceedings.

"Lord Stockley."

Hello, thought Marty, *not commodore?*

"You are familiar with India I believe as you served there with Wellington."

"I am."

"You had dealings with the maharajas at the time."

"Quite successfully," Stewart added.

"I did have some success."

"Did you know the East India Company is embarking on a war with the Maratha Empire?"

"No, I didn't, but it was inevitable," Marty said

"Why is that?" Stewart asked.

"The Company wants control of all trade in the sub-continent and the Maratha are the last major hold outs. They have consistently refused to bow to British rule."

"Do you think they will be aided by an outside power?"

"Any of a dozen who don't want Britain to have control of India."

Marty was beginning to think they were sending him back to do a similar job to the last time.

"What do you think of the Company's methods?" Jenkins said.

"They can be a little heavy handed," Marty said cautiously.

"They can be more than that and that is one reason we want you to go out there."

Marty said nothing, he knew there was more to come.

Stewart leaned forward, "We want you out there as the Military Attaché, your job will be to find out if any of the major powers are aiding the Indians and to provide advice to John Company."

"You mean put an anchor on them."

"Let us say, restrain their worst excesses."

"What am I to do if I find out who is supporting them?"

"What you do best," Stewart said.

"Stop them," Turner said

"Without any traceable involvement by the British," Jenkins added.

"I see. One more question. Why have this meeting here, not in your office?"

"Because there are too many ears there who report back what is said to the Company. We don't want them to be forewarned as they would try and limit your access by lobbying. Once you are out there it will take months for any such restriction on your activities to be sent out," Stewart said.

Marty pursed his lips in thought.

"Who is the current Governor General?"

"Frances Rawdon-Hastings, Marquess Hastings."

"As Military Attaché, I will answer to him?"

"Notionally. He will be informed you answer to me," Jenkins said.

"He will live with that? He could see it as interference."

"He might, but he has voiced concern over the Company's tactics, and he is a military man," Jenkins said.

Marty decided to let that go.

"Is this a family posting?"

"Yes," Turner said before the politicians could answer.

"What about the squadron?"

"You can take your ships; they can be of use in fulfilling your mission and aid the Company Marine," Turner said.

"How long will it take you to get there?"

Marty considered, "If we can maintain two hundred to two hundred and fifty miles a day we could be there in ninety days."

"What? That's half the time of a company ship," Stewart said.

"That's because they practically stop overnight," Turner said. "Marty's ships will maintain their speed twenty-four hours a day. He has bigger crews than the company ships and can run more watches."

"I will take your word for that," Jenkins smiled, "I am no sailor."

"When will you leave?" Turner asked.

"Well, I have to let Caroline and Beth make the retailers in Bond Street rich first, so let's say three weeks?"

"That will be excellent," Jenkins said thinking of the time saved in transit.

The politicians left and Turner closed the door firmly behind them.

"Be careful on this one, Martin, they won't hesitate to throw you to the wolves if it goes badly," he said.

"Nothing new there."

Caroline didn't need three weeks to make the retailers rich, she did it in a week. Marty anticipated that they would be in India for a year at least so she shopped accordingly. He asked why she couldn't get half of it out there, but she knew what she had to get in London and what she could get in India. She did buy him a new campaign table and chair, writing slope, cot, and chest from Charles Stewart, a notable maker of campaign furniture in Charing Cross. He recovered his rifle from Durs Egg which had been converted to the new percussion cap action as well as having a new stock fitted.

Manton had a pair of double-barrelled percussion pistols ready for him when he visited his shop.

"I knew you would be in as soon as you got home and know how much you like your pistols, so I prepared these. They are essentially the same as your flintlocks, but the actions make use of the new percussion caps."

Marty hefted one of the elegant weapons and tried the balance, the main difference he noted was that the hammers were mounted centrally to the barrels rather than the outside. They were beautifully balanced of course and slightly lighter than their flintlock predecessors. They would be more reliable in humid conditions. He decided to buy them but would keep his trusty old brace as well.

The family would travel on the Pride of Purbeck, their private yacht which was a former American privateer. The squadron would escort them. Marty sent Wolfgang written orders and went to their private dock to talk to the master. He was new as their former master had died of the flux unexpectedly.

"Captain Ingram, how are you?" Marty said as he reached the deck.

"Very well, my lord."

"How are preparations for the trip to India?"

"We will be ready. I've had the extra water storage you asked for fitted and the new sails will be arriving tomorrow."

A wagon rumbled up and stopped on the dock. Marty could see the name Fortnum and Mason painted on the side.

"I see my wife has been getting in some private stores."

"Aye, Sir, you shouldn't go short on this trip even if we don't stop at the Cape." They watched hams and wheels of cheese being brought up the gangplank. A porter balanced a crate of preserves on his head and ran up to the deck. He wore a bobbin hat normally found in Billingsgate fish market.

"Have they delivered the other cargo?"

"The furniture? Yes, that came yesterday along with several sea trunks of clothes."

"Have you finalised who will travel on the Pride, Sir?

"Yes. The family, seven of my followers, four of which will have their wives with them."

Matai was married to Tabetha, Sam to Hannah, Zeb to Hilda and surprise, surprise, Roland married Wendy, a young lady he met while shopping in the market. Her father was a grocer who supplied top quality produce. The two had fallen for each other and married quietly and without fuss.

"Mary will come along and the twins' mentor, Mrs Bond."

Ingram made meticulous notes in a fine hand.

"The unmarried men will share a berth?"

"Yes."

"Will the men bring their own stores?"

Marty chuckled, "Lady Caroline has provided for the entire household."

"Very good, Sir, we can be ready in three days."

They weren't due to leave for a week and a half and Marty wasn't sure how Caroline would react.

"I'll let you know tomorrow."

Back at the house he read a report that had arrived from Wolfgang. The squadron would be ready in five days. There had been twenty-seven men who had elected to stay ashore who had been replaced with able seamen known to existing crewmen. Marty reflected that they had at least provided work for some family members the navy had let go.

Caroline stuck her head around the door to his study. "Have you got a minute?"

"Yes, I wanted to talk to you anyway."

"Oh, really?" she said and sat on his lap, arms around his neck.

"You really have the most beautiful eyes," he said.

"Thank you, I never get tired of hearing you say it, but you are buttering me up for something."

"The ships will be ready to sail a week early."

She sat more upright.

"Now you spoiled it," she pouted.

"I'll make it up to you later," Marty leered. She relaxed back into his arms.

"Ooh, I'm looking forward to that."

"Will you be ready?"

"Tonight? Always!"

"No, to leave early."

"Pfft, we are ready now."

"The sky will fall in and there will be a plague or rats!"

She got off his lap and sat on his desk in fake umbrage.

"We didn't need much. Stores for the voyage, clothes for the twins, new dresses for Beth and me. Anything else we can get in India."

"Roland has everything he wants?"

"Yes, and Wendy."

"The little devil didn't tell anyone," Marty said and Caroline laughed.

"How is Billy?"

"He is refusing to leave the ship." Marty checked the report.

"Why?"

"In case we leave him behind."

"Would you?"

"If Shelby said he wasn't fit enough I would."

"And?"

"Shelby says he has made a remarkable recovery. Weeks faster than he expected. The stitches and drains are out. His lung function doesn't seem to be impaired much. The boy is as strong as an ox."

"I can't believe he is fully fit."

"He isn't, but he is well on the road to a full recovery if his recuperation is controlled properly."

"On ship it can, can't it?"

"Most certainly."

Caroline looked thoughtfully out the window; the rain ran down it in rivulets.

"I certainly won't miss this weather, one of the wettest summers ever. London is a mud bath."

"Cheshire is just as bad."

"You have heard from Ryan?"

"Yes, he is worried for the cereal crops. All the rain is going to cut yields and make harvesting difficult."

"What about Dorset?"

"It's the same, the water meadows are flooded so they can't use them for grazing, the potato crop is in danger of rotting in the field and the cereals are like Cheshire."

"Does anything like this weather?"

"Not really, we just have to hope that it changes, and we get some sun to dry things out."

Caroline kissed him on the forehead and left to talk to Roland. Admiral Turner and his wife Juliet were coming for supper.

James and Juliet arrived fashionably fifteen minutes late. Adam greeted them at the door and took them to the drawing room where Marty, Caroline and Beth were waiting for them.

"Good evening, Martin. Caroline, you look ravishing as usual. My goodness who is that? Beth?"

Beth gave him a winsome smile and said, "Uncle James, I'm hardly in disguise."

"Touché."

They drank sherry and chatted. "This mission to India," Marty said, "what do you think I should beware of?"

"We don't know who is backing Maratha so you will have to watch your back as you won't know where any threat is coming from. Most of the big foreign powers have embassies, consulates, or trading houses in Calcutta." Calcutta was the de facto capital of India since the British had taken over. "You will be travelling a lot as the war is to the Northwest of there."

"Do you know anything about where we will live?" Caroline said.

"We own several official residences in the city. All are luxurious and, as Martin is Military Attaché, you will get one of the bigger ones. They come complete with servants."

"You will have to attend endless balls," Juliet said.

Beth looked up at that, "I won't unless Daddy is at home."

"Why is that?" Juliet said.

"Because I will be going with him."

Marty almost spayed the mouthful of fine venison he was chewing over the table. Caroline raised an eyebrow. When he had swallowed and wiped his mouth on a napkin he said, "Why would you want to do that?"

"Because you will be doing 'stuff,' and if I am to become an agent, I need to come with you to learn."

"Don't you think you are a little young?" Juliet said in surprise.

"Daddy was fourteen when he was recruited, and he hadn't been schooled. I am sixteen."

"Going on twenty-five," Marty muttered. Beth frowned at him.

"I am sixteen, almost seventeen and have been schooled in weaponry, bare handed fighting and many of the arts needed for the profession. I know at least as much if not more than anyone coming out of the academy."

"James is with the squadron, why wouldn't your father take him?" James said.

"My little brother is a serving midshipman," Beth said as if that explained everything.

"His interest is more on the sailing side," Marty said. "Since he has been on the Leonidas, he has developed a love for gunnery and navigation. Which isn't to say he isn't interested in undercover work, just that his interest is in more traditional naval activities."

The evening progressed with the conversation turning to more mundane matters. After they had eaten, they retired to the games room where the ladies sat around the fire while James and Marty played billiards.

Juliet asked Beth, "What are the arts you have learnt."

Beth looked at her mother before she answered. Caroline nodded.

"Copying, which you might call forging. Lock picking and getting in and out of places without leaving any trace, surveillance, things like that."

"Oh, my," Juliet breathed, "it all sounds so…"

"Criminal?" Beth grinned earning here a glare from Caroline.

"Dangerous," Juliet said.

"I'm also training in open hand fighting, sword fighting, and shooting."

"She is a crack shot," Caroline smiled.

"Why do you say sword fighting not fencing?"

"When you fence you only use the blade and mainly the tip. When you fight you use the whole sword and your body."

Juliet still didn't understand so Beth fetched two wooden practice swords. When she returned James and Marty had moved some chairs and a table to make a space. Marty took a sword and they faced off.

"We will go through the exercises slowly," he said.

They started as Juliet expected, Marty swung a blow in slow motion at Beth's head. She parried so the blow slipped over her head as she ducked and spun underneath it. She looked to be putting herself in the totally wrong position to make any kind of counterattack, but she continued her spin and used the pommel of the sword to strike at Marty's head. They froze in place just before contact was made.

"But using the pommel Beth can attack from an unexpected direction," Marty said. He nodded and Beth stepped back.

"If you wear gloves while you fight you can utilise the blade and cross guard of the sword."

Beth swung her sword, not to attack Marty directly but at his sword to beat it aside. As the momentum carried her blade around, she grabbed it in her left hand and slid her right down to hold the blade below the cross guard. She drove the reversed sword into Marty's sternum and as he doubled up swung her knee into his face. No mean feat in a long dress and petticoats. She finished with the sword held by its hilt laid across the back of his neck.

"I think I am getting the idea," Juliet said.

"Fight dirty, fight to win," James laughed.

"Ancient knights fought the same way," Beth said slightly miffed at the 'fight dirty' comment, "Daddy has some books from the 1500s which show all the moves."

"Yes, they are called fight books and are tutorials of how to use weapons for total fighting," Marty said.

"Can I see them?" James said.

Beth went to a bookcase set along one of the end walls and took down an ancient book. She placed it carefully on a table and opened it. Inside were illustrations of knights fighting with long swords, maces, short swords, axes, and other weapons.

"I see where you got the moves now, there are a few here I would never have thought of."

"We rehearse them in slow speed to start with and gradually

increase the tempo until we can perform them without thinking at full speed," Beth said.

"That also improves control," Marty said.

The swords were put away and they settled back down around the fire.

"Do you have your own weapons?" Juliet said to Beth.

"I have my own sword and pistols as well as knives and other weapons."

"Other?"

Beth glanced at Marty who shook his head ever so slightly.

"A rifle," Beth said taking his lead not to mention her custom-made brass knuckles, punch dagger, blackjack or stilettos.

Juliet sensed she was holding back but didn't push it.

The conversation turned to more mundane matters until Juliet and James left at around midnight. Juliet would dream of an avenging angel armed with a sword. Her flaming auburn hair streaming in the wind.

Chapter 14: Passage

Their small convoy was joined by a pair of John Company ships as they passed the Downs. Wolfgang sailed close and hailed one. "Ahoy the Earl Spencer!"

"Hello, Unicorn!" the captain shouted back through a speaking trumpet.

"What is your intention?"

"To accompany you until our paths part. What is your destination?"

"Calcutta."

"We are headed to Madras!"

"We will make all sail and not furl at sundown!"

There was a long pause after that. Company captains were renowned for not causing their passengers any discomfort. Wolfgang could see the captain having what looked like a heated discussion with a well-dressed man.

"My Lord Effingham requests you moderate your speed so we can stay with you."

"That's very strange," Lieutenant Brazier said.

"What is Mr Brazier?" Wolfgang asked.

"Earl Effingham died heirless in '16. There is no Lord Effingham."

Brazier was connected to the royal household via his natural father.

"Are you sure?"

"Yes, my father attended the funeral."

Wolfgang sighed. Now he had to decide what to do.

"Bring us up to hailing distance to the Pride."

Marty was surprised when he was summoned to the main deck and saw the Unicorn a pistol shot away. Wolfgang shouted across what had passed.

"Bedamned, they have an imposter aboard," he said to Caroline who had joined him.

"What are you going to do?"

"Well as a government official I suppose I am obliged to investigate. It won't take long."

He ordered the squadron to heave to and signalled the company ships to do the same. They were just off Hastings and the sea was relatively calm.

Dressed in full uniform he was boated across to the Earl Spencer.

"I am Viscount Purbeck, Military Attaché to Governor General of India and Commodore in His Majesty's Navy. I would like to meet Earl Effingham," he said after being greeted.

Earl Spencer's captain sent his first mate to find the earl.

"Is that your squadron?" he asked.

"Yes, we are on route to Calcutta." His abrupt tone said he wasn't in a chatty mood and wasn't lost on the captain.

The first mate returned with a well-dressed man in his middle years. Marty grinned as soon as he saw him.

"My Lord Effingham, how are you? It's been a long time since we last met."

Effingham looked at him in surprise, "Martin, I mean, Lord

Stockley, how are you?"

"I am well, are you in a hurry to get to India?"

"I do have pressing business there and these laggards are telling me they can't do the trip in less than six months."

"The good captain has to take into consideration the other passengers. We will make the passage in half that time. Can I offer you a berth?"

"If I could, I would be forever in your debt."

"Captain, the earl will be transferring to my ship. Please get his luggage into my boat." He turned to Effingham.

"Do you have any staff?"

"No, I'm travelling alone."

Once they were in the boat and heading towards the Pride, Marty turned to the earl and said, "Frances Ridgley, what are you up to? The earl died two years ago."

Francis grinned. "I took it as an alias knowing no one would challenge me, then I saw your ships and bullied the captain into trying to join you."

"No one, except those who knew the earl that is. What are you doing in India?"

"I'm taking over as Head of Intelligence in Calcutta. The only ship I could get was going to Madras."

The boat pulled up at the side of the Pride and Caroline looked down at them.

"Is that Francis?"

"Hello, Lady Caroline," he called and waved.

Marty was first up followed by Francis who was greeted by Billy as soon as he came aboard. He shook his hand and noticed he was not his usual self.

"Are you well?"

"Oh, I'm fine," Billy said.

"Is he hell," Marty said, "took a bullet in the chest when we were ambushed by highwaymen in England. He is still recuperating."

"How long ago was that?" Francis said.

"Just on a month," Billy said.

Marty asked Ingram to get them under way and make all sail. They soon left the lumbering Indiamen behind.

They had a good crossing Southwest across the Atlantic to pick up the westerly trades South of the equator. Then halfway across they got hit by a major storm that scattered the squadron and drove them South. By the time the weather cleared, the Silverthorn was the only ship in sight. A sighting showed they were on the same latitude as the Falkland Islands somewhere below the Cape.

"Where are all the other ships, Daddy?" Edwin said the first time they were able to let the children up on deck.

"The storm scattered them; we will meet up with them again when we get up to Reunion Island."

"Will James be there?"

"Yes, he will be fine," Marty said. The sound of hammers started as men made repairs to the damage to the upperworks which included putting up a jury-rigged topmast.

The Leonidas had ridden the storm better than the Pride and hadn't had to run before it as much as the smaller ships. Consequently, she was much further North and East than them. They came upon the Unicorn in company with the Nymphe after a day's sailing. There was no sign of the Eagle and Endellion.

All three ships had suffered damage to their rigging and were making running repairs.

"Mr Stockley, how is your division?" captain Campbell asked.

"We lost a topman overboard and another killed when the shroud snapped. He was hit by the lashing end and fell to the deck. Apart from that I have two walking wounded with strains."

James frowned, that brought the toll to eight dead and a dozen hurt, six of which would not be able for weeks.

"It was a bad one, please send a signal to the Unicorn. Their number, our number eight D."

Wolfgang, who had his arm in a sling after dislocating his shoulder in the storm, received the message and blew out his cheeks,

"With our and the Nymphe's casualties, that's eighteen dead. I wonder how the smaller ships fared?"

He looked at the state of repairs, "Mr Grey, plot a course for Reunion we will make for the rendezvous as soon as repairs are completed."

He paced, remembering the storm. It had come out of the West. A solid wall of black clouds that looked as if they reached down to the sea. The wind had been ferocious, gusting and veering and the rain had cut the visibility to zero. He remembered the fight, how the men had stood up to be counted. The top man that fell, the four men that were killed when a cannon broke loose. Dislocating his shoulder when he jammed a jackstaff under the wildly swinging two and a half tons of iron and wood. His action and the two men who stood beside him with their own staves had stopped the cannon for long enough for a team to get a rope around it. Shelby had put his shoulder back in, but it wouldn't be right for a long time. Repairs made, they set sail. The weather was clear, the wind favourable, the storm a distant memory.

Reunion came into view ten days later. They hadn't seen any other sails, so made for Le Port and the anchorage.

The Pride and Silverthorn would take twelve days to reach the island by Marty's reckoning. That was if they could make two hundred and forty miles a day.

Frances came on deck for the first time since the storm started. He had been so seasick that Caroline and Mary had to nurse him. Marty could sympathise as even his sea legs had been challenged.

They made their way Northeast without seeing another ship until they got level with Cape Town, somewhat South of Madagascar.

"Sails to the North," the mainmast lookout cried.

"How many?" Ingram called up.

"Looks like three, lateen rigged."

"Silverthorn's signalling."

Marty came up on deck and glanced at the flags flying from the Silverthorn's main.

"Enemy in sight," he said before the ship's boy could look it up in the code book.

"Aye, North of us. Three of them," Ingram grunted as he scanned the horizon with a telescope. He swung back to a point he had just passed. "There they are."

Marty grabbed a glass from the rack and repeated Ingram's movement. A scan along the horizon until he picked up the fleck of white, past it to check there was nothing else then back to the fleck.

"If I was you, I would prepare the hands to go to quarters," Marty said.

"You are familiar with these waters?" Ingram said.

"I have had occasion to sail here a number of times and if I am not mistaken those are Madagascar pirates."

"Can we outsail them?"

"How much do you trust the jury-rigged topmast?"

"I would not want to stress it too much."

"Then the answer is no."

The men went to stations when the approaching ships were hull up over the horizon from the deck. About seven miles distant. Marty guessed that they were assuming they were a couple of small merchant ships with light armaments.

"Would you please signal the Silverthorn, her number and the number twelve," Marty said to Ingram.

The captain had a look that said he didn't understand but did as he was asked. The Silverthorn acknowledged.

"Now if you would be so kind as to get the carronades loaded with canister over small ball."

"Yes, my lord," the captain said and bellowed orders.

"Everything alright, my love?" Caroline asked.

"Pirates," Marty said without looking at her "it would be a good idea to get the children below."

"I'm not going down there," Beth said. Marty turned and looked at her, she had come on deck dressed in her fighting clothes, armed with her sword, pistols, and rifle.

Then he looked at Caroline who was also dressed for war in leather bodice and voluminous trousers.

"Your women appear to be a little warlike," Francis said. He had come on deck armed with a Baker rifle, pistols and sword.

Ingram eyed the Shadows who were forming up behind Caroline and Beth, then saw Sam and Adam step forward and help Marty into his fighting harness.

"I almost feel sorry for them," he said.

"Who?" Barford the first mate asked.

"The pirates, they don't stand a chance."

The pirate ships came on. The Silverthorn closed up with the Pride until they were barely a ship's length apart. The gun ports stayed down.

"How close will we let them get?" Ingram asked.

"Until they are about to come alongside." Marty said.

Ingram swallowed, he wasn't sure the thought that they would let pirates get that close or Marty's calm, unnerved him more.

He looked around his ship. The men were calm, no one seemed worried. In fact, there was a sense of anticipation. Lord Martin's men were spread out along the deck, even the big one who was wounded in England had a multi-barrelled volley gun propped on a cask.

"Steady men," Marty said as the sound of the pirate's screams and war cries echoed across the water.

The silence on the ship was eerie.

The bow gun on the foremost ship fired and a twenty-four-pound ball screamed across the deck.

"Clew up the mainsails!" Marty called.

The screams from the pirate's ships got louder as they took that as a sign their prey were giving up.

They swung around to come up beside the Pride and Silverthorn to board.

"Run out!" Marty called.

The ports shot up and the snub noses of the twenty-four-pound carronades rolled out.

"FIRE!"

The eight guns fired simultaneously with the guns on the Silverthorn a moment behind. A veritable wall of canister and four-pound small ball smashed into the two ships that were a bare fifty feet away.

The screams of victory changed into screams of agony and despair.

While the guns were reloading, rifles barked and the volley gun boomed. Swivel guns coughed loads of death. Then the carronades spoke again.

The lead pirate ship, a large felucca, was decimated. Her side was smashed in, and blood ran from her exposed deck into the sea. Her light timbers had provided no protection at all.

Ingram looked down the deck, Lord Martin's wife and daughter were calmly reloading their rifles. Beth put hers to her shoulder and fired. A man fell. There was no question of quarter.

The third ship had turned tail and run. It had no intention of suffering the fate of its sister ships.

The guns went quiet, and the screams of the pirates could be heard. The pirate ships were sinking, and the silver fins of sharks were congregating. A particularly large specimen with a white tip on its dorsal fin drove into the wreck and grabbed a body before sliding back into the water.

"Make sail captain. The danger has passed," Marty said.

"Aren't we going to rescue them?" Ingram asked.

"They would have thrown you overboard after making you watch them rape and torture our women. If we rescue them, it is only to hang them."

Ingram watched the ship disappear below the surface, the sea was red with blood, the sharks frenzied. He turned away, feeling sick.

"Make all sail," he said.

They came into Le Port to find the frigates waiting for them. There was no sign of the Eagle or Endellion. They waited for three days and made repairs while ships came and went, then a sail was seen approaching from the West. The lookout on the Unicorn, which had the highest mast, identified it as the Eagle. Marty, who was aboard, said, "Signal for Captain Archer to report."

The Eagle limped into port, she had taken a beating from the storm and looked like she had been in a fight.

Trevor Archer came aboard the Unicorn limping and bandaged. Marty had him seen by Shelby before he interviewed him.

"Come in, Trevor, take a chair. Are you badly hurt?" Marty said.

"A few wounds, we had a hard fight to repel pirates. Our rigging was so badly damaged we couldn't get away."

"We experienced the same but managed to fight them off with our combined firepower."

"We came out of the storm way South of our planned course. The mainmast had split, and we were taking on water from a sprung plank. We fished the mast and managed to stay ahead of the leaking after we plugged it with a feathered canvas. Then we saw the Endellion and joined up. She was in as bad a state as we were. Between us we lost eight men dead and thirty hurt.

We made what repairs we could and set off for the rendezvous. Just South of Madagascar we were attacked by four pirate ships. We tried to hold them off with the guns, but they took us from bow and stern. The Endellion was boarded and captured. They did not strike. They fought like tigers but there were just too many of them.

We managed to repel them, then shift a carronade around to bear on the ship at our stern. I put a smasher through her hull. The ship at the bow ran after that and we were able to get away."

"They took the Endellion?"

"Yes, Sir."

Marty went to the door. "Please ask Captain Ackermann to attend me."

When Wolfgang arrived, Marty had Trevor retell his story then said, "I want the squadron to eliminate the pirate threat out of

Madagascar. I did it once before, but it looks like they have built up to be a threat to shipping again."

"We don't need to send the whole squadron to do that," Wolfgang replied. "And I won't leave the Pride without an escort."

Marty acknowledged that with a nod.

"The Leonidas, Nymphe and Silverthorn have enough firepower between them to do the job. The Unicorn and Eagle will escort you to Calcutta," Wolfgang said.

"How long to make repairs Trevor?" Marty asked.

"Can I have use of the carpenters from the Unicorn?"

"Yes of course," Wolfgang said.

"If we can source a new mainmast, a week at most."

"They have a pool here in the port. I will ask if they have anything suitable," Marty said, referring to the pool where new masts were stored, floating in water to stop them drying out.

Trevor was dismissed and went back to the Eagle with Shelby who would attend his wounded. James Campbell was summoned from the Leonidas along with Andrew Stamp from the Nymphe and Terrance Howarth from the Silverthorn. Fletcher and the Carpenter were dispatched to find the Eagle a new mast.

"Gentlemen," Marty said when they were all gathered in Wolfgang's cabin, "I regret to have to tell you that the Endellion was taken by pirates off the South of Madagascar." There were gasps and comments of disbelief. "She was badly wounded in the storm and was swarmed under by sheer numbers. The Eagle barely got away."

He laid a chart of the island on the table.

"Last time I was here, James, you will remember this, we had a standing battle with a fleet of pirates, which we barely won, and then orbited the island, sinking and burning everything bigger than a fishing boat."

James smiled at the memory he had been just a mid then.

"It was rather warm work," he said.

"Well, it probably will be again, they will have ample ships and crews. Break their strength and reduce their capability. You will command being the senior captain. Do the job then get yourselves up to Calcutta."

"What about the Endellion?"

"If you find her and there are any of her crew still alive, bring them and her home. If that is not possible, bring the wrath of the squadron down on those responsible."

"No prisoners?"

"Don't bring any back with you, justice must be seen to be delivered there. Take some for interrogation if you need information but they must be punished according to the rule of law."

Ryan understood, any found guilty would hang.

"Reprovision here, you will find scant chance to resupply there. Let me know when you are ready to sail. Any questions?"

"Can we employ an interpreter? We might want to interrogate some prisoners," James said.

"Certainly. Ask around on the docks they will know of one. Any more questions?"

There were none.

"Dismissed."

Chapter 15: Retribution

Captain Campbell paced his quarterdeck. They were in sight of Madagascar, and he had a plan.

"Signal the Silverthorn, 'go ahead,'" he said to Simon Fitzwarren, his second lieutenant.

The Silverthorn would scout ahead, look into inlets and coves as the eyes of the frigates. Depending on what they found they would either bombard with the ships artillery or send in the marines by boat.

Midshipman Stockley had signal duty; he was the senior mid, but Campbell liked to keep them all grounded so rotated the duty around the three. The other two: Archibald Essex and Gabriel Hudson, were skylarking up in the rigging.

"Silverthorn has acknowledged," James reported.

"Thank you, Mr Stockley, keep an eye on her."

"Aye, aye, Sir," James said.

Fitzwarren winked at James, he was relatively new to the ship having joined in Jamaica when they stopped over on their way back from depositing Napoleon on St Helena. He was a good officer who the men respected and a demon with a sword. James regularly sparred with him.

Since joining the ship, James had discovered a love of gunnery, sailing and navigation. He also enjoyed working with the marines. Like his father he had a passion for all things martial and could, when asked, turn his hand to several underhand skills, although they didn't really hold his attention for long. His captain had noticed his interest and encouraged him by giving him tasks that stretched him. In this way he hoped to mould him into a first-rate officer.

As the Silverthorn got further away, James was struggling to spot his signals so he approached the captain.

"Permission to go aloft, Sir?"

"Take a glass."

"Aye aye, Sir."

He grabbed his favourite glass from the rack and headed up the ratlines. Nimble as a pine marten he swarmed up the mast to the futtock shrouds and hardly paused as he went around the outside, topman fashion. He reached the topsail yard and settled down next to the lookout.

"Afternoon, Mr Stockley," Bert Strange said.

"Afternoon, Bert, anything to report?"

"Nothing except a few fishing boats and the Silverthorn scattering them like a dog on a duck pond."

James scanned the horizon then focussed on the Silverthorn. She was taking in sail and slowing as she approached the coast on the Southeast tip of the island. Paralleled the coast a mile out and headed West as they guessed their best chance of finding the Endellion was on the West coast. He noticed she wasn't flying her colours.

As she sailed majestically along five miles ahead, Terrance Howarth had his crew lolling around the deck as if they were on a pleasure cruise. He was sprawled out on a canvas chair, his feet on a crate. Dressed in a fawn suit with a flouncy shirt he looked like the eponymous playboy out for a pleasure cruise.

They passed Faux Cap and rounded the headland to start running up the West coast. According to his chart, which dated back to Marty's last visit, there was an estuary coming up in the next forty miles or so. It was a likely place for an ambush, but they could attract attention at any time.

A fishing boat was sailing sedately towards them, and the fisherman took the opportunity to try and sell some of his catch. He pulled up at their side matching their speed and held up some fish. Terrance leaned on the rail and pointed to the two biggest and held up a silver shilling. An outrageous offer for two fish. The fisherman, realising he had a real mug on a line, went below and came up staggering under the weight of a tuna that must have weighed fifty pounds. He pointed to the shilling and held up four fingers.

"Four bob for a bloody fish!" spluttered Robey the purser.

"Shut up and pay the man and smile while you do it," Terrance said.

Looking like he had been force-fed unripe lemons, Robey tossed the coins down in exchange for the fish. The fisherman nodded and bowed before waving and heading up the coast to the North.

"Keep us to a walk," Terrance said to allow the fisherman time to get well ahead. He wanted his bait to take as much line as he needed.

By the time they approached the estuary the sun was dipping towards the horizon and they did what any playboy would do, anchored up and, lighting the ship up like a Christmas tree, had a party.

James had finished his watch and was about to go below when he heard the captain call, "All lights out, I do not want to see a single glimmer on this ship."

He decided dinner could wait a minute or two and looked behind at the Nymphe. She too was dark and as he watched she furled most of her sails so that there was very little white to catch the last of the sun's rays. Once it was dark a shuttered lantern was opened at the stern to give the Nymph something to follow.

"Get something to eat, it could be a long night," Angus Frasier said from behind him. James jumped; he hadn't noticed him come up behind him.

"Aye, Sir," he said and ran down below where the minimum of lamps burned for the men to eat by.

He went to the cockpit and wolfed down his ration of boiled beef, pease pudding and biscuit.

"What's going on up top?" Gabriel asked.

"We are sneaking up on the Silverthorn. I think the skipper is setting an ambush."

A Bosun's mate stuck his head through the door and said in a horse whisper, "Go to stations, and keep it quiet."

"Told you so," James grinned and grabbed his sword belt and pistols from his footlocker. Suitably attired, he headed to his station where he commanded the starboard forward nine eighteen pounders. His station was also responsible for firing illumination and signal rockets during a night action. They were held in a rack amidships with different compartments for red, green, blue and illuminating white.

Music drifted over the waves from the Silverthorn where there looked to be a real party going on with men dancing on the deck.

The Unicorn, with the Nymphe in close attendance, slunk closer under reefed topsails to seaward and behind the Silverthorn.

Campbell was careful to keep the ships far enough away not to be illuminated by the Silverthorn's lights. He hove to and waited.

Suddenly a long boat with a dozen oars entered the pool of light around the Silverthorn.

"Rockets away!" called Angus Fraser.

James had already prepared several white illumination rockets and had a slow match prepared. He held the rocket between his fingers at arm's length and lit the fuse. As soon as the rocket ignited, he let it go and it arced into the air, two more followed, fired by his men.

The rockets lit up the scene like daylight.

"Bloody hell, you can walk across them," Bill Gatsby the number one-gun captain said. He was almost right, the sea was covered in long slender boats that were full of men.

"Forward carronades!" the captain shouted, and the two big guns swung around.

Chuff-Boom, sixty-five pounds of grape shot, and canister scythed across the sea from each gun and by the time it reached the boats it had spread to cover a swathe twenty feet wide. Men were plucked out of the boats and thrown into the water; light hulls disintegrated. Then the bow chasers fired, their canister shot spreading out like a cloud.

The Leonidas made more sail and accelerated slowly, heading directly for the largest mass of boats.

The Silverthorn transformed. The party yacht for a playboy with more money than sense, suddenly grew teeth, eight thirty-six-pound carronades shoved their ugly snub noses out of the ports and spat their welcome.

James was so enthralled by what he was seeing it took a shout from the first to remind him of his duty.

"Mr Stockley, pay attention to your duty. Rockets, boy!"

He hastily fired fresh rockets as the first volley were fading. It was just in time as there was a blink of darkness before they ignited.

He turned as there was a squawk from behind him and he turned to see a head and shoulders appear over the rail. He drew and fired a pistol without thinking and the man disappeared, but there were more heads following.

"Repel boarders!" he shouted. His gunners grabbed the nearest thing they could use as a weapon and fought. Men used rams, screws, and jackstaffs as clubs until men arrived from the other side with weapons they collected from the centreline.

He fired his second pistol then dropped it in favour of his sword. A burley gunner brought a huge mallet, used for driving wedges, down on a pirate whose head split like a melon. Another drove a boarding pike through the back of a screaming man who was attacking his mate with two swords. The pirate was slightly built, the gunner had muscles like an ox. He lifted him on the pike and threw him over the side like he was tossing bales with a pitchfork. Then casually held out a hand to help his mate to his feet.

James, being small and fast, dove in and out of the fray, stabbing and slashing before retreating. He became aware of someone beside him.

"Warm work!" laughed Simon Fitzwarren.

James grabbed the arm of a marine as he passed. "Get that man to safety!" he said pointing to a man that was down.

The marine bent and grabbing the man's collar, pulled him away from the fray. He returned and lined up beside James and Simon using his bayonet to good effect. The three plus the gunners drove the pirates from their ship, then dropped eighteen-pound-balls into their boats to smash the hulls and sink them.

The next morning the sun arose on a sea covered in wreckage and dead bodies. Boats rowed to the estuary to see what was there. On the Leonidas several prisoners were knelt in a line across the deck. Mr Rakotomalala, the interpreter James had hired on Reunion, stood beside Captain Campbell. Midshipman Stockley was given charge of the halters that were slung from the mainsail yard.

"Ask them where they are from," Captain Campbell said.

"They say they are from villages along the river."

"Do they know the punishment for piracy?"

"No, Sahib, they do not."

"It's hanging. Do they know what that is?"

"Mr Stockley, select one at random and put a halter on him."

James picked the second one from the right-hand end, who looked to be the oldest. His men dragged him to the first halter and placed it around his neck with the knot at the back.

"If you do not answer my questions that man will be hauled up by the men to die slowly by strangulation. That is the punishment for piracy. If you give me a reason to spare him, I will let you all go. Do you understand?"

"They understand, Sahib."

"Have you seen a ship like that one," he pointed to the Silverthorn, "that was captured two weeks ago."

They all looked at him with stubborn expressions.

The captain sighed; they were going to have to do this the hard way.

"Mr Stockley, I would be obliged if you hauled him up, slowly."

"Take the weight men, now haul away, slowly now," James called.

The wretch's feet left the deck and he squawked as the rope bit into his throat.

"Make them watch, men," the captain ordered.

Men grabbed the remaining prisoners and forced them to watch as the condemned man thrashed and shit himself. It took twenty minutes for him to die.

"Now, select another."

James placed his hand on the shoulder of one at random. The reaction was instantaneous. The man threw himself to the deck at Captain Campbells feet, jabbering and pleading.

"He says that a ship like that was taken to Anantsoño," Rakotomalala said after questioning him in the local Malagasy dialect.

"Who took it?"

"A very powerful captain of the pirates, an Arab. Mustafa Mehmed."

"How many ships does this Mehmed man have?"

"At least twenty, Sahib."

"Are they all based in Anan— whatever it's called?"

"Yes, Sahib, most of his ships are there."

James walked across the deck to the rail and looked at his flotilla. He knew what he had to do.

"Clap this lot in irons, if he is lying, they will all hang. Signal captains and firsts to report aboard."

"Gentlemen," Campbell said, "we will be attacking the port of Anantsoño where we believe the Endellion has been taken. My plan is to blockade the port and bombard it then for the Silverthorn to sail in and cut out the Endellion under cover of our guns."

"Do we know if the men are still aboard?" Andrew Stamp said.

"No, we don't. We will need prisoners to question to launch a rescue mission."

"Will we be mounting a shore action?" Sergeant Bright the acting commander of marines said. Marty had offered him a field promotion as he was replacing Alexander Beaumont, but the grizzled veteran had refused.

"We may if the crew are ashore, or, if the pirates have a base that needs to be stormed, but I would prefer to keep casualties to a minimum. A shore action will be a last resort."

"I will instruct the marines on all ships to be ready."

"Thank you. We will sail first thing in the morning. In the meantime, I would like you all to join me for dinner."

As soon as they could see a grey goose at a mile the sails blossomed, and the Leonidas led the flotilla North with the Nymphe a cable behind and the Silverthorn bringing up the rear, a cable behind her. Campbell looked back and was happy to see that the other two ships were exactly in his wake.

The wind swung against them forcing them to tack to make progress. Consequently, they were still ten miles from Anantsoño when the sun went down. They hadn't seen more than the occasional fishing boat well inshore of them and a single East Indiaman heading South, all day.

"Take us out beyond the horizon we will attack at dawn," Campbell said and once the sun had dropped, he ordered them to creep back in and climbed to the top of the mainmast.

"Mr Stockley, what are you doing up here?" he said.

"Just seeing if I could see the town, Sir."

"Can you?"

"Aye, Sir, there are lights and fires due East."

Campbell swung the night glass he had slung over his shoulder around and looked towards shore. From the masthead he could see lights on the horizon upside down and back to front.

"It doesn't look like a big town," James said. His glass was much smaller than the captain's.

"It is quite spread out, most of the fires are along the shore. Probably ship's crews." He handed his bigger glass to James.

"Oh yes, I can see now."

"What do you think your father would do?"

"With respect, Sir, is that relevant? He isn't here and has different resources than us."

Campbell chuckled, "Good answer."

"But if he was here with the Shadows, he would send them in first to scout the town and locate the crew."

"He would, wouldn't he," Campbell said. "Do we have men who could do the same thing?"

James felt as if he was being tested.

"There are four men I know of who could do something like that."

"Who are they?"

"Barneby, a former thief, Stanfield, convicted roofman, Durrance, former poacher and Stilton."

"A marine?"

"Yes, Sir, he is a scout."

"Is a five-man team enough?"

"They would need to be supported by a shore team that could protect the boat and secure their line of retreat."

"Marines?"

"Boat crew and, say, six marines."

The captain looked at his watch by the moonlight.

"Almost eleven, sunrise is at seven-thirty. Meet me on the quarterdeck in thirty minutes with those men, equipped for a shore reconnaissance."

The captain said no more, slung his glass over his shoulder by its strap and took a stay to the deck.

Oh my! James thought, a surge of adrenaline running through his veins. Then he got himself together and shinnied down a stay to gather the men. Two were in his division, Stanfield was in Archie's and Stilton with the marines. He ran through the ship and had them gathered in fifteen minutes.

"You four will be coming with me on a reconnaissance to try and locate the crew of the Endellion. Get some dark clothes on, no uniform, Stilton, lamp black on your faces and hands. Pistols and knives, marlin spikes for clubs, if you don't have one. You have ten minutes then gather on the quarterdeck. GO!"

The men, startled to be given orders at this time of night, rushed off. James went below and followed his own orders, quickly changing into dark clothes and blacking up. Clipping his pistols to his belt after blowing out the priming he inventoried his weapons.

"Two pistols, blackjack, pair of stilettos, boot knife and belt knife." He got to the quarterdeck to find the men waiting for him.

"Blow out the priming from your pistols we don't want one going off and giving us away."

"Mr Stockley, you appear to be ready," the captain said.

"Yes, Sir, although I would have preferred more time to brief the men."

"You can do that on the trip to shore. Mr Fitzwarren has volunteered to take you in."

Simon grinned at James from behind the captain.

"The cutter is ready."

That was the only order they needed.

"Men, we are going in blind, we don't know the layout of the town. It could be established with buildings or just an armed camp. So, we will take it slowly. Stilton, you will be on point. Eliminate anyone who is in our path, quietly. I will be no more than twenty yards behind you with Barnaby, Stanfield will be twenty yards to the right and Durrance the same on the left. The important thing is we get back to the boat without an alarm being raised."

He looked around their eager faces in the moonlight.

"Understood?"

"Aye, aye, Sir," all four replied.

The sail had been raised on the cutter and they got to the coast in less than an hour using the fires on shore to guide them. They planned to land South of the town and work their way over land, but when they got close enough to go to oars, they discovered it was on the North bank of a river delta.

"There is a sand bar over there that connects to the North shore," Simon said. "I will put you ashore there."

The cutter slid up onto the sandbar and the bowman jumped over to steady it so James and his men could debark. They were followed by Simon and the marines who were also out of uniform. James wasted no time.

"Prime your pistols."

When he was sure everyone had complied, he sent Stilton out. When he had gone twenty paces he followed. They all ran in a half crouch. He had assumed this was the most exposed part of their infiltration but when they reached the end, they found that the town was built on the dunes of a large sandy beach backed by hills. They paused and James did a count of the ships in the estuary and out in the sheltered bay.

"I don't see the Endellion," he whispered to Barnaby.

"It might be further upstream, more secure up there." Barnaby whispered back.

The problem with that, was the glow of campfires between them and there. James hissed and Stilton looked around, James signalled for him to head for the buildings. He led out at a dog trot.

They assumed their pre-planned formation and were soon concealed from the beach by a dune. Stilton disappeared and there was a faint grunt from ahead.

They paused.

Stilton reappeared and waved them on.

James noticed a dark patch against the sand and a flash of moonlight through the cloud showed it was man shaped.

They reached the first huts. The sound of snoring came from inside and none were guarded. A glance through the doors was enough to confirm the crew were not there. More substantial buildings loomed out of the dark. One had, what looked like, candlelight shining through the glassless window. Stilton waited for them to catch up. He signalled 'listen'.

Low voices murmured inside, and a man groaned. There was the sound of a blow and a question asked in broken English.

James slipped forward and very slowly raised his head to glance through the window. He had to stop himself gasping. He ducked back down and scuttled back to his men.

"There are prisoners in there," he whispered, "not our men but civilians. Three women and two men. One of the men is being roughly handled. Stilton, see if there any external guards."

While he was gone, he told the others, "The prisoners are all bound. There are three locals armed with swords that I could see. It is my intention to free them and take them back to the boat with us. But first we finish the reconnaissance."

Stilton reported back that there were no guards outside the building. He was about to order them to follow on when there was a scream.

He went back to the window and saw that two of the locals had grabbed the youngest woman and were dragging her to a space in front of the man.

Christ they are going to rape her! he thought.

That changed the game, he could not stand by and allow that to happen. He dropped and returned to his men.

"Knives and clubs. You two through the front door. Stilton, watch out for anyone coming from the camp. Barnaby you and me will go through the window. Start counting, we go in thirty seconds. All sailors knew that 'one gunner's mate' took about a second."

James counted in his head and as soon as he reached thirty stood and threw his boot knife. It hit one of the men holding the girl, between the shoulder blades, embedded to the hilt. Before he fell James was up and through the window. The other two men burst through the door and took down the second man holding her. The third man had his trousers around his knees and opened his mouth to shout. A marlin spike flew over James' head and struck him in the temple.

All three pirates were dispatched permanently with deft thrusts of knives through their hearts.

James cut the bonds of the man who had been beaten and said, "James Stockley, Midshipman, His Majesty's frigate Leonidas. Can you walk?" The girl appeared beside him; she had pulled together her blouse which had been ripped open.

"He is my father, Jacob Goldstein." She had a faintly German accent. The other prisoners were freed. The second man was around twenty years old.

"You help me with him."

Between the two of them they got him to his feet.

"Come on, we need to get away from here." James deployed his men around the group for the trip back to the boat.

They had not gone far, just to the first huts, when Stilton appeared.

"We need to move fast, there be a group of pirates heading for that house."

James wished he had Billy with him, he could use his muscle right now. All they could do was move as fast as they could.

Stilton had gone from point to rear guard and as they approached the start of the bar and were fully exposed there were shots from behind them. Stilton appeared shortly after.

"Twenty or more coming up fast."

"Take over from me and get the family to the boat. We will hold them off."

Stilton ducked under Goldstein's arm and urged the family along the bar. James and the other three men lined up, pistols at the ready. A group of men appeared out of the dark and a shout told them they had been seen. They came on at a run.

"First pistol, prepare to fire. Retreat ten paces, fire the second then run. Aim low. On my command."

He waited until the pirates were twenty yards away.

"Fire!"

As soon as they fired, they ran back ten paces, knelt and fired their second pistols. It held up the pirates for just a few seconds.

"GO!" James shouted, and they ran for their lives.

James didn't need to look back, he could hear the shouts of the pirates getting closer.

"Lions DOWN," Steven's voice bellowed.

All four threw themselves to the sand just as the marines from the boat fired a volley.

"Up and run," Steven called.

James did and saw the marines were calmly reloading and bringing their guns to their shoulders as he passed them.

A second volley roared out and the marines retreated to the boat. Everyone was aboard and the bowman pushing the bow around into the surf when they fired again.

"Report Mr Stockley," Captain Campbell said.

James was stood to attention in front of the captain's desk. Back in uniform, face and hands scrubbed clean. It was an hour before dawn and the ships were manoeuvring into position to blockade the estuary.

James gave a step-by-step account of the mission without aggrandisement and giving due credit to his men.

"You were going to leave the family until you had finished your reconnaissance?"

"Yes, Sir."

"Even though they could have beaten Mr Goldstein to death."

"They were trying to get something from him, I did not believe they would go that far."

The captain looked down at his hands then back up to James.

"The Goldstein girl told us that the Endellion is moored upriver and that they have been executing the crew for fun. She thinks there are a bare thirty left alive."

"Permission to lead a boat action to rescue them, Sir."

"Your bravery is commendable and so was your leadership during the mission, but Captain Howarth will be in charge of the rescue."

James was disappointed but didn't show it.

"Was that the first person you have killed?"

James paled slightly, "Yes, it was."

"The first is always the hardest, I remember mine to this day. I won't say it gets easier, but we are fighting men, so it is inevitable."

The captain looked at him, concern in his eyes. "If you need to talk about it, I am here."

James looked down then back up, "The man I shot was worse, his chest…"

"It is ironic isn't it that a thrown knife is so much cleaner than a pistol shot."

"Yes, I never imagined."

"Not something your father ever talked about?"

"No, Sir."

James was at his station as the sun rose, his guns loaded and run out.

He could see into the estuary and there was a lot of activity as men ran to their boats to try and get away.

"Rolling broadside, FIRE!" the first shouted and the foremost eighteen pounder fired. The broadside rippled down the ship until all eighteen guns had spoken. It took twenty seconds. Twenty-five seconds later the foremost gun fired again. The Nymphe, moored fifty yards behind the Leonidas, was also ripple firing her broadside and clouds of smoke drifted away on the light breeze to the South.

James could see their fire was having an effect as several boats were broken. A couple had managed to get manned and were under sail.

"Target the lead one," James told the four foremost gun captains.

The guns were firing independently now, and the gunners were calling out instructions to the men with jackstaffs to shift the guns around as they aimed.

Gun number two was the first to fire and James watched the ball head directly for the lead boat only to overshoot it. Gun number three lowered his sights a mite.

"Good shooting!" Angus Frasier shouted as the ball smashed the stern off the boat, vaporising at least one man in the process.

The second boat kept coming and had picked up speed.

"Carronades, stop that boat!" Angus shouted.

The big carronades on the foredeck were already swinging around. James knew they were loaded with small ball and langridge. They spewed fire and smoke blasting their loads across the water leaving an increasing shimmer on the surface as they spread out.

The boat was hit dead amidships, and the side, crew and mast were simply blown away cutting it in half. The second load hit more astern with similar effect.

The carronades turned their attention to the village. Huts and houses were flattened. James wondered if there were women and children there. He didn't like the idea of hurting non-combatants but he was too busy to dwell on it.

After a scant few minutes, the guns shifted, raking the shore and leaving the channel clear. The Silverthorn's boats advanced up the river keeping to the main channel. They were loaded with marines and sailors armed with rifles and pistols. Shots rang out as they spotted an enemy on the bank or returned fire.

The attack was over in under an hour. Thirteen boats destroyed and those pirates who didn't run for the hills were mostly dead. The Silverthorn returned with the remains of the Endellion's crew. Twenty-two men including Phillip Trenchard were carried aboard. They had been starved, beaten, and abused for entertainment.

"I want this place burnt to the ground and bring the prisoners here," an angry James Campbell said.

Detachments of marines left the ships and swept the shore. Any living souls were confined, everything that was still standing burnt. As soon as the first prisoners arrived, the interrogations started.

"Where is Mustafa Mehmed?" was the only question the captain wanted answering.

Several pirates were hung when they couldn't or wouldn't answer until one revealed he was on Mozambique Island. James noticed the grim determination in his captain and realised it didn't bode well for that Mustafa chap.

Campbell decided the Endellion was salvageable and had the Silverthorn take her under tow. They would go to Reunion where the Endellion would be repaired. Once the men were fit enough and the ship was sound, they would sail together to Calcutta. The Leonidas and Nymph set off for Mozambique. The Goldsteins stayed aboard as Mr Goldstein wasn't strong enough to transfer.

The captain called an officers' meeting. James slipped in and stood to the side leaning on the bulkhead.

"Gentlemen, I want to know what any of you know about Mozambique Island," the captain said.

"Owned by the Portuguese, it's not very big," the master said.

"Always been home to pirates especially the Arabs," Mark James the third lieutenant said.

"The port is on the Western side," Angus Frasier said, "stopped there once when escorting an East Indiaman."

"Why on earth did you stop there?" the captain asked.

"We were in need of Jesuit's Bark and our captain had heard you could get anything on the island."

The captain considered as he looked at a chart, he tapped his fingers in a vaguely familiar rhythm.

"We can't attack it because the Portuguese are allies. But we want to get this Mustafa chap and hang him."

He pursed his lips, "Suggestions?"

"We could ask the authorities to arrest him," Simon said.

"Not likely, he will be paying them to ensure they turn a blind eye to him," the master said.

James looked up but thought better of saying anything. The captain noticed, "You have a suggestion, Mr Stockley?"

"I was wondering if we could, sort of, kidnap him."

"That is the kind of thing we have done in the past if we needed to get someone out of either enemy or neutral territory." The captain smiled.

"Sounds like a good idea to me," Angus said with a grin.

"We will have to find him first," Simon said.

"Why not let him find us?" Mark James said.

That was met by curious stares.

"We just burnt most of his fleet. Why not send a party ashore to make a lot of noise about how we spanked the pirates? He is bound to show up to find out what happened."

"A bunch of noisy youngsters maybe," the captain said, turning to his three mids.

"You've done it this time," Gabriel said, "you'll probably get us killed."

"Not until they have well and truly buggered you," Potts their steward said.

"What?" squeaked Gabriel.

"Shut up, Potts, he doesn't need your help to be frightened," Archi said.

"Just sayin' thas all," Potts said unrepentant, "them Arabs is known for it."

Gabriel looked horrified.

James was rummaging in his footlocker and started putting things on the table.

"Bloody hell, 'ave you got a bloody armoury in there?" Potts said, wide eyed as several sets of brass knuckles, a couple of blackjacks, a dozen knives of different types, four loose pistols and a pair in a box, a garrotte, lock picks, a small bottle of fine oil and an intriguing item that was a combination knuckleduster, knife, and gun.

"That's the lot. Now we need to get you two equipped," James said.

All the mids had weapons training, although Gabriel hadn't been in a fight yet. He gave Archi a barker pistol to carry in his coat pocket and a pair of boot knives. Gabriel got a blackjack, the other barker of the pair and a replacement for his dirk. James went for his father's favourite stilettos, strapped to his forearms, a pair of pistols clipped to his belt either side of his body, the lockpicks in his left coat pocket and the knuckleduster gun in his right.

"Can I have one of these as well?" Archi said, picking up a set of brass knuckles.

"Help yourself," James said.

They were laughing over that when Potts stuck his head through the door and said, "Cap'in said to tell you we are entering port."

"Come on, lads, let's go party!" James said.

They were boated ashore with several crewmen to make it look like a normal shore leave and made their way to a likely-looking establishment. The bar, if you could call it that, sold alcohol and supplied hookahs for the Muslims to smoke hashish or tobacco. There were several out on the terrace sat on cushions, smoking, drinking tea and talking.

The boys chose a table that bordered the terrace and ordered wine. As the island was Portuguese, it was a Dow that hadn't travelled very well. It was drinkable but rough. They didn't mind though as they spilled more than they drunk and made a show of getting louder and more boastful as the bottles emptied.

"We bloody slaughtered those pirates on Madagascar," James crowed in a loud voice.

"Not a man left standing, thirteen boats sunk," Archi said. "A toast! To sinking pirates!"

"May the sharks feast on their gizzards!" Gabriel squeaked.

The server came over with a fresh bottle when James signalled him and asked, "You have been hunting pirates?"

"They took one of our ships and murdered our men we have returned the compliment thirteen-fold," James boasted.

"Hung them we didn't kill in the first place," Archie chipped in.

"Where did you do this? Not on this island?"

"No, Madagascar. Some place called Anantsoño, or it was until we burnt it to the ground."

James saw the corner of the server's eye tick when he mentioned the name of the village, so he watched him after he went back to the bar. He saw him take up an empty plate and head out to the terrace. He made for a table with three Arabs sat around it and spoke to one of them, nodding in their direction.

"Hook set," James said and laughed as if one of his mates had told a joke.

The Arabs stayed where they were, but James was aware they were watching them.

"Hey, lads. I've had enough of this boring place, what say we find somewhere a bit livelier."

The boys agreed so they dropped some coins on the table to pay for their drinks and wandered out in the street. They staggered along singing a rude shanty. James spotted two of the Arabs get up and follow them; the third made off.

They came to a place with a couple of women lounging on chairs outside who called to them in Portuguese.

"We are English!" Archie shouted.

"You boys wanna good time?" one of the women said.

"You got decent wine?" James answered.

"We got everything you need, sailor boy: clean girls and good wine."

At sixteen years of age James was still a virgin, but he knew a brothel when he saw one. Archie was also sixteen and Gabriel only fourteen. He surreptitiously glanced towards the Arabs who were peering around the corner of a nearby building.

"Let's give this place a try!" he hiccupped.

"What?" Gabriel squeaked.

James and Archie gathered him up between them and practically frog marched him through curtains that covered the door.

The room inside was dimly lit and as their eyes adjusted, they saw several semi-naked women aged from about fifteen to closer to fifty. A large woman dressed in a corset and skirt swayed up to them.

"Look girls, *man childs*," she said in Portuguese. "Who wants to pluck their cherries." The women laughed and some made rude gestures.

"Excuse me, Madam, we are English," James slurred.

"You choose girls, a real for an hour," she said in broken English.

"Each?" James said

"Sim, for each girl."

James made a show, that set Gabriel giggling, of walking amongst the women and examining them. He came upon a girl of about his age who had coffee-coloured skin and dark eyes. He held out his hand and she took it.

Archie pushed Gabriel forward after whispering in his ear then followed him. He found a girl that was slightly older, and Gabriel chose one who was old enough to be his mother. James flipped three reals to the madam and their chosen women led them out the back.

As soon as they were away from the common room and in a corridor lined with curtained doors. James said, "Any of you speak English?"

"I do a little," Archie's girl said.

"Take us all into one room," James said.

"Pardon, Senhor?"

"All in one room. Bring wine."

The girl nodded and translated for the other two.

"They want to party some more. We will take the lounge. I will get wine."

They entered a medium-sized room with lots of cushions and hookahs. The boys spread out in an arc facing the door and sat, the whores looked confused but sat next to their clients. The drunken youths had miraculously sobered up and indicated that the girls should give them room. Gabriel was pale and nervous but braced himself, emulating the older boys.

The third girl returned with a tray of glasses and a bottle of wine. She looked nervous. James took a pistol from his belt, cocked it, then hid it behind his leg. Archie did the same and after a struggle when the hammer got tangled in his pocket, Gabriel followed suit.

"Sit down behind me," James murmured.

The curtain covering the door moved as if blown by a draft. They waited and heard a man say something.

"Pass the wine, Archie," James said to let whoever was out there know they were in the room.

A second later the curtain was pulled aside, and a large man dressed in Arabian robes came in followed by two others. He looked down on the boys and picked out James.

"Do you speak French?"

James looked at him with a look of fear.

"Yes, I do. Who are you?"

"You boast about killing pirates and sinking ships."

"We did, it's no lie," James said.

The man's face developed a tick by his right eye and his hand went to a large, curved knife on his belt.

"They were my ships and my men; I think I will take you in compensation. Boys get a good price in the slave markets of

Marrakesh."

"Really? You must be Mustafa."

The man grinned, it put an evil cast to his face.

"You have heard of me."

"Yes, I needed to confirm it though."

James raised his pistol and the boys followed suit; the girls screamed.

Mustafa laughed. "You think you can frighten me, little boy?"

He took a step forward and started to pull his knife as his men moved forward.

"I don't want to frighten you, just stop you from leaving."

James shot him in the knee.

All hell broke loose as the rest of the shore party barged through the door to subdue the other two Arabs. They resisted of course and clubs were used to beat them down.

When things quieted, Mustafa was sitting, clutching his knee, his men were trussed up like hogs. The madam stormed in with her bouncers to find out what the hell was going on. She took one look at the guns in the boys' hands and Mustafa's bloody knee and swooned.

"A brothel?" Captain Campbell said.

"Yes, Sir, it provided a more private environment to make the capture than a café or bar," James said.

"You compensated the madam?"

"When she recovered from her faint, I gave her two pieces of eight to pay for the cushions that Mustafa bled on."

"That was generous," Campbell said straight faced.

"It bought her silence while we took the men away."

"I see."

"I also gave the girls an extra real each." James added.

"You did?"

"Yes, Sir. They were quite frightened by the whole thing."

"Very considerate of you, I will see that you are refunded."

"Thank you, Sir."

Campbell scanned the report on his desk one more time then sat back in his chair.

"You took risks but were successful in your mission. Well done. You and the other boys will be required to testify at Mustafa's trial." Campbell said.

"May I ask when that will be?"

"We will hold it as soon as we are back in international waters."

After James left, Campbell was joined by Angus Frasier.

"A chip of the block, that one," Angus said.

"I didn't know his father at that age, but I can imagine he was the same."

"Ruthless. I would never have shot the man in the knee to stop him running. He equipped the boys with his own weapons. You know I had no idea he had an armoury in his sea chest."

"That also goes to form, Lord Martin has a chest just for his weapons."

"We will be ready for the trial in an hour. Foregone conclusion really," Angus said.

"We need to have a record of due process." Campbell said.

"What will the record show about his capture?"

"That he was hiding amongst the prisoners. We never visited this island."

"I will get the halters ready."

"Not yet, I have an idea we can use his execution as a message."

Angus raised his eyebrows in question.

Campbell smiled grimly. "Mahajanga is the other port where the pirates congregate. We will hang him there."

Captain Campbell chaired the trial with the other two captains on the bench. Questions were asked. James acted as interpreter, Simon as his defence. Mustafa stayed silent, refusing to answer questions. His men, likewise, remained silent. The trial was a formality. The boys testified to Mustafa's identity and that he had confessed to being the head of the pirate fleet. As junior officers their testimony was taken as said. Two of the earlier prisoners also identified Mustafa in return for their freedom.

They approached Mahajanga and as they got to half a mile from the beach, where several boats typically used by pirates were pulled up, they fired a cannon. They hove to and waited.

When they did nothing else a crowd formed on the shore. People gesticulated and the sound of their voices drifted across the water. Soon there were several hundred people milling around on the beach and food vendors were selling Nem, Samosa and Brochettes. The smell coming off the shore was a mix of food, sweat and dead fish.

"Bring out the prisoners," Campbell commanded.

The men were lined up along the side. Mustafa stood on his good leg as James's bullet had wrecked his knee. Cries went up from the shore as those with good eyes recognised him.

Up to this point, none of the ships had shown their colours but now, at a signal from Captain Campbell, the Union Jacks were run up. The ships had been allowed to drift in towards the shore until they were just two hundred yards off. The sails were adjusted to hold position.

Three marines in full uniform placed the halters around the condemned men's necks. Drums rattled and, at the captain's order, teams hauled the condemned up. The halters had been positioned navy fashion, with the knots at the back of the necks. Strangled to death by their own weight it took what seemed an age for them to die.

They left them hanging for an hour so that everybody on shore could see them and when they were brought down the bodies were weighted and tossed over the side.

The ship's cutter was launched, and Captain Campbell was rowed to fifty yards off the beach. He used a speaking trumpet to say in French, "Those men were guilty of piracy against British ships and the murder of British citizens. The same fate awaits any others who seek to profit from piracy. In fifteen minutes, we will burn all the boats that are not for fishing on this beach. If you resist, we will bombard the town with our cannon. Anyone who resists will be assumed to be a pirate and killed."

His boat was rowed back to the flotilla where the boats were filling with marines. The guns were run out and once he got to the quarterdeck, he looked at the beach.

"They don't seem to think we are serious, Angus," he said.

About half the original crowd was still there.

"Put a ball into the centre of those boats."

"Aye, aye, Sir," Angus said and gave the order.

One of James' guns was selected, and he decided to lay it himself. He chose a large felucca in the middle of the beach directly in line with his gun and, as the range was so short, aimed directly for it. The gun was loaded with a single round shot and he checked his aim as he took up the tension on the lanyard.

"Fire when ready," Angus said.

James checked there were no people behind the boat and pulled. The flintlock sparked and the gun boomed. The boat was smashed as the eighteen-pound ball travelled along its length and embedded itself in the sand. The effect was immediate. The beach cleared.

"Boats away!" Angus shouted.

The landing was textbook. Half the marines formed a defensive perimeter, setting up swivel guns. The rest set about burning the boats. A few shots were fired from the direction of the town and were answered by the swivel guns. Soon the beach was ablaze, as were a couple of houses from where the shots had come.

When they judged the boats were irretrievably damaged, the recall was given. The marines put on another display of professional soldiering collapsing the perimeter back to their boats and embarking. The prisoners that had talked in return for their freedom were released after being told to spread the word that the next time they came back because of piracy they would burn the town to the ground.

Chapter 16: Calcutta

The Pride, in the company of the Eagle and Unicorn entered the Hoogly River and sailed up stream slowly with the pilot flag flying. A small boat approached and ran up beside the Pride. Without stopping a man transferred and literally popped up onto the deck.

"Panda Gupta at your service, I am the pilot for your trip into Calcutta," he said.

He was small, skinny, and bald. He wore the traditional trousers and loose-fitting coat tied with a sash but was bare foot. He gave off a buzz of energy as he trotted to the wheel.

"Please be so kind as to keep to the main channel, that is to the right of the island," he told the helmsman.

"You can take the flag down now," he said to Captain Ingram who started and looked up. He had quite forgotten it.

They slipped past two islands that looked uninhabited. The river bent to port which meant that the crew had some tricky sail handling to do even though the river was around three miles wide at that point.

Ingram and his first mate were kept busy as there were a host of small boats on the water. He was very conscious of having the Unicorn a cable behind and Wolfgang watching his every move.

"You there! Get out of the bloody way!" the lookout in the bow shouted at a flat bottom boat piled high with cargo that decided to cross their bow. The single crewman was at the rear with a sculling oar giving it all he had to make it across without getting run down.

"Bloody fool!" he shouted as they passed so close behind him he had to stop sculling or lose his oar. The boatman responded with a rude gesture and a stream of Hindi. The pilot went to the rail and berated him as they passed.

"Damn fool!" he said as he returned to the wheel. "Now, Sahib, there is a channel that goes off to the right, we must turn in there."

The channel was about a mile and a half wide and as they entered it, they could still not see Calcutta from the deck.

"How far is it to the city?" Caroline asked Marty.

"If I remember rightly, it's about thirty-five miles up the river from here."

"We can sail all the way up?"

"Oh yes, the river is about a mile wide all the way up and deep enough for even the biggest East Indiaman to navigate."

As he said it a large merchantman flying the East India Company flag approached from upriver.

"Isn't that the Hindustan?" Caroline said.

"It could be, but there are several ships of its type in service."

They were joined by Beth and the twins.

"What is that smell?" Beth said, wrinkling her nose.

"Shit, they put it on the fields," Marty said.

"What kind of manure smells like that?" Beth said emphasising the word manure.

"The human kind," Marty grinned. "All their shit has to go somewhere."

He wandered off to talk to Ingram, chuckling.

"Really, did you have to marry such a peasant?" Beth asked her mother.

"He's just teasing you," Caroline smiled.

Francis Ridgley wandered along the deck, heard the whole exchange and decided to join in.

"Cor, can you smell that?" he said to the ladies as he passed. "Smells like they dumped all the shit from ten thousand people on those fields."

Caroline covered her mouth with a handkerchief to hide her attempts not to laugh. Beth huffed and turned her back on him.

The smell didn't improve even when they came into sight of the city. It changed, taking on a more exotic edge with the smell of spices joining the pervading smell of human waste.

"It smells worse than London," Beth said.

"No sewers here, the locals tend to just squat, and do it where they stand."

"That is disgusting. Who cleans it up?"

"The Dalits."

"Why does it smell worse than Ceylon?" Edmund asked.

"More people crammed into a smaller space," Marty said. "And we are downwind here so getting the full benefit."

They came up to Fort William. "Wow, that is a big fort!" Edmund said.

"There is a big army inside it as well," Francis said as he rejoined them.

"Headquarters of the East India Company army. The fort was built by the company at a cost of two million pounds," Marty informed them.

"What is the big building in the middle?" Caroline asked.

"That is Government House, Martin's new domain is in there," Frances said

The Pride docked right in front of the fort and the squadron ships continued to a navy dock further upriver. A shouted exchange informed the people ashore that a dignitary had arrived, and a messenger was sent to carry the news to those in authority.

"Will we live in there?" Caroline asked.

"Most government officials live inside the walled city in the Southeast quarter. The houses there are quite luxurious I'm told."

The Shadows and the household staff had congregated on deck and Marty looked them over, noticing the excited looks.

A clattering of hooves and several carriages and wagons came out of the gate escorted by a platoon of lancers. Red uniformed and turbaned, the horsemen were very smartly turned out, the sun glinting off the polished steel tips of their lances. The lancers formed up in a line opposite the dock and Marty was glad he had dressed in uniform.

A man with a bicorn hat worn fore and aft and decorated with a white ostrich plume got down from the lead carriage and walked to the gang plank. Marty walked down to meet him.

"Lord Stockley?" he said.

Noting the insignia on his uniform Marty held out his hand and said, "Marquess Hastings, I presume."

He was a tall slim man with grey mid-length hair curled in an old-fashioned style.

"Please call me Frances."

"Martin."

They shook hands.

"Welcome to Calcutta. Not your first visit to India I understand."

"I was here with Wellesley, an interesting time but I never got this far North."

"We need to get you settled as soon as possible. There is a lot to do. I believe the prime minister briefed you himself?"

"Yes."

"Good, enough said." He gave the impression that there were ears and eyes on them.

Marty led him onto the Pride and introduced Caroline. Ingram started unloading the cargo.

"They are going to need more wagons," he said to Frances who was waiting his turn to be introduced.

"All will be provided, see that little man strutting around down there?"

"The one giving all the orders?"

"He is the Commissar of Government House. He will ensure that whatever is needed is supplied. It's a matter of pride for him."

"How do you know that?"

"I have a file on every official, his is quite long. He has worked his way up from a junior clerk where he showed an unusual aptitude for organisation, his life revolves around his position. He is married and has six children. Four of which also work in the house."

"May I introduce Frances Ridgley," Marty said as they reached him.

"Wasn't expecting you for a few months yet," Hastings said and held out his hand.

Francis took it and said, "Martin was kind enough to offer me passage on the Pride. She did the crossing in one hundred days. Even fought off an attack by pirates."

"Really?" Hastings said, looking at Martin enquiringly.

There was nothing for it, but Marty had to tell the tale.

"The Leonidas Nymph and Silverthorn have been dispatched to thin the pirates out a bit and to try and get the Endellion and her crew back. I expect them to join us in a few weeks."

"It's a job that needed doing, but the Company Marine have been busy with the war up here," Hastings said.

"My squadron can take care of any odd jobs that need doing," Marty said.

"The odder the better for your team, what?" Hastings guffawed at his own joke. Marty forced a smile.

Hastings looked down at the dock. "Mr Ramandeep looks to have things well in hand, let's get you and your family to your house. Mr Ridgley you have an apartment allocated inside the fort. Ramandeep will take you there."

The carriages were Indian made and extremely well appointed with well-padded velvet cushions on the seats. Marty, Caroline and Beth travelled with Hastings, the twins with Mary, Tabetha and Hannah were in the coach behind. Hastings was surprised when the Shadows joined them, either climbing up to ride on top or clambering up on the loaded wagons.

"Your men?"

"The Shadows? They are my special team."

"Oh, I read something about them in a dispatch. To be treated as your personal assistants."

Marty chuckled and Beth said dryly, "That's one way to describe them. I would have said a message saying, 'handle with care,' more appropriate."

Caroline smiled indulgently and said, "They are our family protectors when we are together and Martin's shock troops.

"They are all very well armed," Hastings said.

Marty didn't answer. He was busy looking at the sights.

"Is that a semaphore tower?"

"Yes, the company has invested in chains of towers across the territory we control. The towers behind it are St Peter's church."

They circled the fort to the South and Marty could see that there was a substantial city wall.

"The wall was completed in the late 1700s. This has ever been an area of conflict. Much safer now though," he added for the ladies' benefit.

They came to a gate and entered a long tree-lined drive that ended at a substantial two-storey house. The carriage circled a fountain that was the centrepiece of the rotunda in front of the main entrance. As expected, there was a long line of servants waiting.

With the experience they had gained in Ceylon, Marty and Caroline handled the introduction of their own staff and the Shadows in a much better way. As soon as they had walked the line the staff descended on the wagons and started moving them in.

"I will leave you to it, can we meet in my office tomorrow at say ten in the morning?"

"In Government House?"

"Indeed, I will warn the concierge that you are coming."

The house was more than adequate. The majority of the native servants lived in separate buildings in the grounds. The women in one, the men in another. Married couples lived off the grounds. The head of the servants was a middle-aged man of the Vaishyas caste. Shinge ruled the house like a British butler and wore white gloves that he used to check that the girls who cleaned did a perfect job. Woe betides any girl that didn't meet his exacting standards.

Marty and Caroline had a suite within the house that consisted of a bedroom, bathroom, and private sitting room. This gave them a private place away from the large reception rooms where they would entertain guests. Beth had a large bedroom with its own bathroom and the twins shared a similar room with their tutor and Mary in rooms to either side.

The Shadows checked out the security of the grounds and Antton reported to Marty.

"There is a ten-foot-high hedge all the way around the property. Three gates, the main one, one the servants use on the North side and one at the rear used for deliveries. There is a stable with carriages and horses. From the look of it you are expected to use a landau to get around. The grooms and coachmen live above the stables."

"Any riding horses?"

"None that I saw."

Marty would do something about that. He wanted the Shadows to have mounts and horses for the children as well.

"I recommend you get a squad of marines for security. Enough to run walking patrols around the grounds and to have guards on the gates," Antton said.

Marty wrote a note to Wolfgang and Captain O'Driscol inviting them to visit and requesting a guard detachment. There were a couple of boys designated as messengers, so he sent one to the Unicorn.

As Antton was about to leave, Beth came into his study. "Everything all right?" Marty said noting the tell-tale signs she was annoyed at something.

"They have given me two servants," she said.

"You need more?"

"No! I mean they won't let me do anything, if I pick something up one of them appears and asks me if they can help."

"They are just trying to get to know you and what you expect from them."

"Well, I drew the line at my weapons. I told them not to touch them."

"Very wise, they could hurt themselves."

"What about my jewellery?"

Marty cocked his head to one side in query.

"Do I let them touch it?"

"Why shouldn't they?"

"Oh, I don't know, even in Ceylon they weren't this attentive."

"In Ceylon I wasn't an official."

She sat on his knee, "Are there horses?"

"Only for the carriages at the moment, we will go shopping for some soon."

"I suppose I will have to be escorted everywhere."

"I would prefer one of the Shadows to accompany you. It's for your own safety."

"Pfft, I can look after myself."

"I am absolutely sure you can, but I would prefer not to have to explain why you shot someone."

She giggled, "It would be difficult wouldn't it."

"Yes, most young ladies don't carry pistols."

She sobered. "What should I do about the servants?"

"Be nice to them and gently let them know where your boundaries are. They will soon catch on."

Beth stood and kissed Marty on the forehead. "Thank you."

"You're welcome."

She walked to the door and turned before leaving. "Can I go with you when you look at horses?"

"I wouldn't dream of leaving you behind."

"Love you, Daddy!"

The next morning Marty dressed in uniform for his first day at the office. He only wore his knight's pendant, much to Caroline's annoyance as she wanted everyone to know who he was. At nine thirty on the dot Shinge announced that his carriage was ready.

It was the landau, and it had a driver and a footman who stood on a step at the back. He climbed in and they set off at a trot. It felt odd not having at least a couple of the Shadows in close proximity.

The first part of the route took him through an area that was obviously the quarter the British officials lived in. High hedges, beautifully clipped surrounding grand houses that got smaller the closer they got to the fort. Then they passed through a region of small houses with equally small gardens that looked to be the houses of senior married servants.

They approached the South gate of the fort and a guard stopped them. The driver told him who Marty was and they were waved through. The inside of the fort was huge and covered an area a tad under two square miles. It housed ten thousand troops their equipment and mounts. There was even a brigade of horse artillery.

They drove up to the grand entrance of Government House. A man came out and was down the steps before the footman had placed the step for Marty to get out of the carriage. He had to be careful he didn't trip over his sword.

"My Lord Stockley," the liveried man said. "Welcome to Government House. The governor general is expecting you. I am Chopra and I am the concierge. If you need anything just ask me."

Governor General's offices were on the third floor and Marty climbed a grand staircase lined with portraits of former governors and East India Company officials. He stopped by a portrait of Richard Wellesley.

"Looks like his brother," he commented.

"You know the marquess?"

"I am friends with his brother, and I have met him a number of times socially."

"The brother is a soldier I believe."

"His brother is the Duke of Wellington, he defeated Napoleon."

"Oh, my goodness gracious! I am not knowing that."

Marty smiled. "It can be confusing. When he was here, he was just Arthur Wellesley, then he became a viscount and now he is Duke of Wellington."

"And you, Sir, what were you called when you were here last?"

"I was Baron Candor then and a lieutenant."

"You and the duke have both been honoured then."

They came to a large door that was ornately carved. Marty thought it a little ostentatious. Chopra knocked and entered without waiting for an answer. Inside was a room with two people sat behind desks, a young woman, and an older man. British from their appearance.

"Viscount Purbeck to see the governor," Chopra announced.

Marty winced as he had been avoiding making anything of his superior social rank. The woman noticed and looked at him curiously. The man rose, stepped forward and said with a bow, "Thank you, Chopra. Cuthbert Tansey, secretary to the governor. Pleased to meet you. Will you follow me?"

It was obvious that Tansey wasn't going to introduce the woman, so he smiled at her as he was led towards another heavily-carved door. She blushed and looked down at her desk.

This door let into a yard long passage with a door at the other end. Marty thought that strange and made a mental note of the dimensions. The second door led into an extremely large office with a grand mahogany meeting table that could sit twenty easily and an equally impressive desk. The windows were floor to ceiling and let in plenty of light. Each one had a window seat. There was a fireplace, which was cold at that time of year, in front of which were three leather club chairs separated by low tables.

"Martin, welcome," Francis Hastings said as he left his desk chair and walked around to greet him. He nodded to Tansey, "Tansey can you organise some…" he turned to Marty, "…do you prefer coffee or tea?"

"Coffee please."

"Coffee for Lord Stockley and tea for me."

"Come, sit down and we can talk." He led Marty to the chairs by the fireplace after picking up a docket.

"When I got the message from the PM that you were going to be given the position of Military Attaché, I wondered what they were thinking. Then I read the file that came with it. You have an impressive history even though there are significant gaps."

Marty only inclined his head politely.

"You were of great help to the Wellesley's during their tenure, and you are familiar with dealing with the Indians. Do you think they are getting help from a third party?"

"The maharajas are rich and the trade opportunities vast. If the British gain control over the territory, then we will stop them trading with our competitors, especially in opium. It is in our competitor's interest to interfere because if we lose the war, they will be in prime position to take the trade from us. Which will weaken our position here and in China. Losing this war might also trigger a wave of rebellions in the Southern provinces further weakening our empire and trade."

Francis nodded in agreement. "I can see why they sent you, do you need any resources?"

"I have the Shadows, but I could use a secretary."

Just then there was a knock at the door and the young lady from the outer office entered.

"Martin, may I introduce Justine, my niece, she is here to learn secretarial duties. She has a fair hand and knows her way around the diplomatic arena in these parts."

Justine served Marty his coffee and her uncle his tea.

"My lord," she said as she placed the cup on the table beside him.

"Thank you," Martin said.

"Would you like to be Martin's secretary?" Francis said.

"Oh!" she said. "Do you think I could?"

Marty covered his surprise by sipping his coffee and then responded, "You know how to keep an appointment diary, take meeting notes and how to couch correspondence in diplomatic terms?" Marty asked.

"Yes, Sir."

"Then you can be of much use to me."

"Thank you, Sir. When do I start?"

"Right now." Marty rose, "If I may Francis, I would like to see my office and get settled in."

"Of course, old chap, Justine will show you where it is." Marty turned away then had a thought. "Why is this wall so thick?"

Frances grinned. "It's a double wall and the cavity is filled with a foot of cork. Completely soundproof and secure. Yours is the same. By the way there will be a welcome dinner tomorrow night in the ballroom where you will meet the rest of the corps. Justine knows the details."

Justine led him to an office just two doors down from the governor.

"This is yours, Uncle Francis wanted you close by."

Before he entered, he scanned the corridor and spotted a messenger boy loitering on a stool.

"Young man, I have some messages I wish to send."

Once inside, the office he wrote a note for Caroline telling her about the dinner. He thought that the more notice he gave her the better. Then he had a thought.

"Wives are expected to attend the dinner tomorrow?"

"Oh, yes. Your oldest daughter as well."

He amended the note for Beth to attend as well. He wrote a second note asking Adam and Antton to attend him at his office and a third to the concierge informing him that they would be visiting.

"This one for the concierge, these two to my house which is at…"

He looked at Justine.

"It is the Government House in Chandra Road. It has a high fence."

"And marines on the gates," Marty added.

Justine looked surprised.

"My own men."

The boy left.

"Right, let's get started."

He walked through to his office and looked around.

"You will sit there, get a desk and chair." He pointed to a spot that had natural light from the window.

"In here?"

"Yup. You are no use to me out there, Adam will act as door keeper."

"Adam?"

"My valet and one of the Shadows."

"Then who is Antton?"

"Head of the Shadows."

"And the Shadows are?"

"My special team of operatives. I want a current map of Calcutta with the locations of all the foreign powers buildings on it."

Justine wrote on a pad.

"A samovar for the outer office, and another map with the locations of all the semaphore towers."

This is going to be interesting, Justine thought as she left to fill the list.

Marty, meanwhile, went over his office with a fine-tooth comb checking for any listening pipes or peepholes. He was just finishing when Adam stepped into the room with Antton right behind him.

"You called, Sir."

Marty sat on the edge of his oversized desk.

"This is my new office, you both need to know where it is and you, Adam, will be here when I am," he said.

"Is it clean?" Antton asked looking around.

"It is, I just searched it."

"What will I do?" Adam said.

"What you do on ship and provide a layer of security. The outer office is your domain. Nobody gets in without being invited."

"Just you and me?"

A commotion approached from the outer office and two Indian servants entered carrying a desk, followed by Justine and a third carrying a chair.

"This is Justine, she is the governor general's niece and my secretary."

Adam looked at her and blushed, then he looked bashful.

Oh crap, Marty thought reading the signs.

"The maps?" Marty asked to cover the moment.

"The concierge is taking care of that. He says he will bring them this afternoon." She didn't appear to have noticed Adam's befuddlement.

The desk was positioned to his, and her, satisfaction and the servants left. Marty sat at the conference table and indicated that the others should join him.

"Tell me what countries have offices or establishments of any kind in Calcutta," he said to Justine.

She took a moment to gather her thoughts. "The French have recently opened a consulate but have had a trading office for a while. The Spanish have a representative and an office that looks after exports. The Russians have a count who represents them. He lives in a house outside the wall and, according to Uncle Francis, has an overly large staff."

"Do they import or export goods?"

"He trades in precious stones and silk. Brings in timber and leather. He loves to hunt and when he isn't at the auctions or markets is out in the wilds terrorizing the local wildlife."

"Anyone else?"

"The Ottomans have a delegation here. More to keep an eye on us than to actually trade Uncle Frances thinks."

"Are there any countries that have delegations or presence outside of Calcutta in the North?" Marty said.

"The Portuguese are down in Goa, but I don't know of any up here."

There was a knock on the door.

"Anybody home?" Francis Ridgley said.

"Come in and take a seat." Marty said.

"Would you all like tea?" Justine said, and when they all nodded disappeared to get some.

"We were just talking about foreign powers that had representation in the North."

"What with a view to seeing who could be supporting the Marathas?" Frances said.

"Yes."

Frances sat back and steepled his fingers, "Our intelligence indicates that the most likely are the French, who have enclaves on the West coast and in the islands, or the Spanish, who know we have been interfering in South America."

"Looking to get their own back," Antton said.

"What about the Russians?" Adam said.

"Unlikely but anything is possible with the Tsar, he changes allegiances with the wind," the spy master said.

The tea arrived along with a beaming concierge wielding two paper rolls like swords.

"Lord Purbeck, I am having here your maps."

"Excellent, they are up to date?"

"Oh yes, Sahib, one is coming from the British Army Surveyors office the other from the best map maker in Calcutta."

"What do I owe you?"

"Not to worry about that, Sahib, I am thinking you will want more maps, so I asked him to make you an account."

Marty looked at Justine and raised an eyebrow in enquiry while surreptitiously rubbing two fingers and his thumb together in the universal sign for money. She smiled, held up a finger and mouthed 'one rupee'. Marty dug into his waistcoat pocket and passed Chopra a coin.

"Thank you, Sahib, a pleasure to serve you."

They spread the maps out. The army map was a work of art. With each semaphore tower shown clearly. The city map, a large scale one, was clear and showed all the roads with their names. However, none of the locations Marty wanted to know about were marked.

"Right, looks like we have some leg work to do," Marty said. He took the maps and pinned them to a wall which had a cork notice board covering it.

"Antton, I want to know the location and usual information about any of the foreign delegation's residences, offices, or warehouses."

"Yes, boss," he said and got up to leave. "Oh, I almost forgot, Lady Caroline said, you are lucky she brought her wardrobe."

Marty laughed, "Saved me a fortune in dressmaker's fees."

A clank from the outer office announced the arrival of a samovar.

"Adam, make yourself at home and get that samovar working."

Justine waited until Frances had left, then said, "Milord, can I ask a question?"

"It's Martin or Marty when we are alone or with the boys and yes you can."

"Antton isn't English, is he?"

"No, he and two more of my men are Basques, I also have a Frenchman and a Chinaman. Adam, Zeb and Billy are English. Sam is from the West Indies."

She was surprised at the international makeup of the Shadows; she had expected them all to be British Bulldogs.

"He called you boss."

"We are quite informal. Within the team my titles don't mean much."

Adam brought in a pile of dockets, "These just arrived by messenger."

Marty sighed and settled down to go through them.

Chapter 17: Society

The dinner was going to be lavish. The governor general invited not only all the senior government officials but the heads of the East India Company and local Indian dignitaries as well. Caroline and Beth went to great lengths to make an unforgettable impression. Dresses were adjusted to fit perfectly, hair coiffured, jewels cleaned and polished.

Marty had to wear full dress uniform with all his honours and broke out a new hat that had an ostrich plume. He thought it ridiculous he was expected to wear the hot, heavy material and gloves. The dress sword was also an encumbrance and threatened to trip him up in a way his hanger never would. Consequently, he was rather grumpy as they set out.

"Oh, cheer up, Daddy," Beth chided him.

"I'm not grumpy."

"Yes, you are, you have a face as long as last week and you are glaring at people."

"I'm hot and this… sword…"

"Yes, well it does get in the way doesn't it. Do you have to wear it all evening?"

"It will be set aside at the first opportunity."

"Don't you think Mummy looks radiant?" she said, attempting to divert him.

Marty looked admiringly at Caroline then at Beth, "You both look stunning, I don't think I have seen those dresses before."

They were dressed as a matching pair, and it was hard to believe they weren't sisters. Egg shell blue dresses trimmed in intricate Honiton Lace. Caroline wore her honours and her golden tiger topped off with a Ceylon sapphire and diamond necklace, bracelet, and tiara. Beth also had diamonds and sapphires, but her tiara was more of a circlet with a thumb-sized sapphire in the centre.

The carriage stopped in front of Government House and servants rushed to help them down. They got to the entrance of the ballroom where a herald was introducing the guests as they arrived. They stepped forward and the man looked at them enquiringly. "Viscount Stockley of Purbeck, Lady Caroline Stockley and the Honourable Bethany Stockley," Caroline said.

The man stood more upright and dipped a polite bow as he realised, they were the guests of honour. He announced them with extra gusto.

There were audible gasps as they entered, mainly from women who looked in despair at the latest fashion from London, the jewels, and their beauty.

"Martin, welcome," the governor general said. He had his wife on his arm, "this is Flora my wife."

"Flora, may I introduce my wife Caroline and our daughter Bethany."

The ladies peeled off to do the rounds together leaving Marty and Francis together.

"You know they will cause several ladies to have heart attacks and swooning fits," Francis laughed. "I could hear several eating their own livers over the dresses."

"Caroline likes to make an impression," Marty said.

Frances agreed with that then turned to business, "There are a number of dignitaries you need to meet."

"Can I get rid of this damn sword first; we are used to much shorter ones in the navy."

"Of course, can't have you going arse over tit, old boy." He signalled to a servant who took the offending article away.

"Now let's get the introductions done."

Marty looked around and found that a group of men had gathered near to them. One stepped forward. "William, may I introduce our new Military Attaché, Viscount Stockley. Martin, this is William Scott, Commissioner of the Board of Control."

Marty bowed, then shook the hand of the head of the East India Company in Calcutta.

"Lord Stockley, you are a shareholder I believe," Scott said.

He didn't waste any time, Marty thought but plastered a smile on his face and said, "A very minor one since '05."

"A shareholder all the same. You must meet Richard Rocke," he beckoned another dignified-looking man over, "Richard this is Lord Stockley our new Military Attaché, milord may I present Richard Rocke the President of the Board of Directors."

That covers the leading lights of the company, Marty thought as he did the necessary. They chatted for a few minutes sipping drinks that were delivered by servants then Francis deftly moved him on to the next in line. After the best part of an hour, Marty's head was spinning with names, and he sighed with relief when they were called to dine.

It was a sit-down event that, from the array of cutlery, was going to be at least seven courses. He was shown to a place setting with his name on it. Caroline sat opposite, with Beth to her right. To his right sat Flora Hastings, her husband sat at the head of the table and General Sir Thomas Hislop was on his left.

"I say, is that the Waterloo medal?" Sir Thomas, who had spent his entire career in India, said.

"Yes, I had the honour to be there," Marty said.

"Good gad, a navy man at Waterloo, who would have thought," the general spluttered. "But then Hastings told me you are a friend of Wellington, what?"

"I was Head of Intelligence on the peninsula and accompanied him to Belgium."

"You are familiar with land war then?"

"I am indeed, although I am more comfortable with oak walls and a battery of cannon."

Caroline liked Flora and chatted with her across the table while Marty had his time monopolised by the army man next to him. From the sound of it he was having to retell the battle of Waterloo. She did know that the general was a senior commander of the East India Company's army and had a reputation for harshness when dealing with the natives.

They were served an amuse bouche of cucumber and rawas, a local white fish known as Indian salmon. A little palette teaser to get the taste buds working. The next course was a rich mulligatawny soup, spiced with curry powder and thickened with rice. Plates of Sheek kebab, pakoras, bhajis and samosas followed with bowls of minted yoghurt, and chutneys that ranged from sweet to red hot and crispy breads called papadum. Conscious that there were more dishes to come she refrained from eating too many of the delicious treats.

"Don't eat too many, dear," she said to Beth who had taken one of everything, "there are at least another four courses yet."

"I seem to remember these," Beth said.

"You had them when we lived in India before. You were very little then."

Beth nibbled on what seemed to be a ball of onion in batter. It was delicious especially with some of the minted yoghurt. She also tried, to her regret, a red condiment that was both sour and extremely hot. "Tamarind pickle," Flora informed her and took the time to instruct her in the names and strength of each.

Next came the meat dish. A rich mutton concoction they were told was called Kosha Mangsho. Pieces of meat with tomatoes, onions and just enough chilli to make it interesting, served with fluffy long grain rice flavoured with saffron.

They were served wine or Indian pale ale beer. Marty preferred the wine, finding the hoppy, bitter beer too strong for his taste. None of the food had been too spicy yet, however, he remembered some of the fiery dishes he had eaten before and sampled everything before digging in. Jugs of mango and cardamon lassi were on the table and Beth helped herself to that.

In between the courses sorbet flavoured with lemon was served to clear the palate. It was cool and refreshing and Marty thought, just what the doctor ordered.

Then came fried river fish. Marinated with fragrant spices the whole fish was deeply sliced along each side then dipped in a light batter before being fried. Served with salad and thin fried potatoes they were amazing.

Last came trays of Indian sweets, gulab jamun, jilabi, imarti, kaju katli, khirmohan, bowls of kheer, and singori. Marty had a sweet tooth and loved gulab jamun with its cardamom-flavoured syrup.

Once the sweets had been consumed the men went to a games room and lounge to play cards and billiards. The women went to a lounge to drink tea and talk. Well, that is what the men thought, they also played cards. Piquet was popular as was five card loo and whist. Significant sums changed hands as the woman gambled.

Caroline and Beth both played whist and discovered the women played for a penny a point.

"I have never played for money before," Beth said as she won the first game by quite a margin taking money from her mother, Flora and Jane, the wife of Richard Rocke.

"You are young and have an agile mind, that puts us older ladies at a disadvantage," Flora said.

"Ah but what we lack in agility we make up for in wisdom and cunning," Jane said with a rare smile.

Beth liked Jane Rocke, she appeared to be a dour Scottish woman but as she got to know her Beth realised, she had a wickedly dry sense of humour and the ability to cut someone in half with her sharp wit. She also liked a wee dram and carried a hip flask of Meldrum malt.

Jane had an astonishing run of luck over the next three hands and won all her money back. On their way home Beth said to Caroline, "Jane was cheating."

"I know, dear, but sometimes it's best to let things pass."

"I suppose so. She didn't make any money, but it's still dishonest." She looked out at the houses as they passed and noticed a furtive-looking man approaching a house. A woman appeared on the porch and the two embraced before rushing inside.

"Indeed," Beth said to herself.

Marty didn't play cards preferring billiards. He was playing Francis Hastings and they chatted with Sir Thomas who watched them intently.

"Who do you think they are getting weapons from?" Marty said.

"Well, they make some themselves, their gunsmiths are quite accomplished at copying anything they capture."

"They have enough capacity to equip an army?" Marty said as he scored a double.

"I don't believe so," Francis said. "We have captured French-made guns during some of the skirmishes we've had with them." He frowned as Marty had trapped his ball in the corner with the red and was scoring points at will.

"There are a lot of surplus weapons in France since they disbanded most of the great army. Anybody could be buying them up and shipping them over," Marty said. "That's game."

"Well played," Sir Thomas said begrudgingly and handed some coins over to William Scott who had also been watching.

Marty took out a cheroot and lit it from a lamp, retrieved his brandy and took a seat.

"What artillery do they have?" he said.

"Mainly older cannon. They fire a lot of stone shot," Sir Thomas said.

"Stone balls can be deadlier than iron, they shatter, and the fragments spread out. Very effective against infantry."

"True and they have become more adept at using their artillery. Their tactics are much more European," Francis said.

Marty's ears pricked up.

"Since when?"

The last year or so, why?"

"It seems strange that they would suddenly get better at artillery," Marty looked from face to face, "doesn't it?"

"What time did you get back?" Caroline said the next morning.

"The early hours, there is going to be a ball."

"A ball? None of the women mentioned that."

"That's because none of them know about it yet."

Caroline gave him a direct look.

"What are you up to?"

"Me? Nothing. You, however, are going to organise a grand ball for all the foreign dignitaries in Calcutta."

"Me?"

"Justine will help you."

"Who is Justine?"

"Didn't I tell you? She is my secretary."

"Do tell," Caroline said, a dangerous glint in her eye which

Marty noticed immediately and hastened to head off the storm.

"Francis's niece. Training to be a diplomatic secretary. Sweet girl." It didn't work.

"A sweet girl. I see."

"You should meet her," Marty said lamely.

Caroline accompanied him to his office and swept in ahead of him. Adam jumped to his feet when he saw her. Marty shook his head from behind Caroline when he opened his mouth to greet her.

"Your office is in there?"

Marty nodded and Caroline went in.

"Storm clouds, Sir?"

"Could be. Any coffee ready?"

Marty sat on the edge of Adam's desk and sipped his coffee. "Any letters?"

"On your desk. There was a note from Mr Ridgley asking that you visit him in his office."

"That will have to wait."

A peel of laughter came from his office. He looked to the door.

"Storms passed, bring in some tea please," Marty said and went in.

As he expected, once Caroline met Justine, she found she liked her. The two were chatting and laughing merrily. He went to his desk and went through the letters. Adam brought in a tray of tea.

"Can you shut the doors, please Adam. I don't want any visitors for the next hour." Both women looked at him curiously.

"Now you've got to know each other, we can get down to what

needs to be done. I want you to organise a ball to celebrate our arrival in Calcutta. It is to be ostentatious and *the event* of the year that everybody just has to be at. Everybody who is anybody is to be invited, the great, the good and especially the foreign representatives."

"Why the foreigners?"

"Because they are all assuming I am working for British Intelligence, as most Military Attachés do, and if they see me throwing a ball, and more so, hosting it, they are likely to come just to see who I am."

Caroline looked at him her head on its side, her lips pursed,

"That's not all there is to it."

Marty grinned and said nothing until Caroline raised her eyebrows.

"While they are there, Beth, and the Shadows will search their places."

"All of them?" Caroline said and Justine noted she didn't say anything about Beth being involved.

"The French, Spanish and Ottomans."

"She won't want to miss the ball."

"If she wants to follow me, she has to make sacrifices."

Justine followed all of this with her mouth open. "Are you talking about your daughter, Bethany?"

"The very same," Marty said. "Now ladies, I will leave you to it as I need to talk to Ridgley."

Frances Ridgley's office was tucked away in a corner at the end of a long corridor and had no sign on the door. He had already made himself at home and a steaming samovar stood in the corner with his tea set beside it. A small desk stood in front of the window to take advantage of the natural light but looked hardly used. Ridgley was sprawled on a chaise longue beside which stood a low occasional table covered in papers.

"You look comfortable," Marty said as he entered.

"I am, take a seat," Ridgley replied. Marty shifted some papers from the chair to the desk and sat. He looked around expecting to see the usual array of weapons. Ridgley noticed and said, "Looking for the armoury? I'm cutting down." He reached down to the hidden side of the chaise and pulled up a bell-mouthed pistol.

"What did you want to see me about?"

"I heard what was said about the Indian's sudden improvement in artillery tactics and have been going through previous reports. This might be of interest." He handed over a sheet of paper. "It's a report from Elphinstone. Peshwa Baji Rao has been trying to recruit unhappy Marathas who are on his staff and Europeans. He is building up his army and reinforcing the forts at Sinhagad, Raigad and Purandar. Bapu Gokhale is his general of choice."

"You think he has recruited an artilleryman?"

"It's possible."

Marty was silent for a few minutes as he read the report and thought it through.

"Where do I find Gokhale?"

"As far as I know he is near Nashik."

"Where's that?"

Ridgley went to a map pinned to the wall and after a brief scan pointed to a town Northeast of Bombay.

"The trouble with India," Marty said, "is it is too bloody big."

The ball was arranged by a committee headed by Caroline and Justine and consisting of the most influential wives. It would be held in the ballroom of Government House with the band of the Indian 5th battalion supplying the music.

"Martin," Caroline called from Beth's room.

Marty was just getting his cravat adjusted by Adam and frowned as he wondered what Caroline would want him for, as Beth wasn't attending the ball.

"I best go and see what they want," he said and grabbed a biscuit from the tray that Adam had brought up.

He pushed the door open and, as he saw his wife and daughter, breathed in biscuit crumbs which set off an uncontrollable bout of coughing. Adam, who had followed him, slapped him on the back with a huge grin on his face.

Beth was dressed in a figure-hugging black body suit complete with hood, chamois leather soled slippers and a belt equipped with everything she needed for breaking and entering. She stood with her hands on her hips and along with her mother was having a hard time controlling her amusement at Marty's reaction.

As he finally got his breathing under control and his eyes stopped watering, Marty realised his little girl had grown into a full-grown woman with a figure to challenge Caroline's.

"You cannot go out in that!" he gasped.

A dangerous glint came into Beth's eyes, but Caroline was the one to answer.

"Nobody will see her, and she will wear this when she travels."

Caroline held up a dress that looked to be open the length of the front. Beth stepped into it and quickly did up the hook and eye fastenings. When she had finished, she looked to be dressed completely normally, except for the hood which she covered with a hat. It had only taken thirty seconds.

"Did you know about this?" Marty asked Adam.

"We were consulted, Sir."

"Consulted on what?"

"We asked the Shadows what the best design for a costume would be for breaking into houses," Beth said.

Marty had recovered his equilibrium and could see the sense in the design. He had to admit it was eminently practical.

"How fast can you get out of that?" he said, indicating the dress.

Beth demonstrated.

"Quick enough. Weapons?"

"Darts tipped with curare, a pair of throwing knives and two stilettos."

"No guns?"

"Too noisy."

"Garrotte?"

"I'm not strong enough."

Marty nodded and walked around her, examining the belt.

"Lockpicks, a bottle of fine oil and a straw, slim jim, diamond-tipped glass cutter," Beth said.

"Looks like you are good to go. Who goes in with you?"

"Zeb and Chin. Adam on high cover, Antton will drive the carriage. Sam on standby outside the buildings, he is naturally camouflaged."

Marty let her plan the raids on the French and Spanish buildings herself and so far, she seemed to have done a good job.

"Where did they get the carriage?" Marty said.

"It's a Brougham, Antton borrowed it," Beth said

A Brougham was a four-wheeled carriage with an open driving position and an enclosed cab big enough for four people at a squeeze. He assumed that Antton borrowed it without asking the owner.

"Looks like you are all set to go," he said and gave her a hug. "Be careful."

"Always," she said and kissed him on the cheek.

"Are you alright?" Caroline asked as the carriage jolted over the entrance to Fort George. Marty had been unusually quiet during the ride.

"Just getting used to the idea that my little girl is all grown up and wondering what she is doing now."

Beth and her team were enroute to the Spanish trading office which doubled as a residence and was down by the river. Sam and Antton were on the driver's seat, and she shared the cabin with Chin and Zeb. Adam was ahead on horseback so he could be in position when they arrived. She wore the dress in case they were stopped and looked just like a girl out visiting.

"Almost there." Antton leaned down and around so he could be heard through the window.

Beth took off the hat and started unclipping the dress. It took just twenty seconds and she left it so she could step out of it. Chin and Zeb also shed their coats and pulled up the hoods of their black one-piece coveralls. The coach slowed to a walk and there was a double thump on the cabin. Chin was first out followed by Beth then Zeb. All three slipped into the shadows. The carriage continued on without stopping.

A dark window provided access to the private residence, Beth's slim jim dealing quickly with the catch. The three slipped in, Beth closed and locked the window. The house was quiet, the representative was at the ball. There would be servants, but they thought they would be taking advantage of getting an early night or out seeing friends.

They were in a reception room; it was richly furnished and was probably used for entertaining. Beth moved to the double doors and listened. She nodded to Zeb who had his hand on the ornate crystal doorknob. He turned it slowly and cracked the door open. It opened silently.

Beth glanced up and down the dark corridor. The main door was visible at the end. A single lamp lighting the entrance. They hoped the servants would be in their quarters in the basement or rooms in the garret and so far, it looked like that was the case. She slipped across the corridor to the door on the opposite wall. Her gloved hand wrapped around the knob. Locked.

She knelt by the lock and selected a pair of lockpicks by feel. It took just seconds to release the lock.

"Lamps," Beth said, opened the door and stepped in. Chin stayed outside on guard.

Zeb pulled a shuttered lantern from his shoulder bag and lit it, sending a dim beam of light forward. He handed it to Beth and lit a second for himself. The room was obviously the domain of a secretary.

"Search the desk," Beth whispered.

While Zeb searched the desk Beth checked out the cupboards. The first was full of stationery and writing materials. She took a sample of the paper, a block of ink and two metal-nibbed pens. After a short search she found a box of sealing wax sticks and took one of those as well. Just in case they wanted to create an authentic document that appeared to be from the Spaniard.

The second was full of files. They were not indexed, and she decided that the secretary wasn't the organised type. She flicked through them but saw nothing of interest.

The door to the main office was unlocked and Beth carefully ran her hands around the frame before opening it. She felt a slight resistance and stopped.

That's odd, she thought. Her hand went to her belt and found a quill that had the feather removed which she used to run around the slight gap.

"There is a wire attached to this door at the top," she said to Zeb. "Hold it and don't let it move until I tell you."

Once Zeb had the handle, she shone her lantern up at the wire which was attached to the door and ran back to the frame. She followed it with her fingers. "Ease the door." Zeb inched it forward, "Stop."

Her fingers had reached a mechanism. It was a bell with a sprung clapper.

"Someone doesn't want to be disturbed without warning." She unhooked the wire.

The room showed why. As well as a desk and the usual chairs there was an oversized chaise longue with comfortable cushions. There was the faint trace of a woman's scent. A bookcase attracted her attention. She ran her finger down the spines of the books and selected one at random.

"Good grief!" she said as she saw the illustrations inside.

Zeb looked over her shoulder and chuckled. "That could give a man a bad back."

"Wouldn't do much for the woman either," Beth said as she turned the book. It was titled the *Karma Sutra* and was full of illustrations of couples performing sex in every position imaginable.

She put it back and checked another. It was a similar publication.

"No wonder he wants to be warned if someone is coming," she muttered and put it away.

Zeb was searching the desk, she joined him.

"What's this?" she said, pulling a leather braided object out of a bottom drawer. "It's a riding crop, what's he need one of those for in here?"

Zeb sniggered and whispered in her ear.

"Really?" Beth gasped and was thankful the dark hid her blushes.

She renewed her search; thankful she was wearing gloves. At the very bottom of a drawer, she found a letter with a distinctive seal. It had been carefully folded and wrapped in silk cloth. Carefully lying it on the desk she called Zeb.

"This might be important; can you memorise it or copy it?"

Zeb looked it over, "Too long to copy but I can remember it and write it out later. I can make an impression of the seal."

Beth nodded and Zeb started to work a ball of soft clay, he had taken from his pouch, between his fingers. Softening it and warming it. When it was as he wanted, he gently pressed the clay into the seal. After a moment he gently peeled it off and checked the impression.

"Perfect. I could make me own seal from that."

They left the house after reconnecting the bell and locking the door. They waited while Chin fetched Antton and the carriage.

"So does he use the whip on his woman or her on him?" she asked Zeb.

"Them questions you should ask your mum," Zeb said, wary of attracting Caroline's ire.

"Pfft. She won't tell me; she will say I'm too young. Do you think Daddy spanks her?"

"If'n he tried I reckon she would cut his liver out," Zeb said.

That gave her something to think about.

The French consulate had a soldier on guard outside the main entrance, so Antton dropped them off on the street it backed onto. Lights were burning above the stables and in the kitchens on the ground floor. A soldier patrolled the well-lit courtyard.

Beth looked it over and said, "We will have to go in over the rooftops. That house there is closest."

The house next to the consulate was separated from it by a good fifteen feet at roof level. It was four storeys high and had a flat roof like many houses in that area.

"That is a bloody long way down," Zeb said as he peered over the edge.

Beth was eying the landing area on the consulate roof.

"We will have to be careful where we land, there is a skylight there on the left."

"We?" Zeb said, and Chin chuckled.

"You can jump that far, can't you?" Beth said.

"I've never tried," he replied truthfully.

"Watch me," she said and lined up her run.

Beth took a ten-pace runup and launched herself over the gap. She landed comfortably on the other side.

"Come on, Zeb, you are next," she said in a horse whisper.

Zeb swallowed. His eyes were a little wild as he paced back ten paces from the edge. He turned and looked at the gap. Then he walked backwards until his heel hit the wall on the opposite side of the house. He took two big breaths.

Beth watched Zeb. She could almost smell his fear and was about to wave him off when he started running towards her. His eyes were wide, and his arms pumped. His foot hit the edge and he launched himself up and off.

He flew through the air, arms windmilling, legs still running. He landed a foot inside the edge of the roof and Beth grabbed him to kill his momentum.

"You're safe, you did it," she whispered into his ear as she held him. He was shaking.

Chin landed lightly behind her.

"Good jump, Zeb," he grinned.

"Why didn't John tell me you are all bloomin' mad," Zeb gasped and then chuckled. "It was fun though."

They used the skylight to gain entry to the house and made their way down through the floors looking for the consul's office. They found it on the second.

Back at the ball Marty and Caroline circulated and personally greeted every guest. They came to the Spanish representative, Don Rodrigo, and his wife. He was a typical Don. Tall, at five-foot ten, sporting a neatly-trimmed goatee beard and moustache. He was handsome and was well dressed. His wife was not what either Marty or Caroline expected. A short, rather dumpy woman dressed in dark grey. She wore a single broach and no other jewellery. Her hair wasn't styled but rather piled up and held in place by tortoiseshell combes. A lace headpiece covered it. Caroline noticed the pattern was religious in its symbology.

He spoke to Marty in English.

"I understand you spent some time in Valencia."

Marty guessed that his wife didn't speak English so answered in Spanish.

"I spent quite a lot of time on the peninsula during the war, some of it in Valencia. It is a beautiful town."

Doña Lucia smiled a nasty little smile and said, "What were you doing there? I do not remember any British being in that part of Spain until the war was almost over."

"Supporting the partisans," Marty said.

A cloud passed over her face, but she quickly recovered and cracked another false smile. Her husband bowed and moved on to allow the next person to be presented to Marty and Caroline.

"There are a few papers concerning shipments of goods but no mention of weapons," Beth said.

"Yer dad would be looking for things like farm machinery or general goods that are heavy," Zeb said as he picked the lock on a cabinet.

Chin suddenly came into the room, "Someone coming."

Beth went to the door and quickly locked it with her picks. She was just in time as someone tried the handle. There was a pause and then the sound of a key being inserted in the lock. Beth looked wide eyed at Zeb and Chin and the three rushed to hide.

The door opened. Beth was squinting through a gap in the curtains she was hiding behind, and saw a young man enter carrying a candle. He went to the desk and looked across the top. If he was surprised to see papers lying on it he didn't show it. Instead, he manipulated something under the top of the desk in the middle of the foot well. There was a click and he knelt out of sight behind the desk to emerge a moment later with a long key.

He walked across the room to a portrait of a woman and ran his fingers along the top edge. The portrait swung away from the wall revealing a safe into which he inserted the key. Beth couldn't see inside the safe when he swung the door open, but she did hear a clink and saw him put something in his pocket. He closed the safe door, locked it and swung the portrait back into position. Returned the key and after a quick scan left the room.

When she heard the lock click Beth stepped out from behind the curtains, Chin popped up from behind a chair and Zeb slid out from under a chesterfield. Beth went straight to the desk and ran her fingers along the lip. She felt a section of wood that was different and pressed it. With a click a concealed drawer in the left plinth popped open.

"Well, well," she said.

It was very shallow and inside was a small pistol that was loaded and primed, and the key. Emulating the young man she found the catch on the portrait and unlocked the safe.

"Ooh," she said as she got sight of the contents.

A tray of jewels with several pieces missing was the first thing she saw. She guessed they were the consul's wife's. They were locally made. The stones were large and of good quality. She checked the rest of the contents and found several pouches full of gold louis coins.

"That was what you took," she murmured.

Under them were some papers which she scanned, selected one and read it. It was a manifest and had all the things Zeb had said his father would look for. She memorised it and carefully restored the safe's contents to their original positions. It was time to leave.

The ball was well underway when Beth swept in looking radiant. She helped herself to some food and a glass of wine then found she was surrounded by young men.

Marty appeared, made a point of kissing her on the cheeks and said, "Are you feeling better, my dear?"

"Yes, thank you, Daddy, I am much better now," Beth said. The boys hung back a little, intimidated.

Point made, Marty moved on to dance with the wife of the French consul. She was wearing a splendid diamond necklace, tiara and bracelet set.

Beth's dance card soon filled up and she danced the rest of the night away. The young man at the consulate was not amongst the beaus that courted her, and she wondered why he hadn't accompanied his parents to the ball.

She didn't get the chance to tell her father what she had found as by the end of the ball she was exhausted and went straight to bed. The next morning everyone got up late as it was a Sunday and none of them had gotten to bed until the wee small hours of the morning.

Chapter 18: Bethscapades

"Good morning," Marty said as Beth joined him and Caroline for a late breakfast. "How did the mission go last night?"

"Good morning, Mummy, good morning, Daddy," Beth said as she selected fruit and a glass of lassi from the sideboard. Once she was sat and had been served tea she said, "I have put a written report on your desk, but, in a nutshell, we found this seal on a letter which Zeb is transcribing as we speak." She handed over a wax seal that Zeb made from the clay impression.

"That is Joseph Bonaparte's," Marty said after examining it for a moment. "This may explain their behaviour at the ball."

"And the look on her face when you said you supported the partisans," Caroline said.

Marty nodded and put the seal to one side, "Anything else?"

"I found a hidden safe in the French consulate after we watched the consul's son take some gold out of it. I found a manifest in it and thought it odd the consul would store an insignificant document in his safe."

"What was on it?" Caroline said.

"It listed iron goods, farm implements, wine, casks of brandy, casks of lamp oil."

"An odd combination," Marty said.

"That's what I thought," Beth said.

"What do you think we should do now?" Marty asked.

Beth thought for a moment, "Check out their warehouse and see if we can find the goods and if they are what it says on the manifest."

"Good, then that's your next task. Who will you take with you?"

"Just one I think, Billy."

Caroline smiled at Marty as she liked that he let Beth decide what needed to be done. Then she had a thought, "Would it be a good idea if Beth got to know the consul's son?"

"It might," Marty said, "he could be a weak link we can exploit if we can find some leverage."

"What about the Spanish?" Beth asked.

"I want to read that letter first before we decide anything. Focus on the French for now. Take one more Shadow with you as a lookout. Sam is good at that, but you choose."

Beth, Sam, and Billie made their way to the docks that evening. To the casual observer it looked like three sailors walking together. Beth wore men's clothing, and her long auburn hair was tucked under a sailor's knitted hat.

The warehouse they were looking for was relatively new. The French had only acquired the land and built it a year ago. The flag of the Bourbons flew on a pole at the front. The three split up to recce the building from the outside.

Beth wandered along as if she had nothing to do, but she paid close attention to the warehouse and any noises that came from it. It was a quiet night and sound travelled far. There were voices coming through a window grill towards the rear of the building.

She moved in below the window which was about eight feet up.

"We will ship those crates out tomorrow so get them stacked on the loading bay," a gruff voice said.

Another voice complained, "What just the two of us? Can't it wait for the Indians to arrive in the morning?"

"No, we can't. Sir wants them moved tonight," gruff voice snapped in French.

"All right for him. He was out partying with that new British Lord last night."

"Which is why he wants them moved. That new British Lord is the commander of that British squadron that's moored upriver, and he wants to get them crates moved onto the ship first thing."

She moved away and returned to the rendezvous point which was opposite the warehouse entrance. Sam and Billy joined her minutes later.

"Did you see anything?" she asked.

"There is a small door at the far corner we could use to get in. It's got a normal lookin' lock," Billy said.

"Heard some scraping and banging from behind them big doors over there," Sam chipped in.

"That will be the men in there, moving crates to the loading bay for shipping first thing tomorrow. We need to get a look at what's in them and try and find out where they are going," Beth said.

They waited in the shadows and just before midnight, three men left the warehouse via a small door set into the big entry doors.

"Wait," Beth said as Billy made to move in. "Sam follow them. Make sure they don't come back and disturb us."

Sam slipped away and five minutes later Billy led Beth to the rear door. She picked it by feel; thankful her tutors made her pick locks blindfolded.

The lock submitted to her tender caress, and she slowly pushed down on the handle. It stuck, then jerked down. The door was only a year old, but the heat and humidity had warped it.

"They used green wood to make it," Billy muttered as he took over to apply his muscle.

The door popped open. Before Billy could control it, the hinges gave off a loud creak. They froze, ears straining to hear any noise from inside.

"Let's go," Beth said after a minute of silence.

Once inside they used shuttered lanterns to light their way through the stacks of goods.

"There's a lot in here," Billy said.

"Is that unusual?" Beth said.

"I'd have thought they would be trading it, but this looks like it's been here for a while," he said, lifting the edge of a canvas under which was stacked bolts of cloth.

Beth was about to move on when something caught her eye.

"Pull that one out,' she said.

Billy pulled the bolt of cloth out and placed it on top of the stack. Beth looked at it and examined how it was rolled.

"That's odd, you would have thought that they would have rolled it tightly to keep it as small as possible, but this has been rolled loosely."

She looked at the middle, "Let's unroll it."

Billy picked it up and with a jerk sent the roll down the aisle unrolling as it went. When it ended with a puff of dust Beth shone her lamp along it as she moved down to the end.

"What's this?" she said, as she spotted a stain a yard from the end.

"Grease," Billy said. He rubbed his fingers over it and smelt them. "That's pig fat, the French use that for protecting iron goods that are shipped at sea."

"What's it doing on the inside of a roll of fabric? More to the point. Why do they need to import fabric into India? This is cotton. The locally-made stuff is cheaper and just as good."

"Maybe it was used to wrap something." Billy shrugged.

Beth looked at him with a broad grin. "Billy you are a genius. Quick, roll it back up. We will take it with us."

Billy had no idea what she was on about and set about rolling up the cloth. Meanwhile Beth moved to the front of the warehouse.

She froze when she heard a noise at the level of her head and just to her right. She slowly swung the lamp around and found herself almost nose to nose with a large brown rat perched on the top of the stack of goods she was stood beside.

She sucked in a breath and just managed to stifle the scream that was building in her chest. The rat looked at her curiously before scuttling off. Her heart was pounding fit to burst. She took several deep breaths to steady herself.

There was a stack of long crates on the loading ramp. Beth counted them and tried to move one. It was too heavy. She examined a crate carefully and saw that the lid had been nailed down.

"Can you get this open so we can close it again?" she said.

"It will take time," Billy said, "but then we aren't going anywhere." He pulled a crowbar out of his shoulder bag and, after looking around, tore a length of cloth off the bolt. He checked around the entire lid before choosing a spot to insert the bar. He didn't lever it so much as twist it to open a gap. Then he pushed cloth between the bar and the side of the crate and gently levered. Nails gave with a squeak. He moved the bar along the crate and did the same thing again repeating the operation all the way around the lid. Once he had the lid raised a half an inch all around, he wrapped the bar in cloth and handed it to Beth. Pulling out a second bar and wrapping it he said, "You take the opposite side to me and lever when I do."

They moved in parallel down the crate, lifting the lid as squarely as possible and not bending the nails. Once they were done Billy grabbed the lid and pulled it up and open.

"Well, well, well!" Beth said.

Inside was a pile of muskets that had been just stacked on top of each other. She lifted one out. It was coated in pig fat.

"Daddy will want to see this."

The lid was replaced on the crate and carefully hammered shut. A thorough inspection convinced Beth that no one would know it had been opened. She led them to the back door.

Billy had to force the door shut and apply his weight so that Beth could relock it. In the time it had been opened it had warped even more. They had just wrestled it shut when Sam appeared as if out of nowhere.

"You move quietly," Beth said.

"With all the noise you two was makin' I could have brought up an army," he said, rolling eyes that shone white in his black face.

"Bloody doors warped. Here you can carry this," Billy said and handed him the musket.

The trip back home was uneventful, and they were greeted at the gate by a marine guard who let out a piercing whistle as soon as he saw them. Adam met them at the door and led them to the drawing room where Marty and Caroline were waiting.

"Oh! How nice you waited up for me," said Beth with only the slightest hint of sarcasm.

"I was interested to see what you found," Marty said, ignoring it completely.

"This," Beth said and handed over the cloth, "and this." She took the gun from Sam and handed it to Marty.

"Well now," Marty said as he examined the gun and checked the action. "French army issue model 1777. They made millions of them and had warehouses full left unused at the end of the war."

He handed it back to Sam, "Don't clean it, just wrap it in brown waxed paper."

Sam nodded and left the room.

"Now what is this?" Marty said, looking at the cloth.

"I think that is how they smuggled the guns in. There are grease stains on the inside of the roll," Beth said.

Marty checked it over then handed it to Billy.

"Wrap this in brown paper and tie it up snuggly. I want it preserved just as it is."

Billy took it and left.

"There were twenty crates."

"That's a lot of guns," Caroline said.

"Anything else?" Marty said.

"I heard them say they were shipping the guns out tomorrow."

"Did they say where to?"

"No, but they are worried about you."

After a few hours' sleep, Beth emerged yawning in time for lunch. She had an idea about the consul's son but needed some information before she moved. Her father was in his office, so she rode her pony to the fort with Chin as escort.

The nice concierge showed her to Marty's office, and she greeted Adam when she stepped into the outer office, "Hello Adam, is Daddy in?"

"Yes, he is Miss Beth, he's in a meeting with Captain Ackermann."

Just then Justine came out of the office with a note for Adam.

"Hello," Beth said a steely look on her face. She had heard about Justine and didn't approve.

"You must be Bethany," Justine said. "His Lordship, mentioned you might be calling." She turned to Adam, "Can you get that to Captain Howarth as soon as possible please."

Adam took it and went to the door where he called a messenger.

"Sorry, that was important. I am Justine, your father's secretary." She held out her hand and Beth took it stiffly. "I met your mother the other day. You look like her."

"Mother knows?" Beth started to say, then blushed.

"Oh yes, it was Uncle Francis' idea and she and Auntie Flora are happy about it."

"Uncle Francis? Francis Ridgley?" Beth said.

"Oh, no," Justine said, "Uncle Francis is the governor general, Francis Hastings."

Wolfgang came out of the office and swept Beth up in a hug.

"Beth, you look wonderful," he said.

"Thank you, Uncle Wolfgang." Beth still called him that even though she was almost seventeen now.

"If you are here to see your father, he is free now."

"Come on, I'll take you in," Justine said.

"I need some information about the French consul's son," Beth said.

"Like what?" Marty replied.

"His name, where he goes and who his friends are."

"No idea," Marty said and looked across at Justine who was sat at her desk.

"His name is Ghislain, but his friends call him Ghi. He is eighteen. I know that because I was at his birthday party last month. His father is Jean-Claude Blanchette. Mother Annemarie. As for where he goes, that's easier to show you rather than tell," Justine said.

"That would be good," Beth said, softening towards her.

"In fact, there is a party tomorrow night. The daughter of one of the Dutch traders is celebrating her engagement to a lieutenant in the Indian Army. Do you want to come?"

"I don't have an invite."

"Tush, that doesn't matter. It's not a formal ball."

Beth looked to Marty who nodded and said, "You have your mission, do what you think you need to."

"Mission?" Justine said when she was walking her back to the entrance. "Are you a spy as well?"

"I'm learning," Beth said, uncomfortable with talking about it.

"Ooh, how exciting! I shan't breathe a word of course, but if you need any help—"

"I will let you know," Beth finished for her with a smile.

The next morning after breakfast Beth was considering which dress she would wear for the party. She wanted to make an impression but not appear flashy. It would have to be something that set off her hair and made the most of her light complexion. She had taken care not to get sunburn on the voyage over and since she got here.

A knock on the door and her mother stuck her head into the room.

"That's what I thought you would be doing," she said and stepped inside. "What weapons will you be carrying?"

Beth was surprised, she didn't expect her mother to be asking that. It was a daddy question.

"A small pistol in my clutch bag, and maybe a knife," she said.

"This may suit," Caroline said and held out a garter with a slender dagger in a sheath attached. "I wear a similar one all the time."

"How do you get to it? I can't pull up my dress if I'm attacked."

"That's easy, you have a hidden slot in your skirts, about there."

Caroline said, "Mary is a dab hand at making them."

On cue, Mary stepped into the room with her sewing bag.

Beth took off her dress and allowed her mother to tie the garter into place then Mary asked her to put on the dress she had chosen for the party.

"The slot is like a concealed pocket," Mary explained as she worked out the best position for it. "Are you comfortable with the position of the garter?"

"It could be a little higher," Beth said and lifted her skirts to adjust it.

"You will be wearing silk stockings?" Caroline asked.

"Of course, it would be indecent to go out without them."

"It's time you started wearing over the knee ones, you can have a pair of my new ones, they are a lovely ivory colour."

Beth was pleased, her mother had just acknowledged she was a woman now. Once Mary had finished Caroline dismissed her and sat next to Beth on the bed.

"It's time I talked to you about sex," she said.

The next hour was the most embarrassing and revealing of Beth's life.

That evening Antton drove her to the party in the landau, picking up Justine on the way. Beth wore little jewellery except the headpiece given to her by Georgie. It looked like a golden net over the crown of her head leaving her hair free below it and contained cunningly disguised darts and lockpicks.

The party was in a big house on the outskirts of town in a

fashionable area with the traders and was just getting going when the girls arrived.

"Femke, this is Bethany Stockley," Justine introduced her to their hostess, "her father is the new Military Attaché."

"We were at the ball. It was the talk of the town. I saw you there," Femke gushed. In fact, she was so enthused over Beth's presence, she monopolised her for the next hour introducing her to everyone personally. When she finally slipped free, she circulated with the other teenagers slowly homing in on her quarry.

She made sure she was in his line of sight and looked confusedly at her dance card.

"Can I 'elp you?" he purred; his English sexily accented with French.

"Oh, that is very kind of you," she simpered in an empty-headed way, "I have smudged my dance card and have no idea who I am supposed to be dancing with."

"I would be 'appy to dance with you. Bethany is it not?"

"I am, I mean, yes that is my name." She made a show of thinking, "You are Gay?"

"Ghi, it is short for Ghislain," he smiled, then took her hand and led her to the dancefloor.

"Vous ettes Francaise?" she said as they twirled into a Waltz, a dance that was becoming popular, especially with the younger generations. He was a good dancer.

"Yes, I am. You speak French?"

"Yes, as well as some Spanish and Hindi."

"Hindi? Where did you learn that in England?" he said.

"I learnt it in Ceylon, my parents took me there."

"What did they do there?"

"Mummy trades in precious stones, they were buying up most of the island I think."

She didn't miss the avaricious look that passed across his face. It didn't take much effort to get him to ask her out.

"I will have to get Pappa's permission, but I am sure he will have no objection to me being in the company of the son of the French consul." He had boasted about his father's position, frequently, obviously trying to impress her.

"Just send a message to the consulate and I will come to your house to meet you."

Marty asked Beth to visit him in his study.

"I have translated the letter that Zeb transcribed," he said.

Beth sat in the chair by the window and Marty joined her.

"What does it say?"

"It is basically a commendation from King Joseph to Don Rodrigues for his work in tracking down and eliminating a partisan group."

"A collaborator then, no wonder they ended up over here."

"Yes," Marty said, "if he had stayed at home he would probably have been assassinated by now."

"No love for the Spanish king either."

"No, he has no motive to support the Marathas."

"That leaves us with the French consul. Do we know any more about him and his history?"

"A little. Jean-Claude Blanchette was a member of Napoleon's diplomatic corps, responsible for Tuscany. He lost that job when Napoleon went into exile on Alba and was recruited back into the diplomatic corps after Waterloo. He is not a royalist, very much a republican, but fiercely loyal to his country."

"Do you think he is operating under orders from Paris?"

"Ridgley doesn't think so. None of the intelligence from our agents and diplomatic staff there gives any hint that the French would try something like this."

"Are you doing anything about the shipment?"

"My, we are getting into the job," Marty teased.

Beth gave him a look which made him laugh so she crossed her eyes and poked her tongue out.

"The Silverthorn will intercept it when it's at sea. The report from the docks said it was flying a Swedish flag which we know is a nonsense. The Silverthorn will stop and search it on the excuse they are looking for an escaped criminal, if they find weapons then they will impound it."

"But it won't be coming back here," Beth guessed.

"You are getting good at this. No, it's not, they will escort it to Madras. There isn't a French presence there. Oh, before I forget, your brother has transferred to the Silverthorn. Midshipman Shephard has a very nasty attack of dysentery and is in the naval hospital."

"James will enjoy that."

"How did the party go?"

"I think I have Ghi interested. He is egotistical, very status driven and the fact that my daddy is rich, isn't lost on him."

"Just remember he is the mission."

"Oh, I won't, he is not the kind of boy I am interested in."

Marty couldn't resist, "Nothing like Sebastian then."

Beth's earlobes went pink, and a blush crept up her neck.

"If there is nothing else?" she snapped.

"No, you can go." Marty grinned.

She stopped at the door. "When do we expect any letters from Britain to arrive?"

Marty resisted the temptation to tease her further and said seriously, "Not for another couple of months even by Mail Packet. If they are sent by Company ship, four or five months."

Beth let Ghi know her father had given permission as long as she had one of their people with her. A chaperone was the norm, but Ghi didn't expect to find a muscular Basque in the form of Garai tagging along on his date.

Garai gave them space, always present but not intrusive.

"Where do you get your clothes?" Beth asked. "They are very smart but cut differently from what I have seen in Paris."

"They are made locally. A couple of tailors in the city specialise in European styles." Ghi steered them towards a booth which served sugar cane juice.

The vendor crushed the juice from sugar canes using, what looked like, a mangle. To that he added lime juice and ginger to create a refreshing drink. Ghi got them both a glass.

"This is safe to drink," he said and sipped his to prove it.

"It is lovely," she said.

She looked around the street and asked, "What is there to do here? Are there theatres, or music halls?"

"No, no none of that. The Indians have festivals which are fun to watch, but mostly the Europeans here entertain themselves. Father likes to hunt, and Mother attends gatherings held by the other wives." He glanced over to see if Garai was in hearing distance and said softly, "There are other entertainments if you are interested. The Indians play sports which are fun to watch, Polo, Kushti and Kabaddi. You can wager on the games."

"Wager? Does your father let you wager?"

"He doesn't know. Anyway, I am old enough to decide for myself."

You aren't twenty-one yet, she thought and realised this might be the leverage she needed. She looked enthusiastic and said, "Let's go to a game."

"What about your chaperone?"

"Garai won't tell, as long as I don't get into trouble. If it were Antton then, pfft, we wouldn't be able to. He's an absolute tartar."

Garai, who heard that, had to turn away to conceal his grin.

Ghi brightened and said, "There is a Kabaddi contest on Thursday. Do you want to go?"

"Kabaddi? What is that?" Marty asked when Beth reported.

"It's a team sport, a bit like tag. The Indians are crazy for it. The point is I think Ghi likes to gamble, and I want to put him in a position where he does it in front of me."

Marty considered what he would do and suggested, "It would make him more comfortable if you place a bet or two as well."

"I have only ever gambled on cards for pennies. I can play the innocent, let him guide me and even place the bets for me."

"Good, this sounds workable, just remember not to get too excited about the gambling as you are not allowed to do it outside of the mission."

"Spoilsport," she pouted.

"I will be going on a mission soon with most of the Shadows, I assume you want Garai to stay as your chaperone?"

"He will hate being left behind, but yes."

"Did you really call Antton a Tarter?" Marty grinned. Garai had told him when he reported.

"It was a spur of the moment thing, I wanted to put Ghi at ease with Garai."

"Well, it has gone down a storm with the boys. He is getting all sorts of ribbing."

"Oh dear, do I need to apologise to him?"

"No, he's a big boy and can take it."

Marty opened the drawer on his desk and took out a pouch which he emptied on the desk. He sorted out several silver Angelinas, copper Cupperoons, and two gold Carolinas which he put in the pouch.

"Here, your stake money. I want back what is left," he said and tossed her the pouch.

Kabaddi was played on a court that was about forty-five feet by thirty-five. There were fourteen players per side seven of whom could be on the pitch when the team were defending. To Beth it looked chaotic as one player from a team faced the other team who linked hands and tried to capture him before he could tag one of them. It was high energy and they moved fast. There was a raucous crowd of supporters and several shady-looking characters who looked to be taking bets.

Ghi asked someone about who was playing and immediately went and placed a bet. Beth watched for a while, noting the tactics, and trying to understand the game. She noticed that while there were seven players of the defending team on the court there were another half dozen waiting on the side. She soon saw why, as one man was carried off after being knocked unconscious.

"Garai, will you get me one of those flavoured sugar drinks."

Garai nodded and wandered off in the direction of the food sellers.

"Quick, while he is gone, place a bet for me on the defending team," she said to Ghi.

"You have money?" he said incredulously.

"Don't French women?" she replied and handed him an Angelina.

She saw his eyes widen at the glint of gold in her purse which she left open just long enough for him to get a glimpse. He scuttled off to do her bidding and got back before Garai who was carefully pacing himself to give Ghi time.

"I backed the other team," he said.

"Oh," she said all wide eyed, "did I do it wrong?"

He laughed and reassured her that there was no wrong way.

The game progressed. A player from the attacking team, called a raider, had to cross into the other team's half of the pitch and tag as many players as he could in a single breath without getting tackled. To show everyone it was a single breath he had to continuously chant 'Kabaddi'. At the end of his attack, he retreated behind the halfway line to safety.

Beth's team won by the scant margin of two points. Ghi collected her winnings for her. She pretended to be excited and asked him to bet on the next game.

They both won, bet on the third and lost. There was one game to go.

"Let's put it all on the last one!" Beth said, her face flushed with excitement.

"One last fling?" Ghi laughed.

Beth chose her team and gave him all the money she had bet so far and her winnings. He placed her bet then, after a moment arguing with himself, bet all his money on the other one.

The game started and after the first half was all square. In the second half, Ghi's team took a five-point lead. The seventh raider on Beth's team came out. There was just a minute to go.

The raider stalked the centreline.

The defenders paced him.

A shout from the side warned him he had forty seconds left.

"KABADDI, KABADDI, KABADDI, KABADDI," he shouted and launched himself at the defender's chain.

"He scores how many?" Marty said in surprise as he counted Beth's winnings.

"Six, in thirty seconds to win the game by a point."

"Must have been exciting."

"It was, but more important Ghi is now hooked."

"He lost everything?"

"Yes, he is not very good at gambling. He doesn't look at the teams and, as he doesn't speak Hindi, can't get any hints from the other spectators."

"Interesting," Marty said and picked up a local paper.

"Did you know there will be a horse racing meet at the Calcutta course in a week's time?"

"Really?" Beth said and gave Marty a conspiratorial look.

They made the races a family day out, it was a Saturday and almost the entire expatriate community attended as it was a major social event. The women dressed up, wearing new hats of the latest fashion, and carried parasols. The men dressed formally in long-tailed suits and top hats. Champaign was the drink of the day and dainty delicacies were served by servants in splendid uniforms.

The horses were all bloods, imported from Europe or Arabia, from stables owned by either rich British or Indian individuals or syndicates. Each had their own colours. The jockeys Indians, predominantly Sikhs. There were two courses to enable chase and flat racing.

The weather was glorious, the sun glinted off the jewellery worn by the women. The scent of wisteria drifted on the air from the arbour in front of the member's pavilion. Servants circulated as the women chatted and socialised. The men stood together discussing the relative merits of the different mounts circulating in the parade ring. Beth, looking stunning in a pale-yellow dress and a broad-brimmed hat with a yellow ribbon and golden pheasant tail feathers. She found Ghi and conspiratorially said, "All the men are placing bets. Can we?"

"I can place them for you if you have money. But I have a problem. My father has cut my allowance. I only have this."

He held up a gold louis.

"Oh my, that is worth about four pounds! They will never exchange it." She was right. Some bets were large, but none were that big with the bookies. Anything over an Angelina would cause raised eyebrows.

Ghi was crestfallen, and Beth put a hand on his arm in sympathy,

"I could exchange it for you."

He looked at her sceptically,

"You have that much in your purse?"

"No," she admitted, "but, I could cover half of it now and the rest next time we meet."

He looked at the horses being lead around the parade ring. "I can get odds of five to one on the Maharaja's horse," Beth heard him mutter and she could see beads of sweat on his upper lip.

Beth didn't like that horse, it was fidgety and flighty, she had watched them walk around the parade ring and one had caught her eye. It was a gelding, sixteen, and a bit, hands, with a fine Arabian head, a deep chest, and powerful hindquarters. It walked calmly around the ring and didn't sweat up like the Maharaja's horse, which was nervously tossing its head and skittering around against its headcollar. The chase would be over a mile and four furlongs with eight jumps. So, stamina would be an issue.

"I'll do it. Half a louis will fund me for the day," Ghi suddenly said, breaking her reverie.

Beth opened the bag she had slung on her wrist and, being careful not to reveal the pistol, retrieved her purse.

"There you are, a Carolina, three Angelinas and ten cupperons," Beth said and took the louis in exchange.

She glanced around then lent in and kissed him on the cheek,

"And you didn't have to pay an exchange fee. Yet." The look she gave him was full of promise.

He gulped and made his way to the bookie furthest away from the pavilion.

Beth looked at the louis and flipped it. It came down tails.

"Tails you lose," she murmured.

The day was both fun and productive as far as Beth was concerned, Ghi was in her debt, becoming enamoured with her and she had come away with a small profit.

Chapter 19: Gun Running

James was looking forward to serving on the Silverthorn. As the only mid on the ship, he would be effectively second in command to Lieutenant Howarth, Master and Commander. He was approaching the gangplank to his new home along the dock and desperate to make a good impression.

He brought two men with him. Joseph Langley and Eric Haggler. Both were gunners and prodigious fighters that had latched onto James as followers. Joseph doubled as his steward and Eric would at some time be his cox.

He stepped onto the deck and saluted the quarterdeck. "Permission to come aboard, Sir."

"Permission granted, Mr Stockley. Welcome aboard."

James looked forward, admiring the sleek lines of the schooner, then up to the top of the mainmast.

"It's a pleasure to be here, she sails like a witch from what I've seen of her."

Terrance Howarth was unaffected by the praise as it was, in his mind, just a statement of fact. Not that he wasn't proud of his ship, she could keep up with one of the commodore's fast clippers in the right conditions, but he was a pragmatic man.

"Have your men stow your gear. We will sail directly."

"Aye, aye, Sir."

The French ship flying a Swedish flag had left that morning and had a three-hour head start. That was deliberate, they did not want the

French consul to be able to stop her if he spotted them following and for her to be in international waters when they exited the river.

James had no time to settle in, he had to land running.

"Warp us away from the dock Mr Stockley."

James called the orders, his voice warbling between tenor and alto. He was going through that major change in his life that all boys go through and had hair growing on his chest and face not to mention his groin. Unlike his father who had only his ship's daddy to ask, James had been visited several times by Marty who had taken the opportunity to tell him what to expect as they had walked together.

The Silverthorn drifted away from the dock under the pressure of the cables, hauling on a pair of anchored buoys set in the river for just this. As soon as they were sufficiently clear of the dock, he ordered the cables to be brought in and stowed, the boats to be tied astern.

All this time Trevor Howarth watched and evaluated. He completely ignored the fact that James was the commodore's son and judged him on his own merits. He was pleased and liked what he saw. *Got his father's way with the men,* he thought as he watched James chivey a landsman into position. The man was touched, as they say, and had trouble learning anything. He had been taken on because he was the brother of one of his best topmen rather than be condemned to live his life in a bedlam. His lack of intelligence was made up for by prodigious strength which, when directed properly, was a huge benefit to the ship.

Without being told, James ordered the jib and main topsail set to take them down river. The pilot was already aboard and called, "Steerage way!" As soon as they were moving fast enough for the rudder to bite.

"Please be so kind as to set more sail, Captain, we need a bit more speed," the pilot said.

"Mr Stockley! Set the Foresail if you will."

"Aye Sir."

"Come on, lads, latch on and heave away," he said then turned to check on his main muscle. "Here, Dennis, latch on to this un with the rest of the lads." Dennis grinned at him as he got a hold of the rope. He liked James. He was nicer to him than the other one had been and showed him what he wanted done rather than yelled at him.

The sail shot up, the fore gaff rattling as its rings slid up the mast. James' only concern was that they didn't jam.

"Nicely done, lads," he said as they belayed the ropes after trimming it. "Now get those ends coiled Bristol fashion."

He reported to the quarterdeck.

"Nicely done, Mr Stockley, I see Captain Campbell has schooled you well."

"Thank you, Sir. He is most particular that his young gentlemen perform well."

"Yes, I have first-hand experience myself. Now you may stand down and get your things in order. I will take the watch from here."

James went below after watching the shore slip by for a moment as they were passing Fort William. He caught a flash of light from a window then saw seven clear flashes, a gap then three more. The captain stepped up behind him.

"Your father, seven over three," he said.

"God's speed, in the squadron's code," James said a lump in his throat.

"Indeed." Howarth turned away to give James some space.

James took off his hat and waved at the fort. He got a pair of flashes in reply.

Unpacked and settled in by the time the Silverthorn reached the estuary, James was ready to go. The captain handed over the ship to him and went below.

Their assumption was that if the arms were being delivered to Maratha the ship would head for the nearest access point to their empire which was the river Mahanadi. They needed to catch them before they entered.

"Make all sail," he ordered, this was the fun part.

The Silverthorn heeled over as the power of the wind filled her sails and James could hear the thrum of the rigging and swoosh of water running down the hull. His legs automatically adapted to the heel and motion of the ship. He had no need to hold on and moved easily across the deck.

"Fourteen knots and a fathom," the log man called.

"That's the way to do it," he grinned to himself.

He did a calculation in his head. Their prey was three hours ahead and probably making eight to ten knots. If he assumed ten, then they were making four knots on them. In three hours, the prey would cover thirty knots or thirty-seven and a half miles. If they were making four knots or five miles an hour on them then or would take seven and a half hours to catch them. It was one hundred and thirty miles between the two estuaries which gave them around ten and a half hours before the prey entered the Mahanadi River.

Three hours buffer, that's not enough, he thought.

He looked at the sails and the way the ship was progressing.

"Mr Saville, do you think she is driving down a little?" he asked the master.

"Aye, the pressure of the sails is causing the bow to dig in a bit."

"All hands not engaged with sail handling move to the windward side at the stern," he ordered.

It was a tad crowded but with all hands sat in the windward rear quarter the schooner sailed a little more levelly and the bow lifted.

"Fifteen knots and a fathom," reported the log man.

"Now we can catch them in six and a half hours," James said, to himself.

"Sir?" the helmsman said.

"Nothing, was just thinking we will catch them in six and a half hours."

"Middle of the captain's watch then."

James hadn't thought of that, he had imagined the glory of catching the prey on his watch.

The captain came up on time to take his watch, James made his report.

"Fifteen knots, Sir, we should catch then in the next three hours."

"The extra weight on the port quarter has gained us some speed?"

"An extra knot, Sir."

"How much time do we have before they make the river?"

"About six hours, Sir."

"Sail Ho!" the foremast lookout called.

"Where away?" the captain called back.

"Half a point off the port bow."

"Take a glass and go and have a look, James. See if you can identify them."

James! I must be doing alright, James thought as he grabbed a glass from the rack and slung it over his shoulder by its strap. The rigging on a schooner was vastly different from a frigate. Two masted, she only had a pair of square sales at top and royal on the foremast which was as high as the main. He made his way up to the royal yard and made himself comfortable. He looked down, with the heel on the ship he was hanging over the water.

He scanned the horizon with the naked eye, then lifted the glass after pulling out the focus to where he guessed it would suit his eye. He made a mental note to mark his focus point on all the glasses if he would be staying on the Silverthorn.

The focus was close, and he made a minor adjustment, so the horizon was sharp before making a scan. It was clear except for the sail. It was a single ship and he watched it for several minutes as it gradually got closer. He amused himself by working out that the target must be about ten miles away.

"Two hours," he muttered.

"Can you identify it?" the captain called.

He took another long look, and a gust of wind swung their flag around.

"Swedish flag, Sir," he called down.

"Come down."

He lowered himself hand over hand down a stay and landed on the deck with a thump.

"We will go to quarters when we are four miles behind," the captain said, prompting James to fetch his sextant. It was a particularly fine model his father had gifted him. "I will want a noon sighting for the log as well."

James took the angle to the target's masthead. He knew the height of their mast and could calculate using:

Distance = the height/the tangent of the angle

He had memorised his tables at college so only needed a slate to work it out and by taking a sighting every ten minutes calculated the closing speed accurately.

"We should go to quarters in twenty minutes, Sir," he said to the captain once he was sure.

"Very well, I want the guns loaded with chain and grape. If they refuse to stop then we will take down their rigging. Do not run out until I give the command."

The noon sighting was taken ten minutes later by both James and the master. They agreed. "We are at twenty degrees eighty-four minutes by eight-seven degrees fifty-two minutes," the master said.

"Note that in the log please as the position we went to quarters," the captain said. "Make it so, James."

James used his speaking trumpet to call the ship to quarters, the men were ready, and James realised Dennis was standing watching him expectantly. His followers had integrated into the gun teams which had put Dennis at a loose end.

Marty looked over to the captain who had also seen Dennis. He winked and looked away.

I'll be damned if he isn't leaving Dennis to me! James thought.

They came up to a half mile of the target which James could see was named the Faro. The name looked awfully new compared to the rest of the ship and he realised it was painted on a board which had been hurriedly attached to the stern.

"Not a very good job of disguise, is it?" the captain said, and before James could comment followed with, "A shot across their bow as soon as we are alongside."

They were passing a half cable off her starboard side sacrificing the wind gauge for the extra elevation their heel gave them. James looked at their quarterdeck and could see the captain stood by the wheel looking back at him.

"Dennis, how loud can you shout?" James said.

"Dennis shout loud, like a lion John say."

"After the cannon fires, I want you to shout at that ship, I want you to use the trumpet and to shout, 'Heave to, prepare to be inspected!' Can you do that?"

"Heave to, prepare to be ….?"

"Heave to, prepare to be inspected."

"Heave to, prepare to be inspec-ted."

"That's it."

James took him with him to the forward most gun.

"Send it in front of their beakhead at deck height," he said to the gun captain.

Their bow came up alongside the Faro's.

"Fire when ready," James said.

KABOOM! The gun fired, it was an eighteen-pound carronade and sent its mixed load howling across their bow.

"Now, Dennis."

"HEAVE TO. PREPARE TO BE INSPECTED!" he bellowed through the trumpet.

"Lor', they can 'ear that in Greenwich," a wag said, causing a laugh to ripple around the deck.

James made his way back to the quarterdeck.

"Their captain replied with an obscene gesture," the captain said grimly.

"He heard then," James said with a sardonic smile.

"Run out the guns,"

That didn't impress the Faro's captain either.

"Warn him we will bring down his rigging if he doesn't comply."

James was about to shout that across himself when Dennis moved to the side, shook his fist at the Faro and bellowed, "Drop sails, or we shoot them."

James and Trevor exchanged a look and burst out laughing. Dennis looked hurt but James reassured him, "I couldn't have put it better myself."

"Take down their rigging, Mr Stockley," the captain shouted.

The Faro had no choice but submit to being boarded after her rigging was shredded by the Silverthorn's battery.

James was given command of the boarding party and found himself bracketed by Joseph and Eric with Dennis towering over him from behind.

"Midshipman Stockley, His Majesty's ship Silverthorn. I wish to see your papers."

"You have no right to stop us like this. We are a Swedish ship."

"We have every right; we are looking for an escaped criminal that was reported boarding this ship before it departed. We have been in continuous pursuit from Calcutta. Now please show me your papers."

"No."

James was about to make a final demand when Dennis brushed past him, grabbed the captain by the lapels and lifted him off the deck so they were face to face.

"If Mr Stockley wants see your papers you must show him," he said.

James coughed to hide a laugh and stepped up beside them, looking up at the captain whose head was a foot above his.

"Will you show me your papers?"

The captain managed a nod.

"Put him down, Dennis."

Dennis lowered him gently to the deck and smoothed his crumpled lapels.

"Lead on," he said to the captain and then to Dennis, "stay here and keep an eye on their crew. If any make any trouble throw them over the side." He repeated that in French loudly, so the crew heard.

In the captain's cabin he kept his pistol in hand in case the man tried something.

"This is the worst forgery I have ever seen," he said in French as he examined the papers, which were amateurishly done at best.

He noted that the captain reacted.

"You speak French don't you." It wasn't a question.

"Show me your real papers."

The captain didn't move.

"Sit over there. Joseph, keep him covered."

Joseph pulled his pistol, cocked it and pointed it at the captain's head. James laid his pistol on the desk and set about searching. He found no papers. He glanced at the captain who had a smug look on his face. *This English prick is just a boy,* he was thinking.

He has papers, but they are hidden, James thought. He ran his hands along the desktop and under the lip. Finding nothing, he pulled out the drawers and checked inside the desk and under the bottoms.

Nothing.

He sat back in the chair and scanned the cabin as his father had taught him. His eyes relaxed, not looking for anything in particular.

There! Something caught his eye.

He stood and stepped over to the corner of the cabin where the canvas deck covering was curled up at the corner. He knelt and pulled it back.

"You have the key?" he asked the captain as he examined the lock on the strongbox set into the deck.

The captain maintained his silence.

"You want me to search him?" Joseph said.

"No, this won't take a moment," James said and took out his lock picks.

"Aah, there we go. The ship is Le Monge, registered in Marseilles. Owned by a Mr Tresbonnes, fake name if I ever heard one. Captain Gerald Orleans. No manifest."

He folded the papers with the fakes and placed them inside his jacket.

"Gerald Orleans you are under arrest. Take him topside."

With the captain out of the way, he went through the rest of the strong box. He found a sealed letter, the seal was blank, addressed to Peshwa Baji Rao. He was familiar with that name; his father had mentioned it in a tale about their time in India when he was born. He left it alone and added it to the other papers

Back on deck he had the crew locked in the cable tier and instigated a search of the cargo. It wasn't long before a crate was brought up.

"This is the type of crate you said to look out for, Sir," the master at arms said.

James noted that it took three burley seamen to get the crate up on deck.

"Where was it?"

"Forward hold, under a pile of general goods. There are ten including this one in there."

"Any others anywhere else?"

"Not found any yet, Sir."

"Keep looking, there should be another ten somewhere." James looked for Dennis. He was stood five feet away just behind his left shoulder.

"Dennis, be a good chap and open this for me," he said.

Dennis lumbered forward picking up a jackstaff from beside a gun. He jammed the chisel end of the staff between the lid and the side and heaved. The inevitable result of such irresistible pressure was the crate disintegrated. Muskets slid across the deck.

"Guilty as charged," James said.

"Only ten crates?" Howarth said when James reported.

"Yes, Sir. That is all we found, and we about took the ship apart."

"Damn, the intelligence from your father says there were twenty."

"May I make a suggestion, Sir?"

"Go ahead."

"Send the Monge to Madras with a prize crew and we go to Calcutta and talk with my father or at least find out if any other ships left at the same time as this one. They obviously split the shipment to protect themselves against just such an occurrence as this," James said.

"That was what I had in mind. Normally I would send you with the prize, but I think a master's mate will suffice. Detail Vic Pedrick to command it, with orders to have the French crew held indefinitely once they reach Madras. The Company has a prison there."

"How many for the prize crew?"

"Eight hands and two marines. Select men who can do a bit of everything."

"Just like a civilian crew."

"Exactly."

"Can I question the captain before we send them off?" James said.

"Better to do that on the way back. Transfer him over, it will reduce the risk of any attempt to regain control of the ship as well."

James had some ideas on interrogation from the stories that the Shadows had told him when he was growing up of the methods they used. He had Orleans hooded, then squat with his arms held out in front of him against the hull, his weight on the balls of his feet. He ordered Dennis to watch him and knew he could rely on him to not let the man move an inch.

After three hours, at the end of his watch he went to him and let Dennis stand down. Dennis rushed to the leeward side and peed as if he would never stop. The golden stream arching out into the sea.

James made a mental note to make sure he relieved Dennis earlier next time. Then chuckled at the pun.

"Who is that? Please can I move? I am in pain," Orleans groaned.

James leaned close and said quietly, "Where is the other half of the shipment?"

"Please, I do not know."

"Who is your boss?"

He groaned.

"What was your destination?"

"I…"

"You can stay there until your legs cease to work permanently," James stood and turned to leave. The ship hit a bigger than usual wave and Orleans groaned as the roll forced his weight to press on his arms and the balls of his feet.

James turned and said in as flat a voice as he could manage, "The sea is getting up, it's only going to get worse."

The Silverthorn moored directly outside of Fort William which indicated something was afoot. Trevor and James left the ship and went straight to Government House.

"We wish to see the Defence Attaché, Lord Stockley," Trevor said.

"Who are you?" the concierge said. There was something familiar about the younger of the two.

"I'm his son," James said, "and this is Captain Howarth, we need to see him urgently."

"Oh my, I am very sorry, Sahib, but your father left an hour ago."

"Can you get us a carriage?"

A carriage pulled up moments later, several were on standby for use by the people in Government House, and James ordered it to the family home.

"I just hope he hasn't gone off on a mission of his own," James said.

"Then we will defer to Captain Ackermann," Trevor said.

When they got there, they found Marty and the Shadows about to leave. Marty walked over and embraced his son.

"James, Trevor, what are you doing here?"

Trevor explained and Marty frowned. When he had finished Marty said, "Come inside."

"Please ask Miss Bethany to join us in the study," Marty said to a servant as they made their way to his study.

Beth joined a moment after they got there. Trevor's eyes popped when he saw her. James noticed and grinned, his sister had grown up while he had been away and could turn any man's head. Marty, however, was all business.

"It sounds like they split the shipment of guns into at least two parts. Beth, I want you and Garai to see if you can find anything in the consulate tonight. Look for any details like ships' names, appointments with ships' captains, anything that can give us a lead here."

He turned to James, "Did you find out anything else?"

"I persuaded the captain of the French ship to confirm that the consul was his boss. He doesn't know who the real owner is as he's never met him. They were to deliver the goods to a contact in Sonepur."

"Excellent, what did you use to make him talk?" Marty asked, his curiosity getting the better of him.

"The squat, stress position that John told me about."

"He did, did he?" Marty said and a sad look passed across his face as he thought of his friend. He shook himself and brought himself back to the present.

"Keep him on the Silverthorn, see if he lets anything else slip."

He wrote a note, "This is for Frances Ridgley, take it to him. It instructs him to give you all assistance."

He looked at his daughter who had an excited look, "If you find they have done anything other than sent the guns by sea, try and get a message to me. Your mother knows where I will be."

Chapter 20: Pursuit

Marty and the Shadows embarked on the Pride of Purbeck, destination Bombay. From there they planned to head for Nashik to find the artillery specialist and eliminate him. Beth and Garai had their mission to infiltrate the French consulate again and would do that late that night.

James and Trevor headed back to Government House and found Francis Ridgley in his office.

"Gentlemen, what can I do for you?" Francis said, as they walked in.

James handed him the note from Marty and said, "Only half the shipment was on the ship we stopped, we want to try and stop the rest. Can you help us?"

"More specifically," Trevor said, "we are interested if any other ships left at the same time and where they were going."

"That's odd," Francis said, as he tossed Marty's note onto the burner of the samovar, "I had men watching the warehouse and they definitely loaded all twenty cases onto that ship."

Trevor was deep in thought, "We did catch them up quicker than we expected by, what, an hour? That means they could have transferred half the crates to another ship at sea."

"If they did, we have no hope of finding it."

"Well, we know a man who was there," James said grimly.

Frances looked at them quizzically.

"We have the captain on the Silverthorn," Trevor said.

Francis jumped to his feet, "Why didn't you say so! Come on we have work to do."

If Orleans thought that he had been treated harshly by James, he would think the devil himself had arrived when Frances got started.

"I want a plank, two trestles, rope or cord for binding, a towel or cloth of similar material and several buckets of water," he said as he got on deck. "Oh and get us to sea as soon as you can."

Trevor looked at James and raised his eyebrows. James shrugged in return and shouted the orders to get them out into the river and away.

"Who the devil is that?" Frances asked when he saw Dennis stood near to James.

"That be Dennis, he's not right in the 'ead," Joseph, who had been detailed to help him, said, "but Mr Stockley seems to have a knack with him."

"Really?"

"Aye and Dennis has latched onto him. He's likely to rip the arms off anybody who touches young Jim the wrong way."

Frances could believe it, the man was huge!

"Put the plank on the trestles there, when we clear the estuary bring the Frenchman up and tie him to it. Line up the buckets full of water along there. Make the cloth wet before we start. When I nod you stretch the cloth over his mouth and nose and hold his head steady."

They left the river and sailed out into the Bay of Bengal. Orleans was brought up by two marines and bound to the plank.

Frances stood over him then lent down so his mouth was by his ear, "Up to now you have been interrogated by officers and gentlemen. I am neither an officer or a gentleman and have no limits on how far I will go to get what I want. First, I will demonstrate what I am going to be doing to you if you don't answer my questions satisfactorily."

He stood up and nodded. Eric stretched the cloth tight over his face, holding it tight against the sides of his head to stop it turning. Frances picked up a bucket of water and poured it in a steady stream over the cloth directly over his mouth and nose.

He stopped. Orleans was choking, coughing up water and distressed.

"See how uncomfortable life will become?" Frances said, as if this happened every day. "I have an ocean of water to play with and the treatment gets longer every time I have to do it."

James watched and listened; this was chilling. He heard Francis say, "Now. Where will the guns be delivered?"

"Fuck you!" an angry Orleans spat.

Francis didn't hesitate. He nodded to the boys and the cloth was applied. Water was poured. First one bucket then another.

A half-drowned man was asked the question again.

"Sonepur," Orleans coughed.

"When did you transfer the other ten crates to another ship."

"After we were out of sight of land."

"What was the ship and where is it going?"

He didn't answer.

Francis nodded and the cloth was replaced.

"NO! NO! I'll tell you!" his muffled voice screamed. "They are on the Mermaid and she's going to Serat."

The three men sat in Trevor's cabin and shared a glass of port.

"What will you do now?" Francis asked.

"We will return to Calcutta and speak to Captain Ackermann with the intent of leading the fast ships in the squadron in pursuit of the Mermaid."

"Good and we should be able to get Beth's report on her exploration of the consulate."

"You know about that?" James blurted.

"It was in your father's note."

"Oh." James was disappointed that it wasn't some spy trick or something.

About the same time, Beth was getting ready to start her mission. "Knives?" Caroline asked.

"Two stilettos, punch knife," Beth answered.

"Where? Justine asked. She had gone from being scandalised by Beth's skin-tight outfit to being fascinated by the whole affair.

"Stilettos are in arm sheaths and the punch knife on the back of her belt."

Caroline said. "Darts?"

"Right-hand pouch, six darts coated in curare."

"Lockpicks?"

"One set in the left pouch another in my plait."

"Slim jim?"

"In its sheath on my thigh."

"How are the new boots?"

"Very comfortable, the softest leather and chamois soles."

"Why chamois soles?" Justine asked.

"Quiet and excellent grip."

"Is Garai ready?" Caroline asked.

"He is always ready," Beth grinned. "Although, he is a bit miffed at being left behind."

"Chin would have been more suitable for this," Caroline said.

"But not for the other part mother," Beth replied.

Caroline drove the coach with Justine beside her on the driver's seat. Justine carried a rifle but if anything happened Caroline would be the one doing the shooting. Beth and Garai were dropped off in the same place as before and took to the rooftops. Garai made the jump look easy and they were both on the roof of the consulate without being detected. It was two in the morning.

Beth opened the skylight and lowered herself through, Garai, close behind. She led the way to the third floor past the servant's bedrooms. Snores heralded their progress. On the second floor they identified the consul's bedroom and Ghi's from which she could hear feminine giggling.

"Really!" she huffed silently, "Some servant girl I expect." She couldn't help wondering what they were doing and blushed. Thankful for the dark and the hood that covered her head and face.

She opened the office and slipped inside. She locked it behind them and lit a lamp. They went through the office methodically then she opened the safe.

"That's new," she said after carefully looking through the contents. Under the jewellery was a notebook, and when she opened it she could see that it was written in code.

"We don't have time to decode it here, we will have to take it with us."

"Won't that give the game away?" Garai asked.

"It might but it's a risk we will have to take," she said.

They locked the safe and replaced the key in the secret drawer in the desk. Garai listened at the door after the extinguished the lamp. He held up his hand, light footsteps passed in the corridor. He waited, then nodded.

Beth unlocked the door and eased it open. They slipped out, shutting, and locking it behind them then made their way back towards the roof. They got to Ghi's door when it suddenly opened. "Wha?" Ghi got out before Beth chopped him across the throat with the edge of her hand cutting off the cry. She followed up with her shoulder hitting him in the chest and propelling him backwards onto the bed. She ended up astride him, the point of her punch knife almost pricking his eyeball.

"Do not move of make another sound," she whispered.

Ghi's eyes were already wide but widened further as he recognised her voice.

"Beth?"

"Oh damn," she sighed.

"I can kill you now, but that would be messy, so listen very carefully. I know you have been stealing from your father to fund your gambling, I also have the gold louis. Did you know your father had marked them?"

He didn't move as the point of the knife was a mere sixteenth of an inch from his eye. Beth carried on.

"If you say anything about seeing me tonight, I will tell him everything. Do you understand?" She pulled the knife back far enough for him to nod.

"Good."

She slid off him and as she silhouetted against the window, he gasped.

"Do you like it? It's all the rage in my circles," she whispered and did a pirouette. The knife was suddenly at his throat again,

"But do not get any ideas, keep your hands to yourself and your mouth shut."

No one will believe you anyway, she thought as they slipped away.

"Uff, Daddy would probably have this decoded in a trice," Beth complained after she and Caroline had spent a couple of hours trying to crack the code.

"I will send for Frances," Caroline said, giving up.

Ridgley took one look, demanded coffee, and got right down to it.

A second jug was supplied before he completed the task.

"We need to catch up with Martin," he said.

On the deck of the Silverthorn, Caroline hugged Beth and turned to James, "Look after your sister."

"Yes, Mother. Although she will probably end up looking after me as usual," James replied to the amusement of the hands stood within hearing.

They had received Wolfgang's blessing and had been joined by the Eagle, the Endellion still being out of commission. They would try and catch the Pride although, privately, James thought that was impossible given their head start and the speed she could maintain.

Ridgley had deemed what he had found in the journal important enough to join them.

"Our friend the consul, is a high-ranking member of the Parisian lodge of Masons who were, and still are, supporters of Napoleon. His loyalty is more to them than the French government who pay his salary."

Beth nodded. Satisfied she was paying attention he continued.

"They have backed the funding of mercenaries to aid the Maratha Empire in their resistance to British rule. Those mercenaries are specialists in artillery, infantry tactics and cavalry. They come with a cadre of experienced officers and warrants."

Beth suddenly saw where Frances was heading. "Daddy thinks he is going there to take out one man!"

"Exactly, we need to warn him. Ironically the guns are almost irrelevant in the larger scheme of things. Stopping them will hurt them about the same as a mosquito bite."

"What are we going to do with the consul?"

"Now we know what he is up to, and we have the evidence we can either turn him to work for us or expose his activities to the

French government.

"Ooh, Blackmail!" Beth grinned.

Frances shook his head. "The sooner we get you to the academy the better, young lady."

There was a knock on the door and James stuck his head through. "You might want to come on deck and see this."

Intrigued, they followed him up onto the deck.

The crew were lined up along the windward side and James moved a couple to make room for Beth and Frances.

"Oh, my lord!" she exclaimed as an enormous dark shape emerged from the deep blue sea. "Whoooooshh," it said as it blew a mist of spray from its blowhole. It arced down and a huge tail rose out of the water then slid below the surface.

"What was that?"

"A blue whale, the biggest any of the crew has seen."

Another back appeared and vented but this one stayed on the surface.

"Look! There's a small one beside it!" Beth said.

"Probably a mother with her calf," Trever Howarth said.

The whale turned so its eye was above the water, Beth felt as if it was looking right into her soul.

"It looks so gentle," Beth said.

"They are unless you threaten them. The whalers will only take them if they haven't found any Right Whales," Trevor said.

He was very attentive to Beth who in turn was very aware of the effect she had on him. James watched them both with amusement.

Trevor had slowed the ships to enable Beth to see the whales and now ordered them to get back to the chase.

"James, I want our best speed we have fifteen minutes to make up," he said.

"Set all sail, waisters and off watch to the windward side."

They used every trick in the book to squeeze every last fathom of speed out of the ships they could, but James knew the Pride would have the measure of them. They entered Palks Passage between Ceylon and the mainland and sat down to dinner.

"You know the men call you 'our Jim' when they talk about you," Beth said.

"Do they?" James said, "I quite like the idea being called Jim,"

"Midshipman Stockley, on my ship you will be called Sir, or Mister Stockley," Trevor said with a completely straight face."

"Wreckage! Wreckage off the port bow," the call from the lookout filtered down through the open skylight.

Trevor was up and heading for the door before it had ended, James a step behind him.

"Well," Beth said to Ridgley, "that's not good.

"The captain needs a new chef," Francis said, "better food would make him much less impulsive."

"Yes, the soup was very average," Beth said. "Do you think the wreckage is of consequence?"

"It won't be the Pride, but it could be someone who got in their way."

"You have that much faith in my father?"

"Let's just say I have seen him come up trumps against

impossible odds, and that a few pirates would not even slow him down."

They finished the soup, and as the steward cleared he coughed, "Ahem."

"Yes?" Beth said.

"I am afraid that the next course will be delayed."

"What is it?"

"Beef rib, roast just nicely, from a beast that were killed just two days ago," the steward said.

"Delightful," Beth said.

"I like a bit of rare roast beef," Francis said.

Beth sighed, "I honestly think as a day-to-day meat I prefer chicken or pork but once in a while beef is nice if its cooked well."

The boys re-joined them,

"It was the remains of a Dow," Trevor said as he took his seat.

"By the damage it was hit by carronades." James said.

"Any survivors?" Beth said.

"No, the sharks made sure of that," James said as he helped himself to three slices of roast beef.

"Sharks?" Beth said.

James paused with a forkful halfway to his mouth, "Um, they take care of any pirates that are left over." He knew he was entering dangerous territory.

"Are you saying you leave men to the mercies of sharks?" Beth said in a dangerously quiet voice.

James looked at Trevor, imploring him to intervene. The look he got back said, "You're one your own."

Beth and James walked the deck under a full moon. "Do they really leave men to the sharks?" Beth said.

"If we rescue them, they will be hung anyway."

"At least that is quick."

James turned to her, "Hanging, navy fashion, is not clean and it's not quick. They can take up to thirty minutes to die."

"Oh, short rope?"

"Effectively, they are hauled up with the knot at the back."

"That's barbaric."

"It's the way it is."

They reached Bombay and moored next to the Pride. Beth and Francis went across and talked to the captain.

"He left two days ago with the Shadows for Nashik," Beth said when they came back.

"Two days? We are closer than I expected," Trevor Howarth said.

Beth said, "They ran into pirates who held them up for half a day while they sorted them out." She turned to Frances, "We need horses and a local guide."

"She's right, we need to move fast," Frances said.

"Hold on, you cannot follow father on your own," James said then immediately had the feeling he would regret saying it.

"I can spare you and ten marines," Trevor said.

"I would like to take Joseph and Eric," James said.

"You can, if you take Dennis as well," the captain said, "you are the only one he responds to."

James blew out his cheeks, the rewards for kindness were manifold.

Horses were procured and the sixteen set off following in the hoofprints of Marty and the Shadows.

Chapter 21: The Enemy

Marty and the boys arrived in Bombay, a day later than anticipated. They had been attacked while making slow headway on a misty morning between Ceylon and the Indian mainland. The winds had been exceptionally light and the pirates, if that is what they were, had swept down on them in two long boats under sweeps. They had almost succeeded in boarding the Pride over the bow and stern which were unprotected by their carronades. Only a determined defence by the crew, supported by accurate rifle fire from Marty and the Shadows, had saved the day.

But now they were in Bombay and needed to get to Nashik. Marty and Antton found a livery with animals for sale and procured eight saddle horses and four mules. They anticipated covering around twenty miles a day to preserve the horses so it would take six to seven days to get there.

The terrain was expected to be even until they passed through the mountains after Kasara before descending into a large valley. Marty wanted a guide so visited the garrison in the city.

"I would like to see the garrison commander," Marty said to the guard commander at the gate to the garrison.

"And who should I say is calling?" the lanky upper-class fop said, looking down his nose at the civilian in front of him.

"My card," Marty said and handed over a gilt-edged visiting card.

The words on the card seemed to burn their way into the fop's retinas. "My lord," he stuttered, "please come with me. Sergeant!

You have command until I return."

"Lead on, Lieutenant." Marty smiled.

"When did you arrive, Sir?" the lieutenant said, trying to recover some ground.

"This morning, Lieutenant…?"

"Oh sorry, Lieutenant Farmington-Upton, of the Chiswick Farmington-Uptons."

There are more than one? Marty thought with an internal smirk.

They approached a large red brick building that was at the heart of the garrison. Farmington-Upton led him into a cool foyer then up a large curving staircase into an office manned by an adjutant. Marty waited while his card was handed over and the adjutant, who was a captain, stood and bowed.

"Milord, if you would wait one moment for me to announce you, I am sure the major will see you directly." He disappeared through a set of double doors only to reappear within thirty seconds.

"My lord," he said and bowed him through the doors.

Inside was a large office decked out with surprisingly spartan furniture. High-backed chairs faced a plain dark wood desk which had neatly stacked piles of documents, a silver inkwell set in the form of a pair of tigers. On the walls a portrait of the king, a map of this part of India and a tiger's head. Behind his desk was a portrait of a striking woman.

"Major," Marty said and held out his hand, "Martin Stockley, acting Military attaché to the governor general."

"Major Thackery Willems, commanding officer Bombay division, how can I help you?"

"Major, I need to speak to you confidentially," Marty said and waited.

"Gentlemen," the major said, and the officers left the room, closing the doors behind them.

Once they were alone Marty helped himself to a chair and indicated the major should sit.

"You are aware General Hastings is intending to crush the Maratha Empire and bring them under our control?"

"Yes, we are expecting that and have been building up our training and manpower accordingly."

"Did you know the Maratha army is being assisted by foreign nationals? Specifically, artillery specialists?"

"No, although we had noticed a significant improvement in their tactics in the encounters we have had. That would explain a lot."

"Yes, that's what Frances Hastings thinks, and he has asked me to try and correct that."

The major tried to look as if he knew what Marty was saying but had to ask, "What, I mean, how will you do that?"

"By going to Nashik and eliminating the help."

"And you want me to provide an escort?"

"No, that won't be necessary, I have my own team, what I need is a guide. Someone who is familiar with the route and the area around Nashik."

"Aah, now I understand."

He rang a small brass bell, and the adjutant came in.

"Have Captain Sihng attend us."

He turned to Marty, "Captain Sihng is in command of the

Bombay scouts, a command we put in place after Wellesley was here. He was in favour of fast-moving men who could range ahead of the army and provide information of what we would face."

"Yes, that sounds like Arthur."

"You know Wellington?"

"We have had occasion to work together a number of times, here, on the peninsula and in Belgium."

"You were at Waterloo?" The major lent forward expectantly but Marty was saved by a knock at the door and a tall Sikh, who had a familiar cast to his features stepped in, stood to attention, and saluted.

"Captain Sihng, Lord Stockley, has need of a guide familiar with Nashik."

Sihng looked at Marty curiously then said, "I think you know my uncle, my lord."

The penny dropped,

"Rangit Sihng? Yes, I can see the family resemblance. How is the old devil?"

"What's this?" the major asked.

"I had the pleasure of working and fighting alongside Ranjit Sihng the last time I was here with Wellesley. What is he up to these days?"

"My uncle is well and has often talked of his adventures with Lieutenant Stockley and his team of cut throats. He is working with the government in Madras at the moment."

"I say," the major said at the potential insult.

"It's perfectly alright, major his uncle and I are good friends and methinks he knows my men too well."

"If I may," the captain said, "I would like to guide Lord Stockley myself. I am very familiar with the route and the region."

"Who will command the scouts?"

"Lieutenant Randeep is capable and can run it in my absence."

Marty decided the discussion was over, stood and said, "Gentlemen. Tempus Fugit. We will leave in the morning. Civilian attire, Captain. Make sure your weapons are in order and meet us at the dock at first light."

"My weapons are always in order, Sir,"

"I know, I just don't want you to forget it."

The group of mounted men at the dock were a dangerous-looking bunch. Well armed and alert. Jaqvir Sihng walked his horse towards them and knew he didn't need to announce himself. He rode up to the man his uncle had said was one of the best leaders he had ever met.

"Good morning, Sahib," he said.

"Good morning, and while we are on the road you call me Martin or Marty."

"Then you can call me Jack."

"Jack?"

"My name is Jaqvar but I have found that non-Indian speakers have trouble with that."

Marty liked the look of the man who was so like his uncle. He carried a rifle slung across his back on a strap, a curved sword balanced by a curved dagger and a brace of saddle pistols.

"Interesting rifle," Marty said.

"Custom-made Carbine, breech loading, flintlock by Francois Prelat. A present from my uncle."

"May I see it?" Marty said.

Jack handed it over. Marty noted it was primed.

"Expecting trouble?"

"My uncle told me you once said that an unloaded gun was just a club."

"Indeed," Marty hefted it, letting his horse make its own way. "Nice balance." He handed it back.

"My uncle's stories imply you have some interesting skills outside of what a normal naval officer should have."

"I am not a normal naval officer."

"Indeed," Jack smiled.

They rode while it was light and made camp or found a place to stay at sunset. Five days saw them descend into the Aaundha River valley, and that is where it all went terribly wrong.

They were passing the ancient fort at Kavnai through a wooded region. Jack said the fort was unmanned and they were still at least a day from Nashik. They entered a place where the river cut through a gorge when Marty noticed it had gone very quiet. He held up his hand and they stopped. Guns were slung around into the ready position.

"Tell your men to dismount and put their guns down Commodore," a French-accented voice said.

Marty exchanged a look with Jack, "Why don't you come down and take them?" he said.

A chorus of clicks as hammers were drawn back came from every side.

"No, I think you will put them down first," the voice said.

Marty nodded to the boys who dismounted and laid their rifles on the floor.

"Pistols and knives as well."

As soon as they were, apparently, disarmed a man stepped out onto the trail, a rifle in his hands.

"We have been expecting you, I've been waiting here for three days."

"I'm surprised I didn't smell you," Marty said.

"That is a fair comment. Luckily the wind is in our favour."

"How did you know I was coming?"

"Let's just say bad news travels fast. Now step away from your horses and back up the trail keeping your hands out from your sides." He gestured with the rifle.

Marty and the boys backed up as directed. When they were well away from their mounts and guns they were ordered to stop. Men appeared and patted them down, several more knives and a couple of small pistols joined the pile.

"Tsk, tsk, true to form."

"You seem to know an awful lot about me. Now who are you?"

"Robert Bonomi, former officer in his Imperial Majesty's Cavalry now commander of the 1st Marathan Cavalry."

"Pleased to meet you," Marty said.

"That is to be seen, please remount."

Once through the gorge a full troop of cavalry surrounded them.

The cavalrymen were armed with lances as well as rifles and used the sharp-tipped weapons to keep them penned in.

Francis decided at the last minute that he would be better used liaising with his opposite number in Bombay. Beth suspected it was the prospect of being on horseback for five days that did it. So it was that James, Beth and their men were up in the mountains with a clear view ahead when Garai suddenly called a halt. They had ridden hard for four days, travelling well into the night, swapping between remounts. Garai pulled a small telescope from a saddlebag and focussed on a group of riders in the valley below.

"What is it?" James asked and put his own glass to his eye. "Oh bugger."

"Well, what is it?" Beth asked.

"It's your father and the Shadows," Garai said.

Beth looked happy until James handed her his glass and she looked for herself.

"Oh damn. I really don't think that was part of his plan."

"What are we going to do?" Garai said.

"Rescue them of course," Beth said.

"Once we find out where they are being taken," James said.

Marty and the boys had no option but to do as they were told. They were continuously guarded by at least a squad of men and when they weren't riding, they had their legs shackled and linked to the rest by chains. In itself, that wasn't a problem as they could get out of them anytime they chose. But Marty wanted to know how they knew he was coming and to do that he figured being a prisoner was the easiest way to get close to the command.

They approached an encampment spread out across the river floodplain. They passed artillery, both horse and siege, infantry then more cavalry. There was an exotic smell of spices and Indian cooking coming from a huge cook's pavilion. Marty could see cauldrons of rice and piles of flatbreads. Goats were penned in large corals and there were chickens running around free.

Suddenly the layout of the camp changed as did its character. The lines were straighter, tents cleaner, weapons stacked more neatly. A large pavilion was at the centre. They rode up to it.

"Dismount. Commodore, come with me," Bonomi said. Then in French, "Move the rest into the compound, get them fed."

Marty's attention was caught by Antton who nodded towards a nearby hill. A tall pole with two arms which whirled in a choreographed dance stood on the summit.

Well, that explains how the news travelled so fast, he thought.

A shove in his back started him towards the entrance where a pair of European guards stood at parade rest. He stopped and looked them over as if inspecting them, "Tsk, tsk," he said and pointed to the guard's muddy boots.

A snort from behind told him that had amused his escort, but another shove told him he had an appointment inside.

It was dim inside the pavilion, and it took a few seconds for his eyes to adjust from the bright sunlight outside. He blinked owlishly then realised that there were several men standing and sitting inside.

"Gentlemen," Bonomi said, striking a pose, "may I introduce

Commodore, Viscount Stockley of Purbeck."

They turned towards him, and Marty realised that they were all Europeans. Further, their uniforms told that they came from all branches of the army.

"Good afternoon," Marty said, "I am so pleased to meet you all."

He walked over to a chair and sat as if he was meant to be there.

"This is quite a gathering; I assume this is the officer's mess. Would you like to introduce yourselves? You have the advantage of me at the moment," he said with a wry smile.

Bonomi stepped forward and introduced several officers.

Beaufort – Major of infantry

Colmar – Captain of artillery

Laurent – Major of artillery

Moulin – Captain of cavalry

The lieutenants didn't seem to warrant an introduction.

"Pleased to meet you all, it's been a while since I got to practise my French. Since I was in Paris last year in fact. Were any of you at Waterloo?"

No one got time to answer as suddenly, they all leapt to their feet and stood at attention. Marty turned to the entrance. A tall slim man with a shock of hair was silhouetted against the glaring sunlight from outside. He stepped forward and approached Marty who stood.

"Lord Stockley, I am pleased to finally meet you in person. I have heard so much about you. Jean-Baptist Duchand de Sancey, commander of the legion."

Marty gave a very shallow bow, more of a nod. "My pleasure entirely, you were at Waterloo in command of the horse artillery, a member of the Old Guard," Marty said.

"Yes, foul conditions, all that mud."

"Now here supporting the Maratha Empire, but then I suppose one empire is as good as another."

The barb went home and there was a rustle as the men stiffened. The grey-haired general wasn't so easily baited.

"I heard it was you that took our emperor into exile."

"Twice, in fact. This time he won't find it easy to return to France."

"Nothing is impossible," the general said.

"Alas, time is against him," Marty said, "I am afraid he will not live long enough to try. He is quite ill, you know."

This was obviously news to the younger men, but the general just looked sad, "I suspected as much, he complained of stomach pains."

Marty had taken the time during the exchange to study the general and had noted his ring. He was wearing a similar one he had acquired in Jamaica. He made a point of fiddling with the ring, so it caught the light.

"You are a temple member?" the general said.

Marty looked at his ring, it had nicolo intaglio depicting the Square and Compasses motif of the Free Masons within a corn sheaf border. The nicolo onyx had a bluish white upper layer that the intaglio cut through to reveal the brown under layer.

"Yes, the Jamaican lodge."

"Please join me for dinner." The general addressed the room, "Lord Stockley is my guest, please treat him accordingly."

On a hill overlooking the camp Beth and James were watching the camp. They saw them travel through the tents of the Indian troops into an area that was much more geometrically laid out. Beth watched as her father was separated from his men and taken into a large tent and she saw the general arrive in a carriage.

"He's got himself captured," she said.

"Certainly, looks like it," James agreed.

"What are we going to do about it?" Sergeant Bright said.

Beth folded her telescope shut and sighed. "Nothing right now apart from watch and see if we can see a way to get in there undetected."

They watched patiently, seeing who was in the camp, what they wore and what they did. Beth noticed some women going in and out of the big pavilion, they seemed to be carrying the settings tables. She focussed in on them and saw they came from a row of colourful tents behind the pavilion. They were visited often by officers and seemed to be responsible for serving their food which was prepared in an adjacent mess tent.

"I think I have an idea," she said.

They couldn't move until after dark and, even then, only Beth slipped into the camp. She made her way to the pavilion by moving from tent to tent, shadow to shadow, avoiding fires and any areas lit by torches or lamps. When she found them, the women's tents were as she expected and no more than two shared a tent. The one at the far end was empty.

The women not only acted as servants, but washed clothes and provided the officers with other comforts. Beth was well aware of what they were from the giggling and groans coming from some of the tents.

She stole clothes from washing lines, spreading out her thievery to make it harder to spot. She went to the empty tent and used it to dress and shelter until dawn. When the sounds of breakfast being prepared reached her, she slipped out and joined the other girls.

"Oy, who are you?" one girl a year or two older than her said in Parisian French.

"Just got here ain't I," Beth said using the same dialect.

"Where you from?"

"Bastille," Beth said.

"I'm from St. Marguerite. My name's Marie-Anne."

"Béth."

"How did you get out here?' Marie-Anne said.

"Got an offer from some geezer, said I would make good money."

"Yea and the sun will come up at midnight. Oops! Come on, they have the trays ready."

The trays were laden with food. Some with fruit others with bread or meats. Beth took one that had baguettes and a pot of butter and followed the other girls.

Inside she saw that there was a long table with uniformed officers sat down either side. She saw that bread was already placed most of the way down and her tray should go at the end. She worked her way down, men called to her and some made lewd suggestions. She swung her hips and tossed her hair provocatively and got her backside slapped and pinched.

Then she saw him.

Marty was nursing a hangover, his hair ached. The hospitality of the French officers had been generous, and the wine had flowed followed by brandy. Tales had been swapped of experiences at Waterloo and the night had blurred into an alcoholic haze. Now he was paying the price. He'd never had a good head for alcohol, he had pushed it to the limit and, he suspected, a bit beyond.

Now through his bleary eyes he saw a girl approaching with a tray of bread who looked just like Beth. He blinked and stared at her. She looked at him and hesitated for just a second before coming to him and sat on his lap. She stroked his head and leaned in close,

"If I didn't know better, I would say you are hungover old man," she whispered in his ear.

Marty started, then got control. "What are you doing here?" he whispered.

"I came to warn you that they have a mercenary army, not just a couple of advisors, but it looks like you already found that out."

"Get out of here!" he hissed.

"What and leave you to have all the fun." She bounced up and left him with a blown kiss.

"Christ!" Marty said to himself. His headache got worse.

Beth settled down to the routine of service, her looks and the fact she was new got her noticed by the officers and she found she had a natural aptitude for evading groping hands. When service was over, she had acquired a couple of new bruises on her behind but was otherwise unscathed.

"How was that?" Marie-Anne said as she rubbed her feet.

"Easy so far," Beth said and slipped off a shoe to do the same.

"Hard on the feet but harder on your back," a woman laughed.

Beth grinned, that was something she wasn't about to find out.

"Luckily, they will all be out all day training the Indians tomorrow so we can catch up on our sleep. My lieutenant kept me awake half the night. He's bloody insatiable. I should charge him extra."

"Do all of you have a regular man?" Beth asked.

"Not all. Some will lay with any of them but most of the officers want to know their girls are clean so stick to the same ones."

"Who is the civilian?"

"The one you sat on? He arrived yesterday. They was warned he was coming, some sort of agent or assassin for the British according to Jean-Claude."

Beth wanted to ask more but left it so not to draw attention. It got her wondering how they knew.

Marie-Anne was right, it was quiet the next day and she spent her time looking around until lunchtime when a cook called and told her to take a tray to an officer who was ill and confined to his tent. She found it and called out, "Hello! Can I come in? I have your lunch."

"Just a moment!" a young voice called back. "Alright, come in."

The flap was untied so she pushed her way in. The tent was about eight feet by six with a cot to one side, a low table and three-legged stool on the other. A young man, more a boy, of around her age was sat on the cot.

"Put it there please," he said indicating his footlocker.

She noticed he had his ankle splinted.

"What did you do?"

"I trod in a pangolin hole and broke my ankle."

She made sympathetic sounds then asked, "What do you do when you aren't lying around healing,"

"I am an ensign in the infantry. Aid to Major Beaumont."

She sat beside him on the bed, he blushed and started eating.

"I'm new here," she said, "my name is Béth."

"I didn't think I had seen you before. It's probably why they sent you. My name is Pierre."

Beth looked at him quizzically, "Why?"

"What?"

"Why send me if I'm the new girl?"

"The other girls are only interested in making money and as an ensign I don't have much."

"Oh, I see."

"How old are you?"

"Seventeen," Beth said, rounding up.

"Me too." He blushed again and tucked into his meal.

"Who is the Englishman in the mess?"

"I haven't seen him but it's probably Lord Stockey or something like that. Apparently, he is known to the general as someone in British Intelligence."

"It must be wonderful to be close to the senior officers and know what's going on. It is such an important job!" she cooed, all admiring.

"Oh, it's nothing really," he said but sat a little straighter.

"Did the general know him before then?"

"No, but the report said he was at Waterloo."

Beth was bursting to ask where the report had come from but decided she had asked enough. Besides he had finished eating so she picked up the tray and went to leave.

"Béth. Will you come back and talk to me some more?"

"If you want," she said kindly.

Marty was not sure whether to be angry or proud. He was confined to a tent which was quite comfortable but well-guarded. He wasn't allowed to see his men but had been assured that they were being well looked after. The general seemed to be happy to have him confined and made no indication that his life was in danger. From that point of view things were going swimmingly. The fly in the ointment was Beth.

He heard voices outside, then the flap opened, and a girl brought his lunch in. For a moment he thought it was Beth, but it was the usual girl.

"Lunch, Monsieur," she said and put the tray on his low table.

"Where is everyone?"

"They are out playing soldiers with the Indians; they will not be back until tomorrow at the earliest."

"What will you do? No soldiers to play with."

"Get some rest, unless you have some money and an itch to scratch."

"Me? No money they took it all."

"Then you get to sleep alone too," she grinned and flounced out.

He ate his lunch and considered what they had found out. It was clear that Pasha Rao had employed a significant mercenary force but even so, it made up only some ten percent of his army. The threat came from the tactical expertise they brought. He thought about it some more and realised that the bigger threat was, that somehow, intelligence was being passed to them in a very efficient way.

He lay back on his cot and tried to think how he would be able to find out how they did that. The general was cagey about what he said and had deftly parried any questions he had asked. The other officers were also under orders to confine their talk to mundane matters.

He had plenty of time to think about it, apart from an hour where he was escorted on a predetermined route for exercise, he was confined to his tent. The route didn't show him anything, and he didn't see Beth either. He tried not to worry

Voices announced the arrival of lunch, the flap was pulled back by a guard who slapped the girl on the arse as she bent to come in.

"Bent?" he thought. The usual girl was short enough not to have to.

"Hello, how are you?" Beth's familiar voice chirped.

She was all business, placing his breakfast tray on the table, she gave him a sign that told him she was alright and that there was a message. Then she picked up his empty water jug and left dropping the flap as she exited the tent.

Marty checked the tray and, at the bottom of the breadbasket, found a sheet of paper covered in fine writing. In code. He helped himself to bread and butter, slathered in jam and started to read it. It was in their regular code, which he knew so well he could read like English.

"I have befriended a young ensign with a broken ankle, he is on Major Beaumont's staff. He told me that everything the general knows about you, he got from a message that came in on the telegraph. They have an agent in Calcutta who is feeding them information. He doesn't know who it is but apparently, he is in the pay of the consol. I will return for your tray."

Marty tore the message up and ate the pieces, washing them down with bitter coffee. When Beth returned, he said in his best Dorset accent, "Well my lover, you done a proper job. Got a clue where the boom boom store is?"

Beth shook her head.

"T'night at midnight we need a distraction," he drawled distraaaaction out until it was almost unrecognisable.

She signed she understood and left quipping to the guard, "Silly man, talks gibberish."

"He's English, keeps talking to me, thinks if he talks louder and slower, I will understand. What you doing later?"

"Not you, soldier boy," she laughed and walked off with a swing of her hips.

Beth had some free time and wandered through the camp to the artillery camp. The guns were lined up in a neat row with their limbers behind them. Soldiers were polishing the guns, several stopped, and wolf whistled. Beth smiled and flirted.

"That's enough of that, get back to work you useless felons," a loud, authoritative voice barked.

A sergeant, resplendent in his blue coat with its golden arm bands and insignia, walked up to her.

"What are you doing here, this isn't officer country."

"I was just out for some air and saw these magnificent guns, they are awfully big."

"Not the biggest, they are the siege guns. These are cavalry guns, twelve pounders."

"What are the boxes for?"

"Those are limbers and carry the ammunition."

"Mon Dieu! They have gunpowder in them?" Beth feigned fright.

"Not at the moment; that's stored in the magazine right over there outside the camp."

Beth followed his wave of the arm and saw trees. "In the woods?"

"Yes, far enough away to be safe."

Beth chatted for a bit longer then left with the excuse she had to help serve dinner.

She found a secluded spot, shielded from prying eyes, and dug a small mirror out of her pocket. She found the hill where James and the men should still be waiting and flashed a message. She repeated it until a single flash was returned.

Chapter 22: To Catch a Spy

James sat and read the message that was a series of numbers.

"She wants us to blow up the magazine in the woods beyond the horse artillery camp at midnight," he said to Garai.

"Sounds like your father is planning something. We'd better be ready to move fast," Garai said.

"Yes, he and the Shadows will need horses. If it's an escape attempt. I will take care of the magazine. Can you procure some horses? I will need three men; you take the rest."

Garai nodded and went to brief his men.

James knew to set off the magazine he would need a timed charge. He didn't have one of the tool shed's clockwork timers or slow match, so he had to improvise.

He unravelled thread from his spare shirt and platted it into a cord with priming powder rubbed well into it. A test showed it burnt at about a foot in eight seconds. He made up an eight-foot length.

His three men were, of course, Joseph Eric and Dennis. At midnight they slipped down the hill and circled the camp to the woods where Beth had said the magazine was located. There were guards patrolling but under the trees it was very dark and they hugged the pools of light cast by lanterns.

"That is a bloody silly practice this close to a powder store," James thought. However, it would help them immensely as the guards would have no night vision at all.

There were four guards in two pairs outside the entrance. A stick cracked in the dark and they turned at the sound. A huge figure rose in front of one pair and smashed their heads together. The other pair fell when knives slashed across their throats from behind.

James checked his watch; it was ten minutes before midnight. He listened to the night sounds which had started up again. It all sounded normal, so he turned his attention to the door to the powder store. It wasn't locked and opened easily.

"This is too easy," he thought.

He pushed it all the way open, the store wasn't sunk into the ground or reinforced with earth banks around the walls. It was a simple, although large, hut.

He shook his head and entered. Inside were stacks of casks, he found a crowbar and popped the top of one. Inside was powder. Course, uneven, not a bit like the quality of powder the British used.

"I'll be surprised if this stuff even goes bang," he murmured to himself.

He checked a couple of other casks and found the same, then a smaller cask caught his eye. He pulled the bung and found – priming powder for flintlocks. He unwound his improvised fuse and stuffed the end through the bung hole, pushing the bung back in to secure it. He placed the small cask in the middle of a stack of large ones and ran the fuse out of the door.

A quick check of his watch and he lit the fuse using the flintlock on his pistol.

Beth had finished cleaning up the mess after dinner. The officers were back but tired from two days of exercises and had finished early. In fact, the whole camp was quiet. That is until the magazine blew up, then chaos reigned.

She headed straight to her father's tent and saw him stood face to face with a guard who had a levelled musket pointing at his chest. Her hand flicked out and the guard stiffened, toppling over as stiff as a plank. Marty bent and took his musket, cartridge bag and knife.

"Right on time," he said.

"Just in time, more like," she said.

"Let's go find the boys," he said as he dragged the guard into his tent and shut the flap.

Beth knew where the compound was, and they slunk towards it against the backdrop of explosions from the woods. Bleary-eyed soldiers were running around aimlessly until a burning barrel landed by the mess tent and blew up sending whatever was on the stoves flying.

That set off a general panic and men were running in all directions. Marty helped it along by kicking the embers of any fires they passed onto the tents setting fire to them.

The compound was a log palisade surrounding a couple of huts, it was the camp prison and held more people than just the Shadows. The guards looked up as Beth ran towards them a look of panic on her face.

Their looks turned to surprise as soon as she reached them. She pivoted on her left foot, her right swing around in a high kick that took one guard in the side of the head with her heel. Continuing the rotation, she let herself fall to the ground and swept the second guard's legs from under him. Marty appeared and drove the butt of his musket into his head before he had a chance to recover.

"Nice move," he said.

"Savate, Louise taught me," she said referring to the French form of kickboxing.

They opened the compound gates and ran inside to find the Shadows and Jack waiting for them.

"Hello, Martin," Jack said.

"Come on, we need to get out of here," Marty said.

"This way!" Beth led the way.

"What about our weapons?" Jack said thinking of his prized rifle.

"Grab whatever you can," Marty said.

They moved as a group, the Shadows alternating moving and covering in pairs. Beth took a musket from a stack that had been abandoned and paired with Marty.

Discipline was returning to the camp as the officers took command. Some men were detailed to fight fires and others to restore order. They had to move fast.

"Stop! Where are you going?" a sergeant shouted and approached holding a pike.

Marty let him come closer then shot him.

"Move," he shouted.

The boys had managed to pick up guns and swords. They cut down anyone who got in their way and left a trail of bodies across the camp. A shout from behind told them that their escape had been discovered.

"We need to go up there," Beth said, pointing to the hill.

"Why?" Marty said.

"Because that's where James is with the marines."

"James is here as well?" Marty gasped, as they ran.

Beth didn't answer as she was busy disposing of a soldier that had come in from the side. She leapt into him, foot extended kicking him in the gut, following him down so she ended up sitting on his chest and stuck one of her darts in his neck. She didn't wait to see if it took effect but jumped to her feet and followed the rest.

She looked back and saw by the light of the fires that an officer was leading a troop in pursuit.

"Company!" she shouted.

They were close to the edge of the camp and about to enter the cleared zone that surrounded it. The officer shouted an order and the soldiers lined up, with their muskets at the ready no more than fifty yards behind them.

A volley rang out.

"Over here" James called from the smoke of the marine's guns over to the right of where Marty and Beth had been heading. They veered towards him and as soon as they had passed behind the marines, they fired another volley.

"Get to the horses!" James shouted. Marty noticed his voice had settled down to a tenor.

The horses had remounts tied to their stirrups. They headed out at a canter. The marines had scouted an escape route over the last few days, and they followed a trail that was flat enough to ensure the horses wouldn't trip. James upped the pace to a gallop.

Marty wondered how the hell his son knew where to go, there was only a sliver of a new moon and the stars to light their way.

Then he noticed a white rag tied to a bush to his right and the trail turned in that direction.

They galloped for twenty minutes, then James slowed them to a walk.

"We've enough of a head start now," he said.

"Won't they just follow?" Beth said.

"They will when they round up enough horses. The boys left all the gates open and when that powder went up the horses stampeded."

"Adding to the general confusion," Marty said. His horse was blowing, "We should switch mounts."

James pulled his horse up and shouted, "Halt! Remount!"

Miraculously, no one had a horse run into him from behind and they were soon moving again as all they had to do was tighten the remounts' girths.

They arrived in Bombay, dirty, hungry from being on short rations for four days, and saddle sore. They were escorted in by a troop of lancers who had been patrolling the road to Nashik.

Marty paid a brief visit to Major Willems to give him his report and asked him to semaphore a summary to Calcutta. The major was not dismayed that his suspicions of the size of the army he had to his Northeast had been confirmed. His planning didn't change, only accelerated.

"Get us back to Calcutta as fast as you can, the other two ships will escort us," Marty said as he stepped on the deck of the Pride initiating a flurry of shouted orders.

Adam had provided a large pot of hot water and a bowl for him to have a standing bath and laid out his shaving gear.

"Do you think we will ever get our guns back?" Adam asked as he stropped a razor.

"Probably not. I will replace them all, including Jack's."

"Won't find their like in India." Adam put down the razor and started working up a lather with the shaving brush and soap.

"We will find hunting rifles, or commission special builds. They will have to do until we get back to civilisation."

Marty finished sponging off the accumulated dirt of four days hard riding and dried himself off. He pulled on a pair of Nanking trousers and sat in the chair. Adam placed a hot towel around his face and a towel around his shoulders.

The ship moved.

"That was quick," Adam said.

"They were ready to sail," Marty mumbled through the towel.

Adam removed the towel and applied lather with a shaving brush which had the best badger hair bristles. Satisfied he took a razor and stropped it one final time on his palm.

He had had finished one side and was starting on the other when the door opened, and Beth walked in.

"You could have given me time for a proper bath," she said, although to look at her you would never guess what she had been through. Dressed in a pale green dress her hair loose and shining, she was a picture.

Adam finished and handed Marty a towel.

"Tell me about your time in the camp, you chose an – unusual position as your cover," Marty said.

"I wondered when you would get around to asking," Beth said and sat on the transom bench. The sun shone through her hair making it look as if she wore a halo of flame.

"The girls were the only European women in the camp and better they served the officers."

"They are camp followers," Marty said.

"Yes, they were mostly linked to one officer or another."

"And?"

"What are you asking Daddy, dear? Did I 'link up' with an officer?"

Marty scowled at her.

"What if I did? Would you punish me? If I did it to fulfil the mission, would it be wrong?" She was getting angry and upset. "Mother and Louise, both told me that at some point my body may be my best weapon. Are you going to question me after every mission?"

Marty realised that he had been unfair, if he was to let her follow in his footsteps, correction, if she decided to follow in his footsteps, then he would have to accept this as a part of what she did.

He took a deep breath. There was a knock on the door.

"Am I interrupting?" Ridgley said.

"Come in, Frances," Marty turned back to Beth.

"I apologise. I didn't mean to question your methods, but you are my little girl, and I am concerned for you."

She took a breath in turn; she couldn't stay angry at him any more than her mother could.

"As it happens I didn't, I befriended a nice young boy with a broken ankle, but nothing happened."

Marty pulled on a shirt that Adam handed him with a look that said, 'be nice'.

"Did you find out more?"

"Our leak is coming from inside Government House. Pierre heard the general laughing with his major about how the British were so stupid they didn't know that they had a spy in the inner circle."

Frances jumped on that immediately. "Did he say if the spy is Indian or British?"

"No but he did say he thought that he had been there a long time."

Marty paced up and down until Adam handed him a pair of shoes. Then he sat and pulled them on.

"I wish we could contact Hastings."

Beth kissed him on the cheek and excused herself. Once she had left Frances said, "We will deal with that when we get there. I wanted to talk to you about Beth. She is showing exceptional promise. Have you thought about sending her to the academy?"

The three ships went straight upriver without waiting for a pilot and moored directly off Fort William. They had walked about halfway to Government House when a carriage arrived and picked them up.

They were met at the door by the concierge and headed straight to Marty's office after sending a message for Hastings to join them.

However, when they walked in, Hastings was waiting.

"You seemed to be in a hurry so I thought I would save you the trouble of finding me. You are all looking very well."

"Thank you, now this is what we found."

Marty and Frances spent the next thirty minutes telling what had happened and what they found out with Beth chipping in when necessary.

"Good grief, you have had a time of it," Hastings said.

"Comparable to some of his other escapades," Ridgley smiled then got serious. "If I may summarise, we are facing an enemy who has professional European mercenaries led by one of Napoleon's generals. On top of that we have a spy in Government House who is sending them intelligence that should only be known by the governor's inner circle."

Marty looked to Justine, "Can you get us some coffee and tell my wife she can come in."

"How do you know she is here?" Hastings said.

"I know my wife, especially where my daughter is involved."

They discussed, planned and discussed some more. By the time they had finished and gotten home it was eight in the evening. Roland had prepared a special dinner, before which, Marty had a long hot bath. Beth was nowhere to be seen and when Marty asked Caroline where she was, was told, "She asked for a bath and food in her room, Tabetha and Mary are attending her, I think she is going for an extend pampering session."

The next morning James joined them for breakfast,

"There is nothing like a home-cooked breakfast," he said, as he filled his plate with scrambled eggs, bacon, sausage, haggis and kidneys. He had a second plate piled with toast.

Caroline noted the fuzz on his chin and his deepened voice. She resisted the urge to gather him up and hug him.

Beth joined, with the twins and the whole family were together.

"Will you stay on the Silverthorn?" Marty asked.

"Oh, you haven't heard," James said. "Poor Trevor died of dysentery, so I get to stay on."

"Sorry to hear that," Marty said, "did Shelby have any idea what caused it?"

"Best guess, is he ate something from a street vendor."

James cleared his plate and burped.

"Pardon me. How are we going to catch the spy?"

"Is there a spy?" chorused the twins.

"You two run along it's time for your lessons," Caroline said.

"Oh, Mother!" Edwin said. "Can't we stay and help catch the spy?" Constance finished.

"No, not until you are older. Here is Mary to take you to your lessons."

Once the twins were gone, Marty said, "We have been keeping a constant watch on the French consulate, but that has been with locals in Ridgley's employ. The Shadows are taking over the duty and putting the consul, his wife and son under surveillance. Ridgley is going over the records of everyone who works in Government House and Hastings, and I are looking at using the spy to supply false information if we can trap him."

"How do they get the information to the general so fast?" Caroline asked.

"I think they must use a semaphore network which they copied from us," Marty said.

"But isn't the nearest one fifty miles away?" Caroline said.

"Closer to seventy."

A week later, Beth was walking around one of the local markets with Justine. The two had become firm friends and often shopped together. They were looking for material for dresses when they passed a stall selling chickens and other fowl for eating.

"The order for Monsieur Blanchette," a French-accented voice said.

Beth froze in mid-step and used her fan to shield her face as she looked around. A large wicker basket was hoisted up onto the table. She could see it contained pigeons.

"What would anybody do with that many pigeons?" she said.

"What?" Justine said.

"What do the French consulate need with that many pigeons." Beth said and nodded to the basket which was rectangular with a well-made wicker lid held on by leather straps. In the centre of the lid was a small hatch held closed by a leather strap and buckle. "That's a bit elaborate for carrying eating birds."

"They normally just dangle them from their legs," Justine said.

An Indian housewife proved the point as she walked by with a brace of live chickens dangling from her hand.

The basket of pigeons was picked up and carried between the

Frenchman and an Indian servant. They made their way through the market and the girls followed at a safe distance.

"That isn't the consulate," Justine said as the two men went through a gate into a house.

"No, it's not," Beth said and made a note of the street name.

"Hello, Beth," Ridgley said as she let herself into his office, "what can I do for you?"

"Make me a cup of tea, I'm parched,"

Ridgley was surprised, but did as he was bid and placed a freshly-brewed cup in front of her.

"Do you recognise Mughoo Road?"

Frances steepled his fingers in front of his nose, "I think I have seen that before, why?"

"Because a Frenchman picked up a basket of around twenty pigeons from the market in the name of Mr Blanchette."

"The French consul?"

"The very same, it was one of his servants, but they didn't deliver the birds to the consulate."

"To a house in Mughoo Road?" Ridgley guessed.

Beth gave him a smug smile.

Ridgley suddenly smiled as his internal filing system landed on the location. He went to a pile of papers and started sorting through them.

"Here it is." He took a sheet and read it.

"Our friend the concierge lives there."

"How long has he worked here?"

"Let me see. Strewth! Since the place was built."

"Is he the only one of his family who works here?" Beth said.

"Now you mention it he isn't," he went back to the pile and searched again.

"Gotcha! His eldest son works here as well. He is," there was a pause as he scanned the sheet, "in charge of the messengers. Worked here for twelve years." He looked at Beth, a look of enlightenment on his face "Are you thinking what I'm thinking?"

Beth nodded. "Access to all messages, boys stood outside of offices listening to everything that's said. To all intents and purposes invisible."

She jumped to her feet.

"We need to talk to Daddy, come on."

Daddy was in conference with Hastings, so they waited in Adam's office for them to finish. Beth noted where the messenger boys were stood. They couldn't hear what was being said in Marty's office but could hear every word said in Adam's.

"Hello, you two are you waiting for me?" Marty said as he showed Hastings out.

Beth took him by the arm and marched him into his office with Ridgley on their heels. Adam followed shutting the doors.

"We think we know who the spy is," Beth said breathless with excitement.

"You do, do you? Well, who is it? And how do you know it's them?"

Beth told him what they had found and finished with, "Chopra's son Benjamin, lives in the same road as Chopra and is in an ideal position to hear almost every secret and decision in the building."

"Doesn't prove he is a spy," Marty said.

"If the birds that were picked up today are carrier pigeons and they are at his house, that would," Ridgley said.

"I will have the house watched," Marty said. He looked at Beth and saw the flush on her skin and the excited look in her eyes, "I suppose you want to go and have a look?"

"I thought you'd never ask," she said.

Adam, resigned to the fact that he and Justine would be carrying all the important and confidential messages themselves, volunteered to accompany Beth on her latest mission. The city was lavishly decorated for the festival of Kali Puja and the citizens were excitedly gathering. Lanterns burned along all the main streets and statues of the deity were paraded garlanded with hibiscus. Priests offered sweets and made sacrifices of goats and chickens.

There was no one at home and it took the two of them seconds to gain entry.

"Indians don't lock their doors?" Adam said

"Don't seem to," Beth replied, "look, there are the pigeons."

Adam opened the small hatch in the lid of the basket and took out a bird.

"This is not an eating bird. Look there is a leather ring around its leg sealed with lead. It's got a number on it."

He put the bird back.

"They are used to being handled as well."

Beth moved on to search the house. She called Adam over,

"Look at this."

She had found a small writing desk; fine steel nibbed pens and ink were laid out on top. She lifted the writing slope and inside were small sheets of very fine paper. She took a sheet, then noticed something else.

"Well, these banish all doubts," she said as she held up a small cylindrical wooden container with a cap. It was fitted with a leather thong. She put it in her pocket. She continued her search, "Well now what do we have here?" she said. She had found a pouch under a floorboard. It chinked and inside were, "Gold Louis D'Or, just like in the consulate safe." She put the pouch back in the hole and replaced the board. "Let's go, we have seen enough."

"That is definitely a message holder, and that paper when rolled tightly fits it exactly," Ridgley said as they debriefed in Marty's office.

"So, we have our spy, now how to use him to our advantage."

Epilogue

"Beth should go to the academy," Marty said to Caroline as they lay together that night.

"She can't learn here?" Caroline said reluctant to let her daughter go.

"The world is changing, out here we are stuck in an older age. She needs to learn in Europe."

"I can see that, it's just that…"

"She is both our little girl," Marty said and hugged her. "She needs to be with a group of people of her own age and have mentors."

"Louise still teaches there sometimes,"

"Exactly, and she can teach her more about being a female spy than I can."

"Including trapping men into giving up their secrets?"

"What like you did?"

"I did not trap you!" Caroline said and punched him in the ribs. "You ran into my bed willingly."

Marty laughed.

"James will do well on the Silverthorn, they are going to get an independent action to patrol the rivers Tapti and Narbada to show support for the areas under British protection."

"You aren't going?"

"My place is here to support Hastings. Anyway, it's better to leave the running around to the youngsters."

"Are you saying you are past it?"

"Cheeky wench! I'll show you who's past it!"

Beth left for England on a Company Liner, in the new year. It was 1818 and the third Anglo-Maratha war was about to come to a head. In Europe peace reigned, on the surface at least, but the ambitious colonialism of the members of the Vienna Congress and the increasing liberal movements amongst the people meant that it was a simmering pot with the lid held shut by the status quo. At some time it was going to go bang keeping the Stockley dynasty busy for years to come.

Historic Notes

An attempt was made on Wellington's life in Paris, but it was so incompetently executed he didn't even realise he had been shot at. I made up the one in here to make it more entertaining.

The Ottoman Empire was already in decline in the early 1800s. Riven internally by corruption and factions vying for power, To hurry it along the Balkans woke up to the smell of independence in 1815 when the Serbians gained independence of a sort. This spread a desire for independence throughout the empire. The Egyptians in the form of the Wahhabi were next and only brought back under Ottoman control by Muhammad Ali who eventually led his own rebellion. The Greeks backed but the Tsar took a while longer but finally wrested control from the Ottomans in 1821

Annabel had absolutely no chance of getting into any of the medical schools in Great Britain in the early 1800s. The thought of a woman being trained in the medical arts would have been abhorrent to the profession and the institutions. It wasn't until 1865 as Wikipedia tells us that the first woman did qualify and that shocked the establishment so badly they changed the rules to stop it happening again.

In **1865** Garrett Anderson became the first woman to qualify as a doctor in Britain when she passed the examinations of the Society of Apothecaries – they subsequently closed their exams to women to prevent others following her example.
    (Wikipedia)

The navy referred to a hangman's noose as a halter and it was common practice to haul the condemned up, rather than drop them. This resulted in a slow agonising death that could take up to thirty minutes.

The Third Maratha War ran from 1817 to 1819 and was the key to British dominance of the sub-continent. Wikipedia tells us:

The Third Anglo-Maratha War (1817-1819) was the final and decisive conflict between the British East India Company and the Maratha Empire in India. The war left the Company in control of most of India.

With so much at stake no wonder they sent Marty.

Books by Christopher C Tubbs

The Dorset Boy Series.
A Talent for Trouble
The Special Operations Flotilla
Agent Provocateur
In Dangerous Company
The Tempest
Vendetta
The Trojan Horse
La Licorne
Raider
Silverthorn
Exile
Dynasty

The Scarlet Fox Series
Scarlett
A Kind of Freedom
Legacy

The Charlamagne Griffon Chronicles
Buddha's Fist
The Pharoah's Mask

See them all at:

Website: www.thedorsetboy.com
Twitter: @ChristoherCTu3
Facebook: https://www.facebook.com/thedorsetboy/
YouTube: https://youtu.be/KCBR4ITqDi4

Published in E-Book, Paperback and Audio formats on Amazon, Audible and iTunes